OUT OF THIS WORLD

**BY LAWRENCE WATT-EVANS
PUBLISHED BY BALLANTINE BOOKS:**

THE LORDS OF DÛS

The Lure of the Basilisk

The Seven Altars of Dûsarra

The Sword of Bheleu

The Book of Silence

LEGENDS OF ETHSHAR

The Misenchanted Sword

With a Single Spell

The Unwilling Warlord

The Blood of a Dragon

Taking Flight

The Spell of the Black Dagger

The Cyborg and the Sorcerers

The Wizard and the War Machine

Nightside City

Crosstime Traffic

THREE WORLDS TRILOGY

Out of This World (Volume 1)

OUT OF THIS WORLD

LAWRENCE WATT-EVANS

A Del Rey Book

BALLANTINE BOOKS • NEW YORK

A Del Rey Book
Published by Ballantine Books

Copyright © 1993 by Lawrence Watt Evans

Library of Congress Cataloging-in-Publication Data
Watt-Evans, Lawrence, 1954–
     Out of this world / Lawrence Watt-Evans.—1st ed.
        p.   cm.—(Three world trilogy; 1)
     "A Del Rey book."
     ISBN 0-345-37245-X
     I. Title. II. Series: Watt-Evans, Lawrence, 1954–
Three world trilogy; 1.
  PS3573.A859093 1994
  813'.54—dc20   93-22137
                                                    CIP

Designed by Ann Gold
Manufactured in the United States of America
First Edition: March 1994

10 9 8 7 6 5 4 3 2 1

FOR JULIE
BECAUSE SHE'S
LONG OVERDUE FOR ANOTHER

OUT OF THIS WORLD

CHAPTER 1

He was changing lanes, cutting in front of a silver-gray Toyota, when he suddenly felt as if he were being watched, as if someone were desperately trying to get his attention. He was alone in the car, though. He *knew* he was alone in the car.

He swerved back into line and checked his mirrors.

Everything looked normal.

He shook his head, puzzled, and began looking for another opening. His appointment was in five minutes, and he had three miles to go on the highway, another through the city streets. He wasn't going to make it on time, but all the same, he didn't want to be any later than necessary. He ignored the odd sensation, waiting for it to go away.

It refused. Instead of fading, it nagged at him like a sore tooth. Someone was *watching* him, somehow.

When he stopped at a light he looked in the back seat, just in case; of course, no one was there. For a moment he even thought about checking the trunk when he parked, but then he shook his head again. That was ridiculous.

The feeling was very definite. It was almost like one of those psychic things he'd read about—but he didn't believe in those.

The feeling was there, and it wouldn't go away.

He forced himself to ignore it.

■

"Mommy?" Angela, seated cross-legged on the kitchen floor with her Raggedy Ann doll sprawled on her lap, looked up at her mother.

"Yes, honey?" Margaret Thompson went on scrubbing the saucepan, trying to get out every trace of the burnt-on cheese sauce.

"Mr. Nobody's talkin' to me again."

"Oh?" Margaret answered, not really listening. "What's he saying?" She peered critically at the pan, decided it would do, and put it in the drainer.

"He's in terrible trouble, Mommy," Angela told her quite seriously.

"What kind of trouble?" Margaret asked, picking a skillet out of the soapy dishwater.

"There's this bad monster wants to get him and eat him up and make everybody do bad things."

Margaret looked down at her daughter. "Angie, there aren't any monsters. You know that. You tell Mr. Nobody that."

"I *told* him that, Mommy," Angela said very seriously, "but he just keeps talkin' about a monster in the shadows."

Margaret was a bit startled to hear a phrase like "a monster in the shadows" from her three-year-old, but she didn't worry about it. Kids pick up all kinds of things, and besides, Angie was almost four now. She was growing up fast. "Well, if he keeps talking about monsters," Margaret told Angie, "then just don't listen to him. Tell him to be quiet and stop bothering you with that stuff."

"Okay," Angela said, doubtfully. "I'll try."

■

PSYCHIC PREDICTS ARMAGEDDON

Ray Aldridge, noted West Coast psychic advisor, told reporters today that he has it on good authority that Armageddon, the final battle of good and evil, is almost upon us.

"It was the clearest message I've ever gotten from any psychic entity," Dr. Aldridge reported. "It was a warning sent by beneficent aliens far out in the galaxy, telling me that the powers of darkness are building up their forces for the final conquest of Earth. The aliens who contacted me say that the Galactic Empire they represent has tried to fight back Shadow, as they call it, but has been unsuccessful. It's up to us, here on Earth, to defeat it."

When asked how this evil force could be defeated, and what ordinary people could do that telepathic space aliens could not, Dr. Aldridge admitted, "I don't have any idea at all."

■

"Got a good one," called the agent at the desk, holding up an opened letter.

His partner looked up from the file drawer. "What's this one say?"

The man at the desk smiled. "Dear Mr. President," he read from the letter, "the angels from Venus who have been helping me with my garden called me up yesterday on the special telephone in my head to warn me that we're in big trouble. The devil himself . . ." He pointed and said, "That's underlined in red crayon." Then he continued reading. "The devil himself has found out about all the secret messages I've been relaying to you, to keep the Chinese from invading and to tell Americans how to grow better carrots, and he's really mad. I think my neighbor with the sick cat told him. I'm sure she's a witch or one of them Satan cults. The Venusians are going to fight the old bastard and chase him back to hell . . ." The agent paused again and looked up, grinning. " 'Hell' is in all capitals and underlined in red," he said, before turning his gaze back to the letter. He cleared his throat and continued, ". . . chase him back to hell, but they need some help, so if you could send the Eighty-second Airborne to Goshen, Maryland, that's where they expect to meet him. Yours truly, Oram Blaisdell."

"Goshen?" the other man asked, bemused. "Why Goshen? Where the heck is it, anyway?"

"Just north of Gaithersburg, I think," the reader said. "One of those ritzy suburbs with three-acre estates."

"Does this guy live *there*?" The man by the files knew, intellectually, that the nuts whose letters came to this office sometimes lived in fancy suburbs, but it still didn't seem right. He expected them to come from either the inner city or the outermost sticks.

"No, no, of course not," the man at the desk replied. "He lives in Tennessee somewhere."

"Then why'd he pick Goshen? How'd he ever *hear* of Goshen, Maryland?"

The man holding the letter shrugged. "Who knows?" he asked. "Why the Eighty-second? Why Venus? Why carrots?" He tossed the letter aside. "At least that one didn't have Elvis in it."

■

Pel Brown gave the screwdriver another turn and cursed when it slipped out of the slot and scraped across the metal. He dropped the screwdriver to one side, then brushed at the red-enameled surface and leaned over to peer at it, wishing the light were better.

It looked okay.

Better light might be nice, Pel decided, but what he *really* wished was that wagons came ready-assembled. Had *his* father had to put together *his* old wagon? He'd never thought about that before; just one year there it was, under the Christmas tree, and he'd taken it entirely for granted.

Well, this one was going to be a birthday present, rather than for Christmas, but Rachel was probably going to take it for granted just as much as he had. And she probably wouldn't notice if he *did* scratch the paint. That wasn't something a six-year-old cared much about.

She was going to be six. Amazing. Almost ready for first grade.

Of course, the next school year was still almost four months off, but she would be six tomorrow.

She still wouldn't care about scratched paint, though. He sighed and reached for the screwdriver, then froze.

Standing next to the screwdriver was a . . . well, a person. Pel hesitated to call it a man, even in his thoughts; it stood just over a foot high, wrapped in a tattered cloak of coarse brown wool, its black hair pulled back in a tight braid, revealing oversized, pointed ears. It was looking about curiously and uncertainly, taking in the contents of the basement—the furnace, the water heater, and the boxes of stored junk.

It was not a doll; no doll could look that lifelike and alert, no matter how many computer chips were stuffed into it. It wasn't a monkey, either.

And Pel sure hoped it wasn't a hallucination, as up until that moment he hadn't had any reservations at all about his mental health, and he hadn't taken anything stronger than beer in weeks.

The creature had seen him, he was sure, but it wasn't saying anything, wasn't running or hiding or attacking. It was just looking around, a trifle uncertainly, taking in the scenery.

"What the hell are *you*?" Pel asked.

The thing looked up at him and grimaced. "I'm a book-keeper," it replied. "Wouldn't know it from this outfit, would you?" Pel was relieved that it spoke, and spoke English; that probably simplified the situation, because it meant he could just talk to it and get some answers. Its voice was higher-pitched than a man's, but not squeaky or thin at all. Pel had heard grown women whose voices sounded far smaller and more childlike.

"No," Pel said, "I don't mean what do you do, I mean what *are* you?"

"I'm a human being, of course," the creature replied. "A small one. What do I *look* like?"

"You look like some kind of fairy," Pel replied in honest be-musement.

The little person squinted up at Pel. "Are you looking for trouble, buddy?" he demanded. "I'm as much a lady's man as the next guy! If you weren't so damn big I'd punch your lights out!"

"Hey, I'm sorry," Pel said, holding up his hands in apology. "I didn't mean that. I meant an elf or something. I mean, you're a foot tall, with pointed ears—where'd you *come* from?"

Somewhat mollified, the little man said, "That's better. Yeah, I'm a little person. I came from a place called Hrumph—no jokes, I know it's a stupid name! That's what we called it, though, when it still existed. It was in . . . well, in another world."

"Oh, wow," Pel said, who had seen just as many episodes of "Twilight Zone" and "Lost in Space" as most of his generation. "You mean like another dimension?"

The creature looked puzzled. "Dimension? Um . . . I guess." He hesitated. "Not the word I'd have used," he said. "Another world, alternate reality, parallel universe, whatever." He waved vaguely, and his voice trailed off somewhat.

Pel blinked. After a moment of unthinking acceptance, a certain uncomfortable suspicion was growing in the back of his mind.

Outside of movies and TV, things like this didn't happen, did they? Not for real.

"You're putting me on, right? This is a joke?" he asked.

"No, it's . . . it's not a joke." The person—he might not be human, in the usual sense, but after conversing with him Pel certainly thought of him as a person—looked uncomfortable. Not as if he were lying, but as if he were considering throwing up. "Hey," he said, "I don't feel real good just now. Is it hot in here?"

"Hot?" Pel glanced around at the cool, moist basement. If this little person really did come from another world, maybe it was one colder than Earth—but that was silly. He shouldn't be taking it that seriously. "No, it isn't hot," he said.

"No?" The little man was swaying visibly.

"Are you all right?" Pel asked, concerned.

"No," the creature said. "I think . . . I think I better go." He swallowed hard. "Listen, we'll be back, okay? Or someone will. Don't go away!"

Before Pel could answer, the elf, or whatever it was, turned, stumbled away, and walked into the concrete wall.

Pel heard the smack clearly from where he sat. He winced in sympathy.

The little man got to his feet, let out a wail, and again stepped forward.

This time, when he hit the wall, he vanished into it.

Pel stared for a moment.

Then, moving slowly, he reached out and picked up the screwdriver.

He looked at the wall. In the movies, any character who had just seen such a thing would reach out and poke at the place where the little guy had vanished, and maybe nothing would happen, and maybe not. He might get sucked into another world, or he might get killed by some sort of splashy special effects, or monsters might jump out at him.

Pel Brown was not going do that. He had no particular interest in watching the end melt off his screwdriver, or seeing his finger disappear into the fourth dimension, or even just poking the wall. It wouldn't prove anything. If he could hallucinate an elf, he could hallucinate anything.

He waited for a moment, but nothing happened, and he turned back to the wagon, shaking slightly.

Whatever he had just seen, real or not, seemed to be over. Maybe it had been just a weird sort of dream or something, or some kind of flashback to the one hit of mescaline he'd taken back in college, when he was young and stupid.

Or maybe he really had just talked to an elf from another dimension, and this sort of thing happened all the time, but most people didn't talk about it because they didn't want everyone thinking they were nuts. Maybe all those UFO aliens were real, Bigfoot was roaming the woods, and Elvis really *was* alive in outer space somewhere.

Maybe it happened all the time.

And maybe it didn't.

Whatever it was, it was not his problem; he still had to get the wheels on this stupid wagon in time for Rachel's party tomorrow. If the little man came back, Pel thought, he would worry about it then.

■

Amy Jewell leaned back in her lawn chair, the book on her lap forgotten for the moment as she rested her eyes and listened to the pleasant hiss of the sprinkler. The sun was warm on her face, unseasonably warm for early May, and enjoying it seemed more important just now than reading whatever Danielle Steel had to say.

She wasn't sure she was going to bother finishing this one; she was beginning to lose her taste for Steel. And it was good to just lie here, eyes closed, enjoying the warmth, knowing that she had all day with nothing important to do. She liked that about Sundays.

Her eyes snapped open, and she looked up, startled, at the crack of a sonic boom. It sounded as if it was almost directly overhead; she scanned the sky, but she couldn't see any plane.

Then suddenly she *did* see a plane, or something like one, but it wasn't flying, it was falling. It was brightly painted, like the old Braniff jets, mostly purple, and she didn't see any wings, just stubs. And it was *huge*, and it was almost directly overhead and it was falling almost directly toward *her*.

She rolled out of the lawn chair, scrambled to her feet, and ran for the house.

An instant later the thing hit with an immense, booming thud. The shock of its impact rattled windows and the dishes in her kitchen, and a planter at the corner of the patio toppled over, spilling scraggly geraniums across the flagstones. The sprinkler bounced but did not overturn; its spray rattled against the thing's metal side.

The object had completely flattened the back hedge and had torn a major limb off the big sycamore. One of the stubby wings, or fins, or whatever they were had missed the lawn chair by just two or three inches.

It had stayed in one piece, though; it hadn't broken into sections like the crashed airliners she had seen on the TV news. The nose was no more than twenty yards from Amy's back door, while the tail was well across the property line, on Mr. Janssen's vegetable garden.

Amy had reached the back door just as it struck; she turned for a quick glance, paused long enough to lean over and turn off the sprinkler, then slipped inside. From the safety of her kitchen she stared out the window over the sink for a few seconds, then reached for the phone and dialed 911.

911 worked on Sundays, didn't it? Of course it did. Emergencies weren't limited to weekdays.

She didn't wait to hear what the person on the other end said; when she heard the phone picked up she said, "This is Amy Jewell, at 21550 Goshen Road, and an aircraft of some kind just crashed in my back yard."

"Do you need an ambulance?" a woman's voice asked calmly.

"I don't know," Amy said. "There hasn't been any explosion or anything, and the plane looks mostly intact; I don't see any bodies or flame."

"We'll send one. That was 21550 Goshen Road?"

"Yes." Amy heard other voices in the background.

"Even if there hasn't been an explosion *yet*, you might want to get well away from the wreckage. Was it a private plane? We have no reports of any commercial craft in trouble."

"I don't know *what* it is. It's purple."

The voice on the other end was silent for a moment, then asked, "Ma'am, where are you calling from?"

"I'm calling from my kitchen. I can see the plane, or whatever it is, out the window, about fifty feet away, and it's purple, and I never saw a plane like it before. Maybe it's some kind of experimental military thing."

"Fifty *feet*? Ma'am, I strongly suggest you leave the building and get well clear, quickly."

"Yeah," Amy said, staring out the window, "I think you're right." She hung up the phone.

The thing was lying across most of the width of her back yard, easily over a hundred feet long, with leaves and twigs from the sycamore scattered all over it. Amy's yard was three acres, what the real estate people called a "mini-estate," and the aircraft, or whatever it was, seemed to cover most of it, and a fair chunk of the Janssens', as well. Three fins, each shaped differently, projected from the near side, and a fourth jutted up from the top of the tail; the fins were pink and maroon, with yellow lettering that she couldn't make out. The fuselage was mostly purple, with maroon detailing and more yellow lettering. It didn't look like any sort of airplane Amy had ever seen; it had a rather old-fashioned appearance, somehow.

And a hatchway over the central, largest, nearside fin was opening.

Amy knew she should turn and run, go out the front door, and either wait for help or alert the neighbors, but she stared, fascinated.

The hatch swung wide, and a man stepped out. He was tall and blond, wearing a purple uniform with a black belt and high, shiny black boots—it wasn't any design she recognized, but it was clearly a uniform. He had a black holster on his hip—securely closed, to Amy's relief, with a flap that hid whatever weapon was in there; for all she could tell, it might be empty. He held a helmet in one hand, something like a motorcycle helmet; it was purple, too, with a yellow star on the side. He gazed around the yard. He said something.

Long ago Amy Jewell had learned to read lips a little, just for fun. She couldn't hear him through the closed window, but she knew what the man had said.

He had said, "Shit."

He turned and called something back into the hatch, but Amy couldn't make it out, nor could she see his lips.

The man looked perfectly normal and ordinary, except for his rather outlandish attire. He was clean-shaven, and his hair was in a military crew cut that was beginning to grow out. He was tall and broad-shouldered and reminded her a little of Harrison Ford. She could see no sign of any injury; the thing's fall didn't even appear to have seriously mussed his uniform.

He was scanning her back yard, looking over the lawn chair, the still-dripping sprinkler, the spilled geraniums, and the branch that had been torn off the sycamore. He did not look pleased.

Then he spotted her in the window. He waved and cupped his hands around his mouth and called, "Hello!"

Amy stared for a moment.

Then another head appeared in the hatch, looking out—another young man in uniform and crew cut.

Amy decided that she didn't want to talk to these people. They might be harmless—but they might not, and she was alone in the house, the neighbors still being off at their church, and there were at least two of the strangers, and either one was bigger than she was. Those blond crew cuts brought Nazis to mind, which didn't help any.

She didn't think that the plane, or whatever it was, was going to explode. If there were any possibility of that the men would be running to get clear, not standing there looking around as if her back yard was some sort of disaster they had to clean up.

She locked the back door, then went upstairs to her bedroom. She got the little gun her father had given her from the bedside drawer, then crossed to the back windows and looked out again.

There were three men standing in her yard now, looking about. They looked nervous; one of them, the one she hadn't seen at all before, looked downright twitchy, his head jerking back and forth, scanning the shrubbery.

Naturally, he was the one with the gun.

It was quite a large gun, too, not one that would fit in a holster, and not a kind Amy remembered ever seeing before. It looked oddly bulbous but very complicated and ominous. He had it tucked under his right arm, he wasn't pointing it at anyone or anything, but Amy still had to suppress a nervous shudder. She was very glad she hadn't gone out to yell at the men for wrecking her yard; that man looked as if he might have shot her without even meaning to.

The second man righted the fallen lawn chair and sat down—making himself right at home, Amy thought with a stab of resentment. Then he put his head down in his hands, and she felt a twinge of guilt for her feelings. She still didn't have the faintest idea what was going on, but obviously, whatever these people were doing had gone wrong. Let the poor man sit down if he had to.

The big blond who had been the first out cupped his hands around his mouth and called, "Hello, in the house!"

Amy didn't answer. She thought about it, but decided to wait.

"Hello!" he called again.

She put the gun down and opened the window latch, then reconsidered.

"Where are we?" the man shouted. "Can you send for the authorities?"

Amy frowned. That seemed like a strange thing to ask. She opened the window a few inches.

"I already did!" she called.

The man blinked up at her, and the other man, the one with the big gun, turned to look. She ducked down and picked up her own gun.

This was crazy, she told herself. This was absolutely insane. These people were not acting like air-crash survivors at all. And that plane didn't really look that much like a plane.

So who the hell were they, then, and what *was* that thing? They didn't sound like foreigners, not really—though asking her to send for the authorities, rather than to call the cops, was odd phrasing.

That thing they came in—she had a better view of it from upstairs than she had had at ground level. It didn't look like an airplane.

It looked like a spaceship—but not a real spaceship—not the space shuttle or a moon rocket. It looked like something out of an old "Flash Gordon" serial, only *real*—as if those comic-book spaceships had been based on this ship the way comic-book cars were based on real ones.

It bore the same relationship to those cheap models in "Flash Gordon," she thought, that a real 1947 Checker bore to Benny the Cab in *Who Framed Roger Rabbit?*

She blinked. Was someone shooting a movie, maybe? She'd never seen a ship like that in any movie, though. They wouldn't build it full scale and drop it in her back yard, in any case—not without asking her permission.

What the *hell* was going on?

Then she heard the sirens approaching and decided it wasn't her problem anymore.

CHAPTER 2

The nagging in the back of Miletti's head had been there for a few days, and he didn't really consciously notice it anymore—until it abruptly stopped. For a moment he was startled by the sudden mental silence; then he realized what had happened and smiled broadly.

It had stopped.

It was about time.

He had never figured out what caused that odd feeling, but whatever it had been, it was a relief to be rid of it.

■

Angela Thompson burst out crying, and when her mother finally got an explanation, it took a real effort not to slap the girl for getting hysterical over nothing.

"Mr. Nobody stopped talking to me," indeed!

■

Ray Aldridge didn't like it when the messages stopped, but it was no big deal. They weren't providing all that much useful material, anyway—no bulletins from dead millionaires or miracle diet plans. He had gotten along without them for years, and he could get by without them again. He would just go back to making up his own.

■

Oram Blaisdell wasn't so complacent as the others. When the angels from Venus stopped talking to him, he concluded that Satan had somehow killed them all. He got his old twelve-gauge from the back room and went out to his pickup and headed north.

He wasn't any too sure where Goshen, Maryland, might be, but he reckoned he could find it.

He got as far as Radford, Virginia, before the cops picked him up for speeding. Listening to his story, they decided the poor old guy shouldn't be running around loose. They called up his kids back in Paulette.

Between Henry Blaisdell's coaxing and the state troopers' story about a secret government campaign against the Satanists in Goshen, Oram finally decided to go home and mind his own business.

Satan wouldn't get him without a fight, when the time came, but why go looking for trouble where he wasn't wanted?

■

Pel Brown was sitting in his favorite chair, rereading C. S. Forester's *Ship of the Line*, when someone knocked.

He glanced up, annoyed. He had been in the middle of the scene where the *Sutherland*, Hornblower's ship, tears up an entire Italian army on the Spanish shore road, and he resented the interruption. He had been comfortably absorbed in ships' broadsides and Napoleonic politics.

Nancy and Rachel were out shopping, he remembered, partly to return the duplicate tape of *Beauty and the Beast* Rachel had gotten at her party yesterday, but mostly after groceries. They weren't around to answer the knock—but maybe whoever it was would go away.

Whoever it was didn't go away, but knocked again instead.

Why would anyone knock, anyway? Was the doorbell broken?

Sighing heavily, Pel got up out of the recliner and put the book down on the end table, using the unpaid cable TV bill as a bookmark. He plodded to the front door and opened it.

No one was there. The porch and front steps were empty. No one was on the sidewalk or the lawn, either. More annoyed than ever, Pel turned and headed back for the recliner.

The knock sounded again, and he realized it wasn't coming from the front door. It was coming from the door to the basement.

Had Nancy come home without his even noticing it and somehow got herself locked in the basement?

No, because then where was Rachel? She was never this quiet. And besides, he hadn't been *that* involved with the book; he'd have heard them come in.

Maybe a meter reader had come in from outside and needed to talk to him about something?

On Sunday? Not likely.

There was one easy way to find out. He opened the basement door.

The man standing on the steps was a complete stranger. Pel blinked at him, startled.

"Good day, sir," the stranger said. He bowed, right arm across his chest, a hat in his right hand, a feather bobbing on the hat.

"Hi," Pel said. "Who the hell are you?"

"I am called Raven," the stranger replied, with another bow. "And whom do I have the honor of addressing?"

Pel stared for a moment.

He had, he felt, plenty of reason to stare. The man before him was of medium height, maybe five foot eight or so, with curly black hair and a tan. He was wearing a black tunic with silver embroidery and gold trim, black woolen hose on his legs, and a fine black velvet cloak thrown over one shoulder. The hat he held was a wide-brimmed, flat-crowned black felt, with a curling white ostrich plume in the band.

It didn't look like a stage costume, though—the materials were too heavy, and the detailing was too fine, without any of the glitzy look of theatrical attire. The clothes had a solid reality to them.

So did the man who wore them. He had a long nose, dark eyes, and lines at the corners of a thin-lipped mouth; Pel estimated him to be in his late thirties or early forties. He looked more like a mafioso than an actor.

He was waiting for an answer.

"Pel Brown," Pel said at last.

The stranger straightened up a little more and said, "Your servant, sir. Are you the master here?"

"It's my house, if that's what you mean." Pel considered it

odd that the man's speech was rather flowery, in accord with his garb, but his accent was faint and seemed somewhere between Australia and the Bronx, not at all in the traditional British upper-class manner.

"Indeed," Raven said. He moved his eyes.

Pel took the hint and stepped aside. "Come on up out of there," he said.

The man who had introduced himself as Raven obliged, and for the first time Pel realized that the stranger's tunic was belted with a wide band of black leather, and that a sword hung from that belt. Not a dueling foil, as his outfit might have led one to expect, but a sheathed broadsword.

"Come on over here," Pel said.

Raven's eyes darted about, taking in the passageway, the kitchen that was visible through the doorway, the family room, the bookcases, the étagères, the couch, the recliner, the video setup, and the Maxfield Parrish print on the wall.

Pel stepped back and closed the basement door, making sure that it latched and that the lock was set. Then he followed his guest into the family room.

Upon spotting the stranger, the household cat, Silly Cat by name, leaped up from his place on the back of the couch and made a dash for the stairs. He was a timid beast, much given to hiding under the bed, and would hardly ever stay in the same room with an unfamiliar human being.

"Have a seat," Pel said, gesturing to the couch.

"Thank you," Raven said. He sank onto the sofa and seemed startled by how soft the cushions were. His sword got in the way; he swung it to the side and had to unbuckle the belt to get comfortable. He pulled the leather band out, wrapped it around the scabbard, and then laid the whole package gently on the coffee table, carefully not disturbing the two issues of *TV Guide* or the beer-stained coaster. His velvet cloak he draped over the back of the couch, where, Pel was sure, the velvet would pick up cat hairs.

Pel settled back into his recliner, his hand reaching automatically for his book. He stopped himself, leaned forward, and asked, "So, Raven, you said?"

The stranger nodded.

"Okay," Pel said. "So what were you doing in my basement? You have anything to do with the elf who turned up down there night before last?"

"Elf?" Raven's face expressed polite puzzlement.

"Something like that—little guy, about this high." Pel held out his hands to show his tiny visitor's height. "Said he was from Hrumph."

"Oh." Raven nodded. "Aye, that would be Grummetty."

"Grummetty, huh?"

"Aye," Raven said. "A little person. He's no elf; the elven are another sort entirely. Of a time, we called Grummetty's people gnomes, but 'twould seem they find the term offensive now, so we . . . well, most of us try to oblige them. Particularly now, in their days of exile."

"I asked him if he was a fairy," Pel said.

"Alack for that!" Raven exclaimed. A wry grin flickered quickly across his face, then vanished. "He made no mention on that. I'll hope he took not too great an offense at it."

"No, he accepted it as an honest misunderstanding, I think. So, he's a friend of yours?"

"An ally, more than a friend, I would say," Raven replied judiciously.

"Oh," Pel said, accepting the distinction without comprehension. "Well, so you got into my basement the same way he did?"

Raven nodded. "Exactly. It pleases me well to see that you're a man of such quick intelligence."

Pel gave a self-deprecating smile. "Sure. So now that we've got that straight—who the hell *are* you people, and how are you getting into my basement, and why?"

"Well . . ." Raven's eyes roamed the room again, taking in the green wall-to-wall carpeting, the textured ceiling, the green drapes, the sliding glass door to the patio, the books and records, the CDs and videotapes, and the throw pillows that Rachel had stacked on the floor as a fort for her Barbie dolls.

Pel waited.

Raven sighed. " 'Tis a long story," he said, "and I scarce know where to start."

"Begin at the beginning," Pel said, without thinking. "And go on till you come to the end; then stop." The quote from Lewis Carroll was an old favorite.

"Indeed, that's the wisest course for most tales," Raven agreed, "but I think I'd do best to start by asking you a question. What know you, sir, of worlds other than your own?"

"It depends how you mean that," Pel replied cautiously. He did not intend to set himself up for anything.

"What I mean, good sir," Raven replied, "is that I am not of your world. In truth, I know nothing of it save what Grummetty told me and what I have seen for myself. Your pardon, but your world seems to me passing strange; your chamber here reminds of nothing so much as a wizard's secret chamber, yet the door—it is a door?—aye, the door yonder is sheerest glass, is it not? Not some mage's trickery?"

"It's glass," Pel agreed. "Go on."

"Doors of glass," Raven said, shaking his head in amazement.

"Get on with it!" Pel snapped. His patience was wearing thin. If this was all some elaborate stunt he was getting tired of it; he wanted the punchline. If it was real—well, that was another matter entirely. That was frightening.

It was downright terrifying, in fact.

"Your pardon, sir," Raven said, ducking his head. "As I was saying, your world is not my own, nor from what I see here does it much resemble my own, though men are yet men, and the trees and grass I see through the pane seem familiar, and we speak the same tongue."

That fact had already struck Pel. It seemed very unlikely that people from another world would speak English.

"It seems to me that you speak it as the little people do, rather than as my own, yet 'tis certainly the same tongue," Raven continued.

Pel began to wonder if he would ever get to the point. "All right, you're from another world," he said. "How'd you get in my basement?"

" 'Tis the doing of our mage, Elani, with a spell stolen from the foe; she sent first Grummetty, and then myself, to see what manner of world it was that the Imperials had found in their quest for aid against Shadow."

"What?" asked Pel, thoroughly confused. Raven's accent seemed to be thickening, and his phrasing becoming more complex, as he settled into the conversation. The words didn't seem to make sense, but he tried a little free association. "You're in trouble with Lamont Cranston's Chrysler?"

"How's that?" Raven expressed polite puzzlement.

"Never mind," Pel said, waving it aside. "Go on."

Raven nodded. "As I said, 'tis a long tale. Know you aught of Shadow, or perchance of the Imperials?"

"No," Pel said flatly. He decided not to try any Little Anthony jokes.

"I feared as much." The stranger groped for words, then began. "Shadow," he said, "is an evil thing. 'Twas once a mortal wizard, the legends say, but I'd not swear to that. Whatever it is in truth, its magic is great, its slaves and servants many and mighty, and in its realm its power is absolute. For centuries, since before my family's first father began the archives, Shadow has been growing, spreading its power, fighting and defeating and devouring mages and wizards, learning their spells and consuming their power. In its wake come death and terror; castles are thrown down, their inhabitants horribly slain. Villages are burned, the people devoured, the crops and livestock vanished. For centuries, men of good will have struggled against Shadow, have resisted the offers it made of power in its foul realm—but weaker men have sold their souls for empty promises and brief pleasures."

Pel listened appreciatively. Raven told the story well, despite his curious accent. Pel had heard it before, of course, in any number of fantasy novels and movies. "And you've found some way this Shadow can be defeated?" he asked, anticipating the next step in the traditional plot. "Some talisman that can kill it, or something?"

"No," Raven said, startled, "of course not. Such things are the stuff of children's tales. We know of no way Shadow can be fought save by slaying its creatures and combatting its spells, as we have done since my grandfather was a babe."

"No?" It was Pel's turn to be startled.

"No! No, there can be no easy victory—can there?" An odd, hopeful note crept into Raven's voice. "Do you know of some way that Shadow can be defeated? Has something like this happened in your world, and was a way found?"

"No, of course not," Pel replied, confused. "Magic doesn't work in the real world."

For a moment Raven was silent, his face slowly reddening; then he stood up angrily. "You mock me, sir," he said, in a tone that was pure threat.

If this was a joke, Raven was a superb actor; he sounded utterly sincere. Pel blinked up at him, startled anew, and for a long silent moment the two men stared at each other.

"No, I don't," Pel said at last. "I'm sorry. I don't mean any mockery. Go on with your story."

Raven glared for a moment longer, then slowly settled back onto the couch. He stared at the far wall for a moment, where a blonde in white gauze rode a swing before a landscape of impossibly vivid colors.

Pel had always loved that print, but Raven seemed puzzled by it.

At last the stranger said, "Magic does not work in your world, you say?"

"No," Pel said. "At least, we generally don't think so, except for a few loonies. Real magic doesn't work. It never has."

Raven nodded.

"That," he said, "might well account for Grummetty's illness. 'Tis said by some that the little people are magical in origin and yet need a trace of that magic to live. Perhaps in your world that magic is gone, and they cannot exist. Grummetty told us all that he felt as if his own flesh were burning him when he came here, and indeed he was sore ill when he returned to us. At first we feared he might not live, but when his fever broke and his strength began to return, I ventured through the portal. As yet, I've felt no ill here."

"Oh," Pel said. "He said he felt sick. I wondered about that."

Raven nodded. "We sent a little person at the first because he might more easily hide, should danger arise. He said he found no danger save the illness, only a metalsmith at work. Would that be you, sir?"

"I was putting together a wagon for my daughter," Pel explained, a little impatiently. "She just turned six, and we had a party for her yesterday. Now would you go on with your story about the Shadow and what you're doing here?"

"Indeed," Raven said. "And gladly will I speak, an it be that my words can sway. That thing we call Shadow has conquered all my world, now; the darkness is everywhere. From one edge to the other it is supreme, and only in isolated pockets do a few of us still resist its dominion. In truth, we can do little 'gainst it. And having thus triumphed, 'twould seem that the evil seeks new challenge; our surviving free mages, working in secret, spied upon Shadow and learned that it had sought new worlds to conquer—and had in fact found them."

"Earth, you mean?" Pel asked.

Raven stared blankly at him. "Earth?"

"This world, I mean," Pel explained.

"Oh," Raven said, with a glance out through the glass of the sliding door. "You call this Earth? How odd." He shook his head. " 'Tis no matter, though. No, 'twas not this world Shadow found, but another, the realm of the Imperials."

"Oh. Okay, who are *they*?" The tale, Pel thought, was getting unnecessarily long and complicated, and he wished that Raven would get to the point.

"They are men, like us," Raven told him, "and they rule not one world, but many. Not worlds that are reached by magical portals, such as the one that brought me hither, but worlds that float separately in the sky, among the stars, and that can be sailed to in special flying ships—or so I am told. I do not pretend to understand it, not having been there. They call all the worlds gathered under their rule the Galactic Empire, though I know not whence the name derives."

"The Galactic Empire?" Pel objected. "Aren't you mixing genres?"

"What?" Raven asked. His confusion was beginning to have a constant visible admixture of anger, and Pel decided not to provoke him with explanations of the difference between science fiction and fantasy.

"Never mind," Pel replied. "Go on."

"As you will," Raven said, calming. He continued. "When

'twas learned that Shadow sought these other realms, certain mages among those who strove 'gainst the darkness took careful study and discovered the secrets of the spells Shadow had used in its researches—Elani was one such. Those mages then opened portals to the worlds of the Galactic Empire, that they might forewarn the Imperials, and thereby gain their aid in fighting Shadow. However, those who passed through these portals found that the Empire was strange beyond our understanding and was perhaps itself no better than the lesser of two evils. Some, my group among them, therefore resolved not to trust the Imperials, but to proceed on our own."

"So you looked for another, better world, and you found us?" Pel asked.

"No," Raven answered. "The Imperials did that. Once they learned that one other reality existed, and that 'twas ruled by a hostile force, they set about finding another, in hopes of acquiring an ally in their coming battle against Shadow. They have no mages, but they have men and women who can hear the thoughts of others . . ."

"Telepaths?" Pel suggested.

"Aye, telepaths, the very word they use!" Raven agreed, startled.

Pel nodded. For once he'd guessed right about something in Raven's tale. "Go on," he said.

Raven continued, " 'Twould seem that these telepaths had sometimes found traces of thought for which they could not account. Some, it seemed, had leaked through from my own native realm—but some, so it chanced, came from *your* world. Thus, they sought out your reality and attempted to send messages to a few receptive individuals therein. When that yielded no useful results, they devised a means of transporting one of their skyships into whatsoever other realities they might find, and sent that ship hither, to your land. This morning it arrived, and if Elani's spell be sound, not far from here. My group learned about these plans, and our mages opened a portal, that we might communicate with your people—this, that you might have some contact with our realm other than through the Imperials, and that, perhaps, we, too, might benefit from whatever your people can teach us." He frowned. "We had hoped that our messenger might bespeak your rulers ere the ship of the Imperials came, but alas, Grummetty's illness cut short our first attempt, and 'twas not until some hours after the ship was sent that we made another."

Raven spread his hands.

"And here I am," he said, just as Pel heard the whir of the garage door opener.

■

Amy Jewell watched as the last of the crewmen from the spaceship—if that's what it was—climbed reluctantly into the police van.

"What's going to happen to them?" she asked.

The plainclothes cop beside her looked up from his notepad. "Them?" he said, pointing his pen at the van.

Amy nodded.

The cop shrugged. "I don't know," he said. "I never heard of anything like this before. If it's a publicity stunt I expect the movie company will bail them out tomorrow morning—not today, because it's Sunday and the judge won't be in, but probably first thing tomorrow. *If* it's for a movie. And they didn't resist arrest or give us any trouble at all—hell, you probably heard them, they were *asking* to talk to the authorities—so even if they *don't* get bailed out we may not be able to hold them."

Amy nodded again. "I see," she said, though she wasn't sure she did.

"You worried about them?" the cop asked, giving her a shrewd glance.

Amy grimaced. "Not really," she said.

The cop didn't answer.

"What about the airpl—the shi—that thing?" Amy asked, pointing. "How are you going to get it off my lawn?"

The cop frowned. Then he sighed. "I don't know, lady," he said. "That's not my job. I'm sorry, but it's not police business. Either you can move it, because it's your yard, or they can move it, because it's their ship. Either way, they're liable, but you'll probably need to sue them to collect." He glanced at the huge purple object. "The FAA people are supposed to be on their way out here

now, you know, Sunday or not—they want to look at the thing and
figure out how it got here. You probably shouldn't touch anything
until they get here."

A siren started up, then cut off abruptly; a white pumper
truck with GAITHERSBURG–WASHINGTON GROVE FIRE DEPARTMENT let-
tered on the doors in gold pulled away, the engine roaring and the
tires spitting gravel from the roadside. Amy and the cop watched
it go.

"I've gotta say," the plainclothesman remarked, "that this is
the weirdest damn thing I ever heard of."

Amy nodded.

"If worst comes to worst," he suggested, "you could sell tick-
ets and run tours."

"I suppose so," Amy said unenthusiastically. She wasn't really
very interested in the idea; she wanted her yard back, not a tourist
trap. She didn't really need so dubious a source of additional in-
come.

As she watched the pumper depart she spotted a blue sedan
creeping up the road. She thought it looked as if it had writing on
the door, but at that angle and distance she couldn't make it out.

"That's the FAA boys now," the cop said. "I'll be going along.
If you could come to the station tomorrow and let us know
whether you want to press charges or anything, we'd appreciate
it."

"All right," Amy said distractedly.

"That's it, then," the cop said, closing his notepad. "Have a
nice day."

He turned and ambled toward the remaining county police
cruiser as the van pulled away and the blue sedan coasted to a
stop.

CHAPTER 3

Nancy stared stupidly as Raven bowed deeply. Rachel giggled behind her hand and dropped a small plastic shopping bag to the floor.

"Hi, honey," Pel said. He gestured at their unexpected guest. "This is Raven."

"Hi," Nancy said, looking questioningly at Pel as he came to take one of the bags of groceries from her arms.

"Your servant, madame," Raven said, bowing again.

"My wife, Nancy, and my daughter, Rachel," Pel explained as he carried the groceries into the kitchen.

"A pleasure to meet you, I assure you," Raven said.

Nancy murmured something vague, then followed Pel into the kitchen with the other bag.

"Who's *he*?" she demanded. "Why's he dressed like that?"

Pel put the sack on the counter and started putting cans of soup on the pantry cupboard shelves while he tried to think how to answer that.

"He says to call him Raven," he said. "I'm not sure if it's really his name or not. And he's apparently dressed like that because that's what he wears at home."

"Where's home? What's he doing here?"

A can of Campbell's cream of mushroom slipped, and Pel caught it in his other hand.

"I don't know, really," he said. "I mean, I sort of do, but it's . . . well, it's not that it's hard to explain as that nobody would believe the explanation." He paused, considering, and added, "I'm not sure *I* believe it."

Nancy stared at him. "Pel, what are you talking about?" she asked, worried.

Pel looked helplessly around the kitchen, as if hoping the cabinets would tell him what to say.

The cabinets remained blank.

He could hear voices from the family room, he realized—Raven and Rachel were talking. He crossed to the door and leaned through.

"You see?" Raven was saying, "it is indeed a real sword. And sharp—do not you touch it, lest you cut your pretty fingers." He had pulled about a foot of the blade from its sheath, and Rachel was admiring the dull gleam of the metal.

That wasn't cheap chrome, like some of the ceremonial swords Pel had seen, nor stainless steel, nor plain iron. Even from the kitchen door he could see the fine finish, the sort of finish one saw on very expensive carving knives.

Nancy came up behind him and looked over his shoulder.

"Pel," she whispered in his ear, "what's he *doing* here?"

Pel turned and pushed Nancy back into the kitchen.

"He's from some sort of fantasy world," he said. "Where magic works. He's a warrior of some kind, I guess."

"You mean he's crazy? An escaped lunatic?" In an instant, Nancy's expression went from mildly concerned to seriously worried.

"No," Pel told her, "or at least I don't think so. I think he's for real. There's some kind of space warp that comes out in our basement."

The worried look now verged on panic. "Maybe *you're* crazy, too!" Nancy said. "Pel, what are you *talking* about?"

Pel groped unsuccessfully for words and finally just said, "Come on." He took Nancy's hand and pulled her back into the family room, where Rachel was admiring the silver embroidery on Raven's tunic. Raven was watching the girl's little fingers indulgently as they explored the textures.

Raven looked up as the pair entered, and smiled. "A lovely child," he said. "And well spoken."

"Thanks," Pel said.

"In her sixth year, you said. Or was it seventh?"

"She just turned six."

"Ah!"

For a moment the Browns just stood there, and Raven sat, and Rachel ran her fingertips down the silver piping. Then Raven carefully lifted Rachel off his knee, placed her on the couch, and stood up.

"My presence here troubles you, I see," he said, "and I've no wish to trouble anyone."

Pel chewed his lower lip, glancing back and forth between Raven and Nancy, while Raven awaited a reply. He was obviously hoping for a polite denial, but Nancy was obstinately silent as she stared at the stranger.

Raven sighed and picked up his sword. "I'll be going, then," he said.

"I'm sorry," Pel said, "but I can't think of any way to explain you that doesn't sound crazy."

"Ah," Raven said, comprehension dawning, "I see. I'd feared it was something else, that perhaps I'd given offense somehow. I know so little of your world, after all!" He looked hopefully at Nancy.

She remained silent; it was Pel who assured him, "No, you've been charming. But your clothes, and your name . . . well, it's strange."

Raven nodded.

"Madame," he said, "I beg your pardon for intruding, and for my garb, which I take it you find outlandish. In truth, I *am* outlandish—I've come here from another realm entirely."

Pel listened to this with interest; it was remarkable how much more believable that sounded coming from Raven than it did coming from him.

It still wasn't very believable, though, and in fact Nancy obviously still didn't believe it.

Rachel was also skeptical, judging by her expression. Nifty embroidery and shiny swords were all very well, but modern kindergarteners knew better than to believe stories about other worlds. Rachel had independently figured out just weeks before that Santa Claus wasn't real; she was still working on the Easter bunny and the tooth fairy, but she wasn't about to accept Raven at face value.

Raven could see the disbelief as well as Pel could. He sighed. "You doubt me," he said, deliberately understating the case, "and I can scarce blame you, for who in her right mind would believe such an assertion without proof? But perhaps I can convince you. And if not, I'll go, and at least you'll be rid of me." He rose and reached for his sword and belt. "Pel Brown," he said as he fastened the buckle, "if you would be so kind as to lead us to the cellars?"

That was clearly the thing to do, though the idea had not occurred to Pel. "Come on," he said, "everybody down in the basement, and you can see why I believed Raven about where he came from."

They trooped down the stairs, Raven in the lead, then Pel, then Rachel, and last, Nancy. Raven did not hesitate; he walked directly across the basement and into the concrete wall.

Unlike Grummetty, who had whacked his head the first time he tried to return to his own reality, Raven vanished immediately.

Rachel's eyes widened, and her mouth opened.

Nancy turned to her husband and demanded, "Pel, what's going on here?"

"You saw," Pel said. "He vanished into the wall. See, night before last, when I was down here, this little tiny guy, like an elf or something, appeared out of nowhere, and talked to me for a minute, and then disappeared into the wall just the way Raven did." He didn't mention the bump. "Then this afternoon, when you were out, I heard knocking, and there Raven was, in our basement. And he gave me this whole story about another world, and I know it sounds stupid, but I bought it—it sounded real, and he looked real, and I couldn't figure out any other way it could happen."

"Well, he's gone now," Nancy said. Just then Rachel, who had wandered halfway across the basement staring at the spot where Raven had vanished, let out a shriek.

Raven was stepping back out of the blank concrete wall.

Rachel came running back across the basement floor to her parents and flung herself against her father, who bent down and picked her up, hugging her to him.

"It's okay, Rae," he told her, as Nancy laid a comforting hand on the back of the little girl's head, "it's just Raven. It's okay."

The dismay he saw on Raven's face over Rachel's shoulder could not be feigned, Pel was sure.

"My humble apologies, Mistress Rachel," Raven said, going down on one knee and lowering his head. "I'd not meant to startle you. Please, forgive me?"

Rachel lifted her head from her father's chest and peeked behind her. When she saw Raven's posture she pressed her hands against Pel's shoulders, and he lowered her to the ground.

She turned to face Raven, but didn't say anything.

The man in black raised his head and looked at her. "Grant me your pardon, Mistress Rachel, please. Say you forgive me," he begged.

"It's okay," Rachel said, "I think. Isn't it, Daddy?"

"I think so," Pel agreed.

"Thank you," Raven said, rising to his feet and brushing the dust from the knee of his hose. He stood, waiting.

Nancy still didn't say anything.

"Shall we go back upstairs?" Pel suggested.

Nancy didn't say anything, but she turned and marched back up.

A moment later all four of them were back in the family room, and Nancy finally spoke.

"Pel," she said, "come in the kitchen for a moment."

Pel came.

When they were out of sight of Raven and Rachel, Nancy whispered loudly, "Do you really believe him?"

Pel shrugged. "I'm not sure," he said. "I don't have any better explanation."

"It could be some kind of trick," Nancy suggested, "some kind of illusion."

"Sure, I guess it could be," Pel agreed, "but why?"

"*I* don't know," Nancy said, fretting, "but I don't like it."

Pel sighed again. "Nancy," he said, "the guy is not selling me anything. I'm just talking to him. He turned up in the basement, with this whole story about some kind of cosmic war, and I'm just listening to it. That's all. And frankly, I want to hear some more. If you want to go upstairs or something, go ahead."

"All right," she said, "you can talk." She turned and led the way back into the family room, then stopped suddenly.

"Can I get you a drink?" she asked Raven.

He glanced at Pel, then back at Nancy. "Thank you, aye," he said, "I judge I could put a drink to use."

"Um . . . beer?"

"Yes, that would suit me well, thank you."

Nancy spun on her heel and marched back toward the refrigerator while Pel resumed his seat on the recliner. Rachel was sitting on the couch, not touching Raven, Pel noticed, but staring at him intently. His performance in the basement had obviously impressed her.

"Now," Pel said, "you were telling me that you came here to talk to us about maybe joining forces with your people against something you call a Shadow?"

"Yes," Raven said, with a nod. "That's exactly right."

"Shadow is magical, right?"

"Aye," Raven said, " 'tis magical in nature. We know little enough of its true origins, but we know that much. It has gathered to itself all the magic that its evil allowed it, the greater part of all the world's magical might, leaving only crumbs for our wizards to pick at. Because the good magicians were not united against it, it has triumphed."

"But magic doesn't work here. No one in our world *has* any magic."

Nancy appeared from the kitchen, carrying two cans of Miller.

"You have nothing you call magic, perhaps, and nothing like our magicks, it would seem," Raven agreed. "But you have magicks of your own, I am sure, though perhaps you call them by another name. The Galactic Empire calls its magic *science*; do you use that, perhaps?"

"Science isn't magic," Rachel said scornfully.

Raven turned to her, startled.

"She's right," Pel said. "Science isn't magic. It does some pretty amazing things, though."

Nancy put the two cans of beer on the table, then seated herself on the arm of the couch behind Rachel, at the far end from Raven. Pel leaned forward, picked one can up, and popped the top.

Raven blinked, then picked up the other.

"Cold!" he exclaimed, startled, as he quickly put it back down. He stared at it.

Rachel giggled. Pel and Nancy exchanged a glance.

"Maybe he's British," Nancy said, *sotto voce*.

"Course it's cold!" Rachel said. "It just came out of the fridge!"

Raven glanced at her, then reached down and cautiously picked up the beer can. He held it up with one hand while the other explored it carefully, stroking beads of condensation from the side, feeling the smooth, thin metal. He studied it intently.

"I'd wondered," he said, "why you had no bottles or barrels in your cellar. It seems you have other ways of keeping things cool."

"The refrigerator," Pel agreed. "I guess that's some of the scientific magic you were asking about." He remembered his own beer and took a pull on the can.

Raven watched him, then looked at the top of the can he held. "How ... there are letters here, stamped in the metal, or etched, perhaps. I cannot read them."

"Oh," Pel said. He put down his own beer and leaned over. "Let me show you," he said.

He took the can and popped the top, while Raven watched, fascinated. Beer foamed up, and Pel handed it back.

Raven tasted it.

"Good," he said, though his expression contradicted his words.

"It's American beer," Pel remarked. "I like the European stuff better."

"This is a trifle thin, perhaps," Raven agreed.

"So I guess we have technology you don't, like refrigerators," Pel said, leaning back with his beer in hand. "Is that what you came looking for?"

"I'd nothing specific in mind," Raven said, "but if you have this science, or ... technology, did you call it? If you have this, and use it for weapons, perhaps we could use it against Shadow."

"I suppose you could," Pel agreed. "If it works in your world."

"Why shouldn't it?" Nancy demanded, addressing her husband rather than their guest.

"Magic doesn't work here," Pel pointed out.

Raven sipped beer. "There is that," he agreed. "So you do have technology weapons? Ray guns, perhaps, like the Galactic Empire's? Or mayhap you call them blasters? The Imperials use both terms."

"Not exactly," Pel said, amused. "The closest we have to ray guns would be lasers, I guess, and they only work as weapons in the movies."

"In the . . . ?" Raven began.

"Never mind," Pel said, cutting him off. "In stories, I should have said."

"What works in reality, then?"

"Bombs," Pel said. "Guns. Tanks, airplanes, nuclear warheads. Poison gas."

"I know bombs," Raven said, a little hesitantly, "and I think I know what you mean by guns, but these others—what sort of tank is a weapon? What is a nuclear warhead?"

"A nuclear warhead," Pel explained, "is a bomb that can destroy an entire city."

Raven sat silently for a moment, staring at Pel. Rachel got up her nerve to stroke the fine black velvet of his cloak, and Nancy got up to go to the kitchen again.

"How big be these warheads?" Raven asked at last. "Be they real, not just another fancy found in stories?"

"Oh, yes," Pel said, "they're real. But they're very big and heavy, and besides, only a few governments have access to them."

"You don't want them," Nancy said, startling both Pel and Raven. "Besides destroying cities they poison the air and soil, and kill or deform unborn children."

"In truth?" Raven asked, looking at Pel.

"Truly," Pel said, nodding. "They use atomic energy—the same thing that keeps the sun burning—and that produces radiation."

"Our sun burns with magic—I know nothing of yours. But your people fight with these bombs?"

"No," Pel said. "We keep from fighting because we're scared of them."

"Don't forget Hiroshima," Nancy interjected.

Raven looked a question.

"We used them once," Pel admitted.

"Twice," Nancy said.

"Right, twice. On Hiroshima and Nagasaki. Two cities in Japan. That was when the bombs were first invented, at the end of a long war, when we didn't know any better. Almost fifty years ago."

"Ah. So you know they work, then."

"Oh, yes, they work," Pel said bitterly.

"And are they strong enough to break through fortress walls?"

Pel stared at Raven for a moment, then said, "I don't think you understand. A nuclear bomb can totally obliterate an entire city—flatten it, leave nothing but a crater. When they tested them in the desert they fused the sand into glass. The Hiroshima bomb killed a hundred thousand people—and that was a small one, much less powerful than the ones we have now. If you dropped a nuclear bomb on a fortress, *any* fortress, the fortress would be gone. There wouldn't be any walls left."

"Even a magical fortress?"

"There's no such thing."

"There is in *my* world."

Pel had no immediate answer to that, but Nancy said, "It doesn't matter, anyway—you can't get a nuclear warhead, not even a Russian one. They're kept sealed away, heavily guarded. And you wouldn't know how to use one if you had it."

"I see. But guns and bombs and . . . and tanks?"

"You can get guns easily enough. And make bombs. I don't think you could get tanks, though."

Raven nodded. "I see. Thank you." He put down his can of beer and spoke slowly, as if making an effort to phrase clearly what he wanted to say. "I think perhaps I have imposed enough upon your hospitality," he told the Browns. "I'm very grateful for your kindness, but perhaps I had best return home now, to discuss what you have told me with my people."

"You haven't finished your beer," Nancy pointed out.

Raven looked at the can. "I fear my thirst is gone," he said, rising.

"All right," Pel said. "I'm sorry we couldn't be more help."

"I may return, sometime, if you have no objection," Raven said diffidently.

"We'd be glad to see you," Pel replied, getting to his own feet and not adding that he would be glad mostly because it would be further evidence that this wasn't all simply a dream or hallucination.

"I like your cape," Rachel said.

Raven smiled down at her. "I like it, too, child," he said kindly.

Pel led the way to the basement, and together, the Browns watched Raven vanish into the wall again.

As Pel had feared, there were cat hairs on the black velvet cloak.

■

"Are you people finished?" Amy asked.

"I don't know," the FAA man answered, not looking at her, "I really don't."

Amy stared at him without trying to hide her annoyance. "Why don't you know?" she demanded.

"Because I don't know what the hell is going on here," he told her.

She stared at him, and he explained, "That thing out there— it's not an aircraft. There's no way it could ever have flown under its own power. There's no engine, just this weird contraption of crystals and metal plates that doesn't do anything, attached to what looks like a pressure chamber. Some of the equipment aboard is ordinary electrical stuff, and it works fine; other equipment is more of this crystal-and-metal nonsense that doesn't do anything. Those weapons those people were carrying—they have little batteries, but they don't *do* anything. All of them, the big one and the ones that look like pistols, they're harmless. They don't even light up or make noise like my kid's toy ray guns." He shook his head.

"It's some kind of hoax, I guess," he continued, "but why would anyone go to all this trouble? And all the *expense*? Some of the stuff in there looks as if it's made out of gold and platinum, and if it's all a gag, wouldn't copper or tin do just as well? And how did the thing *get* here, anyway? Nobody tracked anything flying around here that shouldn't have been, and this thing would show up on radar like a Christmas tree, not to mention whatever must have carried it in and dropped it." He sighed. "Lady, you've got a really major mystery sitting in your back yard, and I'm glad I'm not the one who has to figure it out."

"You're not?"

"Nope." He smiled uneasily. "I passed the buck. This close to Washington it's all restricted airspace, you know—or just about. So I called the Air Force. They're sending someone out to take a look, and if he's as impressed as I am—which he will be—they'll be doing some serious investigating in the morning. And I think they called the FBI, too. I'm waiting around until their man gets here, and after that it's up to them. I'm hoping he'll just tell me to go home and forget any of this ever happened."

"But . . ." Amy turned and stared around the corner of her house at the huge purple object. "*I* can't go home and forget about it! It's on my land!"

The FAA man shrugged. "I know," he said, "and I'm sorry. You might want to start thinking about how much to ask if the national-security folks decide to buy your property."

"*What?*" Amy whirled back.

"Well, they probably won't," he said, trying unsuccessfully to sound reassuring. "They may just haul the thing away." He paused, then added thoughtfully, "Though I'm not sure how they'd do that."

Amy stared around wildly, looking for a solution and seeing none.

"Listen," she said, "where'd they take the people who were aboard it?"

The FAA man shrugged. "County jail down in Rockville, I guess," he said.

"Thanks," Amy said.

She turned, leaving the FAA man leaning against the maple tree by the driveway, and went into the house. She wasn't sure just whom to call to find out how she could get to talk to those people, the people who had been inside the thing, but she thought she could figure it out eventually.

And if she couldn't, her lawyer could.

She chewed her lower lip. It was probably time to call her lawyer in any case.

But then she remembered—it was Sunday. No one would be in the law offices on Sunday.

"Damn," she said, staring out the kitchen window at the ship. Then she shrugged. "So I'll have to wait 'til morning. It isn't going anywhere."

CHAPTER 4

"**A**ny word yet?"

The lieutenant started, and looked around. The question had come from a woman in a major's uniform, a woman he did not recognize immediately.

"No, ma'am," he said, saluting.

She returned the salute briskly.

"Thorpe should have reported in *hours* ago, even if Cahn couldn't," the major said.

"Yes, ma'am," the lieutenant agreed.

"You haven't done anything about it?" she demanded sharply.

"No, ma'am," the lieutenant answered. "There's nothing in my orders that says I should, and after Major Copley took ill no one told me anything different."

The major's expression made clear what she thought of that argument. "You've dropped all the other contacts with that universe?" she asked.

"Yes, ma'am—at least, the telepaths were instructed to do so, as soon as the ship went through the warp. I was told that we wanted to be sure Captain Cahn didn't have any of our contacts interfering."

"That's right." The major chewed her lower lip for a few seconds, then ordered, "Get another telepath down here—one who's done those interdimensional contacts. I want to know what the hell Thorpe is doing."

"Yes, ma'am." The lieutenant started to reach for the telephone, then stopped.

Why bother? His post was supposed to be monitored at all times; the telepaths had already heard him.

Or if they hadn't, they were in trouble, which would suit him just fine.

■

"And this device of theirs, which they say will destroy an entire city and leave no stone upon another—believe you that it exists and is not but some mad dream, or a tale to frighten strangers?"

Raven turned up his palms. "Who can say?" he replied. "They spoke of it as if 'twere but simple fact; they named names to me that meant nothing but had the ring of truth, yet how am I to know whether they speak lies? I'm but a man, not a wizard who can read men's souls."

The other snorted. "Would that I could!" he said. "I can see a lie betimes, when 'tis spoke, but beyond that I've no more insight into a man's secrets than you, my lord. I'm not one of these the Empire has, who claim to hear the innermost thoughts of others as if they were spoken aloud."

"Telepaths," Raven said.

"Aye," the other agreed, "that's the word."

For a moment the two were silent. Then Raven spoke.

"What of the Empire's expedition to this new world?" he asked. "Have we word of their success, or perchance their failure? Have they made contacts, or perhaps obtained these terrible weapons?"

"Word is not yet received," the wizard replied.

"No?" Raven turned, startled, to look at the door of the chamber, as if he expected it to burst open on cue.

The door did not move.

"Did not Elani open the way for our messenger this hour past?" Raven asked.

The other nodded. "Aye," he said, "that she did, yet there's no word."

Raven stared at him.

"*Why?*" he demanded.

"Because the messenger tells us that the empire has had no word of their sky ship's fate, and our spies can hardly learn what is known to none," the wizard explained.

"No word?" Raven's brows drew together as he frowned. "Why would there be no word? They have their miracle workers, their telepaths—why have they not heard?"

The wizard turned up his palms. "Who knows?" he asked.

■

"I may have to start believing in UFOs and Bigfoot," Nancy said, as she slumped on the couch and stared at the spot where Raven had sat.

"I wouldn't go that far," Pel said.

"Why not?" she asked, turning to face him. "I mean, if we can have swordsmen and elves walking through our basement wall, why are space aliens bringing Elvis back from the dead any less likely?"

Pel opened his mouth, then closed it again and considered the statement. He looked at Raven's unfinished beer, still sitting on the coffee table.

"I don't know," he said at last. "Maybe they aren't any less likely, but the evidence for them is pretty damn weak."

"Yeah, well, what evidence do we have?" Nancy retorted. "We didn't take any pictures or anything; all we've got is some memories and a can of beer. Is that any better than some of the saucer nuts?"

"No," Pel admitted.

"So maybe it didn't really happen at all," Nancy said; Pel noticed a hopeful tone to her voice. "Maybe we imagined it, got ourselves hypnotized somehow into believing it."

Pel took a deep breath, then let it out slowly.

That explanation was actually just about as believable as any other, he had to admit. He didn't like the idea that his mind could play such tricks on him, and he couldn't explain it, but really, a man from another universe wasn't a much better explanation.

He remembered Raven so clearly, though—the embroidery on his tunic, the greasy smudge on one temple, the cat hairs on his cloak, his odd accent. It didn't seem like something he and Nancy would have imagined, not with the weirdly confusing story about evil wizards and galactic empires.

That reminded him of something, and he sat up in the recliner.

"Hey," he said, "there was something he told me before you got home—he said the Galactic Empire sent a spaceship to Earth. Through a whatchamacallit, a gate or a space warp or whatever, somewhere near here."

Nancy looked puzzled.

"So?" she said.

"*So,*" Pel said, "if it was all *real*, then don't you think a spaceship might make the evening news?"

Nancy blinked.

"I don't know," she said slowly, "maybe."

Pel was annoyed at her lack of enthusiasm, but tried not to show it. "Well, if it's on the news, that would settle it, right? It would all be real, if it's on the news."

"And if it's not?" Nancy asked.

Pel shrugged. "Well, then we still don't know for sure," he said. "But we wouldn't be any worse off than we are."

"That's true," she admitted.

"And if it *is* on the news," Pel said with sudden enthusiasm, "this would really be big-time stuff! The first contact with another universe, my *God!*"

Nancy refused to share his excitement as he lifted the remote control and turned on CNN.

■

Amy spoke quietly into the phone as she peered out her kitchen window. A man with what looked like a metal detector was walking across the back yard, swinging it slowly from side to side a few inches above the dewy grass. A team of men was taking photographs from every possible angle, with one of them holding a yellow measuring stick in various positions to provide a scale; about half of them wore Air Force uniforms, while the rest were in mufti.

They had started arriving right around dawn and had apparently reached equilibrium now, with a few leaving whenever more arrived. And Amy's call had finally gotten an answer.

"This is Amy Jewell," she said. "I need to speak to Bob Hough right away."

"I'm sorry," the receptionist at Dutton, Powell, and Hough replied, "but Mr. Hough is on vacation in Cancun. I have the number of his hotel if this is an emergency, but Ms. Nguyen is handling everything for him while he's away."

Amy paused to think who Ms. Nguyen was. There was Susan, the Vietnamese woman who had helped out with the divorce—that must be her.

Susan had probably done most of the work anyway. The women with no titles or authority generally did everything except get the credit. "All right, then I'll talk to Ms. . . . to her," Amy said.

"She's only just gotten in, but I'll see. Just a moment." There was a click, and insipid music began playing softly. Amy watched as the man with the metal detector thing wandered out of sight around the corner, and the photography crew paused to reload.

"Susan Nguyen," a voice said on the phone.

"Susan," Amy said, relieved; the voice was familiar. This was definitely the Susan she remembered. "This is Amy Jewell; I think you helped Bob Hough handle my divorce last year?"

"Oh, yes, Ms. Jewell; how are you?"

"I'm fine, but listen, something really weird happened yesterday. This . . . this thing landed in my back yard. It's like a . . . well, it's like a spaceship out of a comic book or something."

"A spaceship?" Susan replied dubiously.

"Not a *real* one," Amy said hastily. "I think it's some kind of gag—maybe a publicity stunt of some kind."

"Oh," Susan said. "It still seems strange. How big is . . . no, never mind that. What is it you want us to do?"

"I want it out of my yard, that's what I want!" Amy's temper, carefully held in check until now, finally gave out. "I don't want anything to do with it! I want it *out* of here, and I want all these people who are out here looking at it off my land and away from here! And I want damages—it smashed my hedge and scared the hell out of me!"

"Have you called the police?"

Amy said, almost screaming, "They're the ones who started it!" Then she stopped herself, took a deep breath, and forced herself to calm down.

She could sense Susan waiting calmly on the other end of the line.

"I called 911," Amy said at last, "when the thing first fell here, because I thought it was a crashing airplane or something. So the police and the firemen came out and looked at it, and they took away the people who had been in it, and then the FAA came out and looked at it, and they said it wasn't a private plane, it was some kind of military thing. So now . . ."

"Wait a minute, Ms. Jewell," Susan said, interrupting, "there were *people* in it?"

"Yes! About a dozen of them, in silly purple uniforms. One woman and a bunch of men. All white, most of them blond, like a bunch of Nazis, with things like ray guns that didn't work. The police took them all away and charged them with trespassing. And I want you to find them and find out who's responsible and make them get this thing out of here!"

"I see," Susan said. "Was it the county police that took them?"

"I think so," Amy said. "Someone said something about taking them to Rockville, I think."

"Well, that would be the county, then," Susan agreed. "So you want to know who they are, and get the . . . the thing off your property. Anything else?"

"I want these people out of here. The FAA man called the Air Force, and one of them was here all night, sitting in his car, and a lot more got here this morning before I even woke up, and now there are a bunch of people out there taking pictures and measuring everything, and I want them off my land."

"Air Force?" There was a long pause before Susan said, "I'm not sure how much I can do about them, Ms. Jewell, but I'll try."

"I don't care who they are, I want them off my land!" Amy shouted. "Isn't there something in the Constitution about soldiers in people's houses?"

"Third Amendment," Susan replied automatically. "I doubt it applies in this case, but I'll see what I can do. I need to make a few calls, and then I'll probably want to come out there and see just what the situation is. I have your address and phone number in the files; are they still current?"

"I haven't moved," Amy said.

"Good. Just hold on, Ms. Jewell, and I'll see what I can do."

"Thank you," Amy said.

"Good-bye."

"'Bye." She hung up the phone and looked out the window at the photo team. Now they were pacing off the dimensions of her patio.

What business of theirs was that? She clamped her lips tight and turned away.

Maybe, she thought, if she didn't watch, it wouldn't be so annoying.

■

"What I can't figure out," the detective lieutenant said, "is that not one of them wanted to use the phone. You're *sure* of that?"

The booking sergeant nodded. "Absolutely," he said. "We read them their rights individually, just to be on the safe side, and we explained it all, and we told each of them he was entitled to one phone call, and all we got was blank looks. If I didn't know better, I'd *swear* that none of them had ever heard any of it before."

"What, they never saw cop shows on TV?"

"That's what it seemed like. I mean, when I read the line about if you can't afford an attorney one will be appointed for you, I got these looks you wouldn't believe—they were all of them astonished, as if they'd never heard of such a thing. One of them, I mean, man, his jaw dropped open. And one said, 'Really? It's not a trick?' And Jesus, he sounded sincere."

The detective shook his head in wonder.

The sergeant slapped a hand on the desk. "It's *weird*," he said. "I mean, I know there are nuts out there; I've seen plenty of them. I've seen guys dragged in here trying to pick invisible bugs off their skin, and guys hopped up on PCP who needed a dozen men to hold them, and guys that looked as if they'd been dead for a week and I was afraid they'd drop dead on the floor for real before we could get a doctor in. I've had guys swear at me and curse me up one side and down the other. I've had rich guys screaming at me, and street punks being Momma's little angel, but I have *never* seen anything like this bunch!"

"Gave you a lot of trouble?"

"Hell, no—that's what's so strange! They all of them looked around as if this place was something out of a fairy tale, and did just exactly what they were told, and they gave us names and ranks and serial numbers, like they were prisoners of war instead of just busted for trespassing and littering, but they wouldn't tell us anything *else*. They didn't ask for lawyers, didn't make phone calls, nothing. It's as if they really *believe* they're soldiers from another planet!"

"Maybe they do," the detective suggested.

The sergeant spread his hands wide. "*Ten* of them? Ten nuts with the same delusion?"

The detective shrugged. "So they were all ten like that?"

"Well, eight of 'em, anyway. The woman was a little different, I guess. She seemed real upset, where the others were calm as anything. And the captain, as he's supposed to be—he wanted to talk to someone official, and no, I wouldn't do, he wanted somebody from the military or the state department. I told him I couldn't do that, especially on a weekend."

"Did he say why?"

"Well, yeah. He's an envoy, he says, from the Galactic Empire, and he wants to talk to someone about arranging a mutual-defense treaty with Earth, or at least the United States. He can't make a treaty with local cops."

The detective considered that silently for a moment, then asked, "Think it's a movie stunt?"

"At first I did," the sergeant said, "but now . . . I dunno. Wouldn't they have called in the reporters by now? Wouldn't they have made some phone calls? And why would they pick this lady's back yard way the hell out in Goshen? Her lawyer just called, y'know—the lady's really pissed about it."

The detective nodded again. "So they all claim to come from the Galactic Empire?"

"As much as they claim anything, yeah."

"They're consistent?"

"Oh, yeah, absolutely. Not one of them has slipped out of character for as much as an instant, I swear."

The detective sighed. "All right," he said. "Where should I start?"

"Wherever you like," the sergeant said, pushing a clipboard over.

The detective picked it up and scanned the list of names. "Prosser-pine Thorpe?" he said. "Is that the woman?"

"Proserpin-*ah*," the sergeant corrected him. "Yeah, that's her."

"Gave her rank as 'registered master telepath'?"

"That's what she said, yeah."

"She try to read your mind?"

The sergeant just shrugged.

"Not so you could tell, huh?"

"So how am I supposed to know? But she sure didn't talk about it, if she read anybody's mind."

"You said she was nervous?"

"Well, upset about something, anyway. Had a sort of trapped look—like a junkie who suddenly realizes she doesn't know where to get her next fix. You know what I mean?"

"Sure," the detective said. "She a looker?"

The sergeant shrugged. "She's okay," he said. "Nothing I'd leave home for, but okay."

"What the hell," the detective said, dropping the clipboard back on the desk. "I'll start with her."

■

Proserpine Thorpe stared at the walls of her cell, baffled and frustrated.

Nothing. She had been straining her every nerve, focusing all her being on her telepathic sense, and there was simply nothing there.

This universe had some characteristics that nobody had mentioned or thought about in any of the briefings—presumably because nobody knew about them. The ship's main drive didn't work here. The crew's blasters didn't seem to work, either, though she wasn't sure they'd really been tested.

And, it seemed, telepathy didn't work here.

They should have expected this, or at least considered the possibility. After all, they had known that at least some of Shadow's magic didn't work in Imperial space. That demonstrated that there were differences. Why hadn't they considered what *other* differences there might be?

She felt as if her head were packed with wool, shutting out the constant background hum of other people's thoughts, and it was not a comfortable feeling at all. She had never experienced anything like it before.

What was even worse, though, was that no one had yet contacted her.

The plan had been that once they were through the warp she would send a quick verification that they had arrived safely and that she then would devote her attention to the usual duties of a ship's telepath—accompanying Captain Cahn on his diplomatic mission, reading the minds of those around them, advising him when they were lying, and so on and so forth. All of that had obviously become impossible when the ship had crashed twenty miles from their objective and they had all been taken prisoner by the local constabulary, and when most of their equipment wouldn't work.

And she hadn't sent any verification because her telepathy didn't work, either.

Which meant that as far as she could tell, nobody back at Base One had any idea what had happened to them.

So why hadn't they gotten another telepath and contacted her? Surely, she could still receive as well as the natives here could, and her team had managed to make limited contact with half a dozen of the native psychics. Didn't they realize something had gone wrong? She had been here, isolated, all night, and there had been no contact.

Surely they knew something had gone wrong. Surely they had had plenty of time to try to get through.

Then, at last, something stirred in her mind, as if a mouse were moving inside that mass of wool. She tried to focus on it, and as it became clearer, she could sense a sort of shape to the message.

And then it was through—it was Carrie back at Base One, calling her, calling desperately.

"Here!" she thought. "I'm here, Carrie!"

"Prossie!" Relief flooded through the contact, flowing both ways.

She didn't reply with words, but with reassuring thoughts roughly equivalent to "It's okay, Carrie, I'm fine."

Carrie's thoughts caressed hers for a moment, then a question came through, so clear that for a moment Prossie thought she had heard it spoken aloud.

"Prossie," it said. "What *happened?*"

CHAPTER 5

"**N**o telepathy? No antigravity?" The undersecretary frowned at the papers on his desk.

"No, sir," the telepath standing stiffly before him reported, "neither one. It appears that the laws of physics are totally different there—it's not just that the telepathic mutation never happened, or AG wasn't discovered. Not only do they have no telepaths or AG of their own, but ours don't work there; that's why the ship crashed and why Prossie . . . why Telepath Thorpe didn't report in. It's a miracle that there are human beings so much like us in a place so alien, let alone that they speak the same language."

"But they have some sort of technology, don't they?" the official demanded. "I mean, they aren't just using sticks and stones?"

"Thorpe says that they have a *different* technology from ours, sir," the telepath explained, "but it's one that's very nearly as advanced as ours in some ways, sir, maybe even higher. She reports seeing a recording machine of some kind that's unlike anything we've ever imagined, and they appear to have a sophisticated mechanical communications system."

"But if our machines won't work there," the undersecretary asked, tapping the desk, "will their machines work here? Will their *weapons* work here? Or in the Shadow realm?"

"I don't know, sir," the telepath said. "Nobody knows."

"The reports say these people do have advanced weapons," he said. "Did Thorpe say anything about them?"

"Well, sir," the telepath said cautiously, "you have to remem-

50

ber, she was taken into custody before she'd ever had a chance to leave the landing site, and she can't read minds there, she has to rely on her eyes and ears, like anybody else. She spent the night in their jail, and there wasn't much to see there. And I didn't take time to go over every detail; I came directly to you to report."

The undersecretary's manner made his impatience clear as he said, "Yes?"

"So far as I know, she hasn't seen any weapons except the handguns the law enforcers carry," the telepath said, "and she hasn't heard anything about any others."

"Handguns?"

"Yes, sir. Projectile weapons, apparently, like the pistols of a century ago. She saw bullets on the law officers' belts."

"Bullets," the undersecretary said, frowning.

"Yes, sir," the telepath said.

"We're looking for help against the alien super-science of another universe," the undersecretary demanded, "science so advanced that they call it magic, and the best we can find is people who still shoot bullets at each other?"

The telepath shifted uneasily, struggling to stay at attention. "Well, sir, bullets can be very effective, really, and these were civilian law officers, after all, not military personnel. We've all read things in other minds there that hint at much better . . ."

"Which, even if it's true, doesn't mean any of these better weapons would work in our space, or in Shadow's space."

"True, sir," the telepath admitted.

The undersecretary shoved papers across the desk, letting the telepath continue standing at attention. After a moment he looked up.

"The natives think our people are crazy?" he asked. "I mean, certifiably insane?"

The telepath nodded. "Yes, sir," she said. "Either that, or perpetrating a hoax of some kind."

"Will they gas 'em?"

The telepath hesitated. "I don't think so, sir," she said. "When they were taken into custody, the arresting officers read each of the crewmen a statement of rights and privileges. It's Prossie's . . . it's Telepath Thorpe's impression that the culture is relatively nonviolent and benevolent. Her cell is equipped with its own plumbing and electric light, and no one has struck her; she's still wearing her own uniform, in fact, though they did take her helmet and search her for weapons. She's seen no sign of a gallows or whipping post, nor any other means of torture or execution."

The undersecretary stared at her. "Bunch of wimps," he said. "Just like she said. And these are the people we thought might have superweapons for us?"

The telepath didn't respond. She resisted the temptation to ask just who had said what about wimps, and the even stronger temptation to snatch the answer from the undersecretary's mind.

"All right," he said. "Go away. Dismissed." He turned back to his papers.

"Sir?" the telepath said.

The undersecretary looked up. "What is it?" he demanded.

Hesitantly, the telepath asked, "Will we be sending a rescue mission? What should I tell Prossie?"

"I'll be taking it under advisement, Telepath, but you can tell her, provisionally, that we plan no rescue mission," the undersecretary said. "It'd be a waste of time and money and manpower. How would we rescue anyone, anyway, when our warp comes out in midair and our antigravity doesn't work there? And blasters don't work; how would we get them out if our weapons won't fire? No, they're on their own. We can keep in touch, and reopen the warp if they can find a way to get to it, but beyond that I'm writing the whole thing off as a failure. We'll take care of Shadow ourselves."

"But, sir . . ." The telepath didn't finish her protest; even before the undersecretary spoke she had inadvertently, and against all her careful training and discipline, read his response.

"No buts. *Ruthless* was expendable, or we wouldn't have sent her, and she's lost. No point in wasting any more men trying to get her back. Copley probably shouldn't have sent her in the first place, not without more advance work. It sounds to me as if Cahn and his crew aren't badly off—hell, we've got plenty of men on active duty who live in worse than those cells, from what you've said. They may even be let go, and then they'll be free to look around and maybe find a way back. You'll be checking in with Thorpe every so often—say, every forty-eight hours, if your other duties allow. They'll be all right. So we'll get on to other things. Understood?"

"Yes, sir." The telepath offered no further argument. For one thing, she had seen at least part of the real reason underneath undersecretary Bascombe's thoughts.

There were the usual petty political concerns that flavored almost everyone's motivations, the personal jealousies and competitions that every telepath learned to ignore—in this case, the project was associated with Major Copley, who had been falling out of favor even before his appendicitis sent him to the hospital and knocked him out of the inner circle, so continuing it was a bad career move. Underneath that, though, Carrie found a good and logical reason.

If they sent in a rescue mission and shot up a jail in this other universe, they would be making an enemy of the people there, of the dominant nation, the United States of America, as it was called. If the superweapons really *did* exist, they would then be more likely to be turned against the Empire than against Shadow.

She couldn't argue with that.

"Dismissed," the undersecretary said.

■

"Our messenger is bespoke," Valadrakul reported.

Raven sat up and thumped the chalice onto the table by his chair. "And?" he demanded.

"The sky ship is fallen, and its crew prisoners in the land of Earth."

"Ah, evil tidings, 'twould seem," Raven muttered. "Fallen, you say?"

"Aye," the wizard said. "The magicks that hold it aloft failed, when the new realm was reached."

Raven considered that for a moment, then asked, "Wherefore was this word so tardy—was it said?"

The wizard nodded. "Aye," he said, " 'twould seem that the spells of telepaths have no virtue in Earth, as the flying spells have none, and as our own magicks do naught in the Empire."

Raven nodded. "I see," he said. He rubbed his temple, trying to think. "Prisoners, say you? Of whom, and wherefore?"

"Of—an it be I have this right—of the constabulary of the County of Montgomery, in Mary's Land."

"And wherefore?"

"For trespass upon a lady's park, and the unlawful casting of debris upon the land, in that thereupon the ship was fallen."

Raven stared for a moment, then started to speak, then thought better of it.

Valadrakul waited.

"At first," said Raven, at last, "I thought to shout at you, good wizard, and denounce this tale as madness—knights held for letting fall their transport—but upon consideration, I fear you speak only simple truth, for the land of Earth is strange indeed. I saw as much with mine own eyes."

"Aye, marry," Valadrakul replied.

"What does the Empire intend, then? Have we word? Does mount an expedition to free the men, or offer ransom?"

"Nay," said the wizard, "that lordling John Bascombe, him that they call Undersecretary for Interdimensional Affairs, has but moments ago said that such an effort would serve no good purpose, that the people of Earth do not harm prisoners. Among themselves, the mind readers say he fears lest Earth be affronted thereby and fight on the side of Shadow 'gainst the Empire."

"Think you this is truth?" Raven asked.

Valadrakul shrugged. "Who can say?"

"Think you, perhaps, that this Undersecretary Bascombe might himself be a creature of Shadow?"

Valadrakul considered that carefully before replying, "In truth, I know not, but methinks he be otherwise. His reasoning is not valorous, yet 'tis sound enough. Perchance he has such creatures among his counsellors, but I think he be not one himself."

Raven nodded.

"What think you would befall," he said, "should we free these men from durance, and bring them hither?"

Valadrakul spread his hands. "Who can say?" he said.

"Perhaps," Raven said slowly, "Messire Pel Brown can say."

■

There was nothing on the six o'clock news Sunday evening about a spaceship, nor on the ten o'clock on channel five, nor the eleven o'clock; in desperation, Pel even tried CNN and CNN Headline News.

"They wouldn't have anything," Nancy told him. "Not if the networks don't."

Pel protested, "Sometimes they have stuff the networks don't. You remember the 'boys in Baghdad,' don't you?"

"Of course I do," Nancy said, "and I know they break a lot of stories. But that's different, it's all international stuff. They wouldn't have something like this if the networks and locals don't."

"I know," Pel admitted. He put out the cat, and they went to bed.

It gnawed at them both through the night; at breakfast they were both surly, even after coffee.

Nancy spent most of the morning at job interviews, while Rachel was at her kindergarten. Pel made his Monday morning calls, but had no all-day projects or out-of-town appointments, so he was home again for lunch five minutes after Rachel's bus dropped her off.

Ordinarily, a family lunch together was a cheerful event, but the tension still lingered, poisoning the atmosphere; Rachel wolfed her sandwich and left the table, while Pel and Nancy ate in sullen silence.

"It was a joke," Nancy said, without preamble, as she carried her plate to the sink.

Pel didn't have to ask what she was referring to. He shook his head. "How could it be a joke?" he asked.

"What else could it be?"

"I don't know, but it wasn't any joke."

"Of course it was."

"No, it wasn't, damn it."

Nancy turned to face him, hands on hips. "It *had* to be, and don't you swear at me!"

"It was not a fucking *joke*!" Pel shouted.

"Well, then, what the hell *was* it?" she shouted back.

"Daddy?" Rachel said from the doorway.

"*I* don't know what it was, but no goddamn joker would be able to walk through our basement wall like that!"

"It was a *trick*, Pel! A hologram or something!"

"Daddy?"

"You think a *hologram* sat on our couch drinking beer? You think a hologram would wear a velvet cape that Rachel could *feel*?"

Nancy had no immediate rejoinder, and as she fumed, trying to think of one, Rachel was able to get Pel's attention by yanking at his sleeve.

"Daddy!" she yelled, "the man's back!"

For a moment, Pel didn't understand. Nancy was quicker; her mouth opened, then closed, and she demanded, "Where?"

"In the *basement*, of course." Rachel looked as disdainful as only a little girl can. "I heard him knocking and calling for Daddy."

That got through to Pel; he stood up so fast his chair started to topple over backward. He snatched at it and caught it before it fell, jostling the kitchen table. His coffee sloshed onto the place mat; he ignored it as he headed for the basement stairs.

■

"They may be back with a court order," Susan said. "They may even try to condemn your property and take it by eminent domain."

Amy sipped tea before replying. "Then what?" she said.

"Then I try for a restraining order, claiming their order violates your property rights and your right to due process."

Amy glanced out the window at the thing in her back yard; it was still damp from the morning dew and gleamed gold in the sun. "Then what?" she asked.

Susan shrugged. "I don't know," she said. "This isn't really my field. I've never done a national security case before."

Amy shuddered slightly and put down her teacup. "Do you think it's really a national security thing?" she said.

Susan considered carefully before answering. "I don't know." She took a deep breath and continued, "That's what the Air Force people claimed, but if that thing out there is a fake, the way they

say it is, I don't see how they can make a national security claim
stick." She picked up her own cup, which contained instant coffee
rather than tea. "Of course, if it's a fake, there is the question of
how it got here," she added just before she sipped.

"It fell out of the sky," Amy said.

Susan nodded and lowered her cup. "I know it did," she said.
"So does the Air Force; they've measured the thing's mass and the
effects of impact and can probably tell you exactly how far it fell
and how fast it was going when it was hit. What they *can't* tell you,
though, is how it got up in the air in the first place, because they
don't know—and that's what has them so worried."

"So you think they'll be back?"

"Ms. Jewell . . . Amy, I really, honestly don't know."

Amy accepted that and delicately sipped more tea. Susan
gulped coffee.

"At least you kept them from setting up those lights," Amy
said a moment later.

Susan shrugged deprecatingly. "For now," she said.

"Thanks," Amy said. "I know I would never have gotten any
sleep tonight with those things out there." She hesitated, then
asked, "Did you talk to any of the people who were inside it?"

"No," Susan said. "I probably can, if you think it would help,
but I haven't yet."

"Are they in jail?"

Susan looked at her watch. "So far, they probably still are,"
she said, "but the police won't be able to hold them for very long
unless you press charges."

"Me?"

Susan nodded. "They were charged with trespassing, vandalism, and malicious mischief—they dumped that thing on your
land, smashed your hedge, ruined your lawn—you could probably
claim reckless endangerment, too, since you were out there at the
time. But if you don't press charges, the cops will have to let them
go. You don't hold people without a charge, not in the U.S."

"And if I press charges?"

Susan sighed. "None of them could give an address or show
any means of support. None of them had any money or identification except for their 'Galactic Empire' stuff. None of them have

asked for a lawyer or used their phone privileges. They're all staying strictly in character. You can probably get them held for a
couple of weeks, at the outside, since they can't make bond and
the feds don't want them released, but more than that . . ." She
shrugged.

Amy put down her cup and picked up the teabag by the
string, toying idly with it.

"Susan," she said, watching the teabag, "what do you think is
really going on here?"

Susan chewed her lower lip, then admitted, "I don't have any
idea."

Amy looked up. "Do you think they could *really* be from some
Galactic Empire?"

Susan hesitated, then said, "I don't believe in little green
men."

"Neither do I—but how else do you explain those people, and
that thing in my yard?"

Susan frowned. "If they're really from outer space, then why
won't their ship fly?"

"But maybe it *did* fly—how else could it get there?"

"I don't know," Susan said. "I don't understand any of it."
She rubbed her temple. "Maybe if I'd gotten more sleep over the
weekend, but I didn't expect anything like this first thing on a
Monday morning."

"Thank you for coming so early," Amy said gravely. "I appreciate it."

Susan waved away Amy's gratitude. "No problem," she said.
"Shall we get down to Rockville and fill out the papers?"

■

Prossie lay curled up on the cot, staring at nothing.

She was betrayed.

She was trapped here, a prisoner, completely cut off from the
minds of others, and most particularly from the minds of her fellow telepaths, the minds of her family and her community.

She was in jail, for reasons she did not understand—listening
to words without being able to read the minds behind them was
hard for her, and although she had heard the charges against her,

she did not see why they had been leveled at her and the rest of the crew. Their ship had *crashed*; how could that be a crime?

And she knew that there would be no rescue. The brief moment of hope when Carrie had first reached her had died again when the news came through—her people had written her off. They had declared her expendable and expended. Carrie had told her—the mission had been abandoned as a failure, ISS *Ruthless* given up as lost, and she and Captain Cahn and the other eight were considered prisoners of war. No efforts would be made to rescue them.

And since there were no other contacts between the Empire and this Montgomery County, there could be no negotiated freedom, no exchange.

She would rot here, in this bland little cell.

This was almost worse than a dungeon, really. If she were confined behind cold stone walls, in darkness and filth and hunger, she would be able to concentrate herself on resistance, on courage; she would have the romance of all those childhood stories to fall back on, all the tales of heroes who endured monumental suffering along the way to magnificent triumphs. The Earl of the White Mountain, the Man in the Sealed Helm, the people of Camp Eight—all the old stories of famous prisoners came back to her.

What romance was there in concrete block walls, a steel cot, and porcelain fixtures? What suffering did electric light and three meals a day provide?

She was no swashbuckling hero; she wasn't even a real soldier. She was just a telepath, sent along on this expedition because telepathy was the only good way to communicate over long distances.

Maybe, she thought, she should ask for an attorney—the officer had said that if she could not afford one, one would be provided for her.

But no; what good would that do? Why would a native attorney want to help her? How could an attorney get her out if the authorities wanted to hold her? If she got out, where would she go? What would she do?

She wished that Carrie hadn't told her Bascombe's decision.

Captain Cahn and the others presumably didn't know about it, and they were probably stewing in their uncertainty, but that was better than despair.

She curled up more tightly, her head full of telepathic wool, and stared at nothing.

CHAPTER 6

She's not taking it well." The telepath sat slumped in her chair, staring unhappily at the floor.

"Carrie, don't let it get to you," her supervisor said. "Prossie'll be okay, I'm sure of it."

Carrie looked up.

"I'm not," she said. "I read her mind, and I'm not sure at all."

■

There were four of them this time. Nancy hung back as they emerged from the basement, and despite their deferential manner, Pel found their numbers and armament somewhat intimidating himself.

Raven came first and stood to one side, introducing the others as they stepped out into the hall and bowed.

"Stoddard, man-at-arms and a loyal friend to me since I was a lad," Raven said, describing a man who stood six feet tall and wore a dirty and somewhat faded red tabard over a stiff leather garment. Stoddard bowed—more than a mere bob, but not a particularly deep bow. His hair was black and shaggy and his face brown and rugged; besides the tabard and leather, he wore baggy brown hose and brown leather boots. A scabbard hung from his belt, and from the look of it Pel judged his sword to be somewhat heavier than Raven's.

"Squire Donald a' Benton," Raven named the next. His bow was more perfunctory than Stoddard's, his green tunic considerably cleaner, his boots newer. He seemed about half Stoddard's size, and in fact was no taller than Nancy's five foot four, Pel realized. Like Raven and Stoddard, he bore a sword.

His green eyes darted about curiously.

"The mage Valadrakul of Warricken," Raven said, gesturing at the last member of his party. "Now sworn to Stormcrack Keep."

The wizard did not bow at all, but made an odd gesture with one hand instead. Most of his dull brown hair trailed loose, half-way down his back, while the rest hung in two narrow braids in front of either ear; he wore a long black vest, ornately embroidered in red and gold, that reached to mid-calf and mostly concealed a plain black tunic and breeches. The sheath on his belt was too small for a true sword, but it held a good-size knife.

"Mage?" Pel asked.

"A wizard," Raven said, "a magician. One who works spells and brings forth wonders."

Pel nodded and tried not to stare. "This way," he said, motioning toward the family room, herding the visitors ahead of him.

Valadrakul did not fit Pel's image of a wizard. He was neither tall and imposing, nor small and wizened; his face was not long and hawk-nosed. He wore no robes, nor pointed hat, nor long white beard.

Instead, he was of medium height—five-nine, perhaps, or a bit over—and a little fat, with a pale, round face and a full brown beard, clipped short. His hairstyle reminded Pel of Val Kilmer playing the warrior in *Willow*, though it wasn't exactly the same, and his outfit didn't seem like anything in particular. There were no moons and stars, no pentagrams; the embroidery was a grace-ful floral pattern.

Pel stepped down into the family room to find three of the four strangers standing in the center, staring in all directions. Raven stood with the others, but smiled politely at his host and did not stare; after all, he had been here before.

"Have a seat," Pel suggested.

Raven nodded and settled on the couch; the wizard, whose name Pel had not caught, took the other end. Squire Donald started toward the recliner, but threw first Pel and then Raven a questioning glance before sinking gingerly into it.

Stoddard ignored the invitation completely; he stepped back

toward one wall, but continued to stand, arms crossed over his chest and feet braced apart.

Pel looked at his stolid pose and decided not to argue. Sitting down in that leather barrel the man was wearing might be difficult, and he looked as if he were accustomed to standing.

The man-at-arms looked incredibly out of place in that room, in his rough and archaic clothing. The other three weren't so bad, but Stoddard simply didn't fit in such a setting.

With a final glance at him, Pel decided against taking a seat himself; there were no good ones left. Sitting on an end table seemed undignified.

"So," Pel said, addressing Raven, "what brings you back?"

"Why, the same portal as erstwhile, of course," Raven answered smoothly.

"No," Pel said, "I mean, why have you come back?"

Raven smiled an acknowledgment of his slip. "As before," he began, "we seek your aid. Have you heard aught of the sky ship the Imperials sent hither?"

"No," Pel replied, "and we should have, if it's really there."

"Oh, 'tis real, beyond question," Raven said calmly. Then he stopped abruptly and glanced at Valadrakul for confirmation.

" 'Tis real," the wizard said. His voice, which Pel and Nancy had not heard before, was a pleasant tenor. "We've not been deceived, I assure you."

"It wasn't on the news," Pel said doubtfully.

"Nonetheless, the ship is real, and it reached your world," Valadrakul said. "However, its magic did not work here; it plummeted to the earth and has not moved since. Its crew has been taken prisoner by the earl's men. This much we have learned."

"The earl's men?" Pel asked, puzzled.

"The Earl of Montgomery," Raven explained. " 'Twas the county constabulary apprehended the Imperials. Are we not in the County Montgomery here?"

"We're in Montgomery County, yes," Pel said, still puzzled, "but there's no earl. You mean it crashed, and the county police picked them up?"

"A county with no earl? A countess, then?"

"No, Montgomery County's democratic," Pel explained. "Or

Republican, depending. We have a county executive, not an earl."

Raven and Valadrakul exchanged glances. Pel looked at the others; Stoddard was staring straight ahead, paying no attention to anything so far as Pel could determine, while Squire Donald was studying the shelves beside him, fascinated, and might or might not be listening.

For the first time Pel noticed that Nancy wasn't in the room; he turned, and saw Rachel watching from the door to the kitchen. Listening, he could hear Nancy moving about in the kitchen.

"Why call it a county, an there's no count?" Raven asked, annoyed. "Neither earl nor countess, then where's the county? Why not call it a shire?"

Pel shrugged. "I don't know," he said. "We do have a sheriff, I think, so yeah, shire would make more sense, but we call 'em counties anyway."

Raven waved it away. "It matters not a whit, then, who rules here, save that you understand your county police have taken prisoner the ten Imperials who came hither. And yes, their ship fell and could not fly in your skies."

Nancy leaned through the kitchen doorway and called, "Would anyone like a beer? Or anything? I can put the kettle on if you'd like tea or coffee."

Stoddard turned a questioning look at Raven; Squire Donald glanced up from the bookshelves. Raven looked around quickly at all his companions, then up at Nancy.

"Beer would be most welcome, good lady, and our thanks."

Nancy nodded and disappeared.

"All right," Pel said, "so the cops picked up these Imperial storm troopers. Why wasn't it on the news? It's not every day a bunch of people from outer space crash-land around here."

"I know not," Raven said, turning up an empty palm. "Perchance whoever retails your news has not yet learned of it."

Pel considered that. If a spaceship really *had* landed, the government might try to hush it up—but he would be surprised if they actually managed it. He had never bought the Hangar 19—or 18, or whatever the number was—stories for a minute.

"Where'd it land?" he asked.

Raven looked at Valadrakul, who turned up his hands and said, "How are we to know the name of the place? It lies perhaps half a day's journey to the north, traveling on foot."

"But it's in Montgomery County?"

"That, or your shiremen crossed the border."

If the ship had come down somewhere out toward the Howard County line, that might explain how it had stayed off the TV news, so far; there was still a good bit of fairly empty countryside up that way, as Pel knew from driving the back roads to Baltimore on occasion.

"What are they charged with? I mean, why were they arrested?" he asked.

"The charges we were told are trespassing and vandalism," Valadrakul replied. "I fear we have no such word as *vandalism* in our tongue, so we know not what it means."

"It means wrecking things just for fun," Pel explained.

The story didn't sound quite right to him; why would the county cops arrest a bunch of aliens on charges like that? Why weren't the feds all over the place?

Then an explanation occurred to him, one which made the whole thing make sense, including the fact that the news media had not reported anything.

"They don't think it's real, do they?" he asked.

"Your pardon, sir, but what do you say?" Raven replied.

"Nobody thinks the spaceship is real," Pel said. "Whoever found it thinks it's a hoax, right?"

"Indeed," Valadrakul answered, "you may have the truth of it; our reports cannot tell us everything, but 'tis hinted your constables think the crewmen mad. Certes, they do not accept them as envoys."

Raven turned to the wizard. "You'd said naught of that to me," he said, clearly irritated. "I had thought the captors mad, not the prisoners!"

"My apologies," Valadrakul said, bowing his head. "There was much to tell, and in my haste . . ." He turned up a palm.

"I'd like to see these guys," Pel said.

"Guys?" Donald said, looking up.

"A gnomish word," Valadrakul told him, "from a trickster of

days agone, one Guiler by name, called Guy o' the Mews, who was famed for harassing the little folk."

This bizarre false etymology caught Pel's attention for a moment, distracting him.

Just then Nancy stepped in with a tray, carrying five foaming beer mugs. "I didn't think cans would go over well," she said to Pel.

The entire conversation seemed to be going in half a dozen directions at once, and Pel was becoming thoroughly confused. Reversing his earlier decision, he sat down on the edge of the stereo cabinet. "Fine," he told Nancy.

She smiled, not very confidently, and handed Raven a mug. He thanked her, as Pel wondered where she had found five beer mugs, since he only remembered owning four. Taking another look, he realized that the fifth was actually a small vase that they never used. It was about the right size and shape, though it lacked a handle.

She handed the vase to Stoddard, who nodded his head in polite acknowledgment.

Valadrakul and Donald accepted their mugs gratefully, and Pel himself took the last. He held it without drinking while the others sampled the brew.

He could tell they weren't impressed, but that wasn't anything he cared about just now.

"Let me see if I have this straight," he said. "The Galactic Empire sent a ship, with ten men aboard, to make contact with our government—in Washington, I guess?"

He glanced at Valadrakul, who made a sort of one-handed shrug while sipping beer with the other.

"They found out the hard way that some of the machinery doesn't work here, and the ship crashed, somewhere north of here, but still in Montgomery County. Right so far?"

Raven nodded.

"Then the county police came and arrested them all for trespassing," Pel continued, "and hauled them away somewhere—the county jail in Rockville, probably."

Valadrakul nodded this time.

"And they're still there, and the cops think they're crazy because they don't believe any of this stuff about spaceships and galactic empires."

No one objected to any of that.

"All right," Pel said, "I've got all that—so what are *you* people doing here?"

Raven put down his beer—what little was left of it. Pel noticed that Nancy was collecting an empty vase from Stoddard. "More?" she asked.

He nodded, and she slipped away to the kitchen.

"The Empire," Raven explained, "has given up their men as lost—aye, and the lady, as well, for the ship had a woman aboard. The man who has charge of the matter has decided against any attempt at rescue, or any further expedition hither. Thus, these ten are abandoned, at the mercy of their captors. 'Tis a coward's decision, say I, but 'tis made, nonetheless."

Pel nodded.

"The thought came to us," Raven continued, "that perhaps we might find a use for these abandoned men, ourselves. They might tell us much about the Galactic Empire. We might find a worthy ransom, should we offer to send them home. Failing all else, we could at the least find ourselves with nine more brave men in our fight against the creatures of Shadow."

"And a woman," Pel added.

Raven ignored the interruption; his speech rolled on as if Pel hadn't said a word. "We know naught of your world, however, and finding and freeing these Imperials could be a fearsome task. Our portal opens in your cellars and is not so very easily moved, nor can its point of arrival be precisely determined in advance; further, you seemed a good man and kindly disposed toward me. Thus, we came hither to seek your counsel."

Nancy reappeared with the vase refilled.

"You want me to tell you how to get these people out of jail?" Pel said. He saw smiles and nods starting, and asked, "How would I know?"

The smile vanished, and the nods never came. Raven and Valadrakul exchanged an unhappy glance. "We had thought," Raven said, "that you might perchance know something of this prison—its strengths and weaknesses, perhaps, whether a warder might be bribed, somewhat of that nature."

"You want me to help you get these guys out of jail?" Pel asked again.

Nancy looked up from the tray. "Have you talked to their lawyer?" she asked.

Raven and Valadrakul stared at her, startled.

"What's a lawyer?" Raven asked.

■

"Maybe I should talk to them," Amy said, uncertainly, as she toyed nervously with a ballpoint pen.

Susan looked up from the forms she was reading. "Why?" she asked.

"Well, I don't want to be vindictive or anything," Amy explained. "I just want everybody to get their stuff out of my yard and leave me alone."

"And pay for your hedge and your tree and all the other damage," Susan pointed out.

"Yeah," Amy admitted, "that, too."

The desk sergeant shook his head. "I don't think those guys are gonna pay for anything, lady," he said. "They didn't have a cent between them; they haven't called anyone about getting bailed out, nothing."

Amy stared. "They *still* haven't?" she asked.

"Nope. Not one of them. They're all sticking to their story about this Galactic Empire, and most of 'em won't give us anything but name, rank, and serial number."

Amy looked at Susan, who shrugged.

Amy frowned. "If they're real," she said, "then they *can't* pay for anything, can they?"

Susan answered, "Who knows? If they're for real, then it's all beyond me. If they're *not* real, though, and they're carrying it this far . . ."

"If they're *not* real, then screw 'em," Amy said, grabbing the pen. "They're carrying it much too far, and as far as I'm concerned they can rot here. Where do I sign?"

The desk sergeant pointed.

■

Prossie heard someone calling her name, or at any rate something intended for her; she sat up and listened.

To her ears the cell was silent, save for the distant hissing of the highway that passed near the jail. It was her mind that had been touched.

"Carrie?" she said, whispering to make sure her thoughts were in words. "Is that you?"

Her ears still heard nothing, but the words reached her. "Yes, it's me, Prossie," the telepathic voice replied. "How are you doing?"

"Better," Prossie replied, "much better. That woman filed formal charges against us this morning, so they sent an attorney for us, whether we wanted one or not, and he explained some things—oh, Carrie, I wish I'd asked for an attorney sooner!"

Carrie's response was a wordless questioning.

"They aren't going to keep us here," Prossie said, "they *can't* keep us. They have all these complicated rules they follow and guarantees of rights—it's really incredible, if it's all true. We should be free in a few days, I think."

After a moment of mental silence, Carrie asked, "Then what?"

"I don't know," Prossie admitted, "but I'm sure we'll manage somehow. We can work, or live off the land and find some way to get back to the warp eventually, I'm certain of it. It's just a hundred yards above where the ship crashed—that can't be all that inaccessible."

Prossie paused, and listened.

She sensed uneasiness on the other side of the conversation, as if Carrie doubted her, or as if she knew something Prossie did not. She certainly wasn't sharing Prossie's relief.

That troubled Prossie, but she thrust it aside as a new idea struck her.

"Listen, Carrie," she said, "once I'm free, what if I were to track down some of the people we contacted—Miletti, or Blaisdell, or Aldridge? Wouldn't they help us?"

"I don't know," Carrie answered, startled. "I hadn't thought of that. Are you *sure* they'll free you?"

"Well," Prossie admitted, "I have no way of being sure the attorney didn't lie to me—I don't have my telepathy here, so I couldn't check. I hadn't really thought about it—why would he lie?

And if he told the truth, they definitely won't keep me here more than, I think he said thirty days, at most. They might try to send me to a madhouse, though—I think that was what he meant, anyway, though he didn't come right out and say so. But I'm not mad, and I ought to be able to avoid that."

"I see," Carrie said, and again Prossie sensed doubt. "There's something else, though; I don't know if any of the contactees are near where you came out. Some of them were thousands of miles apart. I'll have to see if we have any maps."

"Do it, Carrie, please—for me."

"Sure, Prossie. Hey, whatever happens, it's good to hear you sounding so much more cheerful!"

"It's good to *be* more cheerful, Carrie. Do check those maps for me, please. And thanks."

The contact broke.

Silent, Prossie sat on her bunk, puzzled.

She had been so pleased with her conversation with Jerry de Lillo, the attorney from the public defender's office, that she had not really considered the possibility that it was all a fraud, or that things might not work out as well as Mr. de Lillo said. Carrie, however, seemed to be taking it for granted that there was something wrong somewhere.

Why?

What could Carrie know that she, Prossie, did not? Had they been reading other minds here in Montgomery County, or whatever this place was called?

No, that couldn't be it; she knew perfectly well that contacting anyone in this universe was difficult, and only a handful of people had been sufficiently receptive to manage any sort of communication at all. Out of that handful, only three had been able to both send and receive.

Prossie hadn't been in on all the initial contacts, but she had done her share and had carefully studied the files on those she hadn't personally attempted. None of them had been connected with law enforcement or government.

The chances of locating another new contact who just happened to know something about the fate of the crew of ISS *Ruthless* had to be just about nil. Whatever Carrie had learned, she must have learned back at Base One, or through a contact some-where else in the Empire.

Prossie tried to remember the conversation and spot just where it had begun to go sour.

When Prossie had first mentioned being freed, there had been a lack of certainty, but that was just an insufficiency of evidence—Carrie had been eager to be convinced, at that point. Then Prossie had gone on to describe her hopes for after her release . . .

That was it.

It was when she had mentioned going back through the warp that Carrie had started hiding something.

Any ordinary person would never have noticed it, but Prossie was a telepath; she knew how minds worked. Carrie would never have tried hiding anything from another telepath that way ordinarily, she would have known better, but since Prossie's talent was stifled she must have thought she could get away with it.

It must be that Carrie knew something about the warp that Prossie did not, and Prossie did not have to think very hard about the situation to guess what it might be.

The undersecretary had said that there would be no rescue, that the attempt to contact Earth was being abandoned; the next step was obvious and logical.

They must have shut down the warp.

Prossie slumped back against the wall. They had shut down the warp. The opening between universes was gone.

It would be possible to reopen it, she was sure. It had to be possible.

But would they do it?

CHAPTER 7

"Ted, this is Raven," Pel said.

Ted held out a hand, but Raven was already bowing and did not see it. Discomfited, Ted pulled back his hand and stuck it in his pocket.

"Raven, this is our lawyer, Ted Deranian."

" 'Tis an honor, good sir," Raven said, flourishing his hat as he rose from his bow.

"Uh, yeah," Ted said. He glanced at Pel, silently asking what the hell was going on.

"Raven's not from around here," Pel said hastily. "I mean, he's not just dressed up; that's his native costume."

Ted looked over the black velvet and elaborate embroidery, the sword and the bobbing ostrich plume. "I didn't know they still dressed like that anywhere anymore," he said.

Raven cast a questioning glance at Pel, who quickly said, "Don't worry about it. Come on into the living room and sit down, Ted, let Nancy get you a drink or something."

"Sure," Ted said. He turned toward the living room.

As he did, behind his back but in sight of Pel, Raven jerked his head toward the family room, down at the far end of the hall; Pel shook his head no. There was no need to bring Stoddard or Donald or the wizard into things at this point.

Ted accepted a Scotch and water from Nancy, then settled into the fake-antique wing chair by the front window. Pel gestured for Raven to take the other armchair, while he seated himself on the couch, and Nancy slipped out through the dining room, back to the kitchen.

"Look, Ted," Pel explained, when they were all seated, "Raven's got a problem. Some friends of his are in jail down in Rockville, charged with trespassing and vandalism. They're probably more or less guilty, but it was an accident, nobody meant any harm, and they're all foreigners, they don't understand the American courts, and they haven't got any money for fines or bail or anything. We'd like you to go and look after them, get them out if you can—we need to talk to them, if you can arrange it."

"Foreigners?" Ted pursed his lips and put down his glass. "Do they speak English?"

Pel glanced at Raven, who nodded. "Aye," he said, " 'tis their native tongue."

Pel improvised, "They're from the backwoods of New Zealand someplace, I think."

Ted nodded. "Ordinarily, I'd say no problem," he said. "Do they all dress like, uh, Raven, here?"

Again, Pel glanced at Raven, who answered, "Nay, their garb is like neither mine nor your own."

Pel shrugged.

Ted hesitated, and then said, "I can't place your accent, Raven; where are you from?"

Raven glanced at Pel, then turned up a palm. "I come from Stormcrack Keep, in the Hither Corydians."

"Is that in New Zealand?"

Raven just smiled and didn't answer.

"Listen, would you do me a favor?" Ted asked.

Raven looked politely inquiring.

"Would you say, 'Yonder lies the castle of my father'?"

Puzzled, Raven looked at Pel, whose expression shifted quickly from thunderstricken to suppressed giggling.

"Yonder lies the castle of my father?" Raven said.

"No," Ted said, "declaim it, announce it—you know."

"Ted," Pel interrupted, "Raven isn't Tony Randall, and he doesn't know what you're talking about. The accent's real, he can't help it."

Baffled, Raven looked at Pel, who explained, "It's a line from an old movie . . . oh, never mind." He turned to Ted. "So can you get these people out of jail for us? As soon as possible?

I'll stand bail, if it's not too much, or agree to be responsible for them."

"I'll see what I can do," Ted said, gulping the rest of his Scotch. "If it's just trespassing and vandalism—they broke something?"

"Tore up someone's yard, I think," Pel said.

Ted nodded. "Simplest thing, then, would be to get the complainant to drop the charges; are you good for the damages, Pel, if that's what's wanted?"

Pel had to think for a moment before reluctantly agreeing. "I guess," he said. "If it's not *too* much."

Ted stood up. "Well, thanks for the drink, then, and I guess I better get down to Rockville and see what the story is. Ah . . . do you have names for these people?"

Pel looked at Raven, who said, "Tarry a moment, please." He turned and hurried to the family room, leaving Ted and Pel standing where they were.

Pel looked apologetically at Ted. "Another drink?" he asked.

"No, no," Ted said, "I'm working, and I'm driving, and it's too early anyway."

"Coffee, maybe, or water?"

"No, thanks."

They stood, awkwardly waiting, for another few seconds; then Raven reappeared.

"Your pardon, sirs," he said. "The captain of the crew is one Joshua Cahn; his second is Alster Drummond. The lady with them is Mistress Proserpine Thorpe. Is that sufficient?"

"Should be," Ted said. "Joshua Cahn—how's that spelled, with a *K*?"

"I fear I know not, sir," Raven replied.

"Doesn't matter, I'll find him. Cahn, Drummond, and Thorpe. Got it."

"My thanks, sir, for your efforts in our behalf," Raven said, bowing again as Pel showed Ted to the door.

■

"Somebody named Ted Deranian wants to talk to you," Susan's voice said. "He's a lawyer, has an office in Germantown."

"A lawyer? What does he want to talk to me about?" Amy asked, puzzled.

"About the people from the thing in your back yard. He says he represents a friend of theirs who's willing to pay for the damages if you drop the charges."

Amy looked out her kitchen window at the ship, still lying where it had fallen. The Air Force people had not come back; she hoped they never would, though that did still leave the question of what she was going to do with the thing.

"I thought none of them knew any lawyers," she said.

"I don't think they do," Susan said. "They got Jerry de Lillo from the public defender's office appointed to represent them—he's okay. This isn't him. This Deranian person doesn't claim to be representing anyone directly involved in the case; his client is just a friend of one of them."

"If they're supposed to be from outer space, how can they have friends in Germantown?"

"That's a very good question," Susan said.

Amy considered for a long moment, then said, "I don't suppose it can hurt to talk to him."

"I wouldn't think so," Susan agreed.

"Maybe I'll finally find out what the heck is going on."

"Maybe. Should I send him out there?"

"*Here?* Oh, no. Not here. I can come to your office, or his office—I don't want him here."

"All right. I'd like to sit in, so how about my office? When can you be here?"

■

"I want to talk to them," Amy said. "The people who were in it."

"Fine by me," Ted replied, smiling.

"I mean, I'm making that a condition. If I drop the charges, I want to talk to these people. That's besides payment for the damages."

Ted leaned back in the chair. "Ms. Jewell," he said, "that's fine with me, but I don't know whether they'll say anything. I don't represent them; I'm acting on behalf of a third party."

"Who?"

"His name is Pellinore Brown. He's something of an old friend of mine."

"Pellinore?" Susan said, startled.

Ted swiveled in his chair and said, "His mother got it out of a book somewhere." He turned back to Amy. "Ms. Jewell," he said, "I can't make them talk to you, but how about this—you come to Mr. Brown's house, and I'll bring them there, and the lot of you can talk to each other all you want or not, whatever suits." He smiled. "It should be interesting; I've already met another of Mr. Brown's guests."

Amy considered for a moment, glancing from Ted to Susan and back. Susan shrugged.

"Okay," Amy said.

■

"Somebody's put in for a writ to get those people out of jail," the lieutenant reported, holding the phone.

Major Johnston looked up, then back down at the reports spread on his desk.

Design analysis—nothing. The unidentified machines can't possibly do anything.

Field trials—nothing. The machines *don't* do anything.

Materials analysis—nothing. Steel, glass, simple plastics and ceramics, polished redwood, assorted metals—copper, brass, gold, platinum. Nothing untoward, unless you asked what the gold and platinum were doing there. No unidentified or unusual substances. No petroleum-based plastics, which was odd, and no aluminum, which was even odder. Who ever heard of any sort of flying craft made entirely without aluminum?

Electronics analysis—nothing. Not just nothing comprehensible, like the other reports, but nothing at all. No silicon chips anywhere, not so much as a single printed circuit. Everything electrical was hardwired, with simple copper wires and connectors. No transistors, not even any vacuum tubes—the most advanced equipment aboard that was recognizable at all was solenoids. *Good* solenoids, but solenoids.

This all assumed, of course, that the stuff that looked like random bits of wire, metal, and crystal wasn't some sort of circuitry, but whatever it was, it didn't *do* anything.

Aerodynamics analysis—nothing much. No airfoils. The guidance vanes were just that—guidance vanes. They would provide no lift to speak of. You could drive the thing up to Mach one and it still wouldn't fly, just fall. Air resistance would be very low, the streamlining was perfectly sound, there just wasn't any lift built into it anywhere.

Tracking analysis—nothing. The ship appeared out of nowhere about three hundred feet up, just barely high enough to show up as a blip at the county airport, and immediately plummeted to the ground. It didn't come in from above; if it had flown in below the radar, it had somehow done so without a single report being filed anywhere. No complaints from homeowners, no sightings by UFO spotters, nothing.

Document analysis—still to come.

Somebody was supposed to analyze the food that had been stored aboard the ship, but that hadn't been done yet, either. At first glance it looked ordinary enough—canned goods, freeze-dried stuff, and so forth.

The thing didn't really look like a hoax, exactly; he would have expected hoaxers to rig up fancy displays and use lots of electronics, for effect. Hoaxers wouldn't use gold and platinum; they *would* use aluminum.

Unless, of course, they were very clever hoaxers indeed, trying to not look like a hoax.

The whole damn thing made no sense at all.

"The hell with it," he said, shoving back his chair. He looked up to see the lieutenant still holding the line. "Screw it," he said, "tell 'em they can let 'em go. It looks like we aren't going to figure this one out until someone tells us something, and if those people haven't talked yet . . . just screw it."

"Yes, sir," the lieutenant replied. He uncovered the mouthpiece and spoke into it as Major Johnston angrily shoved the reports to one side and glared at them.

■

"Ms. Thorpe?"

Prossie looked up, startled. The jailer who brought her meals never called her that, never said "Ms.," and it was too early for dinner, anyway—she had only finished her lunch an hour or so ago. She wasn't expecting that wonderful Mr. de Lillo again until tomorrow.

And she hadn't sensed anyone coming, and she still wasn't used to that.

It was a uniformed officer speaking, not the regular jailer. "What is it?" Prossie asked, concentrating on listening for spoken words.

The officer fumbled with the lock as he said, "Ms. Jewell's dropped the charges, and there's someone here with a writ, says he'll take responsibility for you people, so we're letting you all go." He swung open the door of the cell and stood to one side.

"Letting us go?" Prossie blinked.

"Yeah," the man said, "letting you go. Get your things, if you have any, and come on."

"Really?" She did not understand this; why would that woman drop the charges? Who would take responsibility for her and the rest of the crew?

What was really going on here?

"Come *on*, already," the officer said, annoyed. "Do you want to get out or not?"

Prossie didn't dawdle any further. Whatever the explanation might be, she wanted out.

CHAPTER 8

Three cars would be needed—Pel's Ford Taurus, Nancy's little Chevy, and Ted's Lincoln—to transport the ten Imperials to the Brown home. Nancy was seriously unhappy about driving people who had just been in jail; Raven offered to ride along, or to send Stoddard to defend her, but that didn't really help much. While she had met them, they weren't exactly trusted friends.

Eventually she agreed to drive only on condition that Raven ride with her, that she transport only two of the ten prisoners, and that one of them be the woman, Proserpine Thorpe.

At first, Pel and Ted figured that that put four each in the other two cars, which was manageable. Unfortunately, it didn't really leave room for Rachel anywhere except in Ted's car, sitting beside a quondam prisoner, and Nancy objected to that. She wanted her daughter with a parent, not a lawyer—and certainly not home alone, or with the men from Raven's world. The Lincoln could hold six; the Taurus could not.

That called for another shuffle. A prisoner was shifted in the plans, so that the Chevy would carry Raven, Rachel, and Proserpine Thorpe, with Nancy driving. Four men would ride with Pel, and five, including Captain Cahn, with Ted.

That settled, the next problem was that Nancy didn't like the idea of leaving Stoddard, Donald, and Valadrakul unchaperoned in her house. Accordingly, the three men vanished through the basement wall, and the door at the top of the basement stairs was locked.

"That won't stop them, though," Nancy said, fretting. "They

can step right back through, and that big one, Stoddard, I'm sure he can break the lock without half trying."

Pel sighed. "Nan," he said, "a random burglar could break a window and get in just as easily. Why would anyone want to bother? We'll be back in half an hour, probably. It'll be fine."

Reluctantly, Nancy agreed.

Up to this point the discussion of transportation had been theoretical, taking place entirely in the Brown home; now the party moved out, Ted to his car at the curb out front, the others to the garage.

Raven marveled at the vehicles and ran a hand along the roofline of the Chevy while Pel raised the doors. "So smooth!" he said. "Is't lacquer?"

Nancy and Pel glanced at each other. "Um . . . yeah, I think they use lacquer," Pel replied. He opened the door for Raven and held it, while Nancy let Rachel climb into the back seat from the driver's side.

"Why do you build them so low to the ground?" Raven asked as he lowered himself in. "Would it not be better to sit higher, above the splashings of mud and whatnot?"

"Streamlining," Pel said. "Besides, our roads aren't muddy." He slammed the door as Nancy settled in on the other side, then turned away, headed for his own car.

Nancy pulled her seat belt and shoulder strap into place, and looked over to see Raven stroking the upholstery and staring at the various accoutrements, his own straps untouched.

"Fasten your belt," she said.

He started, looked up, and found the buckle. Awkwardly, he pulled it down and, after some fumbling, secured it.

"You, too, Rachel," Nancy said, turning her head.

Rachel displayed her fastened belt. "Already did, Mommy!"

The Ford's engine started up, and Raven jumped again; his hand fell to where the hilt of his sword would have been, had not the Browns convinced him to leave the weapon in the family room. His head snapped around, and he stared as Pel backed the Taurus out of the garage.

" 'Struth!" he said. "They told me of such things in the Empire, but I'd not seen them for myself ere now. 'Tis true, you've no beast to pull it!"

Nancy and Rachel both giggled.

"And that noise!" Raven said. "What makes the noise?"

"The engine," Nancy explained. "The machine that makes it go." She turned her own key, and stepped on the gas.

Raven blanched at the roar—the car's muffler wasn't in the best of shape. Nancy took pity on him and let up on the pedal before backing, slowly and carefully, out of the garage.

Raven watched in delighted wonder as they rolled down the street; he admired the houses, the mown lawns, the floral displays—he had apparently never seen azaleas before. He marveled at the cars everywhere and at how fast they moved and how smoothly—particularly the one he rode in.

"Why, 'tis as good as a wizard's wind!" he remarked.

Rachel giggled again from the back seat, and Nancy smiled a tight little smile. They were still on residential suburban streets.

A moment later, when they pulled onto Interstate 270, Raven stopped talking, admiring, and marveling; he was too busy holding on and fighting sheer terror as Nancy accelerated to about sixty miles per hour and wove in and out of traffic, all of it tearing along at what was, to Raven, an incredible pace.

When they finally pulled into the parking lot in Rockville and slowed to a stop Raven was shaking, odd bits of oaths bubbling incoherently from his lips. Nancy, after unbuckling her seat belt, turned a concerned look toward him.

Rachel, also unbuckled, was leaning over the seat and staring.

"What's the matter with him, Mommy?" she asked.

Nancy glared at her. "I don't think he was ever in a car before, sweetie. He's not used to going so fast."

"By the impaled and bleeding Goddess!" Raven exclaimed.

Nancy frowned and gestured toward Rachel with her head.

He saw the motion and apologized. "Your pardon, lady; I'd bate my tongue, and mean no offense."

Inside the building a few moments later, the cops and court officials stared curiously at a still-shaky Raven. Raven, Nancy, and Rachel were back by the doorway, while Pel and Ted greeted the freed Imperials and introduced themselves.

The purple-uniformed figures stood uneasily, their purple-and-gold helmets tucked under their arms, and their newly returned belts draped across shoulders or dangling from fists. Even their weapons had been given back to them; that had been the cause of some minor argument among members of the jail's staff, but since two of the "blasters" had been disassembled and proven to be absolutely harmless, not even as dangerous as a kid's spark-gun, the return had proceeded.

None of the Imperials spoke for a moment; then one stepped forward and announced, "I'm Captain Joshua Cahn, gentlemen; thank you for your efforts on our behalf." Pel could see no difference between Cahn's uniform and those of the others except a small black insignia on the collar.

"You're welcome, Captain," Ted said, shaking Cahn's hand vigorously.

"I don't know who you are, or why you're doing this," Cahn said.

"We'll explain," Ted told him. "Come on, let's get out of here."

"Will you be taking us back to our ship?"

Ted glanced at Pel, who gave his head a quick, negative jerk.

"Not at first, anyway," Ted said.

Cahn accepted that with a brisk nod. "Where, then?"

"My house," Pel volunteered. "To talk, maybe make some plans."

Cahn snapped another quick nod. "Good enough, then," he said. "Lead the way."

"We'll be traveling in three cars," Pel said.

"Groundcars?" Cahn asked. "Like the others we saw?"

"Groundcars are all we've got here, Captain," Ted said, grinning.

In the parking lot it took only a moment to divide the group up. Raven, with some trepidation, resumed his seat in the front of the Chevy, while Rachel and Proserpine Thorpe climbed in the back. Raven eyed Thorpe with passing interest, but then busied himself fastening his shoulder harness. What had originally struck him as a quaint custom he now saw as an absolute necessity, and he tugged at every point, making sure the straps were secure.

Prossie, in the back, studied Raven. He didn't seem to fit here; his clothing and manner were noticeably different from the others. One possibility occurred to her, but it seemed very unlikely. She debated asking him straight out, but then decided that would be rude, and she did not care to be rude with the people who had just bought her free.

"These groundcars of yours are interesting," she said, casually.

"Aye," Raven said, "that's a word for it."

Rachel giggled; Nancy concentrated on getting the car out of the parking lot and headed in the right direction.

"Not as smooth as they could be, though," Prossie added, as they bumped over the discontinuity between the parking lot and the road.

Raven, now secure in his seat, turned and stared. "Say you so?" he said. "We've none that ride a fifth part so well, whence I've come."

"Well," Prossie admitted, while absorbing Raven's implication that, as she had suspected, he came from somewhere else, "anything with wheels is going to be bumpy."

Rachel looked up at Prossie. "What kind of car hasn't got wheels?" she demanded.

Prossie looked down at the girl. "An aircar, of course." She paused, then added, "But I suppose you don't have them here, do you? If antigravity doesn't work, you couldn't."

"What's Annie Graffiti?" Rachel asked.

"Like Luke Skywalker's landspeeder," Nancy suggested from the front seat. "You remember, when we rented *Star Wars*?"

"Oh," Rachel said. "But I thought that was just in the movies?"

Prossie struggled to follow this; she still had trouble with the accents and the lack of any thought behind the words, and she missed several of the references, but it was clear the little girl had thought aircars were fictional. Prossie smiled. "Not where I come from," she said.

"Then 'tis true," Raven said, "that the machines of this world, and the machines of the Galactic Empire, are different, one from the other?"

"Oh, yes," Prossie agreed, leaning forward between the backs of the front seats, "very true." She paused, then added daringly, "And you, I take it, are from the realm of Shadow?"

"Aye," Raven said, "if you must call it that."

"What do *you* call it, then?" she asked. "The place you come from, I mean?"

"Simply the World," Raven answered. "We call it the World, for ere two years gone we knew no other—at the least, myself, and my companions knew no other; I cannot speak for all the wizards and sages."

Prossie hesitated. She thought she was getting the hang of entirely spoken conversations, but she was still wary of being rude; she had none of her accustomed feedback.

Still, she felt it should be said. She asked, "And you're not one of Shadow's creatures?"

"Nay," Raven barked, startling Nancy and almost causing her to swerve. "I've fought Shadow since I was a lad, and shall fight it ever whilst I live!" He shook a clenched fist to indicate his determination.

"I had to ask," Prossie said apologetically. "I mean, as far as I know, the only people from your world we've ever found in the Empire were constructs Shadow had created—things that are virtually indistinguishable from human beings, but . . . well, they aren't really human."

"Fetches," Raven said, "and homunculi."

"Simulacra, we call them." She wasn't even sure just what words Raven had used.

"What are you two talking about?" Nancy asked, as she steered the car onto the entrance ramp for the interstate.

"Your pardon, lady," Raven said. "We speak of the foul creations of Shadow—things that mock humanity, that appear to the eye as men, that speak fair and feign good will and that then turn on true humans when the time is ripe, all in the service of their evil master. They carry messages for Shadow, and work its will, all the while seeming no more than cheerful peasants or yeomen, or even gentry. Some even take the form of living men; such a one will slay the true man and usurp his place, live his life, even bed his women, until the opportunity arises to wreak ill."

"They aren't really human," Prossie said. "Some of the details are wrong. They don't have appendixes, for example, and the structure of the brain is wrong, and none of them remember anything from their childhoods."

"They *had* no childhoods," Raven told her. "They are not born, nor do they grow as we do; they are made as adults, somehow, by Shadow's magic, brought forth as full-grown and full of hate and treachery."

"Androids, you mean," Nancy said.

"Yes, only we call them simulacra," Prossie said, trying to avoid yet another unfamiliar word.

"Homunculi," Raven said.

"You're scaring me!" Rachel said, loudly and unhappily.

"Ah, mistress, I beg pardon," Raven said, turning and bowing his head.

"I'm sorry," Prossie said. "Uh . . . what was your name again?"

"Rachel," Rachel told her.

"Oh. I'm sorry, Rachel."

Rachel managed a small sniffle and turned away, obviously not accepting the apology.

A few seconds later she changed her mind and turned back. Prossie looked down expectantly.

"It's okay," Rachel said in a small voice, "but don't do it anymore, okay?"

■

Captain Cahn rode in the front seat of the Lincoln, with Spaceman First Elmer Soorn squeezed in between himself and the driver, and three more crewmen in back.

"So," Ted said, as he pulled out of the parking lot, "where are you guys from?"

Spaceman Soorn glanced uneasily at his captain.

Cahn considered the matter briefly before deciding that he might as well tell the truth. He didn't really know what was going on, but he had been sent as an envoy, not a spy. "We were sent here as representatives of the Galactic Empire," he said. "Our ship's home port is called Base One, in the Delta Scorpius system."

Ted threw him a quick grin.

"Sure," he said. "I figured, when I saw the uniforms, that it was something like that. Galactic Empire, huh? Knew it wasn't New Zealand."

Soorn, startled, turned to stare at the driver.

Cahn, moving more thoughtfully and showing no surprise, also focused his attention on Ted.

"I didn't get your name," he said.

"Ted Deranian," Ted said. "Call me Ted."

"Mr. Deranian," Cahn said. "You speak as if meeting emissaries from another universe is not particularly out of the ordinary for you."

"Oh, on the contrary, Captain," Ted said, as he accelerated to pass Nancy's little coupe. "I've never met anything remotely like you folks before. That's why I'm enjoying it so much."

Cahn blinked. "I see," he said. He turned his attention to the road ahead, marveling at the number of different vehicles that were using it.

It had been clear to him that none of the police agents, or other, unidentified personnel he had spoken with since his ship's unfortunate arrival, had believed a word he said. No one had come out and called him a liar; in fact, they had never denied anything, or disagreed with a single datum. They had also virtually never asked him to clarify anything, but had simply noted everything down, with assorted pens and typers, and with their mysterious recording gadgets.

It had become abundantly clear, within a few hours of his arrival, that they all thought him either insane or part of some elaborate conspiracy of deception.

Whether this was because the whole idea of other universes was held to be unacceptably fantastic in this culture, or because agents of Shadow had already infiltrated the society and somehow made sure the Imperial mission was not believed, he could not be certain. Or perhaps the explanation was something else entirely; this was, after all, an alien culture.

Whatever the reason for their disbelief, he had resigned himself to a long imprisonment and to the failure of his mission.

But now he and his crew were unexpectedly free and in the hands of this person who seemed completely undisturbed by mention of the Galactic Empire. He didn't display the annoyance or resignation the law officers had shown.

Captain Cahn did not know what to make of it. Was this man, perhaps, one of Shadow's creatures?

If they had been back in normal space, where telepathy worked, Prossie Thorpe would have been able to tell if the man was truthful, or if he meant them harm—but here, in this strange, warped reality, how was anyone to be sure of anything?

The wisest course of action, he decided, was to be noncommittal and to go along and see what developed.

He sat and silently watched the traffic; his men, taking their cue from him, did the same.

■

First Lieutenant Alster Drummond watched Pel Brown out of the corner of his eye, trying not to be seen doing it.

It was obvious that the Earthman was nervous, having the four spacemen in his vehicle; he had said nothing during the drive and had refused to look at any of his passengers. Drummond had respected the man's emotions and had kept quiet, and the others had followed his example—though it was plain that they, too, were nervous, especially young Peabody, who was seated in the middle of the rear seat and who kept swiveling his head from side to side, like a scanner turret when an ambush is expected.

It might have been useful to say something to soothe the driver—Drummond had not heard his name—but the officer had no idea what to say. He knew nothing about this man, or about his society. Saying the wrong thing would be easy, and finding the right one might be impossible. It seemed better to just stay quiet and see what happened.

They had been in the vehicle for several minutes now, first on the streets, then on a great highway—these people, Drummond saw, having no antigravity, had performed miracles of highway engineering to compensate—and now they were on the streets again, cruising past shops and houses, all scattered among large expanses of grass and trees. Drummond wondered whether this was considered city or country and whether these people *had* any true cities.

The groundcar was slowing; Drummond assumed they were nearing their destination, or at least a transfer point.

"That must be her," Pel said, suddenly.

"Who?" Drummond said, startled.

"There," Pel replied, pointing.

Drummond followed Pel's finger and saw two women, one

tall and fair and the other small and dark and somehow exotic, standing on the sidewalk behind a blue vehicle that was slightly smaller than the one he was in.

A little farther along the curb a big brown groundcar had parked, and Drummond could see Captain Cahn climbing out of it on one side, and the Earthman who had driven it exiting on the other.

Then his view was blocked by the garage wall as Pel pulled the car into place and killed the engine.

Drummond discovered, when he turned to open his door, that the red car that had carried the ship's telepath, Thorpe, was already in the other bay of the garage. He fumbled with the latch and got it open before anyone could come to his assistance.

The men in the back seat did not manage any such feat, and Pel opened the door for them. They emerged, somewhat reluctantly.

People were getting out of the other car, as well—a woman in a peculiar costume of jacket, blouse, and skirt, a man in an even more peculiar and very archaic outfit of black velvet, a little girl in blue pants and a simple red shirt, and, finally, Prossie Thorpe.

"Thorpe," Drummond called, "report!"

Startled, Thorpe turned and saw him and threw a quick salute. "Telepathic silence continuing, Lieutenant," she said. "Still totally dead, both reception and transmission. No other news; an interesting ride."

He nodded, and noticed that the others, the Earth people, were all staring, with various expressions.

Was that fellow in black an Earth person? His clothing did not seem consistent with the others.

But then, there was a great deal of variation in what the Earth people wore, as well as in their skin and hair—they were clearly a very mixed society, with no proper standards of racial discrimination. There had been black men in police uniforms and working at the jail who were apparently treated as equals.

This was an entirely new universe, Drummond reminded himself, with its own rules.

"I saw someone out front," Pel called to Nancy as he crossed to the overhead door. "I think it must be that Jewell woman."

Nancy nodded, while Drummond threw Pel a questioning glance.

"The woman who owns the land where your ship crashed," Pel explained, reaching for the handle. "Out front, there."

Drummond suddenly understood. "What about the other woman?" he asked.

"I don't know," Pel said, shouting over the rumble of the descending door. "Her lawyer, probably."

Drummond nodded. That would seem to make sense. This society obviously made extensive use of hired advocates and elaborate ritual confrontations.

"Shall we all go inside?" Nancy suggested from a small door at the back of the garage. The little girl was beside her, tugging at the handle and hauling the heavy door open.

"Come on," Pel said, making a herding gesture.

The crewmen obeyed.

Once inside, Nancy directed them all to the family room, while Raven slipped away and headed for the basement. Pel opened the front door to admit Ted, Captain Cahn, the remaining crewmen, and two women.

One was small and dark, younger than the other—no more than thirty, surely—with Oriental features. She wore a gray plaid blouse and black wool suit and carried a large black purse. "This is Susan Nguyen," Ted said, gesturing to make it plain that he was introducing her to everyone, rather than to a specific individual. Drummond noticed that he made no mention of her national origin, though she was the only Oriental he had yet seen here on "Earth."

The other woman was of medium height, with thick honey-blond hair cut fairly short but elaborately curled. Pel judged her to be in her late thirties, or at most a well-preserved forty-five; her skin was pale, and she hadn't bothered to use make-up to disguise the fact. She wore a floral print dress, belted tightly. "This must be Amy Jewell, then," he said.

She nodded.

Rachel had recruited crewmen to fetch chairs from the kitchen and dining room to the family room, resulting in a temporary traffic jam as everyone bumped into each other. This was further complicated by Raven's return from the basement, accompanied by Stoddard, Squire Donald, and the wizard Valadrakul. As the chaos gradually subsided and everyone either found seats or places to stand, Nancy looked the entire array over with some dismay. She counted seventeen guests—and she hadn't had a chance to shop.

"Would anyone like coffee?" she asked, a little more loudly than she had intended.

CHAPTER 9

Pel looked over the gathering with an odd feeling of unreality. His house was full of characters out of fiction—spacemen and swordsmen and wizards.

Not actors, though; their clothes were all lived in, serious working clothes, not costumes made just for looks. He could smell sweat and perfume—the perfume, he thought, was coming from Squire Donald. He could see pimples and nose hairs.

These people were just as real as he was.

So if these people were all out of storybooks, did that make *him* a fictional character, too? Was he living out an adventure? If so, he hoped he was the hero, and that there would be a happy ending.

Up until yesterday he had thought he was all through with any chance at adventures and that he had already gotten safely to the living-happily-ever-after part. He had a wife he loved, a delightful daughter, a pleasant home, and his own reasonably successful business.

Maybe he was just background, then, just a spear carrier, some bit player.

Or maybe it wasn't a story at all. After all, what sort of adventure story had both wizards and spacemen? And what were lawyers doing in it?

No, this was no story; this was the real world taking an entirely new and bizarre turn, such as his life hadn't done since college. And it had *never* before taken a turn *this* weird.

"We'll be sending out for pizza a little later," he announced as

Nancy carried in the second tray of coffee. "For supper, I mean. I'm afraid we're not equipped to feed everybody anything more substantial than that."

"Will we be staying here, then?" one of the Imperials asked— Pel did not yet know them all by name, and this was not one he knew.

"What's pizza?" someone else asked, a little more quietly; Pel was not sure who had spoken.

That, at least, was a question he could answer.

"Pizza, for those of you who aren't familiar with it, is a sort of tomato and cheese pie you can eat with your fingers," Pel explained. "I think you'll like it, and it's something we can get delivered easily. As for whether any of you will be staying here for any length of time, I don't know; that's one of the things we need to discuss."

He looked around at the crowded room, and three dozen eyes looked back at him attentively. He was the host, the man in charge; it was his responsibility to get things moving.

"To start at the beginning," he said, "my name is Pellinore Brown, and this is my house; that's my wife Nancy bringing you all tea and coffee, and my daughter Rachel over there in the doorway." He pointed. "We have a cat somewhere, but he's probably hiding under the bed upstairs."

No one laughed; a few polite smiles appeared briefly.

Pel continued, pointing, "That's Ted Deranian, our attorney; some of you owe him a vote of thanks for getting you out of jail."

Ted, who had managed to snag the recliner, and who now sat comfortably enthroned with his feet up, smiled and waved without rising. A polite murmur was heard; when it had subsided, Pel continued.

"Over there," Pel said, pointing to the step down from the hallway, "is Amy Jewell, who owns the land where the Imperial spaceship crashed, and beside her is *her* attorney, Susan Nguyen." The two women were seated side by side on the step; Amy did not react visibly, but Susan acknowledged the introduction with a nervous little nod.

"And," Pel said, looking around to make sure he hadn't missed anyone, "according to what I've been told, the six of us are

the only people here from this planet. We have people here from
three different worlds. I'll let Raven introduce the people from *his*
world."

Raven rose from the white mesh patio chair he was using,
one of three that had been brought in to augment the available
seating. Pel noticed that at some point he had put his sword
back on.

The man in black nodded an acknowledgment and said, "My
thanks, friend Pel Brown. From my world there are at present but
four of us come. I am called Raven of Stormcrack Keep; my
companions"—he pointed—"are the mage Valadrakul, Squire Donald a' Benton, and Stoddard, man-at-arms. We came hither by
magic, seeking aid in the struggle against the Shadow that has
darkened our homeland."

Ted, still ensconced in the recliner, snorted derisively.

"Thanks," Pel said, quickly speaking up before Raven could
go any further. Raven essayed a quick bow to the gathered company, then sat again as Pel said, "And the rest of you are from the
Galactic Empire; Captain Cahn, if you could introduce your
crew?"

"I'm Captain Joshua Cahn, commanding *ISS Ruthless*, de-
tached service, Imperial Fleet," Cahn said, rising from his place on
the couch. "My second in command is First Lieutenant Alster
Drummond, my second officer is Second Lieutenant Geoffrey
Godwin." With each name he pointed. "My men are Peabody,
Smith, Lampert, Cartwright, Soorn, and Mervyn, and our Special
is Registered Master Telepath Proserpine Thorpe."

"Thank you, Captain." Pel took a deep breath.

"Mr. Brown," Captain Cahn said, interrupting whatever Pel
had been about to say, "why are we here? Are we your prisoners?"

"Oh, no, Captain!" Pel said, startled.

"No, you are *mine*," Raven added, rising.

Astonished, Pel turned to see that Raven had his hand on the
hilt of his sword, Squire Donald's hands were ready, and Stoddard
was pulling his blade from its sheath. Valadrakul had made no
move toward his knife, but had raised both hands in a very peculiar spread-fingered gesture that vaguely resembled a martial arts
stance.

"What?" Pel said, baffled. "Raven, what d'you think you're *doing*?"

"Why, claiming my prisoners, friend Pel," Raven replied, "and my thanks to you and your comrade, and your lovely wife, for fetching them for me." He grinned, and Pel remembered that his very first impression of Raven had been of a mafioso in Renaissance dress.

The Earth people all stared in confusion; the Imperials reacted with tension, anger, and befuddlement. Some stood, some started to and then froze, others never moved.

Ted smiled an uneasy smile. Amy muttered, "This is insane," and clutched her purse tightly. Susan watched, her face emotionless.

Captain Cahn did not bother to say anything; he hauled a blaster from the holster on his belt, pointed it at Stoddard, and pulled the trigger.

Nothing happened.

"Damn," he said, "I was afraid of that."

Ted giggled.

"Stoddard, put that thing away," Pel said. "And you, too, Captain; even if it doesn't work, I don't like people pointing guns in my house."

Stoddard glanced at Raven.

"Nobody is anybody's prisoner here," Pel insisted. "Raven, you three may have swords, but there are four of you and fifteen of us, and a drawerful of knives in the kitchen. If there's a fight someone's going to get hurt, and you might lose, and besides, it's just stupid. Put the swords away and let's talk about this, okay?"

"We have more than swords, Pel Brown," Raven said; he kept his right hand on the hilt of his own weapon and gestured at Valadrakul with his left.

"No, you don't," Pel said. "Magic doesn't work any better here than the captain's ray gun."

Raven gave a Hollywood villain's laugh and called, "Valadrakul!"

The wizard's fingers moved in odd, twitching patterns.

For a moment, the room was silent; no one else moved. Then Rachel began crying.

"Rachel!" Nancy cried; she hurried to her daughter's side.

The momentary distraction did not break the tension; after a quick glance, everyone returned to the frozen tableau of a moment before.

Everyone, that is, except Pel, who was standing in the middle of the room grinning.

"Come on, Raven," he said. "Magic doesn't work here."

"Ah . . . my lord," Valadrakul said softly, lowering his hands, "I fear he speaks the truth."

Raven turned to glare at his wizard. "Canst do *nothing*?" he demanded.

"Naught, my lord," Valadrakul said. "Not the merest spell can I bring to fruit."

"As I was saying," Pel said, "three swords against a dozen steak knives isn't anything I'd care to see."

"I understood," Raven said, "that this realm was different, and that magic was not the same here—but to find that a mage can do *nothing* 'gainst armed men?"

"Raven, we have *no* magic here," Pel said. "It's not that magic is different here, it's that there isn't any. *None.* It isn't possible. People have been trying to work magic here for five thousand years, and it . . . Can't. Be. Done."

"Aaah!" Raven flung his hand from the grip of his sword in disgust. "Stoddard, sheathe your blade."

Stoddard obeyed. Squire Donald dropped his hands. Ted giggled inanely again.

"Now," Pel said, exasperated, "can we get on with it?"

No one objected.

"Good," Pel said. "Now, let me see if I have this straight. You people are not from other planets, in the usual sense of planets that orbit stars that you could fly to if you had a working spaceship. You're from alternate realities—places that are in entirely different universes that occupy the same space as ours. Right?" He looked at Raven.

"I cannot gainsay that," Raven said, "though I'd not swear it be true."

Pel looked at Cahn.

"Sounds right to me, allowing for some minor variations in terminology," the captain said.

"Good," Pel said. "Raven, you and your people came here through an opening in the wall of our basement, right?"

Raven nodded.

"Now, how'd you make that opening?"

" 'Twas conjured for us, by the sorceress Elani," Raven said.

"Fine. Now, Captain Cahn, how did you and your people get here?"

Cahn blinked, took a second to consider, and replied, "We flew our ship through a spatial continuum discontinuity—a space warp, we call it."

"And how'd that warp happen?"

Cahn tightened his lips for a moment, glanced at Prossie and then at Drummond, and answered, "It was deliberately created by a process developed by the Empire's Department of Science; I don't know the details."

"But it was done by science, not magic?"

"Oh, yes; magic works no better in Imperial space than it appears to here," Cahn agreed.

"But it seems some of your science doesn't work here either, right?"

"That's right," Cahn admitted. "Though I'd be interested in knowing just how you learned that. It appears that certain physical laws are different here, including some that form the basis for much of our machinery."

"So your ship doesn't fly."

"At the moment, that's correct."

"But if it *did*," Pel asked, "could you fly it back through the warp and go back where you came from?"

Prossie coughed.

"In theory," Cahn said. "It hasn't been done, however."

"Ah. And in any case, your ship *doesn't* fly—so the ten of you are stranded here, right?"

Cahn did not answer that; instead he stared calmly back at Pel.

Pel waved the question aside. "It doesn't matter," he said. "I'm just trying to make sure everyone sees as much of the situation as possible."

"Keep it up, Mr. Brown," Amy called from the hallway step. "You're doing fine so far; it almost makes sense."

Several people, from all three worlds, smiled.

"Thank you," Pel replied. He paused, rubbed at a cheek with his forefinger, and pondered, while everyone else waited expectantly.

"All right," he said, "now let's consider *why* all you people are here. Raven tells me that something he calls Shadow has . . . um . . . conquered?" Raven nodded. "Conquered. Something called Shadow has conquered most of his home world—I guess he just means his own planet, and not whatever others there are in his universe . . ."

Valadrakul cleared his throat. Pel turned his gaze on the wizard. "Yes?"

"Your pardon," the wizard said, "but you misunderstand the nature of our reality. There is but one world; we have no planets in our cosmos, as you would use the term. I would take it that your own cosmos resembles that of the Empire, with a myriad of worldly globes circling many thousands of stars, but our realm is not like that; rather, we have but a single globe, and the sun and moons and stars, and the wanderers that *we* call by the name 'planet,' all travel about it."

"We used to think that, too . . ." Pel began.

Valadrakul cut him off with a shake of his head. "Still you do not understand," he said. "Wizards have *been* to the stars, long ago, and flown behind the sun. We have seen all our universe from afar, hanging alone in a black and empty cosmos. We know its nature."

"All right," Pel said, "I won't argue about it. At any rate, this Shadow thing has conquered most of the world, right?"

"Aye," said three of the four—Stoddard did not speak, but Raven, Donald, and Valadrakul all responded. "May Shadow be eternally damned," Donald added.

"It's conquered *all* the world," Raven said.

Pel nodded. "Right," he said. "And now it's looking for somewhere new, right?"

"Aye," Raven said.

"And that brings us to the Empire," Pel said, turning to Captain Cahn. "Captain?"

"Yes, Mr. Brown?" Cahn said, raising an eyebrow. The gesture was something Leonard Nimoy might have done playing Mr.

Spock, but Cahn, with his close-cropped blond hair and square jaw, didn't look anything at all like Spock. He looked more like someone's idea of the all-American boy.

"This Shadow thing discovered your universe, right?"

"So it appears," Cahn said. "I believe that Telepath Thorpe can probably tell you more about that than I can."

All eyes turned to Prossie. She shrank back against the cushions of the couch.

"Report, Thorpe," Cahn told her.

"Yes, sir," Prossie said, standing quickly and snapping to attention. "About seven years ago," she began, "Imperial Intelligence started getting reports of oddities—strange creatures turning up in places they shouldn't, most often. The creatures in question either vanished or died before any Intelligence personnel or any telepath reached them, and the dead ones didn't explain much—the Department of Science couldn't figure out where they came from, or any conditions under which they could have survived naturally. Some of them seemed to lack vital organs, for example. A few were miniature humans, but most were monstrosities."

Cahn nodded; Pel blinked.

"Hellbeasts and homunculi, most likely," Raven said.

"The Empire investigated," Prossie continued, "and located certain people who were not what they pretended to be. Telepathic interrogation, carried out without the subject being aware of it, revealed that these people, and all of the anomalies, were the products of an extra-universal entity that they knew as 'Shadow.' This entity had sent its creatures to scout out Imperial space, explore it, and to send back reports. Shadow's reasons and long-term intentions were not known to any of its creations."

"Shadow is no fool," Raven remarked. Pel gestured for him to be silent, and he obeyed.

"Up until this point," Prossie went on, "the possibility of inter-universal travel was unknown to the Empire. However, the existence of this extra-universal threat was sufficient reason to begin a crash program at the Department of Science, to find and access other universes. Using knowledge gleaned from Shadow's creatures, telepaths assisted in this research, and in fact were central to it; it was discovered that under certain conditions telepaths could contact minds in other universes, that in fact such contacts had sometimes already occurred inadvertently, but that heretofore their nature had been misunderstood. It was determined that the foremost requirement for inter-universal contact, the one that appears to have been most limiting, is that the minds in question must all think in the same language as the telepath attempting to reach them."

"English?" Ted asked.

Prossie nodded. "It appears," she said, "that a similar limitation must exist on the magic that Shadow used in opening a way between its universe and Imperial space—or perhaps Shadow only discovered the Empire when a telepath accidentally contacted it. In any case, Shadow and its creatures, and most of the other inhabitants of its universe, speak a recognizable dialect of Imperial English. Accordingly, our telepaths were able to contact some of them. Shadow itself, however, was another matter; attempts to read its thoughts were unsuccessful, and sometimes damaging. One telepath died upon contacting Shadow; the autopsy found severe brain damage. After that we were all more careful."

Pel nodded. Amy shuddered.

"Although we could sometimes sense, around the fringes of our perception, beings that spoke other languages, we were unable to establish contact with anything other than English-speaking humans," Prossie continued. "Until very recently this meant that we could only communicate reliably within the Empire, or with Shadow's world. However, a few weeks back we achieved limited contacts with individuals in a third universe—the one we're all in right now."

"It's pretty goddamn unlikely, three different universes, *that* different, where the same species and the same language happened," Ted remarked. "That's the biggest flaw in the story so far— and there are plenty of flaws."

"Given an infinite number of realities," Prossie said, turning slightly to address the recumbent lawyer but staying at attention, "and we have no reason to think that the number is any *less* than infinite, the same species and language would *have* to recur somewhere, eventually."

Ted shifted and leaned the recliner farther back. "I don't buy it," he said, "but go on with your story."

Prossie nodded. "There isn't much more. The Empire's been sure for a long time that Shadow is hostile and dangerous, and we wanted allies against it. Earth looked like a promising possibility. Telepathic contacts weren't clear and reliable enough, however, so the newly developed space warp technology was used to send a diplomatic mission to your largest and most powerful nation." She shrugged. "And here we are."

"The United States isn't the largest nation on Earth," Susan protested.

Prossie slipped from her brace and stared. "It's not?" she asked.

"China is," Rachel piped up from the doorway. "They told us that in kindergarten."

"The United States is the largest country that speaks English," Nancy pointed out.

"That would explain it," Captain Cahn said.

"That's who *you* are," Ted said from his chair, "but who the heck are *they*?" He pointed at Raven and Valadrakul.

"We gave our names, sir," Raven said, a trifle stiffly.

Ted shook his head. "I mean, who the heck are you? Are you good guys, or bad guys, or what? You said you weren't on Shadow's side, so are you on the Empire's side?"

"We are on our *own* side," Raven retorted.

"All right," Pel said, "but it's a good question—what side *is* that?"

Raven made a derisive noise. "Think you," he said, "that though all be conquered, even Shadow can control everything utterly? Think you that, though the fortresses fall, none will continue to bear arms 'gainst the tyrant? I and mine are those who have refused to give up, who have fought on beyond defeat."

"Could you be a bit more specific?" Ted asked.

Raven glared at him.

"Yes," Captain Cahn said. "I wasn't aware of any native resistance to Shadow's rule. Who are you, and how many? How are you organized?"

"Do you think me a fool?" Raven asked, annoyed. Then he stopped, and grinned. "Aye, perchance you do, after that exhibition I made but moments ago. And who could blame you? Yet I'm not such a fool as all that, and I'll not give away secrets before this many, when almost any of you could be a thing of Shadow."

Several of those present glanced uneasily at each other at this suggestion. Prossie realized she was still standing, and sank back onto the couch.

"This is all crazy," Amy muttered.

"Can't you tell us *anything* useful?" Lieutenant Drummond asked.

Raven turned to Valadrakul; the wizard said, "There are many of us, working 'gainst Shadow—but we are scattered, and needs must work in secret. We have organized ourselves in small councils, with no more than a dozen in each, and none but the leader of each council knows any save those within his own group—thus, should we be betrayed, no more than a dozen shall be found and slain."

"Cells," Pel said. "Revolutionary cells."

"And likewise, none save the innermost councils, of which those here have no part, can know our true numbers," Raven pointed out.

"So the four of you make up one cell in this underground?" Pel asked.

"Half a council, rather," Donald volunteered.

"Why didn't you all come?" Captain Cahn asked. "Seems to me that at least you'd be safe here."

Raven shook his head. "Nay," he said.

"Why not?" Cahn persisted.

"I should not say," Raven said, "for I know not whether any of you are tainted by Shadow, nor how far word might spread if spoken here. I'd not have any more known than I must."

"I think it's safe enough here," Pel said. "We're all of us opposed to Shadow, aren't we? Captain Cahn, you and your crew must have been checked over by telepaths before you were sent through the warp."

Cahn nodded. "We were, indeed," he said.

"And Shadow hasn't discovered Earth yet," Pel pointed out, "so none of *us* could be spies."

"We know not whether Earth has been found," Valadrakul corrected him.

"Even if it *has*," Pel pointed out, "there are five billion people on Earth; what are the chances that any of the seven of us here would be spies?"

"Fair enough," Raven said, after a moment's consideration. "Well, then, the truth is that we cannot all be safe here, for three of our council are wee folk—gnomes, as they were once known—who cannot abide this place. And another is the sorceress who maintains the portal; were she to step through, and her magicks thereby fail, we would all be trapped here."

Lieutenant Godwin growled. "We *are* trapped here, I'd think."

Cahn threw him a warning look, and he fell apologetically silent.

"Captain," Raven said, "*can* you return home, an we allow it?"

"I can't say," Cahn replied shortly.

"He probably doesn't know himself," Nancy whispered in Pel's ear.

"If not," Raven said, "we have something to offer you, for your good services."

Cahn cocked an eyebrow at the black-clad foreigner. "And what might that be?" he asked.

"Our sorceress, Elani, has stolen Shadow's gateway spell, and has opened our portal to Earth—and likewise, she can open a portal to your Empire, and thereby send you home."

Prossie made a noise; Pel glanced at her, and she looked away.

CHAPTER 10

"An interesting proposition," Cahn said, in his most noncommittal tone. "And what sort of payment would you want for this service?"

"Why, 'tis obvious, is't not?" Raven asked, spreading his hands. "We wish your aid against Shadow."

"Our aid?" Cahn grimaced. "Mister, we're just ten men—ten people, rather." One hand made a vague gesture in Prossie's direction. "We've got a ship and weapons that don't work here, and that might not work in your universe, either—so what difference will ten men make against a force that has already conquered a world?"

"You are part of the Imperial Fleet, are you not?" Raven asked. "Yours but a single ship in a vast armada, with the power to lay waste whole kingdoms in mere days?"

"Oh, sure," Lieutenant Drummond said, "but the Imperial Fleet is *there*, and we're *here*. We're just the crew of one ship."

"Besides," Godwin added, "as the captain just said, the Fleet's weapons are based on the same principles as the captain's blaster that didn't go off a few minutes ago. They won't work here, and probably won't work on your world, either. We're disarmed—just like your wizard."

Raven ignored Godwin and addressed Drummond. "You are the crew of a *diplomatic* vessel," he pointed out, "sent as envoy and empowered to make pact on behalf of your Emperor."

Pel considered Godwin's comments as Cahn said, "Our authority isn't as broad as all that. We're more a negotiating team than an embassy; anything we agreed to would have to be approved by higher authority, maybe by the Emperor Himself."

"Indeed?"

Cahn nodded. "In fact, the main thing we were sent to nego-
tiate was an exchange of ambassadors. We sure don't have the
power to declare war and send the entire Imperial Fleet through a
warp to fight Shadow, if that's what you were hoping for."

"Raven," Pel said, "there's something here I don't understand.
If magic doesn't work in the Empire, and the Imperial technology
doesn't work in your world, how can they fight?"

Raven blinked in surprise. "Friend Pel," he said, "what mean
you?"

"I *mean*," Pel said, "how can Shadow do anything to the Galactic Empire if magic doesn't work there? And how can the Empire do anything to Shadow?"

Raven turned to Valadrakul, who said, "A good point, sir.
Howsoever, there is some magic that can effect its purpose in other
realms, even while it cannot be conjured there. Consider the gateway spell that manifests in your own cellars—the magic lies entirely in our own world, and yet it functions both ways. Likewise,
consider the magic of the mind that these good people call telepathy." The wizard mispronounced the word, but as he gestured toward Prossie, Pel figured out what he meant. "It works not a whit
here, and this maiden can no more hear your thoughts now than
can any other."

Several people cast startled glances at Prossie or each other
at this revelation. Valadrakul continued, unperturbed. "Yet from
their own land, these mind readers can know what others think in
all our varied realms."

Pel nodded. "Still doesn't seem like Shadow's about to conquer the Empire," he said. "Or for that matter, that the Empire's
about to conquer Shadow. I mean, if each side's major weapons
don't work in the other one's worlds . . ."

"Ah, but Shadow's *greatest* strength is of value in either
realm!" Raven said, interrupting.

"Its creatures, you mean," Prossie said.

"Exactly," Raven said. "Its homunculi can live in the Empire,
and fight there, as can those true humans who are base enough to
choose slavery to Shadow over death in resistance."

"The monsters died, though," Prossie pointed out. "At least
most of them. And the miniatures, too."

"Gnomes," Donald muttered.

"And which would you rather face," Raven asked, "some misshapen thing brought from nightmare, or a well-drilled army? A beast, or a trained assassin?"

"Good point," Cahn conceded.

"And Shadow can be persuasive," Raven said. "Doubt me not, there are those among your own people who would yield willingly to its blandishments, and serve it of their own will. There were such among my own kin."

At that, Stoddard growled—the first sound most of those present had heard from him. Squire Donald spat in disgust, and Pel heard Nancy gasp at the sight of that.

"Don't worry," he whispered to her, "it'll come right out of the carpet."

Cahn nodded toward Raven. "I'm sure you're right," he said. "We've had trouble with spies and traitors before, and I doubt we've managed to breed the tendencies out of the human species in the last few years." He grimaced. "And as Thorpe told you, we've already had problems with Shadow's creatures infiltrating the Empire. Telepaths can spot them, or X-rays, but we only have four hundred telepaths out of thirteen billion citizens, and it's not practical to march everyone past a fluoroscope. Furthermore, Shadow seems to be able to send in duplicates and replace genuine people, so that the checks can't just be done once, they need to be repeated constantly. So we have spies among us, I'm certain."

"I think we all agree that Shadow has to be stopped," Drummond said. "The question is, how?"

"And your answer?" Donald demanded.

Drummond shrugged. "I don't have one," he said.

Cahn expanded upon that. "The Empire is preparing for war," he said. "We're stockpiling ships and weapons, and if ever Shadow attempts the open occupation of any part of Imperial space, it will find us ready to retaliate. We'll blast any colonies we find right out of space. And we're stepping up our security measures—of course, I couldn't give you details, even if I knew them, for fear of compromising them. We're doing everything we can to locate and stamp out any attempts at infiltration. When we find Shadow's creatures, we kill them, immediately."

"A noble effort, to be sure," Raven said, with a note of sarcasm creeping into his voice, "but knowing that Shadow's spies in your Emperor's kitchens will be found and slain gives me no great hope for the liberation of Stormcrack Keep."

"Nor Benton," Donald added.

"Nor anywhere else in our world," Valadrakul agreed.

"Hey," Godwin protested, "who appointed us your rescuers, anyway? We have our *own* homes to worry about, first!"

"And would your homes not be best served," Raven demanded, "by encompassing the utter destruction of Shadow and all its creations, rather than nibbling away at its outer defenses?"

"Of course that would suit our long-term interests," Cahn said, "and it's just that, a *long-term* goal. As yet, we have no way to achieve it." He gestured at Pel. "We'd hoped that these people could give us a weapon to use against Shadow, but I doubt that these super-bombs of theirs would work in your space."

"You can't get any anyway," Pel pointed out.

Cahn drew his blaster, hefted it, pointed it at the ceiling, and pulled the trigger. Nothing happened, not even an audible click.

"Back home," he said, "that would have blown a two-foot hole through the roof. Here, nothing. Our weapons don't work here, and we don't think they work in Shadow's world, either."

"Nor do they," Raven acknowledged. "We've tested them."

For a moment nobody spoke; Pel took them all to be absorbing the implications. Among other things, it was an admission that Raven's people had visited the Empire and had obtained weapons there.

But they hadn't done so openly.

"Well, then," Cahn said finally, "what do you want us to do, when our weapons won't work?"

"Some weapons work everywhere," Raven said, his hand dropping to the hilt of his sword. "Your Empire has great resources, thousands upon thousands of men and machines—you spoke of a populace numbered thirteen billions. Could you not make swords as easily as those . . . those things you carry? Could not your armies march 'gainst Shadow, as did those of Stormcrack Keep in my youth?"

"And where are those armies of your youth now?" Cahn demanded. "Why should we send our people to be slaughtered by that thing's magic?"

Raven frowned and shifted his weight to his other foot before replying, "And what of your science? What of other weapons? We know that what you bear will not function, but have you no other armaments? We know little of what will or will not serve, in any of our three worlds; there may well be weapons known to you, and unknown to Shadow, that would serve as well in our world as your own. We know not whether this world's mighty bombs can destroy Shadow's fortress; mayhap they can, mayhap they cannot. Perhaps your magicians, your science wielders, can discover ways to shield against Shadow's spells; perhaps the men of your world are not as susceptible to those spells as are mine. Dare we not venture the attempt?"

"I'll order the pizza," Nancy whispered in Pel's ear. "I figure five large pies."

He nodded, and she slipped away.

"I'm sure," Cahn said, "that when the Empire has had time to prepare, we *will* make an attempt. The Emperor doesn't want Shadow there anymore than you do, but there's no point in throwing away resources in a premature attack."

"So you wait, and wait—seven years, now, since first Shadow showed its hand in your realm?"

"Seven years, yes," Cahn agreed, "but we haven't been waiting idly—if we had, I wouldn't be here talking to you."

"Not idle, perhaps, yet you wait," Raven insisted. "And I fear that when at last the Empire sees fit to strike, I'll be long in my grave, and our councils lost. Then even if Shadow falls, my people will be but yielding one tyrant for another."

"You're saying the Empire's no better than Shadow?" Cahn asked, his tone threatening.

Raven held up his hands. "Nay, I said it not," he said. " 'Tis certain that your Emperor George cannot help but be preferable to the horrors of Shadow. But is there no other way? Are my people never to return to their own ways, their own rulers?"

"Watch how you talk about the Emperor," Godwin growled.

"His Imperial Majesty George the Eighth generally doesn't interfere much in the lives of his subjects," Cahn said, with enforced calm. "You people will probably have all your own little lords back, if that's what you want—it's just they'll be subject to the Empire."

Raven turned up his palms. "And you do not see why we are dissatisfied with that?"

"I see it," Cahn said, his voice hard. "I just don't see why it's any of my business."

"Ah, Captain," Raven said, suddenly changing manner from supplicant to salesman, "*that* brings us back whence we began. I can take you home to your own world; in exchange, I ask that you aid us against Shadow."

"It's a circle, all right," Cahn agreed, "because I don't see what we can do."

"Isn't there any way you can defeat Shadow, other than a full-scale war?" Pel asked.

Cahn turned to him. "For example?" he asked.

"Well, Shadow's a magician, right? I mean, underneath? Couldn't someone kill him somehow? Wouldn't that do it?"

"Shadow might have been human once," Raven said. "I doubt it still is."

"But could it be killed?"

Raven turned to Valadrakul, who turned up open palms. "Who knows?" he said.

"Well, maybe if someone tried, that would solve the whole problem," Pel suggested. "You know, like if someone had assassinated Hitler in 1938 maybe we wouldn't have had to fight World War II."

Fourteen pairs of eyes stared at him in utter incomprehension. Ted, in his recliner, giggled again; Amy was looking about the room, from face to face, while Susan was watching Raven. Nancy was in the kitchen, and Pel realized he didn't know where Rachel was; she had disappeared.

Probably got bored, he thought to himself. This must all be way over her head.

"Sir," Valadrakul said, "I know nothing of this Hitler, nor any world war, but yes, an we could slay Shadow, we would need no war."

"Well, *can* we slay Shadow?"

Valadrakul turned up a palm again. "Who knows?" he asked again.

"Well, where does Shadow get its power?" Pel asked. "Is there some magic ring we can throw into a volcano or something?"

Stoddard glanced at Raven, who glanced at Valadrakul, but most of those present simply stared at Pel.

"You know, like in *The Lord of the Rings* or something," Pel said.

"Friend Pel," Raven said, speaking gently, "what are you saying? Once before, you spoke of this; we know not what you mean."

"You aren't making sense, Mr. Brown," Cahn said.

"It's a book," Pel explained. "Three books, I mean, by J. R. R. Tolkien. There's this hobbit, see, who finds a magic ring that's the key to the Dark Lord's power, and he throws it into a volcano and melts it, and then the Dark Lord doesn't have any power."

"Nonsense," Valadrakul declared. "What fool of a sorcerer would put all his power in a single talisman? And Shadow uses no talismans at all; Shadow is at the heart of a great mystical matrix, a web of arcane potency built up over centuries. What would such as that need with wands and rings and baubles?"

"I certainly never heard of any such tale as you describe," Cahn added.

"I've heard of it," Susan interjected, "but I never read it."

"What's a hobbit?" one of the crewmen—Cartwright, Pel thought it was—asked.

"An imaginary little person," Pel explained.

"Like a spriggan?" Cartwright suggested.

"I don't know," Pel replied. "What's a spriggan?"

"Like in the stories," Cartwright said. "You know, like Plunkett's stuff."

"Who's Plunkett?" Ted asked.

"Edward Plunkett, the writer," Cartwright said, turning to look at Ted.

"Never heard of him," Ted said.

"Neither did I," Pel added.

"Of course not," Cahn said. "He's from *our* universe, not yours. He wrote picture books, died a couple of years ago."

"Well, I guess we all know things the others don't," Pel agreed.

"Like what that thing is," said Peabody, emboldened by Cartwright's comments. He pointed at the stereo.

"It's a stereo," Pel said. "It plays music."

"Like a melodeon?" Peabody asked.

"I don't think so," Pel said. "Wasn't that some Victorian thing?"

"Boy, has *this* conversation degenerated!" Ted called out to no one in particular. "From saving three different universes to sound equipment!"

"Indeed," Raven said, with a sour glance at Ted, "I must agree. We were discussing whether a way might be found to slay Shadow, without first defeating it in battle."

"I don't know of any," Cahn replied.

"I don't know anything *about* it," Pel said.

"Ah," Valadrakul said, "but you know much it does not."

Most eyes turned toward the wizard, Raven's among them.

"What mean you?" he asked.

"I mean that these gentlemen know many things that we cannot imagine, my lord—these tales of Messieurs Tolkien and Plunkett, an example. Who knows but that they *do* have a way to slay Shadow, but know it not?"

"But if we don't *know* we know it, what good does it do?" Pel asked.

"Perhaps," Valadrakul suggested, holding up a finger, "if men of all three worlds were to gather in ours, and together study the situation, a solution might be found."

Captain Cahn looked around thoughtfully.

"You may have a point, uh . . . wizard," he said. "If we all studied Shadow in your world."

"Yeah, and he may *not* have a point," Pel said. "Listen, I didn't ask for all you people to come here; I didn't ask anyone to put that thing in my basement. I've tried to be helpful, but I'm not going anywhere or studying anything. That's up to you guys."

"Well, I think I'd be willing to chance a visit to wherever these people are based," Cahn said. "I've already risked visiting one alien universe; I don't mind passing through another on the way home and seeing what we can do there." He looked around at his crew. "This would be purely voluntary, men; if you'd rather stay here and wait until rescue comes, that's fine. Or if you want to go back to the ship and see about getting her airborne . . ."

"Oh, no," Amy said, interrupting.

Everyone turned to her, and Pel realized that she had hardly said a word throughout the entire meeting.

"Nobody's going near that ship," she said. "It's on my land, and nobody's messing with it."

"But, madam . . ." Cahn began.

"*No*, Captain!" she said loudly. "I don't know what's going on, really I don't—I've listened to all this, and I have no idea how much of it is for real, if *any* of it is, and if it's not I don't know which of you are in on the gag and which aren't, but whatever the truth is, *nobody* here, not *one* of you, is going to set foot on my land or inside that ship until I *do* know exactly what's going on! And maybe not even then!"

"My lady," Valadrakul said, "everything said here today is purest truth, I swear by the Goddess."

"I don't believe that," Amy replied.

"What part don't you believe?" Cahn asked.

Amy looked around uncertainly. "I don't know," she said. "I'm not sure I believe *any* of it!"

"My lady," Valadrakul said, "we can easily prove to you the reality of our native world; 'tis but a few steps to take you there, along the passage, down the stairs, and across the cellars. A step through the wall, and you can see our world with your own eyes."

"Oh, no," Amy said. "I didn't ask for any ship to fall in my back yard any more than this person wanted a space warp in his basement." She waved at Pel.

Raven turned his attention to Ted, who held up his hands. "Oh, no," he said. "I'm not like Ms. Jewell there; I *do* know what to believe, and I don't believe a word of any of this. I'm enjoying the show, really I am—it's a pretty good story—but I don't for a minute think any of it is real. I suspect I'm asleep and dreaming the whole thing, I really do, but if that's not it then all of you must be crazy. And I'm not letting any escaped lunatics take me any-where, thank you!"

Cahn turned to Nancy, who stood in the kitchen doorway.

"Don't look at *me*," she said.

Valadrakul addressed Susan and said, with a slight bow, "That leaves you, my lady."

"I'm not interested," Susan said, shaking her head. "Not at all. I saw enough of war when I was a little girl."

"Well, then," Raven said, " 'twould seem we have none of Earth who would join us."

"What about those people you contacted telepathically?" Pel asked. "Would any of them want to help?"

Cahn turned to Prossie, who leaned her head back and started counting them off on her fingers.

"Well," she said, "there was Carleton Miletti. Every time we tried to contact him he was doing something dangerous, like driving a groundcar at very high speed, so we didn't force a contact for fear of distracting him and getting him killed, and he never responded to our presence."

"Doesn't sound promising," Pel commented.

"There was Angela Thompson—she's three years old. I don't think she'd be much help. A very sweet little girl, though; she called us Mr. Nobody."

Nancy smiled.

"There was a man named Ray Aldridge who claimed to be a . . . a psychic," Prossie said. "He claimed to read minds and see the future, but we think he was lying. We never found any evidence of any real parapsychic abilities."

"Still," Pel said, "he might do."

Prossie looked up at Pel. "I suppose so," she said. "He lives in a place called California; is that anywhere near here?"

"No," Pel admitted.

"We could phone him, though, and ask him to fly out," Amy suggested.

"Phone?" Squire Donald looked about in polite puzzlement.

"Fly?" Raven turned toward Amy.

"You have aircraft?" Cahn asked, startled.

"Of course we do," Pel said. "Ms. Thorpe, did you get an address for him?"

Prossie shook her head. "No," she said, "but he lives in . . . in Oakville, maybe? Oakmont?"

"Oakland?" Ted suggested.

"That could be it," Prossie agreed.

"Big town," Ted remarked.

"Who else?" Pel asked.

"Well, Oram Blaisdell," Prossie said, "but he's an old man, and his neighbors think he's crazy."

"Where is he?"

"Tessenti? Something like that."

"Tessenti?"

"Tessenti, Tennessy, something—I don't remember."

"Tennessee?" Amy suggested.

"That's it, yes," Prossie said, thankfully.

"Any others?"

"One old woman who died," Prossie said. "She was in a place called Alice Springs—I'm pretty sure that wasn't anywhere near here."

"It's in Australia, I think," Pel said.

"And that's almost all that we even got names for," Prossie said. "There was one more, I think—a girl in another country, who sometimes spoke another language instead of English. Her name was Gwyneth something, I think."

"Sounds Welsh," Nancy remarked.

"That was the other language, yes," Prossie agreed. "She was about fifteen, I think."

"Not much help," Pel said.

"None of them are," Susan agreed.

"Where does this Carleton Miletti live?" Pel asked.

"I don't know," Prossie said. "We never got a strong enough contact to read any place names."

"Damn. Well, this Aldridge—you said he's out in Oakland, California? And he's a psychic advisor?" Pel began walking toward the kitchen as he spoke.

"Uh . . . something like that," Prossie agreed.

"Fine." Pel reached around the kitchen door and picked up the phone receiver; he said, "Just a minute." Then he stepped around the corner and pulled the phone book from the shelf.

"Nancy," he said, thumbing through the black-bordered pages at the front of the directory, "do you know the area code for Oakland?"

"No," she said, unhappily. "Area codes are page twenty-nine, though."

"Got it, I think." He dialed (415) 555-1212.

The motley collection in the other room waited silently while Pel spoke on the phone; a moment later he appeared in the kitchen doorway and announced, "Unlisted. Seems stupid for a psychic to have an unlisted number, but he does."

"Maybe he doesn't want you to phone him unless you're psychic yourself, and can *guess* the number," Ted remarked, grinning. Nobody laughed.

"What about the one in Tennessee?" Amy suggested.

"Oram Blaisdell," Prossie said.

"Yeah," Pel said, "what about him?"

Prossie shook her head. "He probably doesn't even *have* one of those telephone things," she said. "Besides, he's a crazy old man. He thought we were angels talking to him."

"Mr. Brown," Cahn said, "it was a good idea, but forget it. None of the original contactees are going to be any help. It'll be up to my crew and myself to lend whatever aid we can, in exchange for transport home; we won't drag you innocent civilians into it."

"Sir?" Soorn said, uneasily.

Cahn turned.

"Sir," Soorn said, "speaking purely for myself, I would prefer . . . well, you said that this was voluntary?"

"Yes, Spaceman?"

"Sir, I'm afraid I must decline to volunteer. I'd prefer to wait here and hope for rescue. This world doesn't seem all that bad—I mean, dangerous. I'd rather stay here and wait than risk going into some fairyland where this Shadow thing is all-powerful."

Cahn stared at him, and Soorn, after a moment of awkward silence, added, "I saw some of what they found on Lambda Ceti Four, sir. I'm not going."

"All right," Cahn said, "I said it was voluntary, and it is. You can stay here, and fend for yourself."

"Thank you, sir."

"You can't stay *here*," Nancy protested. "I'm sorry, but not in *my* house you don't. I don't know anything about you!"

Soorn looked at her unhappily. "I can find someplace, then, can't I?"

"Maybe a hotel?" Susan said.

"Do you have any money?" Pel asked.

Soorn shook his head.

"Lad," Raven said, "Shadow is powerful, and nominal ruler of all the world, but it's not *all*-powerful. Come with us, and see for yourself! Lend your arm to a worthy battle!"

Soorn looked at him and said nothing.

"Come and take a look," Donald coaxed. "See for yourself! And should our land not please you, our wizards can see you safe home to your Empire, while those who would brave it may stay and fight."

Soorn glanced at Cahn, then at Nancy; neither of them gave any sign of yielding.

"You, too, mistress," Donald said, leaning forward and making a beckoning gesture to Amy, "and you," he said, adding Susan, "come and see our realm! See what it is we wish to save! Then perhaps you'll think more kindly of us. All of you, come and take a look, and if you be not pleased, 'tis but a moment's work to step back through the gate to the cellars here—or should Elani wish it, to the Empire whence most of you came!"

"I could do that?" Amy said. "Just step through and take a look around, and step right back?"

"Why not?" Donald asked, with an expansive gesture.

"Then I'd *know* whether it was real," Amy said.

Donald nodded.

Pel glanced at Nancy. "Y'know, I think I'd like to take a quick look, too," he said. "I've always loved fantasy stories, and ever since that gnome first turned up—I mean, it's scary, but I'd like to take a look."

"You people are all crazy," Nancy said. "Especially you, Pel."

"Oh, don't be such a stick-in-the-mud, Nancy!" Ted said. "Let's *all* go see just what sort of dreamworld I've come up with!"

"Nancy, think of it, seriously—a world where magic is *real*," Pel said.

"*Black* magic," Nancy retorted.

"Not all of it," Pel replied. "That gnome—you'd like seeing him."

"Ha."

"Well, *I'm* going to go look," Pel said, annoyed. "For one thing, as Amy said, how else will we ever be sure this is all real?"

"Are you going to take a camera?" Nancy asked. "And take pictures or something?"

"Sure, why not?" Pel said.

She glared at him, and then turned to Raven and demanded, "Are you *sure* we can step right back?"

"Oh, yes, my lady," he said. "Have we not done so, my comrades and I?"

"You're coming?" Pel asked.

"If you go, I'm going, too," she said. "To keep an eye on you."

"What about Rachel?"

Nancy hesitated. "She's upstairs playing," she said, "but we'll bring her, too. Maybe she'll like seeing those gnomes you talked about."

"She'll want to tell everyone at school about it," Pel said, smiling.

"They'll never believe a word," Nancy retorted. "Not even Jenny would buy a story like that, even if it's true. Which I'm still not entirely convinced of."

Pel shrugged. "You're probably right," he said.

"Then you'll come?" Raven said. "Perchance even a quick glance will tell you somewhat, and some thought may strike you that would serve our cause."

"Not likely," Pel said.

The doorbell rang, and Nancy's hand flew to her mouth.

"The pizza," she said.

Small feet pattered down the stairs as Rachel ran to answer the door.

CHAPTER 11

Amy watched as the self-proclaimed spacemen sampled the pizza. If they were acting, they were doing a very convincing job of it; under other circumstances she wouldn't have doubted for a moment that they had never before seen pizza, or tasted Pepsi. If they had claimed to be foreigners, or from some isolated little place somewhere, that would have been fine.

But they claimed to be, not just from another planet, but from another *universe*.

Believing that would mean changing her entire way of dealing with the world. She had long ago decided that she was never going to be rich or famous, never going to have any wild romances, never going to climb Mount Everest or fly to the moon, or do anything else exciting and dangerous. It was safer and more comfortable to just stay at home and read about all that. She didn't need to do anything herself.

And if the books weren't enough, there were her decorating clients, with all their little stories about where this knickknack or that had come from, or why they had moved here, or what all the gadgets in the kitchen were for. She got customers who were in the foreign service, back stateside for a couple of years, and most of them were eager to tell stories about their time in places like Qatar or Tanzania. She got some buyers who were immigrants, who had *grown up* in places like Morocco or Taiwan or Syria. Listening to them was better than actually going to all those exotic, dangerous places.

Meeting people like that was fine; she could find Syria and

Taiwan on the maps and hear about them on the evening news. But she didn't want to *be* one of them. She didn't want anything exciting to happen to her.

And she had her tidy little ideas of how the world worked, of how everyone was alike, really, the world over. All those people shared a single planet, and despite all the differences in language and culture, they were all part of the same reality, and that reality didn't include purple-and-gold spaceships falling out of the sky, didn't include swordsmen in black velvet or wizards wearing braids.

If she believed these people, it meant losing control of what was real and what wasn't. If magic could be real, if spaceships could appear out of nowhere, how could she ever be sure of *anything*?

It would change her entire perception of the world—and she'd already done that once, when Stan had come home drunk that night, and beaten her, and then left her for that bitch in Florida. She didn't want to do it again. Last time she'd had to learn that the world was not going to look after her, that she couldn't have everything she wanted, that bad things could happen even to her—what would she have to learn this time? That she couldn't trust anything at all, not even the sky overhead?

She wanted to find some nice, rational explanation, like movie publicity stunts or escaped lunatics.

She didn't think she would.

But at least, if she could really take a look at this other world of Raven's, she would *know*, just as she had *known* when Stan knocked her down with his fist, when he swore at her and kicked her.

Better to *know*, and have it over with.

■

The matter of taking a look through the portal was discussed further. The pizza was eaten, and several liters of Pepsi were consumed. And finally, around seven, Pel and Nancy herded everyone down the stairs to the basement. Pel had his old Instamatic in one pocket.

Rachel was staring around wide-eyed at all the funny clothes the different people were wearing.

Raven went down first, to lead the way; he crossed quickly to the appropriate area of blank wall and stood there, waiting.

Stoddard followed immediately and stood a little to one side.

The crew of the *Ruthless* came next, and at Raven's direction lined up against one wall, out of the way. Cahn and Prossie brought up the rear. As Pel watched them descend he heard Soorn's voice, carrying by some fluke of acoustics, as he told one of the others, "I guess it's just as well we're trying this; I don't know if I could ever get used to any world where people eat that 'Pete Sah' stuff."

"I kind of liked it," someone replied—Mervyn, perhaps? Pel was unsure.

"It tasted okay, but it's so *gooey*—and what *were* all those things on top?"

Pel laughed involuntarily, and the conversation stopped abruptly.

Susan descended next, with Amy close behind. Ted followed, and Squire Donald immediately after. That left Valadrakul and the Browns at the head of the stairs.

"Go on," Pel told the wizard.

Valadrakul bowed to Nancy. "After you, my lady."

"I need to check the locks," she replied.

"We're only going to be gone for a minute," Pel protested.

"I don't care," Nancy said. "If we're leaving the house I want it locked up."

Pel opened his mouth to argue, then shut it again.

"All right," he said, "go ahead."

The others all waited patiently while she turned and made sure that yes, the deadbolt was thrown on the front door, and the bar was in place on the sliding door in the family room. The empty pizza boxes, stacked on the family room coffee table, caught her eye. "Maybe I should clean those up," she said uncertainly.

"They can wait," Pel said. "We'll be right back."

She looked around, hesitating. Pel started to speak, but she yielded before he could say a word.

"Oh, all right," she said. She took Rachel's hand and descended the steps.

Valadrakul followed, and Pel came last of all.

As he came down the steps he looked around at the crowd. It seemed somehow more surreal seeing all those people in the basement than it had in the family room; after all, the family room had been used for parties on occasion, and guests there weren't unusual, but the basement was strictly Pel's territory, where nobody else ever ventured.

Or at least, it had been until now.

Now, though, there were eight men in purple uniforms lined up in front of the water heater and related plumbing; there were two well-dressed women and Pel's lawyer over by the gas furnace; and there were four medieval weirdos and two more people in purple uniforms milling about near the boxes of Christmas lights and old baby clothes.

Stoddard stepped forward, slid a palm along the concrete wall; Pel watched as his fingers seemed to sink in at one point.

Then the man-at-arms thrust his entire arm into what still looked like solid concrete. He stepped forward, and vanished into the wall.

"Come on," Squire Donald cried, with a wave of his arm. Then he, too, stepped forward and disappeared.

"All right, men," Cahn said, "you saw how it works. Drummond, take the point."

"Yes, sir." Drummond marched across the dusty floor and, with only the briefest hesitation, strode into the wall.

Pel watched, marveling. It looked unreal, like something from a movie—but at the same time, it wasn't quite like any movie he'd ever seen. No special effects were that good.

Uneasily, Peabody followed Drummond; then went Cartwright, Lampert, and Smith. Smith had his arms curled around in front of himself, and Pel wasn't sure whether he was hiding something, or simply making a protective gesture.

Soorn was next; he stopped and turned to Cahn.

"Captain," he said, "I don't like this."

"Oh, get on with it," Mervyn said, shoving Soorn forward; Soorn lost his balance, put out a hand to catch himself, and toppled through the wall into invisibility.

Mervyn snorted derisively, and followed. Godwin went next.

"Now you, Thorpe," Cahn said.

Prossie obeyed.

Cahn himself went next.

"Ready, ladies?" Ted said. He bounded across the basement in mockery of a ballet dancer, and leaped through.

At the last instant, as he vanished, Pel thought he saw surprise on the attorney's face. He frowned; Ted had been acting very odd ever since he first met Raven, and Pel didn't like it at all.

Amy and Susan looked at each other nervously.

"You don't have to do this," Susan said. "You saw them vanish; they're gone now. You can go upstairs and go home and get the ship hauled away and forget any of it ever happened."

Raven started to answer, and Valadrakul held up a restraining hand.

"No," Amy said. She drew a deep breath and then let it out slowly. "Thanks, Susan, but I want to see. I want to get it over with. I want to know whether it's real or not. I think it'd drive me crazy if I didn't." She threw back her shoulders and marched across the basement, but then she stopped before the wall and reached out tentatively.

Her fingers vanished, and she snatched them back.

They reappeared.

"It's cold!" she said, startled, reaching out again. "And there's nothing there! I mean, nothing solid. It's just like putting your fingers in front of an air conditioner." Her hand vanished, sinking into the wall up to the wrist.

"Our land's but newly freed of winter," Raven remarked. "Spring comes late this year."

Amy threw him a glance, took a deep breath, and stepped forward.

She disappeared.

Susan's expression was plainly unhappy. She tugged at the strap of her purse, a big black leather bag that hung from her shoulder, and then looked around at the handful of people remaining.

"You could wait in the car," Nancy suggested.

Susan shook her head, and without another word stepped into the wall.

Nancy looked at Pel. Rachel pressed up against her mother's side.

"What if we can't get back?" she asked.

"Oh, mistress," Raven said, "fear not! Let me show you." He stepped forward and vanished into the wall.

And, seconds later, he stepped back out, reappearing as suddenly and inexplicably as he had gone.

"See you?" he said. " 'Tis nothing!"

Abruptly Amy reappeared—or rather, her head and shoulders did, thrusting out of the wall, reminding Pel uncomfortably of a mounted hunting trophy.

"Hi," she said, relieved. "Just making sure it really worked both ways."

"Certes, it does," Raven said.

"What's it like?" Nancy called.

Amy had vanished again too quickly to answer.

Rachel giggled, her fear vanished as completely as Captain Cahn's crew. "They look silly," she said.

"All right," Nancy said, "let's go see for ourselves, then."

"Carry me?" Rachel asked, arms raised.

Nancy bent down and picked her up, and carried her through the portal.

Pel gestured to Raven and Valadrakul. "After you," he said.

Valadrakul bowed and stepped through; Raven hesitated.

"You'll come?" he asked. "You'll come, and see my homeland? You'll lend your advice? I value your opinion, friend Pel."

Pel grimaced. "What opinion?" he said. "I'm just going to take a quick look and come right back."

Raven frowned, then quickly recovered his composure. "As you wish," he said.

He stepped through, leaving Pel alone in the basement.

Pel took a deep breath, gathered his nerve, and walked up to the wall. He put out his hand.

As Amy had said, he felt nothing but cool air as his fingers vanished into the wall. He closed his eyes, unable to bring himself to advance with them open, and then took another step.

Coldness swept over him; a shiver ran through his body, starting at the shoulder and sliding down through his spine and into his knees. His eyes snapped open.

For a moment he saw nothing but darkness, felt nothing but the chill, and terror began to grow, weedlike, somewhere in the base of his skull.

Then the door opened, and wan sunlight spilled in, illuminating the inside of the hut.

He was in a hut, a small one, with no light, no windows—only the door. It seemed quite solid, quite real—and it was definitely no part of his basement. It smelled of wood and earth.

Pel let his breath out, and it puffed into visibility in the cold air. Nancy was outside; she and Rachel were standing there, facing away, but Nancy was looking back nervously, watching for Pel.

Raven was in the hut, holding the door open.

The others were all there, scattered about outside; he could hear their voices, and he glimpsed them through the doorway. Pel stepped forward.

The movement felt oddly wrong; the air seemed preternaturally thick, as if he were wading through a foot of water. He looked down, but there was no water, only the hard-packed dirt floor beneath his feet.

The smell of black loam, sawn wood, and pine sap, carried on the sharp, cold air, reached him and swept images of long-ago winter mornings into his mind, mornings when he had gone walking in the woods, or watched his father cut a point on a Christmas tree before fitting it into the inverted cone of the green steel holder. He turned his head to see where the smell came from, and for the first time really noticed the shed around him, and its contents.

On either side, logs were stacked neatly, almost to the low, slanting rafters. Behind him stood a simple wall of rough-hewn planks, with no door nor other opening visible, and he realized he had stepped through it.

He thrust out a hand; it vanished into the wall, up to the wrist, as if the planks were not there.

Reassured that the portal was still there, that he could return home whenever he wanted, he turned his attention elsewhere.

He was one of three people in the woodshed; Raven was another, but the third he did not recognize. He could not see her clearly in the gloom, but she was just below medium height—no more than five foot four, he was sure—with long, dark hair and wearing heavy robes. She was not thin, he was sure of that, but he thought part of her bulk came from her thick garments. One over-sized sleeve caught the light from the door, where he could get a good, clear look at it; it was dull red, and appeared to be wool.

"Hi," he said, giving her a little wave with one hand, and smiling in her general direction. "I'm Pel Brown."

"I am Elani," she said, speaking with an odd, musical accent, completely unlike Raven's nasal twang.

"Shall we have a look at my world, friend Pel?" Raven asked, with a gesture at the door.

Pel nodded. He turned away from Elani, and together the two men stepped out of the woodshed into the world.

Behind them, Elani began mumbling something Pel could not make out.

■

It hadn't been any forty-eight hours, but Carrie had no intention of sticking to a silly limitation like that when it came to her own lost cousin. She settled on her bed and reached out with her mind, reached in that inexplicable direction that led around the corners of reality into the "Earth" universe. She shaped her thoughts to fit Prossie's familiar pattern, and searched down through the name-less irreality for Prossie's thoughts.

She couldn't find them.

Prossie wasn't in that jail anymore.

Carrie could sense a sort of afterimage that she knew was the general vicinity of the jail, perceptible because she had seen it through Prossie's thoughts earlier—but it was dead and empty. No telepath was there, not even one of the pitiful "psychics" of Earth, like that Ray Aldridge or that little girl, Angela. There were guards, and prisoners, but they were all Earth people, all telepathically dead; she could barely sense that they existed, and certainly couldn't communicate with them, in either direction.

Prossie wasn't there.

Well, that was good, wasn't it? She'd been released, then.

Or killed. Maybe Prossie had been wrong about the Earth peo-ple and their soft-hearted rules. Carrie began searching, casting a tel-epathic net farther afield, wider and thinner, hoping for some touch.

For a moment she thought she felt Prossie's presence, but before she could home in on it, it was gone. She pushed on, minute after minute. Sweat began to sheen her forehead; her hands and jaw trembled.

Prossie wasn't there.

She found Carleton Miletti and passed him by; she found Oram Blaisdell, and Angela Thompson, and Ray Aldridge.

She didn't find Prossie.

Miletti and Blaisdell and Aldridge didn't notice the contact, but little Angela sat up in bed and shouted, "Mr. Nobody!"

"Hush," Carrie told her, "hush!"

"What is it, Mr. Nobody? Is something wrong?"

"Not really, Angie. I'm sorry, I didn't mean to bother you."

"You didn't bother me. Whatcha doing?"

Carrie sighed. "I'm looking for a friend of mine."

"Who?"

"Her name is Proserpine Thorpe."

"I'll go ask my mommy!"

Before Carrie could protest, Angie was out of bed and scampering down the stairs, shouting, "Mommy! Mommy!"

Margaret met her at the bottom step, relieved to see that Angie was intact—no visible blood, nothing torn, no broken toys or furniture in sight. "What is it, Angie?" she asked, kneeling so that she could meet her daughter face to face.

"It's Mr. Nobody," Angie explained. "He's lookin' for someone."

Carrie winced slightly. Why was Angie always so certain the voice in her head was a man?

Margaret Thompson sighed. "Is that all?"

Somewhat cowed, Angie said, "That's all."

"I thought Mr. Nobody was gone," Margaret said.

"He was. He came back."

Angie's mother considered that.

She didn't really understand Mr. Nobody. She had never had an invisible playmate as a child; she'd heard about them, read about them in the parenting books, but the whole idea didn't really make much sense to her. And Angie was so utterly certain that Mr. Nobody was real. Her conversations with him didn't seem like anything a three-year-old should be able to invent.

Angie had never claimed to see Mr. Nobody, or to know where he was; she only heard him. That didn't fit what the books described for imaginary companions.

Was it possible that someone really *was* communicating with Angie somehow?

"All right, then, who's Mr. Nobody looking for?" she asked.

For the first time Angie hesitated. Then she said, "Basurpathork."

"Who?" Margaret blinked. She had been expecting a more recognizable name than that.

"Someone named Basurpathork."

Margaret sighed again. A name like that settled it; Angie was just making it up. "I don't know any Ba . . . Pa . . . anyone by that name. Now, you go back to bed and tell Mr. Nobody to let you sleep, and in the morning I'll ask around."

Chastened, Angie said, "All right, Mommy." She turned and made her way slowly back to bed.

And on her own bed, Carrie was fighting back tears. She had only been searching for a few minutes, really, perhaps twenty in all, but that was enough. She was certain. Prossie was not on Earth. And she wasn't back in the Empire, or she'd have made contact herself.

Carrie knew then that her cousin Proserpine, her childhood playmate, was dead. She had to be. What other explanation could there be?

And dying in that hostile other universe, where her mind could not speak, she had died in telepathic silence, in the sort of loneliness that ordinary people lived with every day, but which telepaths contemplated only with dread.

Cut off by that hideous silence, her family hadn't even heard the death cry.

CHAPTER 12

"**H**ey," Pel said as he emerged, "it's daylight!"

"Aye," Raven said, " 'tis an hour or so past dawn, here."

"But it's after seven!"

"Not here, it isn't," Captain Cahn told him.

Pel turned, startled.

Cahn and Valadrakul were standing to one side; to the other side, he realized, were Stoddard, Donald, Susan, and Amy.

"The others went on ahead," Susan told him. "Your little girl was pretty excited."

"Oh," Pel said. "Thanks."

He looked around.

He was standing in a small clearing of bare black dirt. Behind him stood the woodshed. In the center of the clearing was a great flat-topped stump—the tree that had once grown there must have been huge.

Ahead and to the left was a cabin, built of rough-hewn logs and chinked with something grayish; there were no windows on the near side, but a fieldstone chimney bisected it, and to the left of the chimney a brown drape of soft leather hung from a gray wood bar. From the way the drape hung and what he could see below its lower edge, Pel guessed it covered a door.

Between the cabin and the shed, to the left, was a sunny little garden—though it didn't look particularly inviting just now. Most of it consisted of neat, fresh-tilled furrows in the black earth; a few had new green shoots springing up.

Beyond the garden was a steep embankment covered with a tangle of dead weeds, old vines, and fresh growth.

Atop the embankment, and ahead and to the right, was forest—old-growth forest, trees that seemed to soar up almost out of sight before ending in a maze of bud-speckled, crisscrossing branches, brown vines layered onto the black trunks like threadbare carpet, dark green moss spilling down from the crotches and smeared like jam on one side of each trunk—the north, was it? Pel seemed to remember that moss grew thickest on the north sides of trees, sheltered from sun and storm.

To the left the sky, visible through the grays and browns of the lower forest and the green and gold of budding leaves high above, was a rich blue streaked with high, thin clouds; to the right it washed out to uneasy off-white surrounding a pale, almost colorless sun, low in the sky, that seemed dimmer and smaller than natural.

The light of that sun was thin and watery and seemed to spill between trees as if running down sheets of glass, giving the entire landscape a cool, unfriendly appearance.

The air smelled of damp earth and woodsmoke and something faint and unpleasant. It chilled his face and hands, and he could feel his nose preparing to drip. His breath rose in thin white swirls.

He shivered, and not entirely from the cold.

There was no one thing that Pel could point to as being out of place, but the scene seemed subtly wrong. The air in his lungs felt thick and heavy, the ground pulled at his feet, the colors and even the light itself jarred somehow.

Then he realized one thing that was wrong—it was the wrong time of year, as well as the wrong time of day. It was spring, yes, but back home the leaves were out and the azaleas in bloom; here, the trees were still just budding.

If the details had been right, he might have taken a place like this for a rustic retreat, or perhaps a historical re-creation intended to give tourists a glimpse of a bygone life; in that moist chill, the pale light, the heavy air, it didn't seem right.

"If you go around the cabin," someone said, in a high-pitched voice that reminded Pel of Bernadette Peters, "you can get a look at Stormcrack Keep."

Pel turned and saw no one; he looked down, following the voice, and found a tiny person, like the one who had appeared in his basement, the one Raven had called Grummetty.

This one was not Grummetty; it was a woman, even smaller than Grummetty. She came no higher than the middle of Pel's shin. She wore a simple white cotton dress with a thick blue sweater over it for warmth, and had a knitted woolen cap pulled down over her ears. A thick black braid trailed down her back. She was sitting on a rock the size of Pel's fist.

"Oh," Pel said, "is that where Nancy and Rachel went?"

"The lady with the little girl?"

"Yeah."

"That's where they went. Also all those men in the silly purple outfits." She pointed.

"Thank you," Pel said. He followed the pointing finger around the right side of the cabin.

There was a well-worn path consisting of a strip of bare earth between mounds of rotting dead leaves, beaten down until it was too hard to show footprints. Pel followed it.

Every step seemed to take an inordinate amount of effort; he stopped and looked down at his shoes, trying to figure it out.

"Heavier gravity than you're used to," a voice said.

He looked up to find Lieutenant Godwin up ahead, leaning against a tree and grinning at him.

"Heavier gravity?" Pel asked.

Godwin nodded. "I'd judge your planet at, oh, maybe 1.2 gees, tops," he said. "This place has to be at least 1.3. Not a big difference, but if you aren't used to it, I guess it must be pretty disconcerting."

"Earth's one gee," Pel said.

"Well, of course it is, on *your* scale," Godwin agreed. "*Our* scale uses Terra as a standard. I'd say Earth's at least 1.1, probably closer to 1.2."

"But Terra and Earth are the same thing . . ." Pel began.

He stopped, confused.

"No, no," Godwin said. "Your planet's Earth, right? Back home, nobody's called Terra Earth for a century or so. It's Terra."

"But we call *Earth* Terra . . ."

"You do? I thought you called it Earth."

"Well, we do, mostly." Pel stopped again.

"Then why don't we just leave it at that? We probably both have a dozen names for the old home planet, right? But you people said Earth, when we asked, and we call ours Terra. Seems convenient."

"I guess," Pel agreed, reluctantly. Godwin smiled patronizingly.

Pel did not care to be patronized, and resolved to carry on the conversation as if he talked to people from other universes regularly. "So your home planet has lower gravity than this?" he asked.

"Mine? Hard to say—about the same, I'd guess."

"But you just said . . ." Pel began, feeling his resolve vanish.

"No, no, Mr. Brown—*I'm* not from Terra. I'm from Pennington, also known as Kappa Orionis Two. My *grandparents* came from Terra."

"Ah, I see," Pel said.

Lieutenant Godwin did not look like a Martian; with his blond crew cut and broad shoulders and round face he looked like a farmboy from Minnesota. His accent even sounded about right for a farmboy from Minnesota. Still, he was claiming to be from another planet.

"Pennington, huh?" Pel asked.

"Yeah. Grew up on the South Continent, near New Salisbury—and don't pretend you know what I'm talking about, okay?" The patronizing expression became an outright grin.

"Okay, Lieutenant." Pel tried to smile in response, but the result was only a weak grimace.

"I'm going back to the woodshed, see if they've got the gateway set to send us home yet. I'll see you, Mr. Brown." He pushed away from the tree, saluted, ducked past Pel, and marched on.

Pel watched him go.

So they were setting up a portal to send the Imperials back to their own universe? That was quick work.

He didn't blame Godwin for wanting to hurry, though. This place of Raven's was uncomfortable. It was cold and damp and the light was wrong, and if Godwin was to be believed, the gravity was wrong.

Just then the forest and path and cabin all darkened, and Pel looked up.

A cloud had hidden the sun. More clouds seemed to be gathering.

What a nasty, unpleasant place. How could people want to live here? He shivered and walked on.

■

Prossie was not really surprised to discover that her telepathic talent was just as dead in Shadow's realm as it had been on Earth; her head still felt as if it were stuffed with wool that blocked out all the thoughts she would normally have heard.

It was a good thing she would not be here long; she hadn't had a chance to warn Carrie. If the poor girl tried to make contact, she'd be unable to find anyone, and would probably worry.

As soon as she got back into Imperial space—assuming that the wizards could really open the portal they had promised—she would call Carrie, let her know what had happened.

For now, though, she was looking over Shadow's native world; her superiors in Imperial Intelligence would want to know as much as possible about it. Not that she was particularly fond of her superiors, but every telepath worked either in Intelligence or the Signal Corps, or both—that was the price the Empire demanded for letting a bunch of subhuman mutants live—and the better she did her job, the better she would be treated, and the more respect her entire clan would receive.

The gravity was higher than she had expected, maybe a gee and a third. The air was thick and damp, so while the primary's light appeared to be farther toward the blue end of the spectrum than average, that might partly be due to the atmospheric conditions.

The trees looked Terran, as far as she could tell, but she was no botanist. Some certainly looked, even to her untrained eye, like oaks, but she supposed that might be a result of parallel evolution of some sort.

The soil seemed to be rich enough.

The only locals she had seen so far were the ones who had been on Earth, three little people, and the "wizard" Elani. The little people were definitely alive and intelligent, unlike the remains she had seen in Imperial space; and whatever mechanisms the wizard used to create her effects, Prossie had been unable to spot them.

And Stormcrack Keep was a rudimentary fortress, too far away for any serious look at its defenses.

She had gotten that far in her work as an agent of Imperial Intelligence when someone said, "It's like a storybook castle—only it's real, isn't it?"

Prossie turned and found Mrs. Brown standing there, holding her little girl.

"Of course it's real," she said. "Why wouldn't it be?"

■

Amy watched the others traipse off for their look at Stormcrack, but for her own part, she couldn't yet bring herself to move that far away from the gateway home.

And she couldn't leave Susan, who was even more frightened than she was herself.

And why shouldn't they be frightened? It was all real.

Even though Amy didn't want it to be, even though she had desperately hoped it would all turn out to be some incredibly complex fraud, it was all real.

She did want to look at the castle, to see it all—but it would take her a few moments to work up the nerve. She had to adjust.

Her safe little world had come apart at the seams.

Again.

■

Pel could hear voices ahead; he turned a corner, around a huge oak, and found the rest of the party gathered in an open, grassy area, looking out across a wooded valley.

Nancy was holding Rachel in her arms as she spoke to Prossie; Ted was standing nearby, talking to Mervyn. Drummond was arguing with Soorn and Cartwright. Smith, Lampert, and Peabody were sitting on the grass, not talking to anyone, facing away from the path where Pel stood.

Pel stepped forward; Peabody turned and looked at him, and Pel realized he had missed someone.

Grummetty, or someone very much like him, was standing just in front of Peabody. So was somebody even smaller—another gnome, a young one.

"Hi," Pel said.

Several voices returned his greeting.

"See the castle, Daddy?" Rachel asked.

Pel looked out across the valley.

The land dropped away steeply from the clearing, in a slope that was almost a cliff, too steep for large trees to grow on; that provided the first real view of a broad area that Pel had seen since stepping through his basement wall. Up until now, everything had been bounded by trees and walls.

Here, though, he could see.

Below, at the foot of the steep slope, the forest continued, deep green and extending to either side, as endless as a river.

On the other side of the valley—or perhaps canyon—rose another cliff, symmetrical to the one on which they stood, perhaps a half-mile distant.

And atop that cliff stood Stormcrack Keep—such as it was.

The main body of the structure was of windowless stone, at least on the visible side; it was simply a solid, flat-faced mass of masonry. Pel had trouble judging the scale at such a distance, particularly since there were no other referents handy except the outsize trees, but he judged it to be perhaps a hundred feet across and forty feet high.

At one side rose the remains of a round tower, built of the same featureless gray stone. About ten or fifteen feet above the top of the keep wall it was pierced by several tall, narrow windows.

And about ten feet above that, it ended in jagged ruin, roof gone, walls shattered, a few blackened beam ends projecting from the rubble.

The whole thing was in the shadow of a cloud, as was the clearing where the new arrivals were; patches of light and shadow were gliding across the surrounding forests.

Most of the world seemed to be in shadow; the clouds were spreading.

All in all, Pel thought, the castle didn't look like much. He had seen far more interesting and elaborate ones when he toured Europe as a young man.

But Europe wasn't in his basement.

And, obviously, neither was this place, whatever it really was.

Up until now, he thought, he might eventually have been able to convince himself that the whole thing was an underground soundstage, or some sort of illusion done with mirrors and tapes, but that valley, and the castle on the far side—that was no illusion.

A hawk was gliding above the valley; a smaller bird, too far away for identification, vanished behind the ruined tower before the predator could spot it.

It was almost as if they had fallen into a fantasy novel— except that when he read fantasy novels he never had so many of the details: the leaves on the trees, the chill in the air, the slippery spot of mud under one foot, the fibers frayed from that tree root catching the pale sunlight. Fiction never had this solid reality.

"Can we go home now, Daddy?" Rachel asked.

"We figured you'd want to see the castle," Nancy explained, "So we waited . . ."

"It's cold," Rachel interrupted.

Nancy smiled. "But it's cold, and Rachel's tired—it must be about her bedtime, back home."

Pel nodded. "Sure," he said. "I just wanted to see." He put out a hand to the trunk of a nearby oak, and felt the cold, rough bark. "I guess it's all real."

Ted snorted; startled, Pel turned to face him.

"It's all a dream," Ted said. "And this place proves it."

Pel blinked. "What?"

"I'm dreaming, all of this and all of you—I mean, come on, you think this is real? Castles on cliffs? Fairies, or whatever those little guys are?"

Grummetty and the other one turned to glare angrily at Ted.

"Ted," Pel said, "if you're dreaming, what am *I* doing here? We can't be having the same dream!"

"Of course not," Ted agreed. "You aren't here at all; I'm just arguing with my subconscious. It doesn't like it when I know I'm dreaming."

"Come on," Nancy said, taking Pel's arm, "let him think it's a dream if he likes."

With Nancy carrying Rachel on one arm and pressing Pel along with the other, they started back around the cabin. Ted's words nagged at Pel as he walked, and he turned for one more final look at the castle.

A beam of sunlight, breaking through the thickening clouds for a moment, sprayed color across the gray stone, and then vanished.

If they had fallen into a story, now they were about to climb back out. They had just been bit players, spear carriers, part of the background.

"We should take a souvenir," Pel said, "something to prove we were really here."

"Did you bring the camera?" Nancy asked, just as Pel remembered it.

He pulled it out of his pocket. "Hang on," he said, "let me get a picture of the castle."

"Hurry up, Daddy," Rachel said, as Nancy stopped and turned.

Pel hurried; after all, he didn't *want* to be inside a story. He was quite sure that they always looked like a lot more fun from the outside, curled up reading somewhere, rather than living them. He took a quick snapshot of Stormcrack Keep and the surrounding greenery, then turned back toward the woodshed. "Let's go," he said.

He kept the camera ready in his hand, though.

Half a dozen paces down the path he paused and took a picture of the front of the cabin, with its two shuttered windows and leather-hung doorway and the huge trees to either side.

Then he snapped a quick shot of Nancy and Rachel on the path, the woodshed just barely visible through the trees.

Amy appeared as he did.

"I hope I didn't ruin your picture," she said. "I wanted to see the castle."

"Don't worry, it's no problem," Pel assured her. He stepped aside, as did Nancy, to let Amy squeeze by on the narrow path.

"Where's Susan?" Nancy asked.

"She wouldn't come," Amy said. "This whole thing has her really scared; she said she didn't want to get out of sight of that shed we came out of."

Nancy just nodded.

Before she and Pel could continue they heard another set of approaching footsteps; they glanced at each other and stayed where they were.

Lieutenant Godwin was returning. He said nothing, but threw them a quick salute as he strode past.

Pel and Nancy waited for a second or two, but no one else appeared; they turned and walked on, Pel snapping a picture every few steps.

Raven was standing at the end of the path, at the edge of the clearing, when they arrived. He smiled at them and stepped back.

"Saw you the keep?" he asked.

"We saw it," Pel said.

Rachel, curled in her mother's arms, made a noise, but didn't say anything intelligible; Pel realized she was sucking her thumb. It was obviously time to get her home to bed.

"My home, once," Raven said. " 'Tis in the hands of the foe now, and I dare not show my face there."

"Yeah," Pel said. He hesitated, then added, "I'm sorry, Raven. I can't think of any way to help."

"Ah, but you've seen naught as yet but this forester's holdings!"

"That's all we're *going* to see," Nancy announced. "Rachel's worn out, I'm tired, and we've seen enough. We're going home now."

"Ah? Oh, but . . ." Raven glanced at the shed, then uneasily at Pel.

"What's wrong?" Pel asked, suddenly nervous. He felt the muscles in his back tightening.

"Oh, 'tis naught," Raven said, "save that . . . that man Godwin, and the Captain Cahn."

"What about them?" Nancy asked.

"They were here, and you were not, and they spoke fair—I fear Elani is conjuring the portal to *their* realm."

"So?" Pel demanded.

Raven spread his hands. "Friend Pel," he said, "Elani is a sorceress of the first rank, but she can maintain only a single portal at any one time. To open a way to the Empire, she needs must allow the way to Earth to close."

"Damn it, Raven," Pel said angrily, "I *told* you we were only taking a quick look! Has she already begun? Maybe the portal's still open." He started toward the woodshed; he wanted to get *home*, back to normal reality, out of this fantastic setting he had stumbled into.

Raven reached out a restraining hand, and on the far side of the clearing Stoddard stepped over to block the door to the shed with his body.

"No, no, friend Pel," Raven said. "Know you no better? 'Tis folly to interrupt a mage at his work—or hers, as it be in this case."

Pel glared angrily at Raven, but could think of nothing worth saying; he fumed silently.

Rachel took her thumb out of her mouth and announced, "I wanna go home."

"So do I," Nancy said, hugging her closer.

"My lady," Raven said, "I assure you, at that instant that the last of these Imperials is vanished, that would not stay to our aid, then shall I command Elani to restore the way to your home."

"How long will *that* be?" Pel demanded.

Raven turned up his palms. "What know I of such magicks?" he asked. "Perhaps the fifth part of an hour, perhaps twice that—certainly no more than the half of an hour."

"Well," Pel said, reluctantly, "I guess we can stand to wait that long."

Rachel obviously didn't think so; she didn't quite cry, but her expression made it plain that she was holding back tears only by superhuman self-control. "I want Harvey!" she wailed. "I want to go to bed!"

"Harvey?" Raven asked, with an inquiring glance at Pel.

"Her stuffed alligator," Pel explained. "It's her favorite toy; she takes it to bed with her."

"Ah, poor weary poppet," Raven said, giving Rachel a sad, funny little smile. "It shan't be long, I promise you."

Leaves rustled, and Pel turned to find the crew of the *Ruth-*

less marching single-file down the trail toward him, Lieutenant Godwin at their head.

As he looked at the forest, Pel noticed that the daylight had faded; the path was now shadowy and dim. The clouds obscuring the sun were thicker and darker.

That was all they needed—to get caught in a thundershower in this already uncomfortable world.

He stepped aside, and let the Imperials march on past him into the clearing.

Captain Cahn stepped out to confront them, and the march stopped; the crew stood at ease, facing their commander.

"All right, men," he said, "and you, Thorpe—you all know the situation. We're on Shadow's home planet here, and we've been asked to aid the resistance to its rule. Our first duty is to the Empire, of course, and for that reason I've asked these people to open a warp to our own reality, to Base One if possible. Right now the woman Elani is working on it." Pel heard leaves rustle again, and he turned to see Amy and Ted strolling along the path toward the little clearing, side by side, not speaking.

He glanced around and saw Susan standing by the corner of the woodshed, watching silently. They were all back from the clifftop.

"I'll be going through that warp," Cahn announced. "However, if any of you wish to volunteer to remain here and join the resistance, I'm willing to accept that and give orders allowing it. Now, the warp isn't ready yet. You have until it *is* ready to make your own personal decisions." He looked over the nine uniformed people before him, and nodded.

"That's it," he said. "I'll call you when we're ready. Until then, stay in this immediate area."

Leaves rustled yet again; startled, Pel turned to see Grummetty and the other gnome—no, little person—approaching. The other was a young man with a sparse blond beard, wearing a dark green hooded robe. Grummetty was attired just as he had been in Pel's basement, three days before.

Pel was about to say something, to point the little people out to Rachel, who didn't seem to have noticed them yet, when the ground shifted slightly beneath him.

Startled, he glanced down at his feet, then looked at Rachel and Nancy.

They had felt it, too—Nancy was staring at him, and Rachel had raised her head from her mother's shoulder and was looking about, puzzled.

Thunder roared overhead.

"What was . . ." Nancy began.

Then the ground burst open beneath them.

CHAPTER 13

Pel's first thought, as he began to fall backward, was that Ted was right after all. None of this was real; it was all a dream, and now he was waking up. The dream's superficial appearance of sanity and logic was disintegrating, and it was going to turn into the more usual irrational dream nonsense, or maybe a falling dream, maybe he was going to fall through the ground and fall for what would seem like hours, and then he would wake up, and he would be back in bed at home, where nobody had ever walked out of his basement wall with stories about spaceships in people's back yards or evil world-conquering wizards.

Or maybe he was falling out of bed, for the first time in years, and he would wake up on the bedroom floor.

Instead he landed on very solid, very cold, hard-packed ground, landed on his backside and one elbow. Nothing vanished or changed shape or behaved like anything in a dream—except for the head that had thrust up through the earth and knocked him off his feet.

It was black and smooth and hard, with great blazing red eyes and pushed-back pointed ears. More than anything else, it reminded Pel of the terror dogs in the first Ghostbusters movie—but it was larger. Much larger.

Much, much larger.

The head, which was all he could see, looked about the size of a Volkswagen Beetle.

It stank, like fresh sewage.

And no matter how much Pel wanted to think otherwise, it really didn't look like a special effect. It looked real.

Rachel was shrieking, one piercing wordless yell after another, as she watched the thing thrust itself upward. Black dirt
seethed around it, and even over the shrieks Pel could hear the
grinding noises it made.

Nancy started screaming as well, as she backed away with her
daughter clutched tightly to her, but she used words: "Pel, no! Pel!"

Pel scrambled to his feet and backed up a step, watching the
thing.

It was in a pit now; its movements had broken in a circle of
dirt about twenty feet across, and the dirt had fallen inward,
away—to *somewhere*. Pel wondered where. Did the thing have a
burrow down there?

One of the huge trees beside the clearing swayed, and wood
cracked somewhere.

The head was not shaped like a dog's head, not now that he
could see it all; the snout was much shorter, proportionately, than
any dog's. Pel tried to find a comparison—the demon atop Bald
Mountain, in Disney's *Fantasia*, perhaps? There was a resemblance, but that was only an approximation.

The thing didn't look like anything he had ever seen, not
really—not in real life, not in movies, not even just in his imagination. The muzzle wasn't human; the rest of the face wasn't really
anything else.

A demon ape, perhaps? But no ape ever had floppy ears like
that.

The head tilted back, the lower jaw pulling free of the crum-
bling dirt, and then the mouth opened. Pel braced for a roar or a
bellow or a shriek.

None came. Instead of sound, new horrors spilled out, little
black things that crawled and flapped and fluttered, things the size
of a cat or a bat or an insect. They scampered and scuttled, knocking clods of dirt aside, rustling and thumping, but none squealed
or grunted. The only voices Pel heard were human.

Thunder rumbled again; the daylight dimmed further.

People were shouting, Pel realized. He looked past the horrors in the pit and saw people on the far side, the crew of the
Ruthless, and Raven and his comrades. They were crowding back
against the woodshed, calling to each other.

Something hit the back of Pel's head, hard and sharp; he heard wings flapping, felt them beating against him, felt the rush of air, and he smelled rotting meat. He started forward, then turned.

The thing struck again, its claws tangling in his hair—it was glossy black, with wings and talons, and it was flapping and struggling, moving so fast that he couldn't get a good look at it.

It was obviously kin to the things in the pit, the things that had come from the monster's mouth, but it couldn't have come from there, there hadn't been time for any of those to have reached him.

He slapped at it, knocked it away, and it lunged at him again. He knocked it away again, knocked it to the ground, and this time he stamped on it.

He heard bone snap. He stamped again.

The thing was like a lizard with bat's wings, a *big* lizard, with fangs and talons and a four-foot wingspan. He had broken one wing, near the base, and it scurried for cover, limping slightly and dragging the broken wing behind it.

He turned for a glance back at the pit; dozens of creatures had poured from the big one's mouth, and now other things, things like snakes or great worms, things like a cross between a snake and a squid, were burrowing up out of the surrounding soil that the big one had loosened up in surfacing.

Pel started to turn, to head for the woods, but now he saw where the bat-lizard had come from—there were more of them, in the trees, and in the underbrush, and there were other creatures, things like furry dog-size spiders, like fanged black stumps walking on pulled-up roots, like gigantic black rats. Oily fur glistened darkly, white teeth gleamed, eyes of red and gold and cat-green shone.

There were scores of them, all coming silently closer.

"Oh, shit," Pel said, his muscles tensing as he backed away slowly.

The shouting and screaming had faded somewhat, had blended with the grinding of the immense creature in the pit and the rustling of the creatures into a dull cacophony, and Pel heard the sudden loud crack clearly.

At first he thought it was a tree limb snapping; he looked up, startled.

The shouts had suddenly ceased. He turned and looked across the pit, past the huge glaring head, at the people clustered around the woodshed.

Susan Nguyen was braced against the wall of the shed, her big black purse hanging open from one shoulder. She had a short-barreled revolver clutched in both hands, held out in front of her, pointed straight ahead. Something like a large black monkey lay face down on the ground in front of her, oozing thin purple fluid.

Even from this distance, Pel could see she was trembling.

And most of the others were staring at her.

Still trembling, she heaved the gun a few inches to one side and took careful aim at the head in the pit; it was turning slowly toward her.

She fired, and her hands jerked with the recoil. Pel didn't see where the shot went; he heard the gunshot and saw the flash, but that was all.

"Come on!" someone shouted, tugging at Susan's arm.

Pel suddenly realized that there were fewer people over there than there should have been. Squire Donald was gone, and Prossie Thorpe, and maybe others.

"Nancy," he shouted, "run for the shed! Around the pit! They have the portal open!"

Nancy was already moving, carrying Rachel. Pel started after her.

One of the creatures landed black and writhing on a crewman's back—Cartwright's, Pel thought it was—and the man screamed. Susan turned the gun, aimed at the monster, and then stopped as she realized she would have to shoot Cartwright, too.

Godwin was pulling at her arm, and she finally yielded; he yanked her around and thrust her through the door into the shed.

Something flashed red, and one of the monsters near the shed door exploded silently into bits of meat and bone.

"Valadrakul!" someone called.

Another creature exploded, this time with an audible bang.

Something was chewing on Pel's ankle, and he kicked it away and ran.

Godwin was by the door of the shed, herding people in; he grabbed Nancy's shoulder as she came within reach and shoved her through into the darkness.

Pel stopped, ready to turn and join Godwin in guarding the door, but Godwin's hand closed on his upper arm, closed *tight*, and Godwin's voice barked, "No civilians!"

He stumbled into the dark, into the shed that had now added the stink of urine to the smells of pine and earth; someone unseen, someone large who smelled of sweat, took him and thrust him at the back wall.

Pel's hand flew up to fend off a collision with the wall, and the wall wasn't there; he tumbled through the darkness into light, and fell forward rolling on sand, thinking for an instant, once again, that it was all a dream and now he would fall forever, or maybe wake up on the bedroom floor.

Then he landed, grit scraping his arm and cheek.

He blinked, and saw sunlight on fine white sand, sand that was cool against his cheek and hand, while the air was warm.

Sand?

Shouldn't he be back in his own basement?

Someone else tripped over his legs and fell, and Pel gathered his wits sufficiently to roll out of the way as others continued to appear.

He rolled over twice, ending on his back, and then sat up and looked around.

He was definitely not in his basement.

He was sitting on drifted sand, sand that stretched off in all directions, pierced here and there by outcroppings of weathered white stone. A few feet away was the largest outcropping in sight, a diagonally upthrust slab of stone at least ten feet high.

The sand reached the horizon, but the horizon was too low, as if they were all sitting atop a gigantic dune.

As he watched, Amy stepped out of the slab of rock—that was clearly where the portal was. She was bleeding from scratches on her forehead, and something had torn up one side of her skirt.

Pel realized that his own ankle was bleeding; he dabbed at it ineffectually, getting blood on his fingers. The sand seemed to be helping it clot.

He hoped that that thing hadn't been venomous. The wound didn't look bad. It certainly didn't look as worrisome as the surrounding landscape.

This was not his basement. He had a horrible suspicion that it wasn't anywhere on Earth. It would appear that Elani had opened her portal to the Galactic Empire.

The plot thickens, he thought, fighting back an insane urge to giggle.

■

When Prossie fell through the back of the woodshed it was as if a door had been flung open, as if a faucet had been turned on; the wool was gone from her mind, and she could hear again!

For a long moment she gloried in the sensation, letting the shapeless thoughts of the entire galaxy pour through her. She didn't look for meaning, didn't try to find any individual thoughts; it was enough to have the raw "sound" of all those minds reaching her again.

But after a moment the realization came—that sound was weak and distant. Compared to Earth or Shadow's world, it was a thunderous, constant roar, of course, but still . . .

This was not Base One, obviously. There were no telepaths close by. There weren't even any *people* close by—not really— except for the ones who were coming through the warp.

It was only after she had come to this realization that she bothered to use her eyes and noticed the barren wasteland around her.

■

Pel hadn't expected the Empire to be an uninhabited wasteland; that didn't fit very well with any story he had read. He had been thinking more in terms of huge buildings and broad avenues.

Of course, Luke Skywalker's home planet had been a desert, hadn't it? Was that part of the Galactic Empire?

He knew he should stop thinking in terms of falling into a story; this was *real*. The idea, however, wouldn't go away—particularly not when the whole bizarre episode didn't end, but kept on happening. He left the wound on his ankle alone for a moment and looked around.

Nancy was sitting cross-legged on the sand a few feet away, holding Rachel tightly, rocking back and forth, trying to comfort the child. Rachel was crying, and her thin sobs were the only sound Pel could hear.

Susan was standing, watching the portal, her revolver in one hand, her purse hanging from her shoulder, the flap closed now, but the clasp still unfastened.

Squire Donald, too, stood a few feet away, his hands swinging uneasily at his sides, as if looking for something to hold onto.

Prossie Thorpe was walking slowly away, in the direction Pel tentatively identified as east, assuming that it was morning wherever he was. It felt like morning, somehow. She seemed to be paying no attention to anyone else.

■

Carrie sat up abruptly.

"Prossie?" she asked, inadvertently speaking aloud.

The contact was weak; wherever Prossie was, it was still a long way off.

"Hi, Carrie—I just wanted to let you know that I'm all right. We're back in Imperial space, I think, but I don't know just where. I'm going to track down someone local and find out. I'll get back to you when I know more."

"Prossie," Carrie said, "I was so . . . I thought you were dead!"

"For a while," Prossie told her, "I thought so, too."

■

The sun, Pel noticed, was the wrong color—it was very small and intensely white, not the washed-out pale yellow of the sun in Raven's world, but *white*. The sunlight was, for lack of a better term, *richer* than in the forest they had just left, but it was still not right. The air was thin and he felt light-headed.

The person who had tripped over Pel's legs was Soorn; like Pel, he was now sitting on the sand.

Ted had followed Amy out of the stone; he was apparently uninjured.

Two of the little people, Grummetty and the woman, were standing beside Squire Donald—Pel had missed them at first. The woman had her hand to her stomach, as if she were ill, and Grummetty's expression was worried.

A fluttering black thing burst out of the rock, soaring upward into the thin air; Susan started to raise her pistol, but Squire Donald had his sword out before she could take aim. He shouted, "Leave it to me!"

The shout was startling—until he heard it, Pel hadn't realized how quiet this place was. It was as if everything was muffled somehow. Even Donald's shout seemed thin and weak.

The Squire slashed, and the thing tumbled to the sand, one wing hacked halfway off. Once it was down, Donald stepped up and proceeded to methodically chop it to pieces. His movements seemed oddly sharp, almost jerky; experimentally, Pel lifted his own hand, and found it seemed to almost fly up. It was buoyant, as if he were in water.

Even without Godwin telling him, he guessed that wherever he was now, the gravity was weaker than in Raven's world, weaker than on Earth.

Mervyn backed out of the stone, followed closely by Lampert.

"Where the hell are we?" Mervyn asked, as he looked around. As with Squire Donald's shout, his voice was muffled.

Before anyone could answer, Smith appeared, holding up what looked like a plastic club of some kind, and then Peabody. Peabody was holding his right arm in his left, trying to staunch the bleeding of a long gash in his forearm. His uniform sleeve hung in bloodstained tatters, and there were several scratches on his face; blood trickled down one cheek. Pel realized that Mervyn and Lampert and Smith had all been scratched up, as well.

And the club was a two-liter soda bottle, held by the neck—

Pel could make out the Pepsi logo on the crumpled label. Smith must have brought it along from the Browns' basement.

Lieutenant Drummond appeared, limping, with a black creature clinging to his scalp; he snatched it off and flung it away. The creature flapped, tried to fly, but seemed unable to do so. Drummond hauled his blaster from his belt-holster, pointed it at the thing, and squeezed the trigger.

A sharp crack and an electric sizzle sounded, something flashed, and the black thing exploded. The scattered fragments were aflame and shriveled quickly to black ash.

Half a dozen creatures came spilling through the portal then; Drummond blasted two of them out of the air, rather spectacularly, while Squire Donald skewered a third one with his sword.

Raven was next to emerge, sword drawn and dripping with ichor. Close behind came Captain Cahn, Valadrakul on his heels. More creatures accompanied them, and Drummond, Donald, and Raven disposed of several with blaster and blade.

They didn't get them all, Pel noticed, but on the other hand, the survivors weren't attacking; most of them appeared to be wandering aimlessly off across the landscape. A couple of the most gruesome specimens had collapsed, for no apparent reason, to lie twitching on the sands.

Lieutenant Godwin emerged, panting.

"Who's left?" Smith asked.

Peabody looked up from the improvised bandage Mervyn was binding around his gashed arm. "Where's Cartwright?" he asked.

"Down," Godwin said. "We couldn't get him."

"Who's left?" Smith repeated.

"All present but Cartwright, it looks like," Lampert announced.

"What about the Earth people?" Soorn asked.

"We're all here," Amy told him. "Mr. and Mrs. Brown, their little girl, their lawyer, me, Susan—that's everybody."

"What about the locals?" Mervyn asked, looking up from the bandage.

A larger creature, roughly the size and shape of a German Shepherd but slick and black and saber-toothed, burst through the portal; Raven impaled it on his sword, where it writhed briefly and died.

Stoddard appeared close behind it, Elani cradled in his arms; his scabbard flopped about at his side, obviously empty. He staggered out onto the sand and fell to his knees.

A black tentacle reached out, and then abruptly fell to the ground, chopped off where it had emerged from the portal. Pel rose to his feet and moved slowly closer, staring in horrified fascination at the severed limb.

It twitched once, then lay still.

"No more," Raven announced. "The way is closed."

"Well, everybody made it, right?" Amy asked.

"Except Pete Cartwright," Godwin corrected her.

"Where's Dundry?" Grummetty called. "Has anyone seen him?"

"Who?" someone asked.

"Isn't he here?" someone else asked at the same moment.

"Be he not here?" Raven asked, frowning.

Grummetty shook his head.

Elani, trying to get to her feet, said, "I'm sorry, Grummetty. I could hold no longer."

"Perhaps he'll find refuge somewhere," Valadrakul suggested. Pel noticed for the first time that Valadrakul had lost the braid in front of his left ear, along with a patch of skin, leaving a red, oozing spot. Something black, like ash, was smeared across his face and his left hand, while his right was still clean.

Grummetty blinked, and drew his lips tight, but said nothing more.

"What about Cartwright?" Soorn asked.

For a moment no one spoke; then Raven cleared his throat. "You have my deepest sympathies, sir," Raven said, bowing to Captain Cahn, "on the death of your man Cartwright. He fought bravely and well, 'gainst a foe not his own."

Susan made a choking noise.

Nancy stood up, still holding Rachel, but said nothing. Rachel buried her face in her mother's shoulder.

"Captain," Mervyn said, *"where the hell are we?"*

Cahn looked about; so did most of the others, and an uneasy silence fell.

"It sure ain't my basement," Pel remarked, trying unsuccessfully to lighten the mood.

"I want to go home!" Rachel shrieked suddenly.

" 'Twas Elani's spell that brought us hither," Raven said. "Speak, then, lady, and tell us—where are we?"

Elani, finally standing upright, hesitated, and then turned up her palms.

"I don't know," she said.

CHAPTER 14

After a moment of general consternation, Susan demanded, "What do you mean, you don't know?"

" 'Tis plain enough," Elani said, somewhat offended. "I know not where this place might be. I had not the time required to complete my incantation. I had called forth a portal to Messire Godwin's . . ." She hesitated, groping for a word. "World?"

"Universe," Godwin suggested.

"As you will, then—universe," Elani agreed. "But I'd no time to steer it small, and in this . . . this universe there are many . . . worlds? Planets?"

"Aye," Valadrakul said, as he dabbed lightly at the blood that seeped from his cheek, "they do call them by both names."

Elani nodded. "I had no time, as I said, to find the right one, in so many. So I found one where men dwell—that much, I could do—and cast forth the way, and opened it, and here we are."

"There are people here?" Amy said, scanning the empty horizon.

"Aye," Elani said. "Somewhere."

"It's not as bad as it might be, then," Cahn said. "If there really are people somewhere, and it's in our space, then the odds are that it's a part of the Galactic Empire—there aren't more than a dozen rebel worlds in all the galaxy, so far as I know."

"And how many worlds does your empire hold?" Squire Donald asked.

Cahn shrugged. "Not sure of the exact count just now," he said. "Something around thirty-one hundred."

"And how big are these worlds?" Donald asked. "How far must we travel to find whatever people there might be?"

"They come in all sizes," Cahn answered. "From the gravity, assuming a typical planetary density, I'd guess this one at, oh, six or seven thousand miles in diameter. A little smaller than Terra."

Donald nodded. "And your mile is, pray, how many feet?"

"Five thousand," Cahn replied.

Donald accepted that and withdrew to do some calculation.

Pel had listened with mounting discomfort.

This episode—this story, this series of events, whatever it was—was taking an unpleasant direction. He wanted to get out of it now. "That's all very interesting," he said, "but it's time for us to go home. Rachel's exhausted and terrified." He grimaced. "So am I, for that matter."

Raven turned to stare at him. "Friend Pel," he said, "perhaps you do not understand our situation."

"I understand it well enough," Pel said defensively. "I know what's going on. Shadow sent those things, right? The big monster and all the little ones? It found us somehow . . ."

"The portals," Elani said, interrupting. "It sensed the portals. I should have known that it would."

"Yeah, well," Pel said, "so it was the portals. Anyway, it found us, and it chased us all away from that place, whatever it was, and we wound up here, which is too bad for you guys, Raven and you others, I guess, because you can't go home. And it's not great for you others, Captain Cahn and the rest of you, because it looks as if you're out in the middle of nowhere and it may take awhile to get home, but it's not bad, really, because at least you're in the right universe." He paused for breath, and saw Drummond nod.

"Well, for us Earthpeople," Pel continued, "I don't see that it makes any difference. Elani, here, can just open a portal to my basement, and we can go home and Rachel can go to bed and we can just forget any of this ever happened, right?"

Raven and Elani looked at each other unhappily.

"Friend Pel," Raven began.

"*Stop calling me that!*" Pel shouted, his anger sounding

weak and futile in the thin air. "Elani, *right*? You can send us home?"

Silently, Elani shook her head.

"Messire Brown," Valadrakul said, "we are in another realm now, an alternate reality. In this place, our magic cannot work."

"I wanna go home!" Rachel cried.

Pel glared angrily.

"We're *stuck* here?" he said.

Amy, Nancy, and Susan had inched closer during the conversation; now all the Earth people but Ted were facing Raven, Donald, Stoddard, and the two wizards across a few feet of sand.

Raven nodded.

"Yes," he said, "I fear you are."

Pel looked about desperately and saw the crew of the *Ruthless* gathering to one side.

"They got to Earth, didn't they?" he said. "There's *some* way to get back!"

Raven looked at Cahn, who nodded. "If we can get back to Base One," he agreed, "there's the equipment there necessary to open a space warp back to your Earth."

"So how do we get there?" Pel asked. "Where's this Base One? Is it in this area?" A dreadful thought struck him. "Is it . . . is it even on this *planet*?"

"No," Cahn answered. "I don't know where the hell we are, but I know that much."

"We're on Psi Cassiopeia Two, Captain," Prossie Thorpe called from atop a distant outcropping.

Startled, everyone turned.

"I've made contact," she said happily. "Locally, I mean." She pointed eastward. "There's a small colony town about four hundred miles that way—Imperial, of course. If I can convince the governor there that I'm real, and not just a figment of his imagination, he can send a car or a hopper for us."

"Psi Cassiopeia Two?" Smith asked quietly.

Drummond shrugged. "I never heard of it," he muttered. "Must be way out in the middle of nowhere."

"Oh, it is!" Prossie called.

"Thorpe," Cahn called back, "watch it!"

"Sorry, Captain," she said, not sounding sorry at all. "It's so wonderful to have my talent back, though—I can't help it!"

Peabody saw Pel's puzzled look, and explained, "She can't possibly hear us talking, when she's all the way over there—not in this thin air, she can't. So she must be listening telepathically, and that's seriously against regulations, spying on your own people without orders."

Pel nodded, and asked, "What was that about convincing someone she's real?"

Peabody shrugged, then winced at what the motion did to his slashed arm. "I guess she's been calling someone," he said, "and the local brass never heard a telepath before and isn't sure he's hearing one now."

"Why wouldn't he have ever heard one before?" Nancy asked. "I thought you people used them all the time."

"Hey, there are three thousand inhabited planets in the Empire, and only four hundred telepaths," Peabody explained, "and more than half of those four hundred are serving communications duty in the Imperial Fleet. Hardly *anybody* outside the fleet's ever heard a telepath."

"Why are there so few?" Pel asked. "I mean, can't you train more?"

Peabody blinked in surprise, and threw Prossie a quick glance. Her attention was focused entirely on the eastern horizon; her crewmate leaned forward and raised his uninjured hand to shield his mouth as he whispered, " 'Course you can't train more! It's something they're *born* with—you either have it or you don't." He threw Prossie another glance. "I mean, they're all mutants, really."

"Oh," Pel said.

Peabody nodded, and continued, "In fact, they're all one family—all descended from one woman. Prossie's great-great grandmother."

"Oh," Pel said. He considered, and then pointed out, "Well, then, they aren't really mutants—I mean, *she* was, but her kids weren't. The trait bred true, that's all."

Peabody pulled away slightly. "You making excuses for mutants, Mr. Brown?"

"No," Pel said, confused, "I don't think so."

"Good," Peabody said.

∎

Amy looked about her, then settled down and sat cross-legged on the sands.

That five-minute look at another world had gone wrong, just as she had feared it would. Now they needed to find this space warp thing.

Something would probably go wrong there, too.

Still, if everybody else could handle this, so could she. Her world had been snatched away from her, in an incredibly literal way, but she would just have to deal with it. She was still alive; that poor man Cartwright wasn't, she'd seen him fall with that *thing* ripping at his back, tearing away skin and cloth, but she herself was unhurt except for the little scratches that other horrid flying creature had given her—she hoped the scratches wouldn't get infected. Her skirt was torn up, but the scrapes on her leg hadn't even broken the skin.

All that blood, those monsters, that was gruesome, traumatic stuff, but she could handle it. She was a healthy, intelligent woman, and she was not going to let all this mess her up.

She'd been through all that. She could take anything the universe—or universes—cared to throw at her.

She glanced at Susan, who was sitting curled up, almost in fetal position.

Susan was Vietnamese, and hadn't she said something about already having seen enough war? Amy guessed that she must have been through hell as a girl, seen things that made those black monsters look like nothing.

She'd survived, though.

Well, maybe there were *some* things Amy wouldn't be able to handle, but she intended to try. She intended to be, like Susan, a survivor.

No matter what path her life was dragged down.

∎

"See you, friend Pel," Raven said, interrupting Pel's talk with Spaceman Peabody. "Think you not, 'tis just as well that we found ourselves here, and not in your world?"

Pel glared at him. "How do you figure that?" he said.

"Because hence we can go, by means of the 'space warp,' and all of us be sent safely home again. Had we reached your world, then I and mine would be trapped there."

"Would that be so bad?" Pel asked. "I mean, how can you go back? Those monsters were all over everything!" He kicked at a dead one that lay near his feet.

"Oh, I think they'll not stay," Raven said with an airy wave. "Shadow saw us flee and will surely summon home its creatures, so that they might be dispatched elsewhere as needed."

"Maybe," Pel said, unconvinced.

"Where was that, anyway?" Nancy asked. "I mean, that place where we came out. It wasn't your castle, because we saw that across the valley."

"Certes, madam," Raven agreed. "We made our lodgings in the forester's cot of my ancestral lands, for my brother holds Stormcrack as vassal to Shadow, and in disgrace of our family's honor."

"Your *brother*?" Nancy threw Pel a worried glance.

"Aye," Raven said.

Pel decided that a change of subject was called for. "Those monsters that got through, before the portal closed," he said. "What's going to happen to them? Should we hunt them down and kill them?"

Peabody shook his head. "Don't need to," he said. "They'll die on their own."

"Will they?"

"Oh, sure—just ask Soorn. He was on the cleanup crew on Lambda Ceti Four. Those things can't live for long in normal space."

Pel glanced around, not at Soorn, but at Grummetty and the little woman. They were sitting side by side on the sand, arms around each other's shoulders. They looked pale; Pel wasn't certain whether that might be partly due to the abnormally white light.

"What about them?" he asked, surreptitiously pointing a thumb.

Peabody and Raven followed his gesture.

Raven looked grim, and Peabody shrugged his good shoulder.

"I wouldn't make any long-term plans for them," Peabody said.

"Perchance poor Dundry was the fortunate one," Raven said. "An he found shelter, he might outlive us all; an he died, at the least it was quick."

"Dundry was the other one, the one in green?"

"Aye," Raven said, "Alella's son, by her first husband."

"I met Grummetty, but not the others," Pel said. "That's Alella, there?"

"Aye," Raven said. "Grummetty's wife."

"So Dundry was—I mean, is Grummetty's stepson?"

Raven nodded, making no comment on Pel's initial use of the past tense.

Pel took a surreptitious look at Grummetty.

"You know," he said, "Grummetty was in my basement for maybe ten minutes before he started getting sick. *Really* sick. He's been here longer than that, hasn't he? And he looks all right so far."

"Raise no hopes, friend Pel," Raven said. "Mayhap the death is slower here, for 'tis plain truth that this realm is not your own, but death is certain, all the same."

"Unless you can get them back through the . . . the warp in time, anyway," Nancy suggested.

Pel looked at her and realized that Rachel had fallen asleep in her mother's arms.

"Do you want me to take her for a while?" he offered.

"No, that's all right," Nancy said. "We're fine." She hesitated, then asked, "*Can* you get them back through the warp in time?"

Raven looked at Captain Cahn; he wasn't listening. He was discussing something else entirely with some of the others.

Pel looked at Peabody.

"Doubt it," he said, frowning. "I don't know just where the hell we are, even with the name, but if I never heard of it, it's got to be at least a week, probably a lot more, from Base One. If those gnomes could last a week here, we'd probably have caught a few of them alive sometime."

Pel's jaw dropped.

"A *week*?" he shouted.

"Yeah," Peabody said.

Pel turned and grabbed Raven by the front of his embroidered jacket. "A *week*? I can't spend a *week* here! I didn't even want to spend an *hour*! I have a business to run! I left the lights on, and the cat—what's going to happen to our cat?"

"I'm sorry, Pel Brown," Raven said, pulling Pel's hands away from his garments with surprising ease; he was even stronger than he looked.

"Pel," Nancy said worriedly, watching Grummetty and Alella, "this isn't our space any more than it's theirs. Are *we* going to be all right here?"

Pel glared at Raven.

"I know not, my lady," the nobleman said. "But I see no reason to fear. My people and Messire Peabody's have lived in each other's lands for months, even years, and suffered no ill; likewise, the neither took harm from our stay in your own realm. 'Tis only the creatures of Hrumph and Shadow and Elfindom, the creatures of magic, that cannot abide here."

"Sure, lady, don't worry about that," Peabody said. "You'll be fine." He hesitated, then added, "I'm sorry about your cat, though. Maybe the neighbors'll do something?"

"Yeah," Nancy agreed, stroking Rachel's hair, "maybe. He'll have water, at least, if nobody closed the bathroom door."

For a few seconds they were silent, sunk in gloom; then a joyful shout, audible even in the thin air, roused them.

"Aircar on the way!" Prossie called. "No Imperial ships are available, so they're sending a car. Be here in a few hours!"

A ragged cheer went up and quickly faded.

"We need to put up a marker, so it can spot us," Prossie added. "I'll tell them what it is."

That brought on a puzzled silence, followed by disjointed muttering, until finally somebody thought to start collecting the dead monsters, and fragments of monsters, into a heap.

"Should really show up, against all this white," Peabody remarked, wincing, as he used his injured arm to help steady a mashed spider-thing before heaving it onto the growing mound.

Pel, dragging something resembling a saber-toothed wolf,

nodded. He hesitated. "I'm sorry about that man Cartwright," he said. "Was he . . . Did you know him well?"

Peabody turned away from the pile and shrugged. "Well enough," he said. He sighed. "It'll probably be me who has to tell his wife back on Terra."

"Wife?" Nancy, still seated holding Rachel, looked up, startled.

Peabody nodded. "Cute little thing. Her name's Maureen; last I saw she was about seven months pregnant, probably had the kid by now. She and Pete have a place in New Dorset, in North Columbia."

Pel looked uneasily at Nancy; she stared at Peabody in horror.

"They sent him out there with his wife pregnant?" she demanded.

Peabody shrugged again. "Sure. It didn't look all that dangerous. It was supposed to be a diplomatic mission, after all—we didn't know we'd wind up fighting monsters in the middle of nowhere." He gestured at the surrounding landscape. "And we didn't expect to wind up *here*, either, but this doesn't look too bad."

Pel glanced around, at the cold white sand, the various people with torn clothing, bloodstains, and improvised bandages, the pale sun and too-close horizon. He stared for a moment at the heap of fanged, clawed, and tentacled horrors, all of them dead. He took a deep breath of the warm, thin, oddly flavorless air.

"Well, no one's attacking us, anyway," he said.

Peabody grimaced.

"At the moment," Pel added.

"Hours," Nancy said, looking at the corpses. "She said a few hours?"

Pel frowned and nodded.

"I'm going to get some sleep, then," Nancy said. "It must be after ten back home, and I'm tired."

Pel looked at his watch, and saw nothing; the display was blank. The light came on when he pushed the appropriate button, but had nothing to illuminate.

He shrugged. "I don't think it's really that late," he said, "but sure, if you like."

Nancy lowered Rachel gently to the sand, arranged her comfortably, then curled up beside her. Pel watched them silently.

He sat up himself for a while, but eventually, for lack of anything better to do, he joined her.

He was awakened by Peabody jostling him. He blinked, sat up, and looked where the crewman pointed.

At first he didn't see anything. The sun had crossed the sky and was descending toward the western horizon; the air had progressed from warm to hot, while the sand on which he lay had also warmed, though far less. He peered out over the sand and rock, and finally spotted it.

A glittering object had appeared over the horizon and was coming quickly nearer.

"Oh, my God," he said, tensing, "now what?"

"It's okay!" someone shouted. "That's our ride!"

Pel relaxed slightly, but remained wary as the thing neared. Someone—in the dimming light it took Pel a moment to recognize Mervyn—had improvised a small torch, somehow, and was waving it enthusiastically over his head, signaling to the approaching craft.

The vehicle was roughly the size and shape of a car, but had no wheels; instead it cruised along at roughly the height of Pel's head, with no visible means of support.

"It *is* just like Luke Skywalker's landspeeder," Nancy said, sitting up.

Pel looked at her questioningly. "Prossie said they had cars with antigravity—aircars, she called them," Nancy explained, "and I told Rachel they were like the one in *Star Wars*. And they *are*, see?"

Pel nodded. The thing certainly traveled like the one in the movie.

It didn't much resemble it otherwise, though. It wasn't pink and battered. The cockpit wasn't open, and the lines were more bulbous than sleek. It was glossy black, with elaborate brass trim and numerous running lights in various colors, and it reminded Pel more of a 1953 Buick Roadmaster his father had once had than it did of anything else—though of course, the Buick had been festooned with chrome, rather than brass.

By this time the entire assorted party was awake, and everyone had noticed the approaching vehicle. They were all watching it, with varying intensity. Susan was frankly staring, her mouth open; Amy was a bit more restrained, while Ted was grinning like an idiot, as if the thing's appearance were something he had contrived himself that had turned out better than expected. Stoddard was watching other people as much as the aircar itself, judging their reactions to it; Squire Donald's expression was unreadable; Valadrakul's gaze seemed coolly appraising.

Most of the crew of the *Ruthless* seemed mildly relieved and completely unsurprised.

The aircar glided to a standstill and hovered over a slab of white rock, a few yards away. A window whirred open and a white-haired head thrust out.

"Proserpine Thorpe?" the man in the aircar called.

"Here!" Prossie replied, waving cheerfully.

The head swiveled around to peer at the telepath, then turned back to the main party and called, "Captain Cahn?"

"Yes," Cahn answered.

The man nodded, and pulled his head back inside the vehicle. An instant later, with a high-pitched whine, the aircar settled slowly to the ground.

Pel glanced at Nancy, making sure she and Rachel were all right, and then jogged toward it.

As he drew nearer, he saw that the resemblance to an old Buick was less than he had initially thought. The thing was bigger and far more complex, with exposed tubing in several places, running lights in yellow and green and red, and protuberances that Pel couldn't identify at all.

It also bore an elaborate gold seal on its side, showing a lion and unicorn rampant against a sunburst. That was not something Pel had expected—a ringed planet or a spaceship would have struck him as more appropriate. The gold-leaf beasts looked positively medieval, and made a curious contrast with the multicolored lights and all the other signs of a fairly high technology.

By the time Pel reached the aircar's side Captain Cahn had strode the three paces necessary to reach the vehicle and was already bent down, talking quietly with the driver through the open window.

Pel frowned; the vehicle had a pair of bucket seats in front, and two rows of three behind, rather than the two bench seats his father's car had had, but even so, there was no way the entire party could fit into it at once.

"It'll take three trips," the driver said, looking past Cahn, seeing Pel's expression and guessing the reason.

"Couldn't you have sent something larger?" Pel asked, struggling not to shout.

The driver grimaced. "Nope," he said. "This is it. Psi Cass the Deuce isn't exactly London; this bucket's about it for official transport. They were trying to scrounge up more, but for the first run, I'm all you get."

"We'll take the wounded first," Captain Cahn said, in a tone that implied argument was flatly impossible.

The driver nodded. "And I take the telepath, of course, right?"

"Of course," Captain Cahn agreed.

"What about my wife and our daughter?" Pel asked.

"Second trip, probably," the driver replied, reaching for a lever.

Captain Cahn stepped back and turned, looking the group over and choosing who would go.

"Peabody, you go and get that arm looked at," he called. "Drummond, you're in charge, and get the leg taken care of. Wizard . . ." Elani and Valadrakul both looked up. Valadrakul's face was bloody, but he was basically intact; Elani was unmarked, but clearly suffering from exhaustion.

Pel was distracted by the driver clearing his throat. He turned, startled.

The driver's hand was on the polished wood knob atop a black lever, and he was glaring at Pel. Pel blinked.

"Step away, please," the driver said.

"Oh," Pel replied. He took a step back.

The driver pulled the lever, and the aircar made a noise like a vacuum cleaner warming up. It stirred, and then hovered, a few inches off the ground.

As the machine rose Pel felt suddenly off-balance, as if he were about to fall toward the aircar; he backed away another step, and the feeling vanished.

Peabody stepped up, apparently untroubled by any falling sensation; he opened a door and climbed in, then turned and held it open. Valadrakul handed in first Grummetty, and then Alella—they were far too small to board without assistance.

The two little people both rode in a single seat, the center one of the back row, with Peabody to one side. Elani went in next, taking the other side.

"Nobody else's hurt that bad, sir," Peabody said, leaning forward. "Why not take Mrs. Brown and the girl?"

Cahn frowned. "All right," he said, "if they want, but there isn't room for all three of them. If the mother and daughter go, the father waits here. You want to do that, Mr. Brown, or would you rather wait and all go together?"

Pel turned to Nancy.

Nancy looked down at Rachel, who was huddled, sound asleep, in her arms. She looked around at the empty sand, the descending sun, and the gleaming aircar.

"We'll wait," she said.

Cahn looked around.

"You two, then," he said, pointing to Susan and Amy. "I want *somebody* from your world in this group."

The two women glanced at each other, then stepped forward together and boarded.

A moment later the aircar was loaded—Prossie Thorpe rode shotgun in the front, Susan, Amy, and Lieutenant Drummond were in the second row, and Peabody, Elani, and the little people rode in back. Doors slammed, the engine sound rose to an ear-piercing shriek and then upward in pitch into inaudibility, and the vehicle lifted from the ground, swung around, and began to pick up speed, back the direction it had come.

Pel had been standing too close; the backwash of the antigravity drive left him dizzy.

"Next load," Cahn said, "Lieutenant Godwin, you'll be in charge. You'll take the Browns, the other wizard, that Squire Donald, and Ben Lampert. The rest of us should all fit in the third."

There were answering nods, but Pel paid no attention. He was too busy watching the aircar as it disappeared over the horizon.

Despite the hot, dry air, he shivered.

A thought struck him, and he snatched out his camera; it appeared to have survived undamaged, thus far. He pointed it after the aircar, but it was too late; the vehicle was out of sight.

He sighed, and contented himself with snapping a quick shot of the remaining group, scattered on the sands.

CHAPTER 15

Amy found herself seated in the exact center of the aircar, between Susan Nguyen and Lieutenant Drummond. The sound of the engines was not the same as any car or plane she had ridden before; it was a steady whine, and it took a few moments before she could adjust to it and block it out.

Drummond was obviously back on familiar ground—so to speak, since they were cruising about eight feet up. He was leaning back, relaxed and smiling. His injured leg was stretched out, the foot under the seat in front of him, while the other leg was bent, knee out to the side. His blond hair was matted with blood, and Amy wondered what had happened to his helmet. He had had a helmet before, she was certain.

Then she realized where she had seen him with his helmet on—stepping out of the *Ruthless* in her back yard. He had been the first to emerge from the ship.

Despite his wounds, he looked a lot happier now than he had then—and why not? He was on his way home.

Amy wasn't so lucky. She didn't know where she was headed. She *hoped* it was home.

■

The richness of telepathic contact was so wonderful, after the long drought on Earth and in Shadow's realm, that Prossie was tempted to just lean back in her seat and let the whine of the aircar's engine shut out distractions while she soaked in impressions—but she knew she couldn't do that. She had duties to attend to.

She sent a wordless status report to Carrie, back at Base One—Carrie and the family were always her first concern, of course, whatever her official orders might be. And Carrie would keep the higher-ups in the military hierarchy informed and happy, anyway, so that was all right.

Then there were plans to be made here on Psi Cass Two. They would need a ship, to get everybody back to Base One as soon as possible. That barbarian who called himself Raven, and his body-guard Stoddard, and the rest of them, she supposed would all be unspeakably valuable to Imperial Intelligence; Shadow was a top concern, and this was the first time a group of friendly natives from that universe had ever been found.

At least, as far as Prossie knew, it was, and as far as she was concerned that was definitive—if any telepath knew it, now that she was back in normal space and in contact with the family, she would know it, on some deep unconscious level. And if anyone who ever came anywhere near a telepath knew it, or if anyone a telepath contacted from a distance knew it, then the suspicion would leak through.

The telepaths all knew things they didn't know they knew, things that had registered deep in the back of the mind, far below consciousness—it was one of the more useful side effects of their talent, really.

It was also one that they tried not to let normals know about. Prossie wasn't going to tell anyone that she knew how impor-tant these people were; she would let her superiors tell *her* how important they were.

And not just Shadow's people; the Earth people were poten-tially valuable, too. An entire new universe, with its own science—even if much of it didn't work here in the real world, that still had to be valuable.

Not that Undersecretary Bascombe thought so. He thought the Earth people were barbarians.

Prossie knew better; she hadn't snooped deeply, but even a light brush showed her that their minds were rich, sophisticated, crammed with a wealth of stories and information. She couldn't even understand much of what she found in there—especially when she tried this Susan Nguyen, whose background was so different from the others, and who had spent her early childhood speaking an utterly alien language.

Raven and company, on the other hand, *were* barbarians. Oh, they had their own culture, with plenty of elaboration and ritual, and their wizards had a great deal of esoteric knowledge about their "magic," but they had the singlemindedness and ethnocentricity typical of primitives.

She conveyed all that to Carrie, in mental shorthand.

But then she turned her attention to the governor in Town—Psi Cass Two had only one settlement, and nobody had bothered to think up a fancy name for it yet.

A ship. They needed a ship. And Captain Cahn held a special commission as emissary to Earth that, despite what he had told Raven, gave him plenipotentiary powers.

And there were all those people still stuck out in the desert.

She had some arguing to do, to speed things along.

■

Raven watched the vehicle depart. No single part of it touched the sand beneath, and yet these people denied the reality of magic?

What else was their science but another magic?

Yet deny it they did, always and vehemently. It was a curious thing indeed.

Would that the more ordinary, commonplace magic functioned in this hellish realm wherein he had found refuge! Alas, he knew from the reports of his compatriots and their spies that it did not and could not; the currents of power that wizards tapped did not flow here, those lines of the web Shadow had strung did not reach here, in this so-called Milky Empire.

What power was it, then, that these machines used? A pretty puzzle, that; perhaps, were it solved, wizards of Elani and Valadrakul's ilk could draw upon that same source. That was a thought for another day.

For the nonce, the need was to reach the heart of the Empire from this barren outpost, and there to find the portal back to Stormcrack.

And of course, to bring through the Empire's men and machines, to do battle with that infernal Shadow that had fallen upon all the true lands.

Thus, to ride the machines, this aircar, and then some other— would it be as that other vehicle, in the realm named Earth?

Raven did not quail to face man or monster, with blade or less; he feared not death, as must needs come to all in the end. Still, at the memory of that ride his lips tightened.

He did not *trust* these machines, nor the men that built them!

■

Pel's digital watch was still not working. He had no way of telling, therefore, how long the aircar was gone.

It seemed like days. The sun—or rather, the star Psi Cassiopeia—vanished below the horizon not long after the vehicle departed, and the air cooled quickly. Darkness fell suddenly and more completely than the suburbanite Browns were accustomed to; there was no glow of streetlamps and headlights, but only the light of a few million stars.

The stars were brighter and more numerous than Pel ever remembered seeing before, even on trips to the country, but that still hardly made up for the lack of a moon.

The air temperature dropped with astonishing speed once full dark had arrived; where the sands had seemed cool in the heat of the day, they were quickly the warmest thing around.

That, Pel thought, explained why they had been cool in the first place—the sand held the heat far better than the air, which had turned downright chilly.

Captain Cahn used his blaster to heat the rock face where the portal had been, just like Lieutenant Sulu in an old "Star Trek" episode, and the party huddled around it, but in fact the night air was not actually as cold as all that—at its worst, it didn't approach freezing.

There was no food to be had, no supplies of any kind except the half-bottle of Pepsi that Smith had somehow hung onto throughout their adventures; there was nothing to do here, nowhere to go, no place worth exploring, just miles upon miles of empty sand and rock. The remaining travelers, whether from Earth, Terra, or Shadow's realm, had little choice but sleep.

Pel was very glad they had eaten the pizza *before* venturing through the basement wall; that ensured that hunger, while real, was not a serious problem. Rachel did complain, when she was awake, about being thirsty, but she accepted the fact that there was nothing to drink. Captain Cahn was holding the Pepsi in reserve, doling it out in capfuls as he deemed appropriate. He was very cautious about it, and nobody came away satisfied.

The captain did allow Rachel more than her share, Pel had to admit.

At least there were no live monsters, nor even shadows that monsters might hide in. Their situation was not pleasant, but neither was it particularly frightening. Mostly, it was simply dark, dull, and boring, and just chilly enough to make sleep difficult.

Pel had the feeling, sometimes during the long wait, that he ought to be *doing* something. A storybook hero would be doing something—Captain Kirk, or Arnold Schwarzenegger, or Horatio Hornblower wouldn't just sit and wait, would he?

But what could he do?

Besides, he wasn't a hero. If this whole mess was someone's great adventure, it probably wasn't his. He didn't feel like the star, but just a bit player. His role was to go along until he could get back home, out of the story entirely and back to real life.

Some time before dawn, when heating the rock didn't seem to be doing much good anymore, and maybe in part just because he was bored, Cahn set fire to the heap of dead monstrosities—that not only provided some warmth, but served as a beacon for any approaching rescue vehicles to home in on.

Unfortunately, it also stank horribly, making further sleep almost impossible.

The night seemed to drag on forever, but Pel suspected that it was really only five or six hours before Psi Cassiopeia again appeared on the eastern horizon. The star in question seemed to move considerably faster than Earth's sun.

Or rather, he corrected himself, the planet he was on rotated more swiftly than Earth.

The *planet* he was on—somehow, the concept of being on *another planet* was more mind-boggling than being in an entirely different universe.

Were those stars up there really more numerous than what he'd seen from Earth? He had no way of being sure. He was quite certain, though, that he saw no familiar constellations. The familiar planets, Venus and Jupiter and Saturn, were nowhere to be seen; if the Psi Cassiopeia system had other planets, he didn't see them, or at any rate he didn't recognize them as planets.

(There had to be at least one other, he told himself, or this place couldn't be Psi Cassiopeia *Two*, could it?)

The sun had only just cleared the horizon when its light glittered from something moving; Pel happened to be looking in the right direction, and let out a shriek at the sight.

Half a dozen drowsing people started, and a sudden babble arose.

Rachel screamed in terror, and Pel and Nancy rushed to comfort her.

"She was asleep before," Nancy pointed out. "She didn't see it."

"It's okay, Rae," Pel told her, "that's the magic car that's going to get us out of here and take us back—" He stopped. He didn't want to lie about that, to get her hopes up too high. ". . . And take us somewhere we can maybe get a ship that will take us home."

"I wanna go home," Rachel agreed. "I want Harvey."

"Well, then, behave yourself, and we'll do everything we can to get you home. It's a long ride, I'm afraid . . ."

"Anything's better than sitting out here freezing," Nancy interrupted.

"Oh, for sure," Pel agreed, "but three or four hours, or whatever it is, sitting in a car isn't going to be much fun, either."

A moment later, as the aircar slowed to a stop, he added, "And it isn't that cold out here, anyway."

"You're wearing heavier clothes than I am," Nancy retorted— accurately, Pel had to admit. His shirt was definitely warmer than the flimsy blouse Nancy had on.

He had also been willing to sit closer to the smoldering signal fire than Nancy had—she had always been more sensitive to smells than he, and close in the stench was unbearable.

"Daddy," Rachel asked, "are there *more* magic cars?" She pointed.

Pel turned and saw that two more aircars were approaching, a blue one and another black one. His attention had been so focused on the first that he hadn't noticed them before.

"I guess so, Rae," he said.

Nancy frowned. "If they have more than one," she said, "then why didn't they send them all out here the *first* time? Why did we all have to spend the whole damn night out here freezing?"

Pel shrugged. "Ask him," he said, pointing to the driver—who was not, Pel noticed, the same man who had picked up the first group.

Nancy did just that.

"Didn't think of it, ma'am," he replied. "Or, well, actually, you see, the first time we weren't all that sure that the call was genuine, so we didn't want to send everything we had out on a rabbit hunt. We didn't have anything to go on but that telepath's say-so, and we don't have much truck with mutants out here, so we wanted to see she was on the level first. And then we needed Lennie to give us directions, so we had to wait until he got back . . ."

"There must have been *something*," Nancy insisted.

The driver just shrugged. "I guess Lennie couldn't think of anything, ma'am."

The blue aircar was pulling up—it was smaller and sleeker, with a sort of central nose cone that made it resemble a Studebaker or an Edsel, rather than a Buick. Its color was a sort of robin's-egg blue that really didn't seem appropriate at all.

The other black one didn't look like anything Pel had ever seen before. Unlike the first two, it had no brasswork; its trim was painted matte black. Its lines were simpler than the others, and its running lights were few and simple and all yellow. It had a rather nasty air about it that Pel didn't care for; he hurried to load Nancy and Rachel into the back seat of the big one.

Lieutenant Godwin herded Valadrakul, Lampert, and Squire Donald into the middle seat, then took the front passenger seat himself.

Captain Cahn, Ted, and Raven boarded the little black aircar; the blue one took the others.

Pel saw the captain swig down the last trace of Pepsi, hardly

more than a few drops, and then toss the empty onto the floor of
the aircar before he climbed in.

"No luggage?" the driver of the Browns' car called back. "You
folks got everything?"

His answer was a muttered chorus of assent.

"All right, then," the driver said. Engines whined, and one by
one the three aircars lifted off, turned, and sped away. Pel took a
final glance back at the faint column of smoke rising from the
burning pile of dead Shadow-creatures, the odd bits of litter
they had dropped here and there, and the endless rocks and
sand.

That was one campsite he would remember, but would never
miss.

Once they were airborne, the driver announced, "I heard the
other bunch came in real hungry, so I figured you didn't have any
food out here, and I brought shrewsburies."

Godwin and Lampert brightened visibly; the others looked at
each other, puzzled.

It must be food of some sort, obviously, but Pel had no idea
what a shrewsbury might be.

Not that he and the others cared very much. They were rav-
enous, having had nothing to eat for at least half a day.

"They're in the map box," the driver said, pointing to what
Pel would have called a glove compartment.

Godwin opened the indicated container and pulled out a
stack of objects wrapped in foil—not, Pel noted, in plastic, the way
most foods were back home. From the size and shape, Pel guessed
that they were sandwiches of some kind.

Godwin took the top one off the pile, then turned around,
stretching, and passed the rest to Lampert. Lampert gave one each
to Valadrakul and Donald, kept one himself, and passed the remaining four to Pel.

"Last one's mine," the driver called.

Pel took a moment to peel back a corner of the foil on each
packet and look the contents over. They were, indeed, sandwiches;
he guessed that for some reason the Imperials called sandwiches
"shrewsburies" instead. Maybe there hadn't been an Earl of Sandwich in the Galactic Empire.

Or maybe this particular sort of sandwich was called a shrewsbury. The sandwiches, or shrewsburies, all appeared to be the same—white bread, yellow cheese, and a slab of pink lunch meat, the exact nature of which was not clear.

The exact nature of the foil wasn't clear, either, Pel realized; at first glance he had assumed it was aluminum, but it didn't feel quite right.

Could it be tinfoil, perhaps? Some other details of the Galactic Empire seemed oddly old-fashioned; perhaps they still used tin, rather than aluminum, here. Or was their aluminum just processed differently, somehow? *Could* aluminum be different? Metallurgy wasn't something Pel knew about.

Well, it didn't matter. This was another universe, so why should the aluminum foil be the same?

Why should the sandwiches be the same, for that matter?

He didn't know, and right now he didn't much care. He handed one foil-wrapped sandwich to Nancy and one to Rachel, then handed one back to Lampert and unwrapped his own.

It was edible, but unexciting—there was no mayonnaise or other condiment, just bread, meat, and cheese, and the meat was bland some sort of ham loaf, Pel decided.

A jug of lukewarm water was passed around, as well, and at the driver's request the used foil was collected and passed back to the front.

"The stuff isn't cheap, out here," the driver explained. "We reuse the metal."

Food and water improved Pel's condition considerably. However, once the last crumb was gone, the ride was, as Pel had expected, very dull indeed.

Rachel was fascinated for perhaps six or seven minutes by the fact that they were flying, and stared intently out the window as she chewed on her sandwich. She climbed on Nancy's lap for a better view, watching the sand and stone rush by below.

Around the eighth minute, the sandwich gone, she climbed back into her own seat and asked, for the first of what seemed like several hundred times, "When will we get there, Mommy?"

Pel sighed and tried to ignore her.

He wished he had made a last visit to the impromptu latrine

that had been established behind a rock. That particular discomfort at least served to distract him from Rachel's restlessness.

She shifted, squirmed, leaned this way and that, climbed from her seat onto first her mother's lap, and then her father's, before being forcibly placed back where she belonged, with her seat belt fastened securely.

The seat belts, Pel noticed with something approaching astonishment, had actual *buckles*—metal rings with a hinged central prong that went through a hole in the strap, just like the belt he happened to be wearing. He wondered why a civilization that had interstellar travel made do with anything so primitive.

Perhaps an hour after they were picked up, Rachel announced, "I have to go to the bathroom."

Pel, secretly relieved, passed this information forward to Lampert, who passed it on to the driver.

A moment later the vehicle settled to the ground—a stretch of empty sand indistinguishable from where they had started, save that the outcroppings were more scattered, and veined with something grayish, instead of being entirely pure white.

"Five minutes," the driver announced. "Stretch, do your business, whatever, but just five minutes and then we get airborne again."

Five minutes was plenty. The bleak surroundings were hardly an invitation to do anything beyond the necessary. That out of the way, when they were moving once again Rachel curled up quietly and went to sleep.

Pel found himself with no distractions at all, now. He stared out the windows.

The other two aircars were out of sight, presumably gone on ahead, and Pel wondered how the things navigated. The desert below all looked the same, to him.

Just as he thought that, of course, they sailed over a canyon, by far the most distinctive feature he had seen yet. That didn't explain how the driver—or was he a pilot?—knew where to go, though. Pel regretted sitting in back, where he could see nothing of the controls.

This whole new world—whole new *universe*—was all so strange . . .

Pel paused, blinked, and looked down at the upholstery.

There wasn't anything strange about that at all, he corrected himself. The brass-plated door handle and window crank were completely, utterly ordinary, if old-fashioned. Rachel was curled up asleep, fingers tangled in her hair, looking just as sweet as ever; Nancy, on the other side, was leaning against the glass, lost in her own thoughts, and she, too, was familiar.

But outside the car the sun was white, the horizon too near, the ground seven feet away, and instead of rolling over asphalt they were flying over an endless wilderness of lifeless sand.

It was the contrast of the strange and the familiar that was most troublesome, somehow.

For one thing, it made it all seem real. It wasn't a dream, where everything was odd, nor a theme park, where everything was clean and plastic, nor any other sort of fantasy. It was like a visit to a foreign country, in a way—like his trip to Mexico a few years back, where the strange and the familiar had been mixed, where he had bought Coca-Cola with thousand-peso notes, where Mayan ruins had been built of stones no different from those in his own back yard, where the tropic light had been clear and golden, shining on Volkswagens and concrete-block walls as well as palm trees and sandy beaches.

Here the light was wrong, the air was wrong, the gravity itself was wrong; cars flew, and monsters emerged from the earth, but still the door handles were cheap brass, probably plate, and there were little flip-top ashtrays in the armrests.

He didn't like it at all. It was too real. In all his dreams, he had never once imagined cars with flip-top ashtrays in the armrests. In the science fiction books and stories he read no one ever mentioned flip-top ashtrays. If they mentioned ashtrays at all they were exotic devices of some sort, sucking away smoke and ash or evaporating cigarette butts in atomic disintegrators, not just dirty little metal dishes with chintzy lids that clicked open at the flick of a thumbnail.

Ashtrays—did that mean that the Galactic Empire had tobacco? There were no butts or ashes, so Pel could not be sure they actually *were* ashtrays at all, but that was certainly what they looked like.

How closely parallel to Earth *was* the Empire's home world, anyway?

And did he really want to know?

No, he decided, he just wanted to get *home*. Silly Cat (originally Sylvester, but long since shortened) would be seriously upset by now, his food supply probably exhausted, though he could still get water from the toilet—if no one had put the seat down or closed the bathroom door tight.

That mundane little worry somehow made the whole thing worse.

Pel wished he could just dismiss this entire adventure as a dream, as his imagination running amok, even as outright insanity accompanied by hallucinations, but it all felt too real, too solid and detailed. He never worried about toilet seats in his dreams.

He stared out at the sand and rocks sliding by.

■

It might be, Raven bethought himself, that he was become accustomed to the uncanny. Else, it might likewise be that this aircar, as it was, rode higher and more smoothly than the groundcar at Earth, and thus removed from him the worst of the sensations.

He watched the bare sands that flashed beneath, and listened warily to the mutterings of Captain Cahn, in the forward right-hand seat, as he spoke, seemingly to some familiar spirit. The driver of the vehicle said naught, but paid all his heed to his craft—and that as it should be, minding the speed at which they flew.

Beside him, the man called Ted Deranian, the advocate for hire, dozed fitfully, twitching occasionally. Raven glanced at him.

That poor fool still thought the waking world to be a dream; did he then take his dreams for truth? Was he now, perhaps, back in his home, his strange and frightening life untroubled by the common affairs of empires?

Raven smiled to himself at the thought.

■

Pel only realized he had dozed off when he woke up; the whine of the aircar's engine had changed.

They were descending, sinking down into a sort of open-topped box, comprised of four concrete walls painted battleship gray. Pel could see two doors in the wall directly ahead. They were already below the tops of the walls by the time he was awake enough to understand what was happening, so he saw nothing of the surrounding structures except a quick glimpse of black and gray rooftops.

"Welcome to town, folks!" the driver called back over his shoulder.

"What do you call this place?" Pel called back.

"Town," the driver replied, a bit embarrassed. "It's the only one on the planet, so we haven't bothered to give it a real name."

"The only one on the *planet*?" Nancy asked, as she roused Rachel.

" 'Fraid so." With a bump, the aircar was down, and the engine's whine died away suddenly.

Hesitantly, Pel pulled at the door handle.

The door opened and he stepped out, then turned to take Rachel from her mother. When the three of them were out, he took a look around.

They were in a bare, featureless enclosure perhaps fifty feet by eighty, standing on coarse gravel near one corner, surrounded by blank gray walls. The two doors at one end were the only way in or out; the only colors anywhere were the blue aircar, resting in the opposite corner, and the various running lights. The dark hues were in sharp contrast to the bright, pale sky overhead.

The third aircar was in a third corner, but even as Pel first spotted it, its engines came on and it rose upward into the brightness above.

A car door slammed; Pel started, and turned to see that Lampert was standing nearby, one hand on the door as he looked around.

"Doesn't look like much, does it?" he said.

"No," Pel agreed.

The driver slammed his own door, on the other side of the aircar, and called, "Okay, folks, right on in, through the door on the left, please!"

The passengers obeyed, shuffling across the gravel and

through the door; a man in a purple uniform, not quite the same as those worn by the crew of the *Ruthless*, held it open for them. He said nothing as they trudged past.

Inside they found themselves in a large, windowless, and mostly bare room, with concrete walls painted a dull peach color, the floor of gray tile, and the ceiling an off-white. The only furnishings were two rows of white stone benches, and some red-print-on-white posters on the walls. There were four doors, counting the one they had just entered through, one centered in each wall. Light came from white glass globes that hung from the ceiling, looking very much like ordinary electric lights.

Pel would have expected fluorescent fixtures instead, but there were none, only the globes.

People were sitting on the benches—Stoddard, Ted, Smith, Soorn, and Mervyn. They had obviously not yet had a chance to clean themselves up; scabbed-over scratches were still in evidence, sand was in their hair, and their uniforms were wrinkled and frayed. Ted's suit would probably never recover.

Stoddard looked up and smiled as the others trailed in; Soorn waved, and Smith called, "Hello! What kept you?"

Ted grinned foolishly and said nothing.

Mervyn ignored them all; he was leaning back against a wall with his eyes closed, and did not stir. Pel was unsure whether he was asleep or awake.

"Slow old bus," Lampert replied. "How long have you guys been here?"

Smith shrugged. "Maybe ten minutes. They called in the captain and the nut in the velvet just before you people came in. The two of them, and that one—" He pointed to Ted, who waved in reply. "—were here before we were. Don't know how long."

"The nut in the velvet" was obviously Raven. Pel hadn't thought of him in those terms.

If that was how they saw Raven, Pel wondered how the crewmen saw him—the nut with the kid? It was probably something just that impersonal and unflattering.

The man in the purple uniform closed the door and stood silently against the wall. Nancy and Rachel settled cautiously onto an empty bench.

"Oh, I guess I got here about ten minutes before you," Ted said to Smith. "I must say, this is the longest and most compli cated dream I can ever remember having. I wonder if I have a lot of dreams like this and I just don't remember them when I'm awake?"

Smith grimaced and turned slightly away from Ted. Pel felt his own stomach shift uneasily.

That sandwich had been some time ago, and he never had gotten enough to drink, but still, Pel knew that his discomfort wasn't merely physical. It was Ted making him nervous. Ted was acting crazy—literally insane.

Well, Pel told himself, if they could just get him safely back home to Germantown, Maryland, it wouldn't matter if he thought he had dreamed the whole thing.

Pel wished he could think of it as *when* instead of *if.*

CHAPTER 16

Raven listened with approval as Captain Cahn conversed with the local lordling, the so-called governor. This Cahn had the makings of a good commander, and such was recognized even in so dismal a place as this. Put him in armor and a sword in his hand, and he'd be fit for the service of Stormcrack, fit even to lead a hundred men.

Ah, but to get him there . . .

Best to say nothing and leave it all to Cahn. These misbegotten fools doubtless thought Raven mad; were he to speak it would serve no good. Leave it, then, in terms of the Empire's good, the Empire's authority, and say nothing of the need to fight Shadow.

■

Prossie watched in admiration as Captain Cahn told the governor what to do. It was really quite educational; he didn't shout, didn't argue, didn't ask anything. He used a sort of tight, determined anger to drive his thoughts and words, but Prossie doubted a non-telepath would sense any of that—the Captain was calm and efficient, simply taking his authority as a given.

And of course, it was quite real. The Empire had given its emissary pretty much a free hand and the legal power to go with it.

The governor couldn't really know that, though. He had no telepath to verify anything—Prossie worked for Cahn, and the governor didn't know enough about telepaths to realize that that meant Cahn had the Empire's full blessing. His orders had always come by ship, prior to this.

For all he could prove, Cahn could be a rebel, a mutineer, a lunatic—but when Cahn spoke the governor never doubted for a moment that he was just what he claimed to be.

Prossie could see the theory of how to do it, of course, but she couldn't possibly have done it herself; quite aside from the near-universal antipathy to telepaths, and aside from her sex, she just didn't have the knack. Watching Cahn was like listening to a first-rate musician. Prossie might read the same notes, might pick them out, but she didn't have the talent to make the same music.

Cahn was magnificent. Prossie had been relaying messages to the governor, had been telling him much the same thing that Cahn was now saying, and had been virtually ignored, because she simply didn't have Cahn's presence and aura of authority; the governor had made a few tentative gestures, but no more than that. Now that the Captain was here in person, though, he was getting instant compliance.

It took less than fifteen minutes to establish martial law, with Cahn himself in charge, and to commandeer much of what they needed.

■

The stay in the waiting room hadn't been long—twelve minutes, according to Godwin, whose analog watch seemed to have survived better than Pel's digital one. Half a dozen of the purple-uniformed men had then appeared and escorted the party out.

The next stop was a crowded men's room—at least, for everyone except Nancy and Rachel, who had a ladies' room to themselves. Soap, towels, and various brushes were provided, and Pel emerged feeling much better than he had entered. Clothes were still torn and wrinkled, faces unshaven, but at least the worst of the dirt had been cleared away.

The facilities were indistinguishable from what Pel would have expected in a men's room back on Earth, in, say, a bus station or a rest station on an interstate—white tile, bare bulbs in wire cages overhead, green-painted steel partitions, white porcelain fixtures.

It was only when he ran water in the sink, and found himself bothered by something about how it flowed, that Pel was re-minded that this was *not* Earth.

The difference wasn't really very great at all, he decided, watching the water, but *any* change in how water flowed was enough to make him uneasy.

It was slower, he realized. In the lighter gravity of Psi Cassi-opeia Two, objects—including water—fell more slowly.

He had more or less adjusted to how the air and gravity *felt*, but he had had few opportunities to see anything fall. He stared.

Then he shrugged, and went on washing.

After cleanup came food—cafeteria food, served in a more or less standard-issue cafeteria, but that was quite good enough for the Browns at this point. Rachel gobbled two hot dogs—which were labelled "hot reds"—along with several dozen sugared french fries and large quantities of canned milk; Nancy tried the maca-roni salad, frowned, and then settled on ham slices, green salad, and cold tea.

Pel took a "Homburg shrewsbury," which looked like a cheese-burger, and discovered that there was cornmeal and chopped onion in the meat, which appeared to be a blend of pork and beef, rather than pure beef.

Another quirk in the local cuisine, obviously, like the confec-tioner's sugar on Rachel's fries, or for that matter, the word "shrewsbury" replacing "sandwich."

It was edible, though, and he ate it, washing it down with wa-tery root beer.

"Everything tastes funny," Rachel said, staring at her empty plate.

"Well, we're on another planet," Nancy said, throwing an un-easy glance at the smear of macaroni salad on the edge of her plate.

Pel said nothing; he had sampled a french fry and decided against eating any more. Rachel was quite right; everything *did* taste funny.

Well, why shouldn't it? This wasn't their own land. Foreign food was *always* strange at first.

He hoped that the stuff would nourish them. This was not only another planet, as Nancy had pointed out, but another *uni-verse*. The molecules in the food could well be arranged differently—he vaguely recalled reading something about right-handed and left-handed proteins.

Well, the crew of the *Ruthless* hadn't had any visible problems with the pizza.

He wondered about the people from Shadow's universe—was this food strange to them, too?

What about the little people? Were they all right?

The later arrivals had not seen anyone from the first carload since arriving in Town, nor had Cahn and Raven rejoined them. The purple uniforms had denied knowing anything at all except where the group was to go next.

Pel stared down at the table, which was topped with black glass.

The cafeteria wasn't quite standard issue, really. The tables were steel and glass, and the chair seats were made of something like fiberglass on steel frames. It struck Pel suddenly that except for some trim in the aircar, he hadn't seen any wood in this entire place—none of the rooms had any woodwork; the chairs and benches and tables were all stone or steel or glass. Plastics and paper products were present, but scarce—the men's room had been equipped with fluffy white terrycloth towels, rather than paper towels. The cafeteria plates were ceramic, the napkins cloth, the flatware steel.

He hadn't seen any trees, anywhere, on this planet. There was nothing to make paper or wood out of. And most plastics were made from petroleum, weren't they? Petroleum came from dead dinosaurs—well, maybe not dinosaurs, but dead things from millions of years ago. A planet as lifeless as this probably had no oil deposits. For all Pel knew, there was no native life here at all.

"Okay, folks," someone called, "let's clean up and move on."

"Hell," Pel muttered, "let them clean it up themselves." He did not find himself exactly brimming over with gratitude for the treatment he and his family had received here; while it was true they had been cleaned up and fed, they had hardly been pampered. After waiting around without any explanation, or any contact except the silent guards, Pel was hardly in a mood to show his hosts much consideration. He stood up and headed for the door, leaving his tray where it was.

Nancy and Rachel followed.

In a moment, the full dozen—the Browns, Valadrakul, Stoddard, Donald, Ted, Godwin, Smith, Soorn, Mervyn, and Lampert—were marching down another bare concrete corridor, with purple-clad guards ahead and behind.

Double doors swung open, and while two guards held them, others indicated that the visitors were to turn right into another corridor—but this one was not entirely empty. Captain Cahn and Raven of Stormcrack Keep were waiting there.

Smiles broke out, but after a few quick words of greeting there was no conversation.

Fourteen strong, the party continued down this new corridor, and through another set of doors—glass doors, this time—into a large glassed-in vestibule.

Pel scarcely had time to look out at the vast expanse of flat gray before he was swept on through another set of doors, out onto the gravel pavement.

Gravel—the tar in asphalt is another petroleum by-product, Pel realized.

For the first time he saw the exterior of the building he and the others had been in—a blank white concrete facade, only two stories, few windows. It extended several hundred yards in a gentle concave arc; the glass vestibule was the rightmost one of three, spaced well apart along the curve.

Red letters were painted above each of the vestibules, reading, "Welcome to Psi Cassiopeia II." The lettering had clearly been done by hand, and the letters were shaped a bit oddly.

That was to his left; to his right the gravel pavement ran for perhaps a hundred feet, and then gave way to white concrete.

The broad strip of gravel ran the full length of the building, however, and in fact continued on past each end of the arc; it appeared to Pel that it formed a full circle, around the circular concrete.

And on the concrete—

There were three of them.

The smallest and farthest away, almost directly across the circle from them, was about the size of a tractor-trailer combination, back on Pel's Earth; it had once been painted white, with red trim, but the paint had worn away in several places, exposing dull gray metal. A small bubble cockpit protruded from the top; two huge, swept-back fins adorned the sides. It rested on three legs; a hatch in its belly was open, and a ladder descended from the hatch to the pavement. Its lines were graceful, but it had obviously seen better days.

Flash Gordon, twenty years after, Pel thought.

He had never seen the *Ruthless*; had it looked something like that?

The largest, its bullet-shaped nose near the middle of the circle, was gigantic—the size of an ocean liner, perhaps, its tail assembly projecting well out over the gravel ring on the far side. It was also squat and ugly, its gray paint obviously several layers thick; its surface was dented here and there. Three glass-and-steel observation blisters, reminding Pel of the gun turrets of a B-17, protruded near the nose. There were no fins or foils or trim, simply the immense cylinder, rounded at one end, flaring slightly at the other. Two support struts kept the thing from rolling over on its side in one direction; Pel assumed there were similar struts on the opposite side. He could see the outlines of three hatches in the behemoth's side, any one of them large enough for the smallest ship to fit through sideways, but all three were closed.

A freighter, probably, Pel guessed.

They were headed toward the third and closest spaceship—the three craft had to be spaceships, Pel mused. This one was midway between the others in size, and apparently newer, with green and gold paint that had not yet begun to flake or peel. The stern was adorned with a profusion of gracefully swept-back fins. A door in the side was open, and a boarding stair was in place.

"The others are already aboard," someone said.

It suddenly struck Pel that they were being herded aboard a spaceship—they were going to leave Psi Cassiopeia Two.

"Hey," he said, "we're leaving?"

Captain Cahn heard him, and turned to reply, "Yes, Mr. Brown—they're giving us a ride back to Base One, just as we wanted. Nine days, I'm told, and we should be back there, ready to send you and your family home to, uh . . . to Earth."

"But I thought . . . didn't your telepath Thorpe say there weren't any ships available, when we were out on the desert?"

Cahn nodded. "They *weren't* available—that freighter just got in this morning; they couldn't find the owner of that little one back there, and the liner here was just down, hadn't cleared quarantine yet. And none of these are Imperial property, you know; we've had to invoke martial law to get the use of the liner. Don't worry, Mr. Brown, we're doing the best we can to get you home just as fast as possible."

"But we haven't *seen* anything here yet!"

Someone snorted; someone else chuckled.

"Believe me, Mr. Brown," Cahn answered, amused, "you've seen everything worth seeing on *this* planet!"

Pel didn't argue; for one thing, Nancy was glaring at him. It was quite obvious that she wanted him to shut up and not do anything that might delay their return home, and he belatedly realized that *he* didn't want himself to do anything that might delay their return home, either.

Still, it seemed wrong, somehow, to visit another planet, an outpost of the vast Galactic Empire, and see nothing but a few hundred miles of desert and the spaceport waiting rooms.

This was another *planet*, after all, thousands of miles across, big enough for whole oceans and continents, entire new civilizations—and all he'd seen was a little of one town.

Maybe rushing home as quickly as possible wasn't all that necessary . . .

He cut his chain of thought right there.

Getting home as fast as possible *was* necessary. He had responsibilities there, Silly Cat not the least of them. He had a home and a business and friends and family, all of whom would be wondering what had become of him.

And while he might be in the Galactic Empire, he didn't have so much as a toothbrush with him.

The possibility of coming back here later, properly prepared, occurred to him. It was an idea, certainly.

If Earth had anything the Galactic Empire wanted, then they could probably open a healthy tourist trade; who wouldn't want to visit an entire new universe, with strange new worlds, different air and light and gravity—and where everybody spoke English?

The business prospects in that began to percolate through his mind. That was certainly full of marketing possibilities, and marketing was what he did, after all.

But on the other hand, the Empire didn't seem to be a particularly friendly place, and seemed to be unhappy about the very existence of other universes. It might well be that they wouldn't want tourists.

And Earth might not, in fact, have anything they wanted—would a culture with interstellar travel and the resources of a galaxy be interested in a single planet's output?

Looking around, Pel thought that they just might, at that. Psi Cassiopeia Two was a backwater, admittedly, but it seemed to him that what he'd seen of the Empire and its works wasn't all that impressive, in many ways. They did have antigravity, which was amazing and wonderful and useful and all that, and they had blasters, which were effective enough, but they seemed to be rather backward in their use of metals, and he hadn't seen anything using any sort of electronics anywhere—no digital clocks, no LED readouts anywhere, certainly no computers. No one had even mentioned television.

There were innumerable possibilities, not just in tourism, but in trade of all sorts.

Where Shadow's universe fit into this he wasn't sure. And of course, he had no idea what the difficulties of inter-universal travel might be; so far, it had seemed simple enough, stepping through portals, but those had been magical portals, opened from Shadow's realm—the technologically created space warps the Empire used might not be so easy.

Scientifically created space warps, he corrected himself—the Empire didn't seem to like the word "technology" much, and preferred to call it "science."

Had the Empire considered the possibility of trade?

Oh, they must have, he told himself. How could they not? Just because nobody had mentioned it to him, because everything anyone had said so far was about diplomatic or military interactions, that didn't mean that no one had thought about trade.

Somebody must have thought of it. Surely, once the preliminaries of opening relations and dealing with Shadow were done, the Empire didn't intend to just shut itself off from Earth again!

He stumbled slightly, the toe of his shoe catching in an uneven patch of gravel, and brought himself back to the present reality. Right now, nobody was talking about doing business between universes, because right now they all needed to get back to Base One and pick up where they had left off, in coping with Shadow and its creatures.

Raven probably wasn't concerned with trade possibilities at all—he just wanted Stormcrack Keep back. Captain Cahn was just doing what he was told to do by his superiors, and not worrying about long-term consequences.

And there wasn't really much point in his worrying about them, either, he decided. He squeezed Rachel's hand, and on a sudden whim, leaned over and kissed Nancy on the cheek.

They stepped up from the gravel to the concrete pad and marched on toward the ship. Pel could see her name now, painted on the side near the nose, in gleaming gold letters—*Emerald Princess*.

Captain Cahn stepped to one side at the foot of the steps, and started counting noses; Raven's boots clanged loudly on the metal steps as he led the way up, into the waiting vessel.

The narrow steps created a slight bottleneck, and the Browns had to wait their turns for a few seconds while Stoddard and Valadrakul and the rest sorted themselves out.

"Nine days," Nancy whispered, leaning over close so Rachel wouldn't hear. "The cat will be frantic!"

"*Everyone* will be frantic," Pel whispered back. "And unless these guys prove they're real, somehow, no one's going to believe our explanations."

"Well, we'll just say we were kidnapped by a UFO," Nancy said. "It's almost the truth, isn't it?"

Pel started to protest; this was real life, not the absurd fantasies of little men with big heads who went around mutilating cattle. Then he stopped, before a word had escaped him.

After all, if one other universe was trying to contact Earth and botching it, why couldn't there have been dozens, over the years? What if all those flying saucer stories were true?

Now *that* was a terrifying thought. Pel had grown up with science fiction and fantasy, in books and in movies and on TV, and while he enjoyed the stuff immensely, he'd always been very clear on where the line was between fantasy and reality.

Flying saucers and UFO abductions and psychics and all the rest of the material found in tabloid headlines he had always put on the "fantasy" side—and he'd considered them bad fantasy, at that.

But here he was, boarding a spaceship, and that woman, Prossie Thorpe, was a telepath—a psychic, in other words. He'd been abducted from Earth, after a fashion, and had found himself in a world of little men—though Grummetty's appearance in his basement had hardly been the stereotypical close encounter of the third kind. Grummetty had seemed thoroughly down to earth, despite his impossible size.

The stairway was clear, and Captain Cahn was waving them forward; Nancy went first, leading Rachel by the hand. Pel brought up the rear, with a steadying hand on Rachel's back.

As they climbed toward the warmly lit doorway into the ship, Pel considered UFOs and the Galactic Empire.

This ship made *sense*, though. The people had an *explanation* for what was happening—the whole thing about Shadow and space warps and telepaths all fit together. The space creatures in the UFO stories never made sense, flying around conducting mysterious experiments with no rhyme or reason to them, kidnapping people at random.

But on the other hand, would the *Emerald Princess* and all the rest make any sense to, say, an Australian aborigine?

Pel didn't know anything about Australian aborigines, but he suspected that it wouldn't.

Then he was at the door, being helped in by Susan Nguyen, of all people; she was wearing an unfamiliar outfit, a white blouse and maroon wool skirt combination cut oddly.

The door, or hatch, or whatever it was opened into a small chamber, presumably an air lock, painted in a friendly mustard color; a wine-colored drapery on one side incompletely hid a bank of gadgetry of some sort, probably the pressure controls.

The inner door was open; he stepped through into a room, or cabin, or compartment, whatever the correct term was, about the size and shape of a one-car garage. Amy Jewell, in white and maroon like her attorney, was standing there, welcoming people aboard; behind her was Spaceman Peabody, his arm in a cast and sling, the rest of him in one of the purple uniforms the guards had worn, rather than his own ruined outfit. Grummetty and Alella were perched atop a cabinet bolted to one wall—their clothes were the same, but somewhat cleaner.

A loud clang interrupted Pel before he could say more than a quick general hello; the last arrival, Captain Cahn, was aboard, and had just slammed the outer air-lock door shut.

Now he was in the lounge, closing and locking the inner door as well.

Pel had looked first at the people, but now he considered the chamber in which he found himself.

The walls were covered in rich yellow wallpaper, flocked in a stylized floral design; the floor was covered in lush plum-colored carpet. The several doors leading elsewhere were dark polished wood, set with round, brass-rimmed windows. Plum-upholstered seating was bolted to the floor—two round things, like circular sofas, that reminded Pel of an old-fashioned hotel lobby. Light came from lantern-like brass fixtures on every wall. The overall impression, he decided, was of a turn-of-the-century ocean liner.

The *Titanic*, for example.

As Pel greeted the others he wished he hadn't thought of that particular comparison.

CHAPTER 17

As had been obvious from the first glance at its interior, *Emerald Princess* was a luxury vessel; that it had stopped at Psi Cassiopeia Two was, Amy later learned, merely a lucky chance. Psi Cass the Deuce, as it was known, happened to lie along the route between Omicron Cygnus Three, better known as Avalon, and Alpha Ophiuchus Three, better known as Ishmael. Noticing that fact on the charts, the party of Avalonian tourists who had chartered *Emerald Princess*, bored by the long flight, had decided to stop in at Psi Cass, unaware that the planet was home to nothing more interesting than a small and rather dismal mining colony.

Amy hadn't noticed any mines, but she was assured that Psi Cass the Deuce was a mining colony.

From the point of view of the Avalonians their timing had been absolutely abominable. Pleas of injustice, threats of punitive action, and attempted bribery were all insufficient to prevent Captain Cahn and the local governor from using their authority, as agents of the Empire, to seize the ship temporarily, in order to transport the crew of *Ruthless*, along with people from two other universes, to Base One with all possible haste.

A suggestion that the freighter, or the battered little scout, be used instead was rejected; the freighter had no room for passengers and was too slow, and the scout was simply too small for the entire group.

The *Princess* was perfect.

Getting the entire group safely from Psi Cass the Deuce to Base One was obviously a matter of importance. If there had been any doubt of that, orders authorizing the seizure had come through, by way of Registered Telepath Thorpe, even before Captain Cahn had added his voice to the governor's in suggesting it.

That the governor had hesitated when Prossie relayed orders, and had only paid heed when Cahn showed up and started talking, was not mentioned in Amy's hearing.

Nor did anyone mention that the more desperate charter passengers had tried to throw doubt on Thorpe's reliability and trustworthiness. Once convinced, however, the governor had been unyielding, and when word reached the captain he was seriously offended. While it might be true that Thorpe, being a telepath, was a damnable mutant bitch, as one man had called her, she was *his* damnable mutant bitch, and no mere civilians were going to impugn her honesty and get away with it.

Cahn had made no explicit threats, but he did calmly point out that interfering with a ranking Imperial military officer in the performance of assigned duties could draw the death penalty. This remark was passed aboard by the same Town guards who had first informed Captain Gifford that his ship was being claimed by the Empire.

That ended the debate, and the frustrated passengers and crew of *Emerald Princess* had mostly huddled in the control room or the aft salon, complaining bitterly to each other, while the first batch of refugees, as they were now called, came aboard and sorted themselves out in the forward lounge.

This was the party that had been put aboard the first aircar, under the command of the limping but still mobile Lieutenant Alster Drummond; his second in command was Spaceman James Peabody, with his chewed-up arm. Prossie Thorpe was undamaged, and they had in tow Susan, Elani, Grummetty, and Alella, in addition to Amy.

This group, led by an armed and wary Lieutenant Drummond, came aboard while the later groups were still eating. They were greeted in the forward lounge by Captain Gifford and his chief steward.

Both sides seemed nervous, as if expecting a nasty confrontation; the sight of Drummond's hand on the butt of his blaster didn't help any. Blasters were not subtle little things, either; nobody would fail to notice the hardware.

Peabody, with his injured arm, made no move toward his own weapon. Prossie Thorpe, as a Special, carried no sidearm. Elani was carrying the two little people, who were both now seriously ill, and none of that threesome was very clear on just what was going on; they were also unarmed.

Still, that blaster was there, ready to draw.

And Amy noticed not just Drummond's weapon, but also that Susan's hand had strayed into her big black purse, as if fiddling with something; they were both stepping out of the air lock into the lounge before Amy realized what Susan was doing.

Susan had a gun of her own in that handbag, the pistol she'd fired at the monsters back in Raven's place—Raven's world, though Amy really didn't like thinking in terms of multiple worlds.

Did that mean Susan was ready to get into a firefight with these people? Amy couldn't really imagine that; she was glad that she had left her own gun safely at home. Using it to defend her house against Captain Cahn's men would have been one thing, and she thought she might have done that, but getting into a battle here, with all these people who presumably knew far more than she did about what was going on—no. No way.

But Susan was Susan; if she wanted to have her gun ready, Amy wasn't going to try to stop her.

And maybe she was right.

The spaceship's captain was eyeing his unwanted guests cautiously, very much aware of Lieutenant Drummond's blaster, but probably with no idea at all that Susan was armed.

For a moment they all stood there, not speaking.

Oddly, what finally broke the silence and settled the situation peacefully was Amy—to be precise, her appearance. When the chief steward finally looked past the tall, threatening blond man in the rumpled, worn, and bloodstained Imperial uniform and saw the deep, half-cleaned scratches on Amy's forehead and tattered condition of her flowered dress, his protective instincts took over. Here was a female in distress, and one who was to be a passenger aboard his ship, at that.

"Come in, my dear," he said, beckoning, "and we'll get you fixed up and find you something to wear!"

Susan made a small, wordless noise, and tugged at the jacket of her suit. Her hand was no longer in her purse, and Amy felt a definite relief upon seeing that.

"You, too," the steward said.

"If that's all right," the captain said, glaring at Drummond.

"Absolutely," Drummond said, smiling. "Excellent idea. We're going to be stuck with each other for a while; I don't suppose anyone's going to like it, but there's no reason we can't make it as comfortable as possible."

The captain thawed slightly.

"I'm not going to interfere with the way you run your ship, Captain," Drummond continued, "and I'm sure Captain Cahn won't, either, just so long as you get us all to Base One as quickly as possible."

Captain Gifford nodded. "Yes, sir," he said.

■

Pel and most of the others were blithely unaware of any prior conflict as they trickled in through the air lock. It didn't even occur to Pel to wonder whose ship he was on, or where the crew was, until someone else brought the subject up.

The earlier arrivals, once aboard and with Drummond's authority accepted, had sorted out the accommodations. Despite the complaints, the refugees posed no serious hardship to anyone. In fact, the ship wasn't even crowded; all the original complement had to do was double up, so that the unmarried passengers were two to a stateroom instead of one, and that provided enough space to fit the twenty-two refugees in at three or four to a room. Crew quarters, far less luxurious to begin with, were not disturbed at all.

The Browns were given a cabin for the three of them, with a double bed for Pel and Nancy and a folding cot for Rachel.

Susan, Amy, Elani, and Prossie, the four unmarried women in the group, took the largest cabin aboard—a suite, actually, with a tiny sitting room and miniscule bedroom, one of two suites aboard the vessel.

Raven, Stoddard, and Drummond were grouped together, as were Godwin, Ted, and Valadrakul. Peabody, Lampert, and Squire Donald were assigned to a single room. The more observant noticed that this put at least one Imperial in each group of men—

either one lieutenant or two spacemen—but nobody bothered to comment on the fact.

The other suite, opposite the one the unmarried women shared, went to Captain Cahn, who claimed the bedroom for himself, and left Smith, Soorn, and Mervyn occupying the sitting room.

The little people, Grummetty and Alella, were given an unused storage locker; since the ship's furnishings weren't suited to them, nobody saw any point in giving them a stateroom. They made no objection; the locker suited them just fine.

Besides, they were really too sick by then to care very much.

While these assignments were being made up forward, the twenty original passengers divided themselves into pairs for the ten remaining staterooms. Since that happened to work out to a nice even two to a room, there were no serious accusations of added unfairness or injustice.

By the time these arrangements were settled and explained Pel was thoroughly bored with the whole affair. He had begun to tune out the chatter and wonder how much time this group would waste before getting under way.

Nine days to Base One, they said, and there were bound to be delays there, as well—the Galactic Empire seemed to be full of delays. They did some things quickly and well—Prossie had made the original telepathic contact with Town within minutes—but others they seemed to dawdle on. It had taken forever, it seemed, to actually pick everyone up.

He probably wouldn't be home for another two weeks, at this rate. He was still worried about Silly Cat. He was pretty sure he had left the lid up on the upstairs toilet, but the poor beast might well starve before Pel and Nancy and Rachel got home to feed him.

And God only knew what would become of Pel's business after more than a week of missed appointments. He had a report to write up for that computer dealer in Rockville, explaining why their radio ads weren't working—that wasn't getting done while he was here, instead of home.

"Mr. Brown," a steward said, startling him out of his gloomy thoughts.

"Yes?" Pel turned and found himself facing a young man in a white jacket and dark pants, with his crewcut and bristling mustache looking oddly mismatched.

"This way." The steward gestured toward a brightly lit passageway.

"To where?"

"Your cabin, sir."

"Oh," Pel replied, feeling foolish. He brushed Nancy's arm to make sure she was paying attention, then followed the young crewman. Nancy and Rachel came close on his heels.

Their cabin was the fourth door on the left; it was moderate in size, perhaps ten feet square, with its own miniature bathroom and a more generous closet, all of it decorated in shades of blue. A square of royal-blue velvet drapery hung above the bed.

The steward bowed and left, closing the door gently.

While Nancy and Rachel were examining the closet, Pel kneeled on the bed and pulled the curtain aside, revealing, as he had expected, a porthole.

At least, it looked like a porthole, but then he reconsidered. Perhaps it was a backlit painting on glass.

He shifted his angle of view slightly, and decided no, it was definitely a real window.

Beyond the porthole the sky was black and full of stars; the ship had taken off.

Pel had felt no jarring, no acceleration, but with antigravity that didn't seem to mean much. He stopped to listen, and could hear a faint, steady, high-pitched hum, but nothing like the roar of jet engines or rockets.

But then, with antigravity drive, why would you need rockets?

And there wasn't any weightlessness, but presumably, if the Empire had antigravity, they could also provide artificial gravity.

That took some of the fun out of a trip among the stars.

Then he paused in his chain of thought. *Were* those stars? Something looked wrong. They looked fake, somehow.

Was this a video screen, rather than a real porthole, perhaps? Or was it a glass painting after all, done with some unfamiliar technique?

If it was video, it was some kind he'd never seen before, something that made the best HDTV stuff he'd seen look primitive. It was *not* video. And he couldn't imagine any technique that would give a painting such a flawless illusion of depth. Was it a hologram, perhaps?

No, it had to be a real porthole. But then, what was it that looked wrong? He stared out at the star-spattered darkness for a moment, and finally figured it out.

The stars weren't twinkling. They burned as sharp and clear as tiny headlights, out there in the emptiness.

No air, he realized. There was no atmosphere blocking his view.

He had never really thought of stars on a clear night as "twinkling," despite the popular descriptions—not the way Christmas lights twinkled, or those spinning mirror balls. Stars didn't blink on and off, or anything even remotely similar to blinking.

He had to admit, however, that in comparison with the steady, sharp brilliance he saw now, stars back on Earth were dim, fidgety things. The intense points of light beyond the port looked quite unstarlike in their stability, their unchanging blaze.

Tearing his gaze away, he turned his attention back to the others. Nancy was bent over, bouncing her hands, stiff-armed, on the cot's mattress to show Rachel that the cot was sturdy enough to hold her.

"We're moving," Pel said.

Nancy looked up, startled; first she looked at Pel's face, and then past him at the porthole.

"Oh," she said.

"You stay here," Pel said. "I'm going back to the lounge."

Nancy nodded.

■

The stars of the Galactic Empire, Raven noted, did not shine as the stars of home, but instead with a clear, hard light that was not particularly pleasant to look upon. He closed the little drapery.

A ship that sailed above the sky, and yet they disdained all talk of magic. Incomprehensible, these Imperials. The reports he had received had never fully conveyed their strangeness.

Consider, he thought to himself, that their lord governor's palace, just departed, was built of bare stone, ugly and harsh—not even a fine stone like marble, nor any polished thing, but that unpleasant substance they called "concrete." Consider that it was, insofar as he had seen, furnished in the rudest fashion, almost unadorned, and lit everywhere in a harsh and discomforting manner.

And then compare this vessel upon which they now rode, this mere transport, that by rights might be cramped and malodorous, bare of all luxuries, as had been every ship Raven had heretofore sailed upon.

Instead, though the chambers were small, it was rich in comforts, with the finest of fabrics and woods, with polished brasses and the warm glow of artificial fires. There was no rocking or sway, no stench; the ceilings rose well clear of even Stoddard's head. The beds were fine and soft.

What sort of people were these, who made their vehicles finer than the homes of their lords?

It was wisely said that men devote the most thoughts to that which is to them most important and lavish the most care upon that they value most highly. Did then the Imperials place the transport of goods more highly than the administration of their colonies? An it were so, it spoke ill of them.

Or might it be perhaps that attention was paid to such craft as this because the distances in this realm were so great that more time was spent upon the journey than at the end thereof? This passage was to be nine days, which was no great time—but was this place just departed the most far-flung of the Imperial possessions?

It was all a mystery; indeed, the minds of all those around him, save his own handful of faithful allies, were as inscrutable as cats. Further, worrying at such a knot did nothing to aid him in all that mattered, to wit, the defeat of Shadow and the liberation of Stormcrack Keep.

He would, he swore, worry it no more. He flung himself upon the bed and closed his eyes, resolved to rest whilst the opportunity availed itself.

■

Pel made his way back up the passageway, moving carefully—
somehow, the knowledge that the ship was under way made the
floor seem less steady than it had a few moments earlier.

He reached the lounge without incident. Amy and Susan were
there, on one of the sofas, and Smith was leaning against a wall
nearby, chatting with them—and trying to pick Amy up, Pel decided. A white-jacketed, brown-haired man Pel didn't recognize
was standing quietly in one corner, observing.

Maybe he had designs on Susan, Pel mused, and was waiting
for Smith and Amy to leave. He was presumably a crewman—
another steward, perhaps.

Pel wandered in his direction, and the steward, or whatever
he was, spotted his approach and quirked his eyebrows upward
questioningly.

"Hi," Pel said.

"Hello," the other replied. "Was there something you wanted,
sir?"

"I was wondering about our departure." He deliberately
phrased this question with a certain ambiguity.

"It went quite smoothly, sir—all things considered. Captain
Gifford piloted the ship himself."

Pel nodded.

"Are there any, um . . . viewports?"

"Yes, sir, of course—isn't there a port in your stateroom?"

Pel admitted there was. "But what I wanted," he explained,
"was to get a look back at the planet."

The steward pursed his lips thoughtfully, then pulled a gold
pocket watch from his jacket and glanced at it.

"Come with me, sir," he said, as he put the watch away.

Pel followed as the steward led the way aft, explaining, "You
won't be able to see much, sir; that military officer, Captain Cahn,
has insisted on maximum acceleration, so we've already come a
long way."

Pel nodded. He wasn't all that interested in seeing the
close-up details, but he did want a look at the planet. He had never
seen a planet from space.

He had never *been* in space before.

He was now, though. He supposed he should be impressed, or

awed, or something, but he wasn't. Somehow, the mere fact that he was on a real starship, flying through outer space, didn't seem all that mind-boggling anymore.

Maybe, he thought wryly, he was all boggled out. The shock at Grummetty's appearance, at Raven, at the crew of the *Ruthless*, at stepping through into Raven's world, at the attack of the monsters, at finding himself on some strange planet he'd never heard of—he was having real trouble being boggled anymore.

The steward opened a door, and the two of them stepped into the aft salon.

Though still compact, it was a good deal more elaborate than the forward lounge; the crystal chandelier was the most obvious exemplar. The room was decorated in several shades of green, with gold and silver trim, and was inhabited by perhaps a dozen people, most of whom Pel did not recognize.

Before Pel had had a chance to look at any of the details, however, a familiar voice cried, "Ah, two more figments of my imagination!"

"Ted?" Pel turned, and saw his lawyer grinning maniacally at him.

"This one," Ted announced to everyone present, "is a simulacrum of a client of mine, one Pellinore Brown, free-lance marketing consultant. It was he who supposedly got me involved in all this."

Pel glanced at the steward, who discreetly shrugged.

"He's been trying to tell us," an elegant redhead in a green evening gown explained, "that we're all just part of a dream he's having. I haven't decided if he's serious or not, and if he *is* serious, I haven't decided if he's crazy or just confused."

"Ted," Pel said, "what are you talking about?"

Ted leaned forward, still grinning. "I'm *talking*," he said, "about this interminable, boring, complicated dream I'm having. I've never had one quite like this before—at least, not that I can remember. This one just seems to go on and on."

"Have you been drinking?" Pel asked, uneasily.

"I don't know," Ted replied, "have I? I really don't remember just *when* I went to sleep. Maybe I *was* drinking. That might have something to do with it."

"No," Pel said, "I meant here, now."

"In the dream? No, I haven't been dreaming about booze, o figment of mine. Odd thing to ask—are you a subconscious worry that I might wind up an alcoholic, maybe? I've heard that alcoholics dream about booze, but as far as I recall, I've never done that. Maybe I've been suppressing it, eh? Maybe you're some little bit of my mind trying to break through a wall of denial and suppression, to warn me off the sauce before it's too late. But hell, figment, it's nowhere near that late, is it?"

"Ted, I'm not a figment. You're not dreaming. This is real." Pel hesitated, then added, "At least, I think it is."

"Well, if you're not a figment, what are you doing in my dream?" He smiled a humorless, challenging smile. "Are you a telepath, Brown? Sending psychic messages to me while I sleep? Is that why there are telepaths in this dream? I never thought about telepathy much before, that I can recall. So are you sending this to me?"

Pel glanced uneasily about; everyone else in the room, save the steward and the bartender at the far end, was staring at the two of them. The steward was carefully not looking anywhere; the bartender was polishing glasses.

"No, Ted," Pel said, "this is *real*. You are *not* dreaming. I swear you aren't. You're making a fool of yourself."

Ted shook his head vigorously and held up his hands as if pushing the very thought away.

"No, no, Pel," he said, "or figment, or alter ego, or whatever the hell you really are. This *is* a dream. It has to be."

Desperately, Pel said, "*No*, Ted! I know it's all strange, but it's *real!*"

"Nope," Ted replied. "Can't be. You think I don't know a dream when I see it? A bunch of bad swipes from Tolkien and Buck Rogers, all twisted around? Gotta be a dream."

"It *isn't*, Ted . . ."

"Pel, look," Ted interrupted, "I'm open-minded and all that, and if a spaceship landed on the White House lawn tomorrow I'd accept that—though I'd be amazed as hell, believe me. But this stuff is all too much. I mean, you hire me to bail a bunch of spacemen out on behalf of some guy out of Shakespeare by way of

Brooklyn, and then we all eat pizza together and walk through your basement wall into somebody's back yard in Appalachia, except there's a castle on the next ridge, and then a bunch of El Greco monsters jump out at us and chase us through the wall into a bleached-out desert where the horizon's too close so it looks like a cheap Hollywood set, and we sit around for a few minutes except that dream time can stretch all out of shape so it seems like hours, and we get picked up by a flying Oldsmobile . . ."

"Buick," Pel corrected him. "I thought it looked more like a Buick."

"No," Ted said, shaking his head. "*You* went in the Buick. I was in the other one, the little one. But you're right, it wasn't much like an Oldsmobile. Reminded me a little of this primer-black Camaro my nephew has, actually."

"Ted . . ."

"*Anyway.* So I fly off in this car with the Shakespearean guy and the spaceship captain and a driver who thinks he's CIA, and halfway there the captain starts getting psychic flashes or something and talking to the air and telling us stuff, and none of it makes any sense, so then we land at what looks like the Pittsburgh Greyhound station and eat a dinner that all tastes like tofu, and then we get aboard a spaceship that looks like the Emerald City turned sideways on the outside, and like a French whorehouse inside, and here we are."

"That's right, here we . . ." Pel began, soothingly.

Ted paid no attention to Pel's interruption; he demanded, "And you're trying to tell me all this crap is *real?*"

"*Yes*, damn it!" Pel glared at Ted. "Yes, it's real, and I'm telling you that!"

Ted stared back, his expression merely mild surprise—no anger, no doubt at all.

"But, figment," he said, "it's *silly.*"

"*Life* is silly, Ted," Pel told him. "I mean, think about it—isn't it all a bit ridiculous? But it's real. And all this is real, too."

Ted simply grinned foolishly at him.

"Sir," the steward suggested quietly, "if you want to see Psi Cassiopeia Two . . ."

"Right," Pel said, turning away from the silent Ted. "Lead the way."

The steward led the way to the curved rear wall, where a window, perhaps two feet high and six feet wide, was centered.

This gave a view looking back over the tail assembly; Pel stretched up, peering out the topmost part of the glass, trying to see the planet. The tail of the ship was apparently hiding it.

All he could see was stars.

And the stars were mostly various shades of orange; they covered a range from pale yellow to deep red. Pel supposed the glass was tinted, though the green paint on the ship's tail looked its natural color.

"Where is it?" he asked.

The steward pointed. "Right there," he said, "that big faint one."

"Big one?" Pel followed the pointing finger, and found a pale orange dot of light, virtually indistinguishable from all the others, save that it seemed marginally larger and not very bright.

It did have one odd feature, he realized after staring for a few seconds. It was shrinking, while all the other stars remained constant.

"I didn't realize we'd come so far," he said at last.

"Oh, yes, sir," the steward said, beaming modestly. "*Emerald Princess* is a very fast ship."

"How fast?" Pel asked, looking away from the window. "Nine days to Base One—how fast is that?"

"Oh, our top speed is around point three."

"Of C?"

"No, sir—I don't know that term. I mean, point three light-years per hour."

Pel turned to stare at him. "Light-years per hour? It's faster than light?"

The steward smiled at him, almost smirking. "Well, of *course* it is, sir," he said. "How else is interstellar travel possible?"

"You don't use space warps or something like that?" Pel asked.

The steward looked puzzled. "No, sir," he said.

Pel turned back to the glass. "Is that . . . the color out there . . ."

The steward glanced at the window. "Yes, sir, the red shift is quite visible now, isn't it? You'll see a bit more of that, but then in a little while, when we pass the speed of light, you won't be able to see anything at all looking out in this direction."

"So what happens then, do we pop into hyperspace or something?"

"Hyperspace?"

Pel turned, exasperated. "Look, *I* don't know your terminology! I mean, you can't go faster than light in normal space, right?"

"You can't?" The steward looked baffled. "Why not? What other kind of space is there?"

"*I* don't know," Pel snarled. His grasp of the theory of relativity was sufficiently weak that he had no intention of trying to explain it to someone—and most particularly, someone who worked on a spaceship and ought to *know* all that stuff. He glanced out the window again, and an unpleasant thought struck him.

Maybe this wasn't normal space, as he understood the term. It certainly wasn't *his* space.

Maybe this universe had entirely different rules.

Maybe here, everything he knew was wrong. Everything he had learned in a lifetime of dealing with his own world was open to question.

He had been thinking of his situation in terms of having stumbled into a science fiction story of some sort—something with spaceships and ray guns and monsters, but still grounded in logic and common sense. But if the laws of physics were different, then *anything* might be possible.

It wasn't science fiction at all, it was fantasy. He might as well be in the twilight zone.

Or in a dream.

He backed away, then turned, all his confusion and frustration boiling up in him at once.

He found the elegant redhead standing there waiting for him. "Mr. Brown, is it?" she asked.

"Excuse me," he said, pushing past her. Right now he did not want to talk to some stranger from another universe, no matter what she looked like.

She turned to stare, and the other strangers made way for him as he stamped across the room to Ted.

Ted, bemused, watched him come.

Pel grabbed the lawyer by his lapels.

"Listen," he said, "what would it take to convince you that this is real, and not a dream? Would a punch in the nose do it? I mean, if it hurt, just like real life?"

Ted considered this quite seriously. He looked around the room, at the oddly but splendidly dressed passengers, at the dimming orange stars beyond the window, at the crystal chandelier and the brass railings.

"I don't think so," he said. "It'd probably just mean I fell out of bed. It might wake me up, though."

Pel nodded.

"Let's see," he said, as he swung.

The steward was almost in time to stop him, and his restraining arm, flung up in front of Pel's, slowed the impact; Ted staggered. His nose was red and starting to bleed, but he didn't fall, and nothing broke. He made no protest, no defense, and no counterattack. After the blow had landed he simply stood, staring blankly at Pel.

"*Sir,*" the steward began, shocked.

"Oh, shut up," Pel replied, as he stalked off toward his cabin.

CHAPTER 18

By the time they were two days out from Psi Cassiopeia Two, Pel understood why the original complement aboard the *Princess* had wanted to land there in the first place.

Space travel was *boring*.

It was very nearly as boring as, though far more comfortable than, sitting out in the desert waiting for the aircar to come back.

Obviously, anything that broke the monotony would be welcome, even if it was just a stopover somewhere like Town—which Pel, angrily remembering Ted's words, had to admit probably did resemble the Pittsburgh bus station more than it did anything else.

So much for the romance and adventure of being in another universe.

The fact that none of them had so much as a toothbrush in the way of supplies didn't help any. Having to either wear the same clothes constantly or borrow ill-fitting substitutes from condescending strangers was a constant irritation for them all; Amy and Susan had wound up with spare stewardess uniforms, but there hadn't been enough of those to go around even for the women, so the crew and the original passengers had made donations to the poor, pitiful refugees.

"Condescending" was the politest word Pel could apply to their attitude. He would have paid his entire fortune for a well-packed suitcase—preferably one with a couple of paperbacks in it. A nice trashy novel would have been just right for passing the time.

Pel had initially assumed that the ship would have some sort of library, or a theater of some sort—just a VCR hooked to a TV would have been wonderful. This assumption had not panned out; some of the paying passengers had brought their own books, but there was no library, and none of the people native to this universe seemed to understand what he was talking about when he mentioned "TV," or "video," or "VCR."

Movies they understood, films, motion pictures—though Pel had the impression that they only knew silents, that the Empire hadn't yet developed talkies. In any case, there weren't any films on board.

And books were too bulky. Keeping a good selection would have been, a steward told him, completely impractical; far better to let the passengers bring their own and swap.

None of the passengers seemed interested in simply *loaning* books to the refugees, and of course, the refugees had nothing to offer in trade.

This was not to say that there was nothing at all on board for entertainment; on the contrary, the *Princess* was, the stewards assured him, fully equipped in that regard. They carried a plentiful supply of playing cards, poker chips, backgammon boards, dice, and other gaming devices.

Pel was not quite ready to resort to such mundane pastimes—for one thing, he had no money with him, which really made poker and other gambling games rather pointless. He had never much liked backgammon, never even learned craps.

There were other card games, and he knew he would probably resort to them shortly, but for now he was still hoping to find something more exotic. He didn't want to be like those people who go to Europe and eat at McDonald's; he wanted to sample the local culture.

Unfortunately, the local culture was not cooperating. The native passengers, after the incident in the aft salon, avoided him even more than they avoided the other refugees. The crew spoke to him, but kept relations strictly businesslike and formal.

Nancy and Rachel had found something to occupy *their* time—caring for the two little people, who were growing weaker and weaker with no visible cause for their illness. The two of them were in constant pain now, and unable to move, and Nancy had taken it upon herself to stay with them and tend them as best she could, feeding them thin soup and aspirin, sponging off the heavy perspiration that bathed them, and talking to them soothingly. Rachel was acting as her mother's messenger, running whatever errands needed to be run.

That was all very well, and in fact Pel was proud to see it, but there wasn't room or need for another person in the storage compartment the little people occupied. That left him unable to help out, and without the company of his wife and daughter.

The others all seemed to have found ways to stay busy, as well—except for Ted, and Pel was avoiding him.

There wasn't even anything to see out the ports; to the stern the stars had red-shifted into invisibility, while ahead they had blue-shifted into areas of the spectrum hazardous enough that the ports were kept closed.

This left him sufficiently desperate for entertainment to stand around asking stupid questions of the crew.

"How does antigravity work, anyway?" he said casually.

The navigator looked up from the periscope, annoyed. "What?" he asked.

Pel repeated his question.

"How the hell should I know?" the navigator snarled.

"Well, I just thought . . ." Pel began. "I mean, I don't know *anything* about it, not even schoolboy stuff; we don't have it where I come from."

The navigator returned to the eyepiece, but said, "It's simple enough. Matter absorbs gravitons, so that particles are drawn toward each other by the streams of gravitons flowing into them—that's gravity, right?"

Pel made a noise of agreement, but was in fact bewildered; that was not at *all* the explanation he remembered from high school physics.

But then, why should it be? This was another universe, with its own laws.

"Well, antigravity makes solid matter spit the gravitons back out again, that's all," the navigator explained patiently, never moving his eyes from the periscope. "So it counteracts gravity. And if we make it spit the gravitons out all in one direction, we can use it like a rocket, only of course it's far more powerful."

"Oh," Pel said.

It would appear, he thought, that gravity did not work here in anything like the way it did back home. No wonder *Ruthless* had dropped like a rock.

"How do you get matter to emit gravitons?" he asked.

The navigator let out an exasperated sigh and looked up from the lens. "You compress it until the space it occupies collapses, of course," he said. "You take a lump of uranium, or something else really massive, and run a vibratory current through it to destabilize it, and then you apply pressure."

Pel started to ask another question, then saw the navigator's expression and thought better of it. "Thanks," he said.

He started to turn away, and then something else occurred to him. "If we're traveling faster than light," he asked, "how can you see to navigate?"

"I'm not *seeing* anything," the navigator said, "I'm reading the gravity fields."

"Oh," Pel said.

The whole thing sounded crazy. That bit about making the space an object occupied collapse sounded a little like black hole theory, but the rest of the explanation didn't, and how would creating a miniature black hole result in antigravity? That didn't make any sense.

It was clear that he had come upon this other universe's version of quantum physics, and that he wasn't going to make sense of it any time soon. He wandered off, baffled.

The navigator had at least answered him with more than monosyllables, however, so he drifted back an hour or two later and hovered nearby, trying to think of something intelligent to ask.

He was still working on the phrasing of a question about telling one star from another when the spectra had shifted when the navigator said, "Shit."

This was almost the first time Pel had heard any citizen of the Galactic Empire use foul language. He blinked in surprise.

The navigator adjusted something and stared into the eyepiece, then repeated, somewhat louder, "Shit!"

"What is it?" Pel asked.

The navigator didn't answer; instead he turned and pushed

Pel aside as he reached for a button and pushed it hard. A bell chimed somewhere.

That done, the crewman looked at Pel as if only now discovering his presence.

"You'd better get to your cabin," he said, "and lock the door. And if you have any weapons, get them."

"Why?" Pel asked. "What is it?"

"I don't know," the navigator said, "not for sure, but we're slowing down. It looks like something's got a gravity beam on us."

"A gravity beam?" Pel was getting tired of feeling stupid and lost and asking dumb questions, but he couldn't help himself. "What's that mean?"

"It means someone's slowing us down and pulling us in."

Pel blinked. "It does?"

The navigator made a disgusted noise and pushed the button again. "Yes, it does," he said.

"How does that work, though?"

"Where the hell are they?" the navigator asked, not speaking to Pel.

"Who?"

"The captain. It works . . . well, I told you we spit out a stream of gravitons from our main drive, right?"

Pel nodded.

"Well, you can spot that beam pretty easily and track where it came from, and then if you fire a faster, more powerful beam back along the same line, it cancels out our main drive—and in fact . . ."

A buzzer sounded, and a distant, dull thump reverberated through the flooring beneath Pel's feet. He felt suddenly lighter; his gorge rose in his throat, and his ears hurt.

"*Damn!*" the crewman said. "In fact, it can blow out the drive completely, which it just did, and then we're just coasting until we can get it running again, and that gravity beam can reel us in like a fish on a line."

Pel started to say something, and almost choked; the crewman glanced up and asked, "Feeling light-headed?"

Pel nodded.

"With the drive blown we don't even have the full on-board

gravity," the man explained. "We're on emergency power. Most ships don't even have this sort of backup, but the *Princess* is top of the line—on an ordinary ship you'd be drifting a foot off the floor right about now. And those bastards would probably like that just fine; we'd be even more helpless."

"But why?" Pel asked, with his composure back but still utterly baffled, more confused than worried. "Who would want to do that?"

"Pirates," the navigator said.

And then the alarms went off, and an officer chased Pel out of the room.

■

Prossie had been asleep, afloat in the pleasant current of dreams, both her own and others she soaked up from her surroundings. She had picked up some wonderful imagery from somewhere nearby, from one of the non-telepaths aboard *Emerald Princess*, and had tangled it into the warm, comforting network of her own family. A faint touch of the pain and hurt and heat and worry from the forward storage locker had wormed its way into her sleeping thoughts, but so far it was just a little background noise, and had not turned the dreams into nightmares.

Then the alarm bell sounded, and she snapped awake, as much from the psychic shock of a score of other minds being startled as from the actual physical sound.

She felt the disciplined worry of the crew, the confusion of passengers, but the rule was "Don't snoop," so she didn't snoop. She called Captain Cahn for orders.

He didn't know what was going on, and latched onto her light contact.

"Find out," he told her.

She thought a question.

"Just find out," he replied. "No rules to get in the way until we know."

She dropped the contact and reached out elsewhere. She found Captain Gifford, found the navigator—

And woke up Carrie, back at Base One, with her mental shout. Captain Cahn heard it, too.

Then she stopped worrying about anybody else for the next few minutes, as she found her uniform and began carefully searching for anything else that would mark her for what she was—an Imperial telepath. She had to hide it all, or better still, destroy it; she had to remove all the evidence.

Because everybody knew what rebels and pirates and anyone else who feared the Empire did to telepaths. No outlaw could risk, even for a moment, having someone around who could relay their very thoughts to the Imperial military.

If the pirates reached *Emerald Princess* and spotted her for a telepath, killing her would be the first thing they did.

They wouldn't even take the time to rape her first.

■

Pel stood in the passageway, dazed, for several minutes, watching crewmen hurrying back and forth, most of them looking worried and determined and purposeful. A few looked angry, or frightened, or as dazed as Pel. He kept himself pressed flat against one wall, out of the way.

After a time it occurred to him that there were probably better places to be. The navigator had told him to go to his cabin; that sounded like a good idea.

Pirates—had the man been serious?

Something was obviously wrong, and the navigator certainly hadn't *sounded* as if he were joking, but pirates?

Space pirates?

That sounded so *silly*, like something out of a low-budget, straight-to-video movie, that Pel found it hard to believe it could be serious. *Pirates?*

Pirates were a childhood game, something out of kids' adventure stories or old films. They were an absurd anachronism, a word that brought an image of peg legs and parrots and that ridiculous accent. Captain Hook and Errol Flynn and "Arr, me buckos"—those were pirates.

Pel smiled uneasily as he began inching toward his cabin, still keeping his back to the wall and staying out of the way of oncoming traffic in either direction. Pirates?

Ted wouldn't believe in any pirates—but then, he didn't believe in *any* of this. Raven and the rest from that world probably wouldn't have any trouble with the concept, though, and Rachel might think it was exciting—or scary.

And he didn't know about the other Earth people, Nancy and Amy and Susan . . .

Susan.

Susan Nguyen.

Pel grimaced. She probably wouldn't think there was anything funny or unbelievable about pirates at all. Pel had no idea how she had gotten to the U.S.—she might even be native-born, really—but she was obviously Vietnamese by ancestry, and plenty of Vietnamese refugees knew firsthand that pirates weren't just something out of old adventure stories.

And Pel and his family were refugees now, like those boat people . . .

Suddenly Pel didn't see anything particularly amusing about the idea of space pirates anymore. He picked up his pace.

The cabin was empty, and he remembered belatedly that Nancy would still be tending to Grummetty and Alella. He turned back and headed that way.

At the door of the storage locker he found Rachel sitting against the bulkhead to one side, arms wrapped around her knees and her head down. She didn't stir when he approached.

That wasn't how she would react to the alarms, or to talk about pirates; Pel knew his daughter better than that.

"What's the matter?" he asked her.

She shook her head and didn't answer, didn't look up.

"Rachel?"

She refused to speak, refused to move.

The locked door opened and Nancy peered out. "Oh, Pel," she said, "it's you."

"Yeah," Pel said. "What's wrong?" He belatedly remembered why Nancy was there in the first place. "Are they worse?" he asked.

Nancy nodded. "Grummetty's dead," she said. "About ten minutes ago." Her voice was unsteady.

Pel felt his own throat drying and tightening at the news.

"Oh," he said helplessly, "I'm sorry." He paused for a second or two, out of respect for the little man, and then said, "Listen, the ship's in trouble." He couldn't bring himself to mention pirates, not yet; it still sounded stupid.

"I heard the bells," Nancy said. "What's wrong?"

"I don't know exactly," Pel said, "but the navigator said we're under some kind of attack—something that shuts down the antigravity."

"Is it Shadow?" Nancy asked. "Is it sending more of those creatures?"

Pel had not even thought of that; what if it *was* Shadow that was responsible, and not pirates?

"I don't know," he admitted. "I don't think it could be the creatures, because they can't live in this universe any more than Grummetty could, but it could be people working for Shadow, I guess."

"Are they shooting at us? At the ship, I mean?"

"I don't know," Pel repeated. "Listen, I really don't know much of anything, but we *are* under some kind of attack, and the navigator said we should get to our cabins and lock the doors and wait there."

Nancy shook her head. "I can't leave Alella," she said. "You take Rachel, and I'll stay here."

Pel chewed on his lower lip, considering, and then nodded. "Come on, Rae," he said, "let's get back to our room."

Rachel looked up unhappily. "I want Harvey," she said.

"I know you do," Pel said, "but he's not here. Now, come on, and we can cuddle up together, if you like."

"Is Grummetty *really* dead?"

"If your mother says so," Pel said, "then I'm afraid he is. Your mom's pretty reliable about these things."

"I don't want him to be dead."

An officer trotted past, almost running. Something was buzzing loudly somewhere forward.

A storybook hero would find some way to make himself useful, find some way to save the ship, but Pel was no storybook hero; he knew that more certainly than ever. Right now, dealing with Rachel seemed much more important than saving the ship. He knelt down and spoke softly to his daughter.

"I don't either, Rae, but we have to go. Right now. Come on!" He reached over and took her hand, and then stood up again. She allowed herself to be pulled upright, and followed him, unresisting, as he led her by the hand back to their cabin.

There, they sat on the bed and waited.

■

Amy had decided to make one more attempt to convince Ted that he was awake, and that everything that had happened was real.

For one thing, she wanted to be sure that she was convinced herself; for another, she thought Ted might be useful somehow if he once started taking things seriously.

She had been leading the conversation gently in that direction, listening to Ted ramble on about how everyone misunderstood what lawyers really did, when the alarm bells sounded. She looked up, startled.

"I wonder what that is?" she asked.

Ted shrugged, looked around, and saw nothing different about the aft salon. "I guess I haven't decided yet," he said.

Amy frowned.

A crewman ran through, without so much as glancing at them. The two Earth people watched him go.

"Or maybe we should go see," Ted said, getting to his feet, "just what I've come up with this time."

■

The tocsin roused Raven from a doze. He frowned; he had slept far too much and too easily, of late. Perhaps the strain of these strange adventures in fantastic lands was telling upon him, and were it so it would be sorry news indeed; he would need all his powers when he led attacks against Shadow.

"A bell?" he asked no one in specific. "Wherefore does it ring?"

"I know not," Stoddard replied. "Perchance the lieutenant can say?"

"An he be here," Raven agreed.

"It's an alarm," Drummond said, hurriedly pulling on a boot. "I don't know why."

"An alarm?" Raven said, swinging his feet to the floor and sitting upright. "Be the ship endangered?"

"I said I don't *know*," Drummond snarled. "I'll go find out." He stood, boots on.

"Shall we accompany?"

Drummond hesitated, thinking.

"No," he said at last. "No, you two stay here. And don't cause any trouble. You're valuable; if there's some kind of fight we don't want you getting yourselves killed."

"I've no fear to give my life in a good cause," Raven said. "Better to die waging war 'gainst evil than to live in an evil world."

"This isn't any war against evil," Drummond said. "It's probably some stupid mix-up. You just stay out of trouble."

"I reserve, sir, the right to judge my best role myself," Raven retorted. "I am no child."

"Fine," Drummond said, "fine. Just stay out of it this time, though, okay?"

Then he was gone, the door closing behind him.

" 'Tis not our fight," Stoddard said. " 'Tis not our world, so how could be?"

Raven looked at his sword, leaning against the nightstand, but did not reach for it. "Shadow has its agents in this realm, as in ours," he said, settling back. "But 'til we know more, best to bide."

■

Somehow Pel had assumed, from what the navigator had said, that the pirates, whoever they were, would be arriving, however they would arrive, within a few minutes, but instead he and Rachel sat on the bed, hugging each other and whispering quietly, for what seemed like hours. Nothing happened; no one burst in, or even knocked; there were no loud noises, no screams, no explosions, no sign that anything out of the ordinary was going on. A few times they heard footsteps passing the door, sometimes running, sometimes not.

Rachel fell asleep after perhaps a quarter of an hour, and Pel tucked her into bed. Then he sat, alone, waiting.

And still nothing happened.

He wished fervently for a book to read, or a TV to watch, or *something* to pass the time. A deck of cards to play solitaire would have been a taste of heaven, and he wished he had taken one when he had the chance.

His watch still wasn't working; after some thought he had concluded that as near as he could figure, liquid crystals didn't exist in Imperial space, and probably *couldn't* exist. He wasn't sure about chip technology in general, whether it was impossible or just hadn't yet been developed.

Whatever the exact reasons, he had no way to tell how long he sat there, watching Rachel sleep and waiting for the pirates. It was very inconsiderate, he decided, to not provide every cabin with a working clock.

He lay back on the bed, trying to think of what he should be doing and reaching no conclusions at all. Nothing that he came up with seemed very important, and they all involved leaving the room, and that meant leaving Rachel alone, which seemed like a very bad idea.

■

Amy had reluctantly followed Ted to the forward lounge, where they watched the confusion and worry. Three times, crewmen ordered them to leave, to go back to their cabins, but Ted simply ignored them—he didn't need to obey orders from figments of his imagination. Amy followed his lead; she wanted to see what was happening, not be cooped up in the suite with Susan and Elani and Prossie.

Nobody had time to argue with them, or force them, and they stayed in the lounge.

They stayed there right up until the pirates boarded the *Princess* and burst in through the air lock.

Ted looked at the gray-uniformed men, at the heavy blasters they held, and shook his head. "No, no," he said. "I don't like this part. It's nasty, and I don't want any more of that. The monsters were bad enough."

"On the floor," a man in a gray coverall ordered.

Ted ignored the order; instead he stepped up and reached out for the man's blaster. "Give me that," he said.

"He's crazy," someone called.

Ted's hand started to close on the barrel of the blaster, and the man holding it said, "I'll give it to you, all right."

■

A dream it's all a dream it's a fucking *dream* it can't be real.

The pain blazed through the side of his head, screaming agony that ripped at his consciousness.

It's a dream.

It *has* to be a dream.

But a dream can't hurt like this.

I must have fallen out of bed, that's what happened, I fell out of bed and hit my head on the floor, and it hurts like hell, why can't I wake up? God, is it a concussion or something?

Why can't I wake up?

As he fell, as he struggled to remain conscious, Ted remembered an old story called "The Knight's Tale," from a book of puzzles, a book called *Mazes and Labyrinths*, a story about a mysterious death. The man in the story had dreamed his own death, and had died in his sleep as a result.

Could that happen? Could he really die from this stupid interminable dream?

No, the knight had lied. And he couldn't possibly sleep through pain like this. He would wake up any second now, he knew he would wake up, and the dream would be over.

Please, God, it would be over!

■

"Get away from there," someone ordered.

Nancy looked up, startled.

"What is that, anyway?" the man in the gray coverall demanded. He was standing in the doorway of the storage area with a blaster in his hand.

"Alella," Nancy said. "She's dead, too."

The man looked at the little corpse.

"What is that, some kind of freak? Or just a doll?"

"She's . . . she was a little person," Nancy said.

"You sure it's dead?"

Nancy just stared at him; the inside of her chest seemed hollow and aching.

"Whatever, just leave it and come out of there."

Nancy didn't move.

"Damn it, bitch! Get out here!"

In some part of her mind Nancy knew that she should do what the man in gray wanted; he had that gun, and he was getting angry, and it wouldn't do Alella or Grummetty any good to linger here.

That logical, sensible part of her was overwhelmed, though, by the grief and emptiness she felt, and she still didn't move.

With a wordless growl, the man reached in and grabbed her by the hair, one-handed, the other hand keeping the blaster at ready. He tightened his grip until, even through her grief, she felt the pain; a small gasp escaped her.

Then he dragged her out into the corridor.

Exhausted from her long hours tending the little people and from all the cumulative strain of being swept out of her own world, awash in despair, she never did find the strength to scream.

■

When the door opened, Raven expected to see Lieutenant Drummond enter. By the time he saw the stranger's face it was too late.

"Touch that sword and I'll blow your fucking head off," the man in gray told him.

Stoddard glanced at Raven, who gave a quick negative jerk of the head. The weapon in the stranger's hand would not have worked back in the real world, nor in Pel Brown's Earth, but this ship sailed in the Empire's skies, where such devices were effective indeed.

"Surely, sir," Raven answered. "Whatever please you."

Stoddard accepted this hint, and made no move for his weapons.

"Get out here." The man gestured with his blaster.

"Certes. Might I ask, though, whether Lieutenant Drummond . . ."

"No questions."

Raven shrugged and obeyed.

He had no fear of any fight, but unarmed men against one of the Empire's fire-weapons was a senseless waste. He would heed, for the present, Lieutenant Drummond's advice. Perhaps this was some jurisdictional squabble between Imperial factions, or a disagreement over the succession to the throne, but in any case, this gray-clad fellow with the rude speech gave no impression of being one of Shadow's monsters. Surely, in time, all would be made clear, and when matters were settled Raven and his companions would be free.

And perhaps whatever faction this person represented would be more eager to fight Shadow than had been Captain Cahn and his crew.

■

Pel was awakened by a pounding on the door; it was only when he started up that he realized he had dozed off.

He turned the knob, struck once again by the incongruity of ordinary wooden doors, with knobs and hinges, aboard a spaceship.

The door was shoved open, the knob yanking out of his hand before he could react, and he found himself facing three unfamiliar men in gray uniforms. Two of them held drawn blasters; one needed a shave.

"Out," one of them ordered.

"What . . ." Pel began.

"*Out,*" the man repeated, gesturing with his weapon.

Pel reluctantly stepped out into the passageway, then turned and said, "My daughter . . ."

"That her?" One of the men pointed at Rachel, still asleep.

"Yes," Pel said.

"Get her."

Pel obeyed. He crossed quickly to the cot and stooped over her, then stood again, lifting the girl to his shoulder. She protested sleepily, then flopped against him, her arms around his neck.

"Out," came the order.

Nervously, Pel returned to the corridor.

"That way," he was told, and one of the men herded him forward, toward the lounge, while the others vanished into the cabin.

Farther aft, down the passage, Pel could see armed men at other cabin doors, and ahead he could see a knot of people.

In the lounge he found the ship's doctor bent over Ted Deranian, who lay on the floor, arms flung out to either side. One side of Ted's head was . . .

Pel couldn't see it clearly. He couldn't bring himself to look at it, but he couldn't look away, either. There was black, and red, wet and shining, and the hair was gone. He was glad Rachel was asleep, and not able to see it.

"What happened?" he asked.

"I don't know," someone said.

"He tried to play hero," Amy answered. "When they came charging in here Ted tried to take away one of their guns, and the man with the gun shot him. He didn't have time to aim, though, so he's still alive." She made a choked little noise, apparently suppressing a hysterical giggle, and said, "I mean, the man didn't have time to aim, so Ted's still alive."

Pel realized that the doctor was feeling Ted's chest, rather than his head, but before he could ask anything, Amy added, "They kicked him after he fell; we think a couple of ribs are broken."

"Was anyone else hurt?" Pel looked around, checking who was present.

There was Susan, standing quietly, and Prossie Thorpe, and Soorn, and Valadrakul. There were three, four, five of the *Princess'* original passengers, and three of her crew, in addition to the doctor.

"Where's Nancy?" Pel asked.

Amy turned and glanced about, worried. "I don't know," she said, "wasn't she with you?"

"No," Pel said, "she stayed with Alella."

Raven and Stoddard emerged from the corridor behind Pel, their swords gone, a blaster leveled at their backs. Beyond them Pel could see more of the original passengers, and farther back Captain Cahn and two of his crewmen.

"All right," one of the gray-clad men ordered. "Through there. Let's go." He pointed toward the air lock.

"What about my wife?" Pel called.

"Don't worry about it," another man ordered him. "Just move."

Pel started to say something, and the man shoved a blaster under his nose with one hand, pointing to the air lock with the other. "Move," he said.

Pel moved.

CHAPTER 19

The corridors of the pirate ship—if that's what it actually was—were gray-painted metal and resembled the inside of a submarine Pel had once toured. This vessel was far more what he had always expected a spaceship to look like than *Emerald Princess* had been.

He had little time to study it, though; he was hurried to a large, bare chamber, where he and some of the others were locked in, without any further explanation.

For a moment after the heavy steel door slammed shut Pel stared at it, expecting something more to happen. When nothing did, he turned to consider his surroundings.

A row of stained, bare mattresses lay along one of the long walls; at the far end were two small bathrooms, the doors standing open. There were no other furnishings, no windows, no other doors. In the room with him were Amy and Susan; the navigator of *Emerald Princess*; two passengers, one a young man, one a middle-aged woman; and of course, Rachel.

"What happened?" Amy asked. "Who are those people? Where are we?"

"Pirates, right?" Pel asked, looking at the navigator.

He nodded. "Pirates," he said. "From one of the rebel worlds out on the fringe, I suppose. Though I don't know why they picked on the *Princess*; I'd think there were juicier targets out there."

"And those juicier targets are probably better guarded," the young man said knowingly. "The *Princess* was small enough that we weren't worried about pirates, and we didn't have any defenses. Made us a sitting duck."

The navigator's expression made it plain that he wasn't impressed with this logic. "There's a good reason we weren't worried," he said. "A gravity gun's an expensive thing to operate, and bringing in a ship in mid-flight isn't any picnic; the *Princess* shouldn't have been worth the trouble."

"Well, how much trouble was it, really?" the young man argued. "The ship itself—she's a nice little boat, and they've got her for next to nothing, really. And the passengers—we had money and jewels along, some of us, and they can probably collect ransoms on most of us . . ."

"No, they can't," the navigator interrupted. "How the hell could they collect any ransoms? If they tell anyone where they are, so someone can make the payment, the Empire'll hunt them down and wipe them out."

"Well, there's still the ship . . ."

"I suppose," the navigator admitted, "but it still seems strange. The ship isn't anything all that special."

Amy, Pel, and Susan exchanged glances.

"Do you think it might have had anything to do with us?" Amy asked.

"I don't know," Pel said. "Could Shadow have tracked us somehow?"

"Why would it bother?" Amy asked.

"Does it need reasons?" Susan said. "It tried to kill us once, back in that forest; it could just be trying to finish what it started."

"In that case," Pel argued, "why didn't it already kill us? I mean, why didn't these pirates just shoot everybody?" A thought struck him, and he added, "And even if they aren't working for Shadow, if it was the ship they wanted, why didn't they shoot us?"

That question made everyone uneasy; Amy cast a glance at the mattresses.

"Those stains don't all look like blood," she said uncertainly.

Pel followed her gaze. "No," he agreed, "they don't. I think if they were just going to kill us, they'd already have done it."

"They killed some," the navigator said.

The others all turned to face him.

"They did?" Amy asked.

"Yeah," the navigator said. "There was some fighting. One of the spacemen, that man Jim Peabody, he pulled a gun and picked off two pirates, and they blew his head off, in the starboard crew compartment. And when they found someone hiding in one of the storage lockers they dragged her out and beat her, and ..." He glanced at Rachel, who was drowsing but not fully asleep, and then finished, "And worse, and I'm pretty sure they killed her when they were done."

"Her?" Pel asked, suddenly nauseated, his ears starting to ring. He had seen Prossie alive and unhurt, and some of the original female passengers, and Amy and Susan were here with him. Nancy was missing, though. "Her?"

It didn't have to be Nancy, he told himself. There were some missing females among the ship's original passengers, too, weren't there?

"A woman," the navigator said, "one of your group. I saw part of it and got a look at her, when they were done, but I don't know her name."

Elani was still unaccounted for—but hiding in a storage locker?

"Nancy," Pel said, gasping, "my wife."

There was a long moment of silence as Pel's strangled words sank in.

"Oh, God, Pel," Amy said, "I'm sorry."

"Mommy?" Rachel asked, waking. "Where's Mommy?"

■

Raven considered his surroundings with interested distaste.

It would seem that the luxury of the other ship was not a universal trait of sky ships in the Empire's world. This sorry vessel—assuming that this was indeed the interior of another ship—was just as drab as the governor's installation in Town, perhaps even more so.

Well, he had endured hardship before, and would undoubtedly do so again, in his battle against Shadow.

All that troubled him was that he still had no notion of who had captured him, or why. Pirates, the others taken with him said—but pirates in whose pay? Freebooters or privateers?

■

Amy watched miserably as Pel tried to comfort his sobbing daughter. She wished she could help, but she hadn't been able to do any more than provide a used tissue out of her purse. No one had actually told the child directly that her mother was dead, but none of them had denied it, either.

This was perhaps the worst moment yet in the long string of dislocations and horrors that she had been living through ever since that damned spaceship fell out of the sky on her back yard. Monsters bursting up out of the ground, being stranded in an alien desert, all the other things had been frightening and uncomfortable, but nothing that equaled the feeling of sick helplessness she felt right now.

"Why *didn't* they just shoot us?" she muttered.

The young male passenger heard her, and cast a sideways glance at Pel before muttering in reply, "I've heard some rumors."

Startled, Amy turned to look at him. "What rumors?" she asked.

"Well, they *are* just rumors," he said, "but you heard the crewman there mention the rebel planets. There are some nasty rumors about them."

"What rumors?"

"Supposedly—and I don't know, it's just what I've heard, but supposedly they've revived the slave trade."

Amy stared at him. For a long moment his words failed to connect with anything. Slave trade? What was that? What did it have to do with anything? What did it have to do with *her*?

Then it clicked into place.

She had been captured by pirates. Spaceships and drab gray uniforms notwithstanding, she had been captured by pirates.

And they were going to sell her into slavery.

The image of the "wenches" being auctioned off in Disney World's "Pirates of the Caribbean" came unbidden to her mind. She had ridden through with her ex-husband years ago, and had found that bit of scenery slightly offensive and oddly uncomfortable, though she knew it was intended to be harmless fun. Now, in retrospect, it seemed downright horrible—there was nothing at all amusing about auctioning people off.

But this wasn't the eighteenth-century Caribbean; she was in a spaceship. The Galactic Empire had antigravity and ray guns; didn't that mean it was more advanced than Earth? Didn't that mean they would have no use for slaves, would have no tolerance for slavery?

Didn't they have robots, or something?

"What sort of slaves?" she asked.

The passenger shrugged. "Labor for the mines and farms, I suppose," he said, "and . . . well, other things." He blushed faintly.

He actually blushed. It wasn't a bright red, but it was unmistakably a blush. Amy hadn't seen a man blush in years. She didn't inquire any further.

"I still don't understand," the female passenger announced, "why they picked on the *Princess*. There must be dozens of ships out there that would have been worth more—the big liners, or freighters. Why pick on *us*?"

"Maybe it was random," the navigator suggested. "Maybe they just saw the gravity field and attacked because it was close, without even knowing what ship it was."

"That seems stupid," the young man said. "What if they hit a warship that way?"

"I hadn't thought of that," the navigator admitted.

"They must have known what ship it was," the woman said.

"I guess they must have," the navigator agreed.

"How could they?" Amy asked. "I mean, aren't we sort of in the middle of nowhere? And they couldn't have gotten close enough to *see* it until after they'd decided to attack, could they?"

"Shadow," Susan suggested, gripping her big black purse tightly. Noticing the bag, Amy wondered whether it had been searched; no one had bothered to check her own. "It was Shadow," Susan said.

"What's Shadow?" the female passenger asked.

Susan looked helplessly at Amy, then glanced at Pel and Rachel, still huddled together in the corner.

"It's this thing from . . . from another universe," Amy explained. "It's why we're here."

"Why who is where?" the young man asked. "Do you mean why all of us are *here*, in this room?"

Amy shook her head. "No," she said, "I mean it's why Susan

and Pel and the rest of us are in your universe." She sighed. "It's a long story."

The passengers and the navigator glanced at one another, puzzled.

"Are you claiming you're from another universe?" the young man asked.

Amy nodded.

"We are," she said. "That's why we were important enough to need your ship to get us to . . . to wherever they were taking us. Some military base, I think."

The navigator nodded. "Base One," he said. "It's the head-quarters for the entire Imperial military."

Amy nodded again.

"So this Shadow thing," the navigator asked, "it's from your universe? It followed you, you think?"

"No," Amy said, "it's from a third one. There are three. Some of those other people are from Shadow's world, but we aren't."

"But it followed you?"

"Maybe," Amy said. "We don't know."

"This Shadow," the young man asked, "just what is it, exactly?"

Amy looked at Susan, who shrugged.

"We don't know that, either," Amy said. "I don't think anybody does, really."

"How could it have known anything about us, anyway?" the middle-aged woman asked. "Does it have a telepath working for it, or something?"

"I don't know," Amy said. "Maybe Shadow didn't have anything to do with it; maybe the pirates just have a telepath of their own."

The navigator shook his head. "All the telepaths work for the Empire," he said. "They always have."

"Maybe one went rogue," the young man suggested.

"If that ever happened," the navigator said, "the Empire would hunt it down and kill it."

"I wonder what happened to Prossie?" Amy said, more to herself than anyone else.

"Prossie?"

"Is that the bitch telepath that came aboard with you people?" the woman asked.

Startled by the harsh term, Amy didn't answer immediately.

"She was in the lounge," the navigator said. "I saw her there right before they brought us across."

"If the pirates know she's a telepath . . ." the young man began.

"She's probably *working* for them," the woman snarled. "She probably called them down on us!"

"She's an Imperial officer," the navigator objected. "And her entire family works for the Empire. Why would she work for pirates?"

"Because she's a stinking mutant, and she hates everybody normal!" the woman replied angrily.

"I don't think that's true," Amy objected. "I've talked with Prossie—I don't think she hates anybody."

"Well, of course you wouldn't think so," the woman retorted. "She can read your mind and act however you want her to act, do whatever it takes to fool you, and you'd never know the difference."

Startled by the woman's anger, Amy didn't reply.

"If she's not working for the pirates," the young man said, "she's the best hope we've got."

Amy and Susan looked at him inquiringly.

"Well, it's obvious—she can call for help. Maybe she already has. If she's not working for them, they've made a big mistake not killing her the minute they got aboard."

"Maybe they don't know she's a telepath," Susan suggested quietly.

"She was in uniform," the female passenger said scornfully. "Of *course* they know."

"But she wasn't," Susan said. "In the lounge she was wearing a dress."

"Her uniform was aboard the *Princess*, though," the young man pointed out. "When they find it, they'll know."

"Well, let's hope they don't find it, then," the navigator said.

"Of course they'll find it eventually," the woman said. "I mean, won't they strip everything out of the ship?"

Amy glanced at Susan's purse again.

"They might not look at it closely enough," the navigator suggested. "And even if they do, she's probably already called for help."

"But when they find it, they'll kill her," the young man pointed out. "That would make it harder for any pursuit to track us."

"Serve the bitch right," the woman muttered, "snooping in people's head. Mutants."

"They may have killed her already," the navigator said, "but let's hope not."

"Can she really call for help from way out in space?" Amy asked. "I didn't know telepaths could do that. I thought they had to be close to someone." She remembered the distance from Town to where the portal had first delivered them all to Psi Cass the Deuce, and corrected herself. "I mean, on the same planet, anyway."

"Oh, sure," the young man said. "She could call the other telepaths from clear across the galaxy. I don't know about reading minds, or anything to do with normal people, but telepaths can reach *each other*, no matter *how* far apart they are. That's why the Empire uses them; they're the fastest form of interstellar communication we've got."

"Then the pirates couldn't have a telepath working for them, could they?" Susan asked. "Wouldn't he or she be spotted by the Empire's telepaths?"

"What if he were?" the woman asked. "Those mutants all stick together against us. They wouldn't squeal on one of their own."

Nobody bothered to argue with that—not because they agreed, since in fact none of the others believed it, but because there was no way to prove anything.

A moment later, the young man said, "Suppose they had their own *family* of telepaths. I mean, suppose the telepathic mutation happened *again*, and this time working for the rebel worlds instead of the Empire?"

"The Empire's telepaths would have spotted them," the navigator said.

"Are you sure?" the young man asked. "Suppose they communicated on a slightly different level, as it were; suppose that there was some sort of mutual interference, in fact, so that the two families blanked each other out, couldn't detect each other."

"You're just guessing," the navigator said. "I never heard about anything like that."

The young man shrugged. "Sure, I'm guessing," he said. "But it *could* be true."

"I still think it was Shadow," Susan said.

■

The discussion, and sometimes argument, continued off and on for hours, perhaps days; no one was quite sure how long they were confined to that room and ignored. Long enough to grow very hungry, certainly, and no one brought any food. They were left entirely to their own devices.

They took turns sleeping; there were enough mattresses for everybody, but it seemed like a good idea to always have someone awake.

Rachel gradually calmed down; sleeping helped. She and Pel listened to some of the conversations, but neither of them had much to add. Topics included the nature of their captors, their destination, the fate of the other people who had been aboard *Emerald Princess*, and other such matters.

The navigator confirmed, out of Rachel's hearing, that the woman he had seen raped and murdered fit Nancy's description, and not Elani's.

More generally, the four Earth people learned that the Galactic Empire did not actually rule the entire galaxy, or even the majority of it; most of it was still uninhabited, at least by humans—and so far, no intelligent aliens had been encountered, though that didn't mean there weren't any. The female passenger, whose name turned out to be Arietta Benton, took any suggestion that a nonhuman could be sentient as a personal affront, apparently on theological grounds; the navigator and the other passenger were more open-minded, but neither one had ever heard anything more than tall tales about aliens.

Even among human-inhabited worlds, the Empire was not as

all-powerful as it might have liked. The galaxy was vast, and space travel fairly cheap and easy; anyone who could get a ship could reasonably hope to find himself an uninhabited planet of his own. It might take a few years of looking, and if the Empire found the planet later it would promptly be conquered, but people were willing to try it. A good many of them succeeded and set up their own little fiefdoms.

Nobody was sure just how many of these independent worlds were out there—that was inherent in their nature, since if they were sufficiently well-known to be counted, they would already have been conquered.

The male passenger, Alex Gorney, was of the opinion there were a hundred or more rebel worlds; the navigator, Lieutenant Martin, put the number much lower, at maybe half a dozen. "Ships aren't *that* easy to come by!" he insisted.

Gorney argued that one ship could colonize a dozen worlds, and Martin agreed it *could*, but maintained it wouldn't. One habitable planet, after all, was big enough for a few dozen miniature empires.

All three of them, Gorney, Benton, and Martin, agreed that the sort of people who wound up on the rebel worlds tended toward the fringes of sanity. The colonies the Empire had found so far had ranged from eccentric to downright bizarre; some had destroyed themselves before the Empire ever got there, and atrocity stories were common.

Naturally, some had turned to piracy. And some had turned to slavery. Not to mention those that had taken up communalism, theocracy, torture, murder, cannibalism, and any number of other barbaric practices.

The Earth people listened to these explanations—Amy with visibly growing worry, Susan with a veneer of calm acceptance, Pel far too concerned with Nancy's fate and Rachel's reaction to care much at first.

As time wore on, though, the subject percolated in Pel's mind, and finally he found himself sitting on his mattress grinning wryly at the thought.

The clean, hard frontier, where men were strong and brave; the fine new worlds beloved of science fiction writers, away from the decadence and bureaucracy of old, worn-out, overpopulated Earth—all that was a cliché, of course.

And here was the reality, it appeared—pirates and slavers and lunatics.

That he and his daughter were about to be delivered into the hands of these pirates, slavers, and lunatics did not fully register until the hour—day or night he could not tell—when Lieutenant Martin shook him awake and said, "The drive's shut down. We've landed."

CHAPTER 20

They were all awake when the door finally opened, all of them dressed and waiting. Martin and Gorney were standing straight and tall, waiting to face whatever might come; the others were sitting in a group on two of the mattresses, waiting with more resignation than defiance.

"Come on," one of the gray-clad pirates ordered, "out of there."

"Where are you taking us?" Benton demanded. "To see the captain?"

"Just get out here," the pirate said, gesturing with a blaster.

Pel, Susan, and Amy got to their feet, Pel giving Rachel a reassuring hug. Benton crossed her arms over her chest and looked defiant.

"I want to know where you're taking us," she announced.

The pirate in the doorway cast a disgusted glance over his shoulder, then stepped aside. Two men entered, stepping past him; they carried no guns, but in Pel's opinion they didn't need them. Both of them were huge, built like linebackers or pro wrestlers.

Pel glanced doubtfully at Amy, who returned the look uncertainly. Susan stepped out of the way immediately, her back against one wall. She didn't meet anyone else's eyes. She held her black purse tight to her side and didn't move.

Gorney and Martin stood firm, unyielding and motionless, between the door and Benton.

The first of the oversized pirates reached out and grabbed Martin around the throat, one-handed. Pel immediately remembered the scene in *Star Wars* where Darth Vader picked up a rebel one-handed and broke his neck; the pirate was not doing anything quite so dramatic as that, but the gesture was still extremely effective.

Martin's hands flew up, trying to pry the death grip loose; Gorney, horrified, flung his own weight on the outstretched arm.

The other large pirate marched past, undaunted, to where Benton sat on the mattress, glaring up at him. He pushed past Pel and Amy as if they weren't there, and neither of them dared resist; instead they backed away, one on each side. Pel almost stepped on Rachel in his retreat.

"You coming?" the pirate asked, as he looked down at the disobedient captive.

"No," Benton began, a bit less steadily than before, "not until . . ."

That was as far as she got; the pirate kicked her in the belly, hard. The air burst out of her lungs, and she curled forward, gasping. Rachel let out a little wail and buried her face in her father's shirt, clutching the fabric with both hands; Pel put a soothing hand on her head.

The pirate reached down with one hand and roughly yanked Benton upright. She didn't resist; the fight had gone out of her with her breath. She was unable to walk at first, and the pirate dragged her by one arm until, halfway to the door, she got her feet under her.

Martin and Gorney had been unable to release Martin from the other pirate's stranglehold; now, though, the grip was suddenly released, and Martin almost fell.

"Come on," the pirate said.

There was no further resistance; the entire party allowed itself to be herded out of the room, and on out of the ship.

■

The holding facility had rough concrete walls and rows of steel benches, but not everybody used them. Some stood along the walls, some crouched on the floor. The room was cavernous, big enough that even without crowding everyone together the entire party of dozens occupied less than a fourth of it. Light came from a row of clerestory windows, far overhead. A narrow corridor at one end led to toilet facilities. The place was dusty and cool and had a faint unpleasant odor to it, compounded of mildew, sweat, urine, and other, less definable traces.

Pel looked over the crowd.

In addition to the handful he had been with aboard the pirate ship, he spotted Lieutenant Drummond and Captain Cahn, Raven, Valadrakul, Elani, Squire Donald and Stoddard, Prossie Thorpe, Smith, Lampert, Soorn, and Mervyn. Ted Deranian, his head a mass of bandages, sat dazed in one corner, and Pel was relieved to see him alive. Most of the passengers and crew of *Emerald Princess* were present, but Pel had never become familiar enough with them to put names to them all or say if any were missing.

He looked back to Prossie Thorpe. She was alive—that was promising. She was out of uniform, now wearing a ragged bathrobe rather than the borrowed dress she had been in before; maybe their captors didn't know she was a telepath. Maybe, even now, she was relaying messages to the Galactic Empire.

He didn't want to draw attention to her. He returned to scanning the crowd, looking for familiar faces.

Nancy was not there. Neither was Peabody, nor Lieutenant Godwin, nor Alella.

There were three doorways, with pirates guarding each of them; each pirate held a blaster. Susan, Pel noticed, was standing with her back to the wall once again, stiff and tense, trying to watch all three guards at once.

"Now what?" someone whispered.

"Shut up," one of the pirates called—not angrily, just giving a necessary order. The hand holding the blaster lifted somewhat.

Silence descended, broken by shuffling feet and rustling clothes. Someone coughed.

One of the doors opened, and three more of the gray-clad pirates entered, accompanied by a tall man in blue coveralls. The four of them strode into the room with an air of calm and certain purpose, then stopped.

"All right, everyone hold still," one of the pirates bellowed. "Sit down, and hold still."

With varying degrees of reluctance, those who were standing

obeyed. Susan's descent was so quick Pel thought at first she had fallen.

When everyone was seated, the man in blue stretched out a finger and began counting heads. Pel could see his lips moving; he wasn't sure if he could hear muttered numbers or not.

"Forty-three," the man announced.

"You missed one," the smallest of the accompanying pirates said. "I counted myself. Did you see the little girl, there?"

Rachel raised her head from Pel's lap and blinked.

"You're right," the man in blue said. "Missed her. Forty-four, then, and the dead midget. Forty-two healthy adults at fifty crowns each, and half each for the kid and the one with his head shot up. That's twenty-one fifty, plus twenty for the freak, makes twenty-one seventy."

"What, half for the kid and the dummy?" the small pirate protested. "Come on! He's just got his hair burned off, he's not hurt bad! And she's older than she looks!"

The man in blue shook his head. "She's not twelve," he said. "She's not even eight. Just take a look at her. Hell, *ask* her!"

"I'm six," Rachel volunteered.

"There, see?"

"All right," the pirate conceded, "but the one with the bandage . . ."

The man in blue sighed. "Oh, hell, it's not worth the argument. Twenty-one ninety."

"Ninety-*five*."

"Right, ninety-five."

One of the other pirates handed him a clipboard and a pen—Pel noticed they looked much like the same implements back on Earth. The man in blue filled out a few lines, then signed at the bottom, tore off the sheet, and handed it to the small pirate. He smiled, folded it, and tucked it away in an inside pocket.

All the pirates were smiling, in fact—not just the four in the central party, but the three at the doors as well.

Then the party of five turned and marched back out, leaving the captives where they were.

"What the hell was that about?" Pel asked, half to himself, before he remembered that the guards preferred silence.

"Prize money," the nearest guard replied, smiling. "That chit's sixty crowns for every man on the ship—double shares for the officers, and a bonus for the captain."

"Sixty-five, I make it," one of the other guards called.

"Whatever," the first replied, grinning. "Enough to get good and drunk. And that's just on these—prize court hasn't even looked at the ship yet!"

"Shut up, both of you," the third guard snapped.

They shut up, and Pel sat, thinking. This was the first time any of the pirates had deigned to answer any questions at all, and he rather hoped it was the beginning of a trend.

Prize money—he knew about prize money, more or less, from the novels he had read. It was a method of rewarding ships' crews for capturing enemy vessels in wartime, by buying their captures from them. It had been dropped over a century ago back on Earth, and with good reason. The whole system struck Pel as a really barbaric idea. It made the crews greedy, made them more interested in catching enemy merchant shipping off-guard than in winning battles.

And even at its worst, back on Earth, he thought it had only been applied to ships and cargo, not to *people*.

Why would anyone pay prize money for people?

He could think of a few possibilities, and he didn't like any of them very much. The only good one was also the least likely—that it was just a humanitarian gesture, a way of convincing the pirates to deliver prisoners alive, rather than dead.

Somehow, Pel couldn't imagine any government making such a gesture.

Of course, that assumed that they were dealing with a government here. If they were, then perhaps "pirates" wasn't the right term for their captors at all; "privateers" might be more accurate, or perhaps they were actually part of the navy—or space force, or whatever the correct term was—of this particular world. Or country, if the government in question didn't run the entire planet.

One of the doors opened, and half a dozen men in dark blue uniforms ambled in. Most of the prisoners watched intently.

"Okay, boys," one of them called, "you can go."

Mervyn got to his feet, and the man in blue called, "Not you, stupid."

Mervyn sat down again, as the three gray-clad guards, grinning and slapping one another on the back, jogged out of the room. The newcomers split into pairs, and took up posts at the three doors.

"You people might as well settle in," one of them called. "You're staying here tonight, and you'll go out in the morning, around nine, I think." He pulled a watch from his pocket and glanced at it. "That's fourteen hours. We'll get you in some breakfast before that, I guess, but for now, you might as well sleep."

"May we talk?" someone asked; Pel didn't see who it was.

"Nope," the guard said, smiling. "Sorry. No escape plans. And if any of you gets within five yards of a door, we'll shoot you dead, no warnings." He drew a blaster, then leaned back against the wall beside the door. "Good night!"

■

Dazed, Ted looked out at the gathered prisoners.

This dream went on and on and it was so boring! Why hadn't the pain in his head woken him up? He must be lying on the floor, he might have a concussion, and he had always thought he had a better imagination than this.

Why wouldn't it stop?

Maybe he was dead, not dreaming, maybe he was dead and this was some antechamber of hell.

But no, he didn't believe in any of that, he hadn't believed in it since he was eight, not really, maybe he *never* had.

He was dreaming.

He had slept and woken, he had eaten, he had been hit and burned and abused, and the dream still went on and on and didn't end, and he really wished he would wake up.

He would need to talk to someone about this, he really would. He'd never seen a psychiatrist, never wanted to, but a dream like this might change his mind.

Maybe if he attacked one of the guards, he'd be shot, and that would wake him up . . .

Or maybe he'd die. Maybe he was really hurt from falling out of bed, maybe he'd had a heart attack, or a stroke.

He wouldn't risk it.

But he wished he would wake up.

■

Raven pursed his lips angrily.

How utterly foolish, to have fallen prisoner in some petty little raid like this!

It was clear to him now that this was no grand factional dispute, nor any great crusade against the Empire; instead this was some minor warlord's action, an attempt to gather a little loot without drawing the Empire's wrath. *Emerald Princess* would be reported lost, doubtless, but the loss ascribed to wind or weather, monsoon or monster. Even were pirates suspected, how could they know which or where?

And so here he was, Raven of Stormcrack Keep, about to be held for ransom, or sold to slavery, and there was naught he could do to prevent it.

Thus was his struggle to end, then?

Or might he yet win free? Might he draw the aid of whatever warlord was responsible, by promises of booty from Shadow's conquered lands?

That was a thought to consider, most certainly.

First, though, to survive that long. Would that someone would spare him somewhat to eat!

■

They hadn't eaten, Pel realized, for at least a day and a half; poor Rachel was starving, her stomach hurting. "Breakfast soon," he whispered in her ear, as she shifted on the bench beside him, trying unsuccessfully to get to sleep.

She whimpered.

They had dozed fitfully for hours, surrounded by others doing the same. Some of them snored, or at least breathed loudly and sometimes irregularly; some tossed and turned. At least once, someone had fallen off a bench with much commotion and noise.

The guards at the doors were replaced every four hours, as nearly as Pel could judge; after the first change they all wore the dark blue uniforms, rather than the drab gray of the pirates.

He wondered just where they all were, and who these people were, and what was really going on.

And he wondered what he was doing here, and what had really happened to Nancy. Was she truly dead?

She couldn't be. He looked down at Rachel.

Nancy couldn't be dead. Martin the navigator must have been wrong, somehow. The whole thing had to be a mistake.

Nancy couldn't be dead.

He looked up, swallowing hard, his eyes wet.

The line of windows had been visible as a slightly lighter strip of darkness, sprinkled with stars; now, though, the stars seemed to be fading, the darkness lightening.

Dawn?

He hoped so, if only because of the promise of breakfast.

■

Amy felt as if she had just gotten to sleep when the banging woke her. Someone was beating on a metal tray, making a great clanging racket.

"All right, you people," a man shouted, "up and at 'em! Breakfast in five minutes!"

The struggle between hunger and fatigue raged for a long moment, but amid the general stirring and muttering, bringing home the realization that they weren't going to let her sleep anyway, hunger won out. She got to her feet, stretched, and yawned.

The inside of her mouth felt gummy, and she was sure her breath stank, but that wasn't anybody's business but her own anymore. Stan had been given to rude remarks about it, back when she was married.

He had also been given to rude remarks whenever she put on weight, and she'd noticed that her breath always smelled worse when she was dieting, which had created a no-win situation—one of many in her relationship with him, even before the whole thing went down the tubes once and for all.

Stan wasn't here, though. He wasn't even in this *universe*, if all this was really happening.

If it was really happening, she repeated to herself. Ted's dream theory did have a certain undeniable appeal to it.

But she couldn't imagine herself dreaming about bad breath, and there was Ted with his head bandaged up, and the echoes from the blank walls, the rattle of the metal benches, all the solid little details made the dream theory seem pretty untenable. She couldn't manage to believe it, though she rather wished she could.

Who was it that could believe six impossible things before breakfast?

Well, it wasn't her; she seemed to be stuck with a choice of believing one or the other of two, either this was all real or it was all a dream, and she was having trouble accepting either of the available options.

But there just wasn't any third choice.

"Breakfast! This way to breakfast!" shouted a man at one of the doors. People were beginning to line up there, Amy saw; she tugged her maroon stewardess skirt into place, hung her battered purse on her shoulder, looked around and saw she had nothing else to pick up, and then ambled in that general direction.

The door opened into a short, gloomy, gray-walled passage-way. At the far end of the passage the prisoners found themselves in a cafeteria that closely resembled the holding room they had slept in, save that there were tables between the rows of benches, and a serving counter across one end. The line that had formed in the holding room and moved down the little corridor now swerved directly to the serving area without breaking formation; gray metal trays were stacked at the near end, waiting.

Back in Town, on Psi Cass the Deuce, they'd all had to sit and wait, and then had gotten fed—but it had gone much more quickly, and they'd been treated more considerately, and the place, drab as it was, hadn't smelled or looked anywhere near as unpleasant.

Amy's stomach pinched at her as she waited her turn; she could smell coffee, could smell food. The contrast with the odor of the waiting room was drastic indeed.

It had been much too long since she had eaten. It had been much too long since *any* of them had eaten; she could hear stomachs growling.

The one good thing about that was that it meant the line moved quickly; each person was eager to fill his or her tray and get it to a table. No one was kept waiting a moment longer than necessary.

Breakfast was biscuits and sausage and corn flakes and

coffee—no eggs, no orange juice, no fruit. The biscuits were fluffy, but almost tasteless; the sausage plainly contained as much filler as meat; and the coffee was thin, watery, and cool.

The corn flakes were fine, except that there was no milk or sugar or fruit to put on them.

It had been long enough since her last meal that Amy ate everything on her plate anyway, and went back for seconds on the biscuit and sausage.

As she worked her way through the narrow gap between benches, back toward her seat, she saw Rachel Brown twisting about in her place, her face set in a scowl. "I don't like this stuff!" she said. "Don't they have any milk, or soda, or anything?"

"No," her father told her, "they don't. Just coffee."

"They have water," someone—Lampert, Amy remembered his name now, Ben Lampert—said from across the table. "Would you like me to get you some?"

Pel looked down at his frowning daughter.

"Well, it's better than *this* stuff," Rachel said, pushing her cup away and spilling coffee onto her tray.

Pel caught the cup and righted it while it still held half its contents; Amy stopped watching and proceeded back to her own seat.

The food ran out before everyone had eaten his or her fill, but Amy no longer heard stomachs complaining; everyone had at least eaten *something*. Now they sat, looking about, talking quietly with their neighbors.

Amy had Susan on one side, and an unfamiliar middle-aged man on the other; across the table were strangers, save for Bill Mervyn, one seat to her right.

"Any idea what's going on?" she asked Susan.

Susan, lips tight, shook her head no. She clutched at her purse.

Mervyn looked up from his empty coffee cup, at Amy. "I don't know if . . ." he began, then stopped.

Amy looked back at him. "You don't know what?"

"Well," Mervyn said, reluctantly, "I think I can *guess* what's going on, but you won't like it. You'd probably be better off not knowing."

"No," Susan said, "we would not."

"Especially not now, now that you've said anything," Amy added.

Mervyn sighed and looked back at his cup; the coffee had run out, as well as the food.

"Well," he said, "when I was on *Devastation*—that's ISS *Devastation*, Captain Morley, that was my ship before *Ruthless* . . ."

Amy nodded. "Go on."

"When I was on *Devastation*, we did a run on one of the rebel worlds out on the fringes of the Empire. They'd been supporting pirates, same as these people here, and they used the people the pirates brought back as slave labor. Auctioned them off. And about half a dozen ships got away—these might even be the same people."

"So you think . . ."

"I think they're feeding us because hungry slaves don't look as good to the buyers, and hungry people are more likely to do stupid, desperate things, like trying to escape."

"Only at first," Susan said. "Go without food long enough and you don't have the strength anymore. You need to choose your time carefully." She adjusted her purse on the bench beside her.

"Well, that's true," Mervyn acknowledged, "but they want us healthy."

Amy and Susan nodded reluctant agreement. "At least we have that much," Susan said. "I've known worse."

Amy glanced at her attorney, startled, but Susan was not looking in her direction.

She had known worse?

Amy decided not to pursue that. For a moment, the two of them sat, contemplating their situation. Amy was, once again, finding it all hard to believe; slavery? She, Amy Jewell, was going to be sold into slavery by pirates?

That was something out of stories, something out of the past . . .

Then she stopped and glanced at Susan again.

"I've known worse," Susan had said.

Susan was Vietnamese, and her family had escaped to Thailand by boat when she was a child. Amy didn't know any of the details; she had never asked, and Susan had never volunteered anything.

Still, Amy had heard stories about the boat people. Robbed, raped, murdered by pirates; stuck in camps and abandoned by civilized governments on all sides—to Susan, this might well seem all *too* real and familiar.

To *most* people outside the United States, Amy supposed, this wouldn't seem so outrageous. The world was full of cruelty and injustice, it always had been; why should this other world be any different?

She told herself that, and she knew enough history to know it was true, but still, she didn't really *believe* it, in her heart and her gut. All her life she had been safe, had been protected, had known what the rules were. She didn't walk through certain neighborhoods at night, she generally kept her doors locked, she stayed out of bars, and that was enough; her world was safe and serene.

It wasn't perfect; she'd had her bad moments when her marriage fell apart, when her dorm was broken into in her long-ago junior year of college, when she wrecked her car on that trip to Phoenix, but those seeming disasters looked pretty trivial in retrospect. She had worried that Stan would walk out, would leave her broke, would take the house away from her, might even slap her; she had feared that she might lose all her things, all her money and mementos, that she would never be able to sleep again without worrying; she had wondered how long it would take to get home without a car, where she would stay, how she would pay for everything, what would happen to her insurance rates.

Stan had done worse than slap her, but she had survived it, and it hadn't been so very bad, she hadn't wound up broke at all, or anywhere near it. And when it was over she was rid of him and that was all right.

She hadn't been robbed again, she had burglar alarms, and all her things were safe at home waiting for her.

She had flown home, bought a new car, and paid her bills off eventually.

So she had worried about all those things, and they had all turned out all right in the end—but she had never, in all her life prior to the crash of *Ruthless*, had to worry about where her next meal was coming from, or whether she would be alive to eat it; never worried about whether she would ever again see her house, her family, her friends, her entire *world*.

She had sometimes feared rape, robbery, and murder—but piracy? Slavery?

And in *another universe*?

It was absurd; it was crazy.

And it was true, wasn't it?

Or would she be rescued at the last minute? Would the cops come, the neighbors, the lawyers, the way they had after the robbery, the way they had after Stan had beat her? Prossie Thorpe was still alive, Amy had seen her; had *she* called the cops, the Imperial soldiers, this time?

And would they come?

"Your attention!" someone shouted above the room's babble. "Your attention, please!"

The hum of conversation and general hubbub faded. A man in a blue uniform was standing on a chair against one wall, his arms spread wide.

"Next step is hygienic," he announced. "I'm sure most of you haven't had a good bath in days, and you may have . . . well, you could probably use one."

Amy threw Susan a glance; the lawyer shrugged. Other people were also trading looks, worried or questioning.

"We don't have facilities for individual baths," the announcer continued. "Instead we have showers, one for the men, one for the ladies. If the men would please leave the cafeteria through *that* door—" He pointed. "—And the ladies through *that* one . . ."

"Now?" someone asked.

"Whenever you're ready," the announcer replied.

Showers.

They were prisoners being herded into mass showers.

Amy tried very hard not to think of what that immediately brought to mind.

Did any of these other people, the ones not from Earth, have anything like that in their histories? Had this monstrous, inhuman Shadow that they talked about ever sunk to the level of the Nazis?

Had the Galactic Empire ever faced an evil to equal the one the Allies had conquered?

Very probably, she thought; after all, Stalin had killed as many as Hitler, and Pol Pot and a dozen others had tried. There had been murderous dictators all through history. The people of the Empire, and the people of Shadow's world, all looked human enough; they probably had plenty of murderous dictators in their own histories.

But had those dictators used poisoned showers? Was anyone else here making the same connection she was?

Probably not. She was probably just being paranoid. And Prossie Thorp must have called for help. Even the people at Auschwitz had been saved eventually, when the Allied troops came marching in.

A few of them had been saved, anyway.

A few of them.

She turned to Susan. "What do you think?" she asked. "Should we go?"

The lawyer shrugged.

"Do we really have a choice?" she asked.

CHAPTER 21

Pel Brown was arguing with the announcer as Amy left the cafeteria. She couldn't make out the words, and decided against snooping; instead she just followed the little crowd through the indicated door.

Once inside, she looked around the bare little room and noticed that there were no lockers in the changing room, just cardboard boxes—stacks of them, gray inside, blue outside, with loose-fitting lids. There were no markers, no pens, no labels, no serial numbers, and Amy found herself very suspicious indeed.

How would they ever get the right stuff back?

Did anyone ever expect to return anything?

"Just put your clothes in there, dearie," the blue-uniformed woman with the billy club told her. "They'll be safe."

"How'll I find the right box?" Amy asked. "I mean, afterward?"

The guard, or matron, or whatever she was looked annoyed. "Write your name on it if you like," she said.

"There aren't any pens," Amy pointed out.

"We ran out; don't you have anything in that purse you're carrying?"

Amy was not satisfied, but she began fishing in her purse, looking for a pen. If nothing else, it let her stay dressed a moment longer. The room was not particularly warm—and there were those other fears, not entirely suppressed.

Around her the other women were slowly, reluctantly removing their clothes. The first shower was turned on in the tiled room beyond and for a moment Amy froze, listening for the hiss of gas.

There was no gas; just water, splashing on the tiles. Someone squealed. "It's cold!"

"It'll warm up," the guard called.

Amy felt an altogether unreasonable rush of relief, and was annoyed at herself. Had she really thought they were about to be gassed?

Did she really know they weren't going to be killed by some other method?

She shook her head. She was being paranoid again, and it wasn't going to do anybody any good. Her hand brushed through the contents of her purse, and for a moment she could see an old Bic, and then something slid over, and it was lost again.

Someone knocked on the door from the cafeteria, interrupting her thoughts, and a male voice called, "Is there an Amy Jewell or a Susan . . . Susan Goyen in there?"

Amy looked up, then quickly scanned the room. Susan was already naked and about to step into the shower room, but incongruously, she still had her purse, held so the matron could not see it.

"I'm Amy Jewell," Amy called back.

"We have a . . . could you come to the door, please?"

Cautiously, Amy approached the door. It swung open a few inches, then stopped.

"Excuse me, miss," the voice said, and Amy recognized it as the man who had made the announcement about showers. "I don't want to intrude on anybody's privacy."

"It's okay," Amy said, leaning around the edge of the door, "I'm still decent. What is it?" She looked out.

The cafeteria was almost empty now, and a man in a dirty apron was collecting trays and debris. The announcer was standing with his back to the door, holding it open with one hand.

His other hand was on Rachel Brown's shoulder.

"We have a bit of a problem here," he said. "It seems this little girl doesn't have her mother here. She wants to stay with her father, but I'm afraid we have very strict rules about that; we just *can't* let her through the men's side. So could you please take charge of her for now? Her father says she knows you."

Amy looked down at the child; Rachel looked back, her eyes wide. She had been crying, and Amy had the distinct impression that the wrong word would start more tears flowing.

Amy had never been very good with children and had always been relieved that she and Stan had never had any. Still, this poor thing needed *somebody* to look after her, and her mother, Amy remembered . . . well, her mother wasn't here.

And it was only for a few minutes.

"Would that be okay, Rachel?" she said. "It'll just be until we're washed up, and then you'll be back with your father, I'm sure."

The announcer's face was carefully expressionless, and Amy suddenly knew, beyond any question, that it would not just be a few minutes before Rachel was returned to her father. She knew that these people had no intention of ever returning the child to her father, and she knew that this time she wasn't just being paranoid. Still, she could hardly back out now.

And they weren't planning to return those personal belongings, either. She threw a glance at Susan and her purse; Susan was being smart, if she could get away with it.

Just what they *did* plan, Amy didn't know. She pushed that thought aside, though, at least for the moment, and forced herself to smile at the girl.

Rachel stared at her for a moment, then pulled away from the announcer's hand and slipped through the door.

■

Pel watched Rachel go, then reluctantly allowed himself to be pushed through the door into the men's changing room.

He took his clothes off with dull mechanical efficiency, trying not to think. Nancy was dead, and now Rachel had been taken away; he was lost two universes away from home—he didn't *dare* think. He knew that Rachel was supposed to rejoin him after they had showered, but on some level he didn't dare believe that, *couldn't* believe it, because the possibility of disappointment was too horrible to contemplate. Better to give her up as lost now, while he knew she was still alive and in the hands of someone who, if not exactly a trusted friend, was at least familiar and not obviously hostile or alien.

If he let himself think, he knew he would start anticipating Rachel's return, would start wondering if Nancy was *really* dead, would start planning a return to Earth—and Rachel was gone, Nancy was dead, and he would never get home; he knew that and dared not let himself hope.

So he dared not let himself think. He peeled off his worn clothes quickly and dropped them in the box provided, focusing his eyes and mind on the texture of the concrete floor, the scuff marks on the steel bench, the grain in the box's cardboard—all of it simple visual data that occupied his attention and filled his mind.

Some part of him probably wondered how he would reclaim the right box, but right now he really couldn't worry about it.

Mechanically, he walked naked into the shower room, where the other men were already bathing themselves; Cahn and his surviving men, passengers and crew of *Emerald Princess*, Raven and his companions. Ted Deranian was not merely bathing, he was singing quietly.

Pel plodded into the room, but made no move toward the showerheads.

And behind him, between the shower room and the changing room, a heavy steel door dropped into place.

The others started, turned, shouted. Pel didn't bother; he stood, spray from the showers splashing his legs, water running down across his ankles, and onto the tile floor.

He had known. Something like that had to be coming. He had known. And it didn't matter anymore.

Nancy was dead. Rachel was surely gone now, closed off by that metal barrier, as he had known she would be. He was trapped. He was doomed.

They were going to kill him. They were going to kill everybody. He was going to die. Maybe he was already dead. Maybe this was hell, this Galactic Empire, not part of any living reality at all.

Maybe he was mad.

Maybe he was dreaming—but no. That was Ted's theory, and he had seen what happened to Ted. Besides, that was the way to false hope, because every dreamer must wake eventually.

Pel knew he was not going to wake up.

■

This mass ablution was distasteful, but Raven had acquiesced, had taken off his garments and placed them neatly in one of the odd little boxes provided. He had stepped into the water chamber and had allowed the water to wash over him. He was not yet ready to draw attention to himself, beyond the comments already made upon his attire.

When the portcullis fell, though, he cursed his own foolishness in playing along this far.

Now, with his clothes gone, what was to mark him apart from the common mass of humanity? How was he to assert his identity?

True, the clothes would not have been proof, for the veriest madman might contrive himself the appropriate garb to support his tales, but they were all he had, save his own words.

Now, he had only his tongue and his wits.

Further, this locking away seemed a sign that the lordling that had captured them was done with them and was now consigning them to whatever fate awaited them.

Slavery, most likely—a sorry life tilling the soil somewhere, back bent to the hoe and burnt by the sun.

Cold anger grew in his chest as warm water spilled down his side. Raven of Stormcrack Keep, a mere tender of vegetables?

Not so long as breath remained in him!

■

Amy stared at the steel door. After an initial yip of surprise she hadn't bothered to shout or scream or protest; some of the other women, though, were not so resigned. Three of the passengers from *Emerald Princess* were pounding on the metal with their bare wet hands, calling out until the shower room echoed deafeningly.

Slaves, Amy thought, they were going to be slaves. Bill Mervyn was right. That was why the door had dropped, she was certain—buyers would want to see what they were getting. No fancy packaging, no clothes. The showers were genuine enough, because the slavers wanted their merchandise clean, but they also wanted them naked, and how else could that be accomplished without argument?

She looked down at Rachel, who was looking up at her in silent puzzlement.

"It's okay, honey," she said. "They don't want us going back that way, that's all. They aren't going to hurt us."

At least, she thought, not yet. Slavers wouldn't be eager to damage the merchandise.

But the new owners . . .

The new owners could be anybody and anything. Sadists, perverts—or just people looking for cheap labor.

If she were lucky, whoever bought her would just want cheap labor.

"All right, ladies," the matron called, "out this way, when you're done washing."

Amy turned and found that the drab gray door at the far end of the shower room, the door that had looked so much like access to a broom closet or furnace room that nobody had consciously noticed it at all, was now open. The matron was standing there, her billy club in her hand, her blue uniform starting to sag and darken with the moisture in the air.

Amy managed a smile as she told Rachel, "Come on; we might as well get on with it."

"What about our clothes?" someone shouted; other voices chimed in.

Amy, Rachel, and Susan didn't bother shouting, but they heard the matron's explanation. "We'll have them waiting when you're dried off. This way, please."

The women from Earth exchanged glances. They knew better. They would not be getting their clothes back—at least, not for some time yet. Amy wondered if Rachel knew, too.

Susan's purse was not in sight, and Amy had no idea what her attorney had done with it.

■

Pel toweled himself off quickly, though he had never gotten all that wet; then he stood and waited.

This was no dream, no fairy tale. He wasn't going to wake up back home. This shower room wasn't going to melt away like morning mist. He wasn't going to get out of here by wishing. He couldn't get back to his own world that easily.

This was real life, and real life was never that simple, there were never any ruby slippers.

In the stories everything came out right in the end. In the stories someone would rescue them, Nancy would still be alive, it would all be a mistake.

This was no story.

Someone might rescue them. It did happen. There were possibilities. There was Prossie Thorpe—or at least, there had been Prossie Thorpe, he had seen her in the waiting room, maybe even in the dining hall, but she might be dead by now. Death only took an instant.

And there might be some way to save himself. The hero of a story would do that, he wouldn't wait to be rescued. In stories there was always a way out.

But in real life, sometimes there was and sometimes there wasn't. Sometimes the hostages were rescued; sometimes they died. Sometimes the innocent were saved; sometimes they were slaughtered.

Real life was never as tidy as the stories.

"You done?" one of the guards asked.

He nodded.

"Toss me the towel, then, and I'll see if we're ready for you."

Pel obeyed, and stood naked and waiting, while the other men, seeing their protests did no good, finished drying themselves and stood about chatting uneasily.

There were three guards, each with a baton—no blasters, no blades. It occurred to Pel that the thirty or so prisoners could easily overpower them. In the stories, the hero would organize them and they'd do it, they'd overpower the guards—but then what?

Thirty men, naked and unarmed, on a hostile planet, with no idea where they were—what could they do?

In the stories they'd find a way, but this was no story.

Three guards were plenty.

A loud click was audible over the general background noise; Pel turned to see that the door opposite the shower room, a door that had been locked, was now open. One of the three blue-clad men stood beside it, baton at ready.

"Okay, one at a time," he called. "You!" He pointed at Pel. "You ready? You first."

Slowly and deliberately, Pel crossed the room.

This was it; he was about to die.

This was the last minute, when the rescuers would burst in with blasters ready—in the stories.

In real life, it was when the victims died like sheep.

Would it be a bullet? A shot from a blaster? Would they cut his throat, butcher him like an animal?

He didn't know, and wasn't really sure he cared. He stepped through the door.

Two men were waiting for him in the corridor.

"Hands behind your back," one of them ordered, as the other grasped his upper left arm. Pel obeyed, and cuffs were slapped on.

He didn't get a good look at them and couldn't turn his head far enough to see them once they were in place, but he could tell from the feel that these were not the slim steel bands used by modern police; they were wider and heavier than that, like old-fashioned manacles.

He considered that dispassionately. Would he be blindfolded, next? Posed against a wall for a firing squad, perhaps? Led up the steps of a gallows?

The guard who had cuffed him took his right arm, the other still held his left. He was led down the corridor and through another door.

As the door opened Pel blinked and tried to stop, but the pressure on his arms forced him onward. Suddenly horribly aware of his nakedness, he struggled, but to no avail. He felt his scrotum contracting, as if he had just plunged into cold water.

He was being dragged out onto a stage, in front of a crowd of at least a hundred people, men and women; those he could see were dressed in strange but elegant clothing.

This was *worse* than death, worse than the gallows or firing squad. He trembled, and might have screamed if one of his guards hadn't jerked him back and shoved a gag in his mouth.

The stage was lit, but so was the audience; he was on display, but this was no play, no mere performance.

An announcer stood behind a lectern at the far side of the stage. "Lot number one," he called, "a healthy adult male, age and history uncertain. What am I bid?"

■

Raven stood straight and proud as the auctioneer called out the bids. He thrust out his chest, threw back his shoulders, and set his jaw.

If he were sold as a mere farmhand or miner he would stand no chance of gaining authority's ear. Were he to be bought as a conscript for the guard, as a bodyguard perhaps, or as someone's personal attendant, his chances were that much better.

He had heard the bidding on other men, and he allowed himself a smile when he heard the auctioneer call out, "Four hundred! Four hundred and ten! Do I hear . . . I have four hundred and ten!"

The smile broadened when he heard a woman's voice from the audience and the bid jumped to 425.

None of the others ahead of him had gone for so much. He had guessed that four hundred was the ceiling for simple labor. If he went for more than that . . .

■

Amy could hear the remarks as she was led out.

"No yearling this time, hey?"

"Drooping a little."

"Is this somebody's grandmother?"

She started to react, to glare at the audience, then stopped herself. This wasn't some stupid movie; acting up wouldn't impress anyone with her spunk. It would probably just get her a whack from one of those damned billy clubs.

Just as arguing with Stan hadn't impressed him, hadn't cowed him, hadn't won him over, hadn't gotten an apology. It just got her hit and finished off the ruins of their marriage.

The lights were on the audience as well as the stage, so that bids could be spotted, and Amy looked out at the bidders, but she didn't glare, didn't make any stupid defiant gestures. This was no movie.

If it *were* a movie, of course, rescue would probably arrive right about now. And there were so many things about this that seemed unreal—castles and monsters and spaceships—that why *shouldn't* there be a last-minute rescue? All those Imperial troopers in their spiffy purple uniforms ought to be good for *something*, and surely Prossie Thorpe had had plenty of time to send a telepathic cry for help.

In fact, why hadn't help already come?

She had glimpsed Prossie Thorpe briefly in the showers and in the drying room; she should have asked. She had been busy with Rachel, though, and when she had looked elsewhere it had been at Susan and her mysterious vanishing handbag, or the passengers off the *Princess* banging on the door.

Mostly she had paid attention to Rachel. Now she and Rachel had been separated by the guards anyway, to be auctioned off individually.

The thought of that poor little girl being sold like an animal was ghastly. It couldn't be allowed. Something would have to happen to prevent it.

Prossie Thorpe was the only hope, though. *Did* the pirates and slavers know that Prossie was a telepath? They were treating her like anyone else. Did they have some way of blocking her telepathy?

How would they know what she was? How could they block something that could work between universes?

Help had to be coming. It had to be on the way.

But there was no sign of it. She was standing naked on a bare stage, about to be auctioned off, and she could see the cracks in the plaster walls, could smell the cologne someone in the front row was wearing, could hear someone whispering, but she couldn't see or hear or smell any sign that anyone was coming to save her. No ships rumbling overhead, no soldiers shouting, just rustling clothes and muttered asides, and somewhere behind her the clink of manacles.

"What am I bid?" the auctioneer called, and the moment of silence before the reply was the most embarrassing few seconds in Amy's entire life.

■

Pel wondered how much 280 crowns actually was. It didn't sound
like very much.

But then, why should he be worth much? Somehow he didn't
think a place like this would have much use for a marketing consultant, and without that he was just another warm body, another
set of not-very-developed muscles.

He didn't put up any fight when his new owner came and collected him; he was so relieved to be off that stage, away from all
those staring eyes, that he was almost glad to see the man who had
paid 280 crowns for him. The whole experience had been exhaust-
ing, terrifying, unbearable; he was more certain than ever that he
had somehow found himself captive in hell.

Rachel—would they auction *Rachel* off that way?

Who would buy a six-year-old girl, and why?

He was so involved with his own thoughts, with trying to
keep them away from certain subjects, that he barely noticed when
he was loaded into an airbus, barely noticed when he was turned
over to someone else, when he was led into the mineshaft, or when
the manacles were removed.

The overseer had to slap him to get his attention.

"All right, new boy," he said. "You listening now?"

Pel nodded, gently touching his stinging cheek.

"You're new, you don't seem too bright, we'll keep it simple
for you. Those guys over there are breaking rock; your job is getting that rock off the floor and into the carts, so we can get it out
of here. You can use your hands, or if you ask nice we'll give you
a shovel." The overseer glowered at him, hands on hips, the overhead light emphasizing his downturned features with streaks of
shadow.

Pel took the hint. "Please, sir," he said, "may I have a
shovel?"

One of the workers at the rockface grinned and kicked a
shovel over toward Pel; it clattered loudly in the enclosed space.
Watching the overseer's face, ready to duck or drop the shovel, Pel
cautiously picked it up.

The overseer gave a snort and turned away.

Pel, holding the shovel but not moving, watched him go. He

made no move to smash in the overseer's skull with the edge of the shovel; the urge was there, at least slightly, but he knew it would do no good. It couldn't be that easy.

Then the overseer was out of sight and the opportunity had passed.

"Hey, new boy," one of the workers called, "you got a name?"

"Pel," Pel admitted, turning.

"I'm Jack. You really stupid, or just confused?"

"Disoriented, mostly," Pel answered.

"Yeah. I figured. Well, it's not really all that bad here; we get food and shelter and as long as we get the ore out they don't bother us. You'll get clothes, too."

Pel registered for the first time that the other men—there were half a dozen in sight—wore pants and boots. No shirts—but then, the mineshaft was hot. Sweat gleamed on every side in the light of the four electric work lights that hung from the shaft's ceiling.

"They'll give you your duds at supper tonight," Jack told him, "after we change shifts. You do the first day naked to remind you that you ain't worth shit, but after that they'd just as soon you didn't get scratched up."

"We change shifts?" Pel asked.

Jack nodded. "We got two shifts, twelve hours each, work here; meals before and after, and they send down food and water around mid-shift."

"Are we . . ." Pel swallowed; his throat was suddenly dry. "Are we the day shift or the night shift?"

Jack smiled. "Neither one; guess you *are* new. Local day is something like seventeen hours, so everybody just ignores it; all the clocks are on Terran time."

"Oh."

"We're the Blue Shift; the other one's Red. Somebody's idea of a joke, I guess. You'll get a cot, share it with someone on Red Shift."

Pel nodded. He stood, the shovel in his hands, trying to absorb all this.

"Hey, buddy," another man called, "enough with the lessons. Get to work."

Pel looked at Jack, who nodded and pointed to the pile of ore and slag. "There you are," he said.

The rock was on one side, the empty cart on the other, and Pel between, with his shovel. The rock was fist-size lumps; the cart was a battered black metal box on steel wheels; the shovel was a shovel.

He started shoveling.

■

Amy looked over the interior of the aircar apprehensively. She didn't like the situation at all.

She had seen most of the others, male and female, sold to men in various uniforms and formed into gangs—obviously destined for manual labor somewhere. A few who had had specific skills announced had drawn higher-than-average bids and had presumably been bound for jobs that could use their talents.

But the auctioneer had announced Susan with an audible leer in his voice. "A really *nice* young woman," he had said, grinning. "History unknown, looks a bit exotic." And the bidding had been enthusiastic—she had gone for eleven hundred and something, higher than anyone else Amy saw sold. Susan was small and slender, with no known skills, so nobody was buying her as a laborer. It was obvious what her value was.

And one of the bidders for Susan—one of the losing bidders—had been the one who bought Amy for 510. He hadn't bid on anyone else after that; he had just stood in his spot along the right-hand wall, watching her, waiting until he could claim her. He wore no uniform, no fancy clothes, just a dull white shirt and black slacks; he had no clipboard, no notes, none of the totems and devices the other buyers flourished.

And when the paperwork was done, and he could collect her, he hadn't said a word; he had just grabbed her by one manacled wrist and had dragged her out to the parking lot where his aircar waited.

That had given her her first glimpse of the outside world on whatever planet this was, save for the quick dash across bare concrete from the pirate ship to the holding facility, and she had been interested by the look around, despite her worries. They were clearly in a city—she really hadn't been sure of that from the glimpse between the ship and the entrance tunnel. None of the buildings in sight from the parking lot were over three stories high, but the streets were lined solidly with masonry, showing no gaps in the stone and concrete facades. The architecture ran to colonnades and pilasters, with little ornamentation—it reminded her of old pictures of the Soviet Union under Stalin.

Then she had been shoved into the rear seat of the aircar, and a moment later they were airborne, just the two of them. She wondered if she should say something, anything, but she had no idea what would be appropriate. After all, she had never been auctioned off before.

She studied the interior of the aircar.

The dark red upholstery was worn; a tear in the back of the rear seat had been darned with heavy thread, but the off-white stuffing still showed through. The nap of the rough fabric scratched her bare bottom, her manacled hands made it difficult to sit back, and she shifted repeatedly in an unsuccessful attempt to find a comfortable position.

If she had been wearing anything, she thought, she would have been much more comfortable.

The windows were clean; the cranks to open them had been removed, she noticed, leaving bare threaded metal. The metal was dull, not shiny—the removal wasn't recent.

The rear shelf, behind the seat, was dusty and empty. The front seat was more of the same, dark red fabric, worn but clean and serviceable.

The driver—well, the driver was medium height, heavy, with a round, sweaty face. His expression seemed to vary from hostile and blank to an unpleasant smile, and his gaze had never yet met her own. All she could see of him now was the back of his head, thick black hair that could have used a shampoo and trim.

He hadn't said a word to her.

And he had just *bought* her, for 510 crowns, however much that was.

However much it actually came to, it was less than half what Susan had been valued at; Amy wondered if she should be offended by the difference. Of course, Susan was at least ten years younger, and ten pounds thinner—or maybe twenty. She wasn't sagging anywhere yet, the way Amy was.

She was just as sold, though. Amy had seen her standing motionless on the stage, her face calm and resigned; almost everyone else who had stood there had been visibly nervous, trembling or sweating, glancing in all directions as if expecting sudden rescue.

It was about time for that rescue, Amy thought. It was *past* time. Prossie Thorpe must have called for help days ago; wasn't it due to arrive by now?

After all, in the movies help always arrived before anything really terrible could happen, didn't it? And this whole thing, spaceships falling out of the sky into her yard, Raven and Shadow and the Galactic Empire—wasn't it all something out of the movies?

If help didn't come soon . . .

She didn't want to think about it.

Not just for herself, but all the others. What was going to happen to Susan? What had become of Rachel? Amy hadn't seen her out on that stage; the girl had been pulled away by the female guards and put at the rear of the female line. Maybe they had the decency not to make slaves of little girls, Amy thought; maybe they would find a good home for her.

And maybe not.

CHAPTER 22

The aircar set down on a gravel square in the front yard of a rambling one-story house; the little patch of pavement was surrounded on all sides by grass, and that, in turn, was surrounded on every side by cornfields. The crops stood from knee- to waist-high, and stretched off as far as Amy could see in every direction. In the distance she could see the wind drawing patterned ripples in the fields, but where she stood the air was still.

A few scraggly oak trees had been planted near the house, but as yet none were much taller than Amy, and while she wasn't short, she was hardly Amazonian.

The driver got out, slammed the front door, then turned and opened the rear.

"Get out," he said.

Amy got out, not hurriedly, but not hanging back, either. The manacles made it a bit awkward.

Once she was out the gravel hurt her bare feet, and she danced a painful two steps to the grass. "Ow," she said.

"Come on," the man ordered, turning away from her and toward the house.

Amy looked around.

She stood beside a gravel square, connected by a gravel path to a concrete stoop; the house behind that stoop was half-timbered, with something like orange clay forming most of the walls, while the frame and trim were dark, unpainted wood. The roof was thatch. The windows were large, with only a few large panes, which seemed at variance with the rest of the architecture.

A front lawn of neatly trimmed grass extended out from the house and around the gravel landing area. On all sides of the lawn green corn plants marched in neat rows across the reddish earth.

The idea of escape struck her. Her feet were free; the man had made no move to stop her when she hopped off the gravel, and now she was a good five feet away, out of his reach. He didn't look much like an athlete. If she were to turn and start running, she thought she could probably outrace him and outlast him.

But where would she go?

She couldn't see any human-made structure except the house and aircar, anywhere. She was naked, her hands chained, on an unknown and hostile planet. There weren't any lawyers or cops to help her this time, no friends or family she could hope to contact.

Where *could* she go?

Reluctantly, she turned and followed her captor toward the house.

■

When Raven was first informed of his duties he balked. The rightful lord of Stormcrack Keep, kept to play the stud for some fat old mare?

"Why else would someone pay five hundred crowns for you?" asked his new mistress' majordomo, who had bid for and bought him on the woman's behalf.

Raven had no quick reply.

In truth, he had no reply at all; he knew too little of his new home to make any guesses.

And upon further consideration, he decided that perhaps this was for the best. A woman who could afford such luxuries must needs be powerful indeed, in the local hierarchy, and what better way to ingratiate himself than by such services as she was demanding?

Nor was there any great hurry; she had ordered that he be fed and pampered for a day or two, that he might be up to the task.

He had not as yet seen her; her agents had collected him after the auction. As he ate and drank he found himself imagining what she might look like. A wealthy woman, they told him, and as his purchase demonstrated; she was presumably not of noble birth, for these people, degenerate barbarians that they were, put no store by ancestry, but he would make allowances for that. And no great beauty, surely, else she would have no need to buy a man's services. Still, doubtless she would have her virtues.

Doubtless.

■

The food was boring, with a peculiar off taste to it, but it was nourishing. Pel found the work boring, as well, and tiring, but not particularly difficult—it called for endurance, but no great strength or skill. No one abused him; the overseer checked in maybe once an hour, billy club in hand, and then went on to inspect the other work gangs. There were no whips, no groaning wheels, no one dying of exhaustion, none of the clichés of slave-worked mines that Hollywood had taught him. The men worked hard, but were a long way from killing themselves, and as long as the broken rock came out of the shaft on schedule nobody bothered them.

In fact, the workers exchanged bitter jokes about their situation, and laughed at them.

Pel didn't laugh with them. He was gradually coming out of his funk, but was not yet ready to laugh at anything.

There was a sort of dull comfort in the steady work, in pushing the shovel under the rock, lifting it, and dumping it into the cart. It kept his body busy, kept him moving, so that he couldn't sink completely into apathy and despair, but it still left him free to think if he wanted to.

And it tired him, so that when he was off-shift he slept soundly.

That twelve hours on, twelve hours off was deceptive, he discovered. His gang, along with the rest of Blue Shift, was only permitted to leave their shaft when their replacements from Red Shift had arrived and actually begun working. Walking back out to the refectory and dormitory, being checked out by the clerk at the shaft mouth, finding a seat in the refectory—that took half an hour or more. The refectory crew wasn't in any great hurry, either. And the meals were fairly leisurely; no one rushed.

On top of that, if he wanted his sweat-soaked pants laundered, he had to wash them himself, in the lavatory sinks—and most of the men did just that, because odors lingered in the unventilated shafts. Each slave had been issued one pair of pants, and one pair of wool-lined boots—no socks. Not much could be done about the smell from the boots, but washing the pants out each night was a social necessity. Lines for drying ran the length of the dormitory halls, and every night a pair of damp trousers hung over each bed; if a man was too exhausted to wash them, at the very least he hung them to air out. Aside from the smell, moisture seethed constantly in the cool night air; anything left damp with sweat and *not* hung out was an invitation to mildew and rot.

With the walk to and from his work area, the leisurely meals, the washing up, and the lines everywhere, Pel found he only had about nine hours to sleep, and no time left at all for any sort of diversion. Nine hours was not excessive at all, given the unaccustomed heavy labor.

He could speak to the other slaves, of course—on the job, at the table, in the lavatories and dorms. At first, though, he didn't. They were strangers, not even from his world, and he was still too caught up in his losses.

The men around him accepted that; nobody bothered him. Occasionally someone would try to include him in a discussion, but nobody forced it, nobody pressured him.

But he gradually came out of his funk, and by the third day he was thinking again, thinking about just one thing, the one thing that any storybook hero, or any sane man, would think about.

Escape.

■

As Amy and the black-haired man approached the house the front door opened, and a woman appeared. She was short and dumpy, in her forties, her dull brown hair tied back. A shapeless brown floral-print dress covered her from throat to ankle.

She looked critically at Amy.

Amy was reminded anew that she, herself, wasn't wearing anything at all. Even an ugly brown dress would have been an improvement.

She hadn't exactly had a choice, though, and at least the

weather was reasonably warm. Walking around naked in snow would have been much worse.

"I see you got one," the woman said.

The man didn't bother to reply.

"What'd she cost?"

"Five hundred," the man growled, pushing past the woman into the house.

Amy was mincing across the gravel to the stoop by then, trying to keep her feet intact. The woman watched with interest. "That's not too bad, five hundred," she said. "And she's got nice hair, it looks like—hard to be sure, the mess it's in."

The man growled something Amy couldn't make out as she gratefully stepped up onto the smooth concrete and found herself face to face with the woman in brown. She hesitated, looking down slightly at this person, apparently the mistress of the house.

"Go on," the woman said, gesturing, "get inside."

Amy got inside.

The door opened into a large, open room; the floor was gray concrete spread with bright rag rugs, the walls papered in a wine-red pattern of stripes and blossoms on primrose. Most of the furniture used black iron frames to support upholstered seats and backs, the iron seemingly in rough imitation of early American woodwork.

The man who had bought her stood by an open door; beyond, Amy could see a cheerful bedroom. "Come here," he ordered.

Amy glanced at the woman.

"Guess I'll go take a walk," the woman in brown said. She stepped out the door, closing it behind her.

"Come here, bitch, if you want those cuffs off," the man called.

Amy hesitated.

Wasn't it about time for the space cavalry to come charging over the hill? Hadn't Prossie done *anything*? Couldn't the Empire find her?

The memory of Stan was far clearer than she wanted, just now. This man didn't look anything like him, but something in his voice had the same ugly edge Stan had developed.

"Get the fuck over here, bitch!"

Reluctantly, Amy crossed the room, stumbling over the up-turned edge of one of the rugs. The man stepped back into the bedroom as she approached, and to one side.

"On the bed," he ordered, "on your knees."

"Why?" Amy demanded, her throat dry.

"Why do you *think*?" he retorted. "If I just wanted someone to do housework, I could've gotten someone cheaper than you—a kid or somebody's grandmother. I couldn't afford that black-haired one, but you'll do."

"You're planning . . ." She swallowed, moistening her throat, and tried again. "Planning to rape me?"

"What the hell else did I buy you for?"

The woman was outside somewhere; as far as Amy knew, if she could overpower this one man, she would be safe, at least for the moment. Amy considered kicking him in the crotch, but he was off to the side, the angle was wrong—he could dodge. And she was still manacled, her hands behind her back, which would throw her balance off.

She didn't have any weapons, but neither did her captor, so far as she could see.

She was still trying to think of something when his patience ran out and he grabbed for her arm, saying, "Get *over* there!"

She dodged, turned, and ran, with no plan at all except to get away.

With a growl, he ran after her.

She was turning, trying to get her hand on the door handle, when he caught up with her and punched her in the belly.

The air rushed out of her lungs, and she felt a sudden constriction, a cramping of her diaphragm, as if she were about to vomit. She doubled over, and his other hand came down on the back of her head, knocking her off balance. She fell to her knees, slamming her right knee hard against the concrete floor; before she could regain her balance he drove both hands, clenched together, against the back of her head, knocking her forward. She caught herself on one shoulder just before her face hit one of the rugs, but then the man's booted foot came down on the back of her neck and pressed her cheek down against the coiled fabric.

"Stupid bitch," he growled. "Where the hell would you have gone, bare-ass naked and with your hands chained?" Holding her down with his foot, he unfastened his belt. "Get it through your head, I *own* you. You do what I tell you, or I'll beat the shit out of you. Give me too much trouble, and I'll kill you—and don't think it'll do me any harm, either; on this planet, nobody thinks twice about killing a slave. I've done it once already." He fumbled at the buttons on his fly; from the corner of her eye Amy could see his fingers working.

This was the time for a rescue, all right. This was it, the last minute, when help was supposed to come.

It didn't.

He bent over her and grabbed her manacled hands, pushed them up behind her back with one hand while the other stroked slowly down her side and across her buttocks. She squirmed, trying to pull away, and he shoved the cuffs viciously.

She had her breath back now, but if she struggled she knew it wouldn't help any.

She screamed.

That didn't help, either. He laughed, a harsh, nervous laugh, as he knelt behind her.

And rescue didn't come.

■

Raven's first impression was of an infinite field of lace and fine fabric beneath a mountain of flesh. As the door closed behind him he thought that this was surely some mistake, that the bed already held two or three people; was he expected to service them all?

Then she lifted her head from the pillows and beckoned to him, and even in the dim orange light, even among the myriad of pillows and cushions and hangings, her shape became clear, the huge masses of her belly and breasts and thighs.

The partial erection beneath his robe, prompted by anticipation and imagination, vanished.

"Come here," she said, in a thin soprano, "come and sit beside me." She patted the bed, her fingers like thick pale sausages.

Reluctantly, he obeyed.

The odor of perfume and her own scent, horribly sweet and

cloying, reached him even before he sat down beside her. He did not look at her.

"Take off that silly robe," she told him.

He stood and slowly removed the robe, letting it fall to the floor.

He had not considered what would happen if he were unable to perform. It was simply not a question that had ever arisen for him before. Refusal, yes, he had thought about that—and he had decided against it. Inability had never occurred to him. He turned to face her, trying to think of other women, beautiful women.

A little plumpness was a good thing in a woman, certainly, a little flesh on the bones, and he wouldn't have wanted one of those gaunt, bony scarecrows he had seen betimes, with hipbones that would grind against you and ribs that would dig into your own, but this great pile of powdered flesh scarcely looked human at all, the skin was coarse and pasty, with none of the smooth resilience of a woman's . . .

Yet she *was* a woman, and he could smell her musk. She was waiting for him, she held the power of life and death over him. However repulsive she might be, she wanted him to make love to her.

And however repulsive she might be, he would have to try.

CHAPTER 23

There was only one way out of the mine, so far as Pel could determine. That was through the building complex that included the dormitory and refectory, as well as a great deal of industrial equipment he couldn't identify—machines that sorted and processed the rocks that were sent up in the carts. Pel never got a clear look at most of that area; he had no business there. He saw glimpses when he came up out of the shaft; he heard the distant rumblings as he ate or slept.

He had come in that way, but the airbus had landed in an enclosed courtyard, at the bottom of an airshaft somewhere—he would not go out by that route.

There were no side shafts, no back way out of the mine itself, so far as he could determine.

Where he emerged from the shaft each day the cart tracks ran straight ahead, through a large black pair of swinging doors; he and the other workers always turned right into a gray-painted corridor that ran between the refectory and kitchen on the left, the dormitory and lavatory on the right.

He figured that the ore must eventually leave the complex somehow, and probably not by air, but trying to follow it seemed far too risky; judging by the sound, he was as likely to find himself in a crusher or a furnace as outside.

So any escape route would have to be from the living areas, rather than the work areas.

That didn't look very promising, either. The dormitory's light and air came from a handful of small clerestory windows—this planet's architectural preferences, and in fact those of the entire Galactic Empire, from what Pel had seen, seemed to run to clerestories. Getting up to them would not be easy, and since he could not look out, he had no idea what lay beyond.

He tried watching for shadows when the sun shone—or rather, whatever star served as the sun here; the light was a little more orange than seemed natural. He determined that a chimney or similar structure stood near one window, but beyond that he could learn nothing that way.

The adjoining lavatory was arranged similarly, and the single clerestory there was frosted and barred. A filthy skylight added a little more light, but no more hope for his escape.

The refectory had a row of tall, narrow, heavily barred windows looking out on a small, paved courtyard—little more than an overgrown air shaft, really. It did have a gate into a passageway at one end, but Pel was unable to see where that gate led.

That left the kitchen, and ordinary workers were not allowed in there. The slaves were not heavily guarded, in general, but at meals the two doors to the kitchen *were* watched, a billy-club-wielding overseer standing by each.

Food had to come in somewhere, Pel decided, and where it came in, he could go out.

Through the kitchens, then—that was the way to go. That was where he would find a way out of the mine complex.

Even though he was still somewhat dazed with grief and the confusion of his situation, he was rather proud of working this out. This was the sort of thing that a storybook hero would do, Horatio Hornblower or Captain Kirk or whoever—work out the best way to escape, plan it all out logically and then carry it through.

In a movie or a novel, of course, this whole episode, being captured by pirates and sold into slavery and all the rest of it, this would all just be a minor episode on the way to the big final confrontation with Shadow, the climactic battle that would save the world—but screw all that, Pel told himself; he would settle for just getting home safely. Let someone else worry about Shadow, or about the Galactic Empire, or about Earth itself; he had his own problems.

A World War II POW wouldn't have worried about assassinating Hitler (though he might dream of it); he'd worry about getting home alive.

And that was what Pel was doing. Take it one step at a time, he told himself, and the first step would be to get out of the mine complex by way of the kitchens.

Of course, he would still be stranded on a hostile planet, with nothing but his pants and the boots on his feet and whatever he could grab on the way out. He would still need to find Rachel somehow—but he might be able to bring back help to rescue her if he could just get off the planet. Besides, if he was ever to get home to Earth, he would need to find some way to get back to Base One.

Stowing away, perhaps, or stealing a ship—though he realized he had no idea how to navigate a spaceship.

Stowing away, then. He would make his break through the kitchen, hide wherever he could, and find his way to the nearest spaceport. That was the only possible route. If he found any friendly faces along the way, he would see about finding and freeing Rachel.

No storybook hero could do any better, he was sure.

He arrived at these conclusions without ever mentioning a word about escape to any of his fellow slaves; it was only after he had reached this point in his plans that he decided to risk a few whispered questions while working.

Jack, the unofficial leader of his work gang, picked up on his hints immediately. He put down the pick he had been swinging.

"Thinking about making a run for it?" he said, sympathetically. "We all think about it, sometimes. I suppose you were figuring on the kitchen route? You don't look like the sort who plans on going out the dorm windows. Or hadn't you got that far?"

"I was thinking about the kitchen," Pel admitted, dismayed that this didn't seem to be news.

"Doesn't hurt to think, I guess," Jack said, nodding. "We've had a few people try it, but nobody's ever made it. A couple have gotten themselves killed. Farthest anybody ever got without dying . . ."

"How do you know they died?" Pel interrupted.

"Because they hauled the bodies back to show us, of course,"

Jack replied, unruffled. "Wouldn't do anyone any good to let any rumors about successful escapes get started. They don't want to kill us, after all; we cost good money."

Pel grimaced.

"Anyway," Jack went on, "the farthest anyone's gotten is the back courtyard. See, when you go through the kitchen, there's just one door outside, and that goes into a walled courtyard where they keep the trash cans and so forth, with this big sliding iron door at the back—and the door's been closed every time anyone's gotten that far. Apparently it's always closed when anybody from inside is on that side of the passageway."

"It can't always be shut," Pel protested.

"Of course not," Jack agreed. "But it is during meals, and the rest of the time the kitchen's locked."

"So nobody's gotten past that door?"

"That's right. And nobody's going to. There are only two ways to get even that far, and neither of them is going to be real popular."

"What two?" Pel asked.

"First, you can rush it—ten or fifteen guys charge in there, and the guards can't stop them all. Everybody knows that; the guards don't even try if they see it's a whole mob. What they do do is sound an alarm, and when everybody goes charging out into the courtyard to try to haul that door open, they find a bunch of thugs with blasters looking down at them from the walls."

Pel nodded.

"And the second way," Jack said, "is to create a diversion, so that one or two people can slip through. That's tough—those guards aren't stupid, or at least, whoever gave them their orders isn't. And there are cooks and people in the kitchens; you can't sneak past them, you have to make a dash for it. The cooks won't bother you—that's not their job—but you can't hide either, because they'll see you. So you'll get out to the courtyard, and you can't move that door, it takes more than one man to get it open, and before you can come up with anything else the guards will catch on and come out after you and beat the shit out of you."

Pel thought for a moment, pushing his shovel as he did. He had been disappointed to hear that all his plans were old hat, but surely, there was some overlooked possibility here, one that he could spot.

He had a rule of thumb from his marketing work that came to mind, a question he always asked himself: When you have two possibilities, can you combine them?

"Well," he suggested, "what if you did that, got one or two guys through to the courtyard, and *then* ten or twelve guys stormed through, and caught the guards from behind?"

Jack blinked. "I don't know," he admitted. "I don't think that one's been tried while I've been here."

"I think we should try it," Pel said.

Jack didn't answer for a long moment. He lifted his pick and hefted it thoughtfully, eyeing Pel.

"Maybe we should," he said.

■

When he was done he fished a key from somewhere, unfastened the manacles, and stood aside, dangling the cuffs from one hand. Amy didn't move.

"All right, bitch," he said, "get up and clean yourself off, and then let's get some clothes on you."

Amy didn't move; she crouched, trembling with fury and shame, on the floor.

Even Stan had never done that to her.

"Oh, come on," he said, kicking her in the side. "You weren't any goddamn virgin."

She still refused to move.

"Goddamn stupid bitch," he muttered. He pushed her aside with his foot, the rug where her face and arms rested slipping easily, and opened the front door.

Amy considered a lunge for his leg, now that her hands were free. She shifted her weight, judging the distance.

He glanced down and saw the movement; cautiously, he stepped farther away.

"Beth," he called, "get in here, will you?"

Amy bit her lower lip. The woman would be coming back, and in a minute it would be two against one. This was probably the best chance she would ever get; he probably thought she was cowed and helpless. She lifted herself up on one arm, then threw herself sideways, grabbing at the man's leg, trying to throw him off balance. If he fell, she saw, he would hit his head against the wall or the doorframe.

She hit him, but not as hard as she had hoped; the distance was too great. He stumbled back and dropped the manacles, but caught himself, and kicked her in the face.

The cuffs clattered on the hard floor just as his boot hit her jaw, and for a moment Amy confused the sound with what she saw and felt and thought she was hearing her bones rattle. She staggered, but did not fall.

"Shit," he said. He disentangled himself, stepping back a few feet.

Amy tried to bring herself upright and get out the front door, all at once, but she was still stooped and still inside when one hand closed on the back of her neck. Awkward and off balance, she was unable to resist as he rammed her head forward, driving her forehead against the doorframe.

Dazed, she slid back to the floor.

He reached down, grabbed her arm just below the shoulder, and hauled her up to her knees.

"Listen, stupid," he said, "I *told* you, there's nowhere to go. So just settle down and live with it, all right? You might even get to like it, if you give it a chance."

Dazed, her vision blurred, aching in a dozen places, Amy reluctantly nodded.

She would wait.

She would not yield, but she would wait.

■

She allowed him a second attempt, and a third.

It made no difference; the sight of her unmanned him.

At the second trial Raven had managed to drive himself from shame to rage, in hopes that his anger would bring his blood to move, would allow him to function, but it did no good. The blood suffused his face and chest, his hands trembled with it—but not his loins.

At the third trial he forced himself not to see her, conjured up in his mind's eye all the women he had loved before, from sweet little Elenor to the fiery Alison, and still, at her touch, all his lust had faded, he had withered, and again he had failed.

She had him whipped, of course; he had expected that.

And then she sold him.

■

Talk about large-scale diversions and massed rushes was all very well, but Pel didn't expect it to work. He had his own ideas, ideas he didn't intend to share.

Jack might well be an informer, after all. He seemed to know almost *too* much.

The information about the courtyard door was probably accurate, though, and could be useful.

Pel didn't really expect his first attempt to work; it was more in the nature of a scouting expedition. It was extremely difficult to manage the first step, he found; it wasn't until the third attempt that he was able to stay awake long enough during his off shift without anyone realizing he was still awake. The heavy lifting and hauling was responsible, he knew.

Eventually, though, he did manage it, and found himself the only person conscious in the entire dormitory.

It was daylight, as it happened, and light slanted in through the windows overhead, so he was able to see clearly. Darkness could have made things more difficult—or given him additional cover, and he wasn't sure which would be more significant. Carefully, he arose from his cot and stole as silently as he could across the floor to the door.

It was locked.

He had expected that, really. He turned and crept to the lavatory. That door was never locked; after all, someone might well need the facilities at any time.

And the lavatory had another door, opening onto the central passage. That should be locked, too—but he had noticed that the latch was rusty. In the damp air of the building practically anything ferrous was likely to rust.

He had not only noticed that, he had done something about it, hammering at it surreptitiously whenever he could, trying to knock it out of shape.

His efforts had had the desired result; the door hadn't latched properly. By giving the knob a good hard tug to the left he was able to spring the door open.

Then he was out in the passageway, where he tiptoed quickly to the refectory. The doors between the dining hall and the corridor were open—Pel had noticed that they never seemed to move, from one shift to the next, and had concluded that nobody ever bothered closing them.

The doors to the kitchen were locked, of course, just as they were supposed to be.

He crossed to the tall, narrow windows, and measured the gaps between the bars. They weren't as wide as he had hoped; he would not be able to slip out that way.

He was improvising, scouting out the situation; he had no coherent plan yet. He stood for a long moment, looking around, trying to think of some way to get through the windows, or through the kitchen.

When did they post those guards at the kitchen doors?

He would come back to that.

He slipped back into the corridor and crept down toward the mine.

And that was where the guard spotted him.

He was beaten methodically, without any particular animus, and then thrown back in his cot.

He lay there, planning the next step.

■

The man's name was Walter, but Amy was not permitted to call him anything but "master." Beth was just Beth; Amy wasn't sure of the reason for this difference.

Amy's duties were simple enough; she was to keep the house and its contents clean. Later on, if they trusted her enough, she could help tend the corn, and Beth would take over part of the cleaning, but for the present Amy was not permitted outside the house. Amy was also to be available to Walter whenever he felt the urge—which was fairly often.

She was given a simple white shift, undergarments, slippers, and an apron. She slept on the floor, with a rug underneath and a blanket on top. When she refused an order or resisted in any way,

Walter would beat her into submission. If a beating didn't convince her, she would not be fed until she relented. The manacles were kept handy, and on occasion, when she had disobeyed, they were used to secure her to furniture, where she could watch Walter and Beth eat.

She did not resist very often—enough to maintain her self-respect, but not enough to seriously endanger her health. She knew that she wasn't going to do herself any good by starving, or letting Walter break bones. If she was ever to get out of this unbearable situation she would have to keep herself reasonably fit.

She thought about escape, but knew she had nowhere to go. She could not get far on foot in any case, and had no idea how to fly the aircar—even if she could start it without the key, which was doubtful. She had heard of hotwiring a car's ignition but didn't know how it was done, and in any case aircars were not necessarily the same as the cars back on Earth in such details as ignition switches.

Walter was not interested in speaking with her, and besides, he spent most of his time out of the house. Beth was out much of the time as well, but less, and she was willing to talk, and even answer questions—at least, sometimes.

She explained about the inconveniently short day, and the arrangements they had made to deal with it. She explained the basics of corn farming, and showed Amy how to handle unfamiliar household equipment.

She answered more personal questions, too.

Yes, Amy was the only slave they had at present; they had had two others at one point, both women, both subject to Walter's whims, but last year's crop had been very bad and first Walter had sold the little one, Maggie, and then the other one, Sheila, had died.

At first, Beth insisted that Sheila had gotten sick and died before they could get a doctor for her, but eventually she admitted that Walter had gotten drunk and angry one night and had strangled her. She was buried out back. Beth pointed out the grave, visible from the back windows.

Amy had thought that the bare ground there was a small garden patch; now she stared at it and felt ill.

"He's not going to really hurt you, though," Beth said. "He couldn't afford to buy *another* slave."

Somehow, Amy did not find that very comforting.

■

When Raven learned the identity of his new owner, and what the man wanted of him, he realized that this was Arabella's final insult, her final comment on his own sexual prowess, or lack thereof.

It was, he supposed, to be expected.

He put it to his buyer directly, in blunt terms—how much fun could there be if Raven had to be beaten into submission every time? Raven was stronger than this new owner, so that other slaves would have to do the beating, would be required to hold him down. Was that what this Roland wanted?

What point in owning him, then?

Roland did make one test of Raven's resolve; thus convinced, and nursing a black eye as a result, he put Raven up for sale.

That was after the flogging, of course.

There were no buyers at first; nobody cared to risk any money until they knew whether or not the slave would live.

■

Reaching the clerestory windows wasn't as difficult as Pel had feared; standing a cot on end and climbing the ladderlike frame lifted him high enough to reach the sill.

The other slaves simply watched, with amused interest; they made no effort to help him, but didn't hinder him, either. Nobody called for the guards. They all just watched as he chinned himself on the sill, threw up first one arm and then the other, his feet waving wildly all the time.

He hung there for a moment, looking out through the window at gray asphalt roofing and, some distance away, the tumbled gray stone of a mountainside. There were no obvious hazards or obstacles.

Encouraged, he struggled to inch upward, to swing one leg up.

It was harder than it had looked in all those old movies, all those times Indiana Jones had hung from a cliff by his fingers or whatever, but eventually he got himself out the window onto the roof.

He got cautiously to his feet and looked around.

He stood on a long, narrow rectangle of slate-gray roofing, extending the full length of the dormitory and lavatory, but only about six feet wide. The "chimney" he had located by its shadow was close by, and he now discovered it to be a vent-pipe from the lavatory's plumbing.

Behind him, the windows were set in a sheer wall extending much higher than he had expected—it had to be at least twenty feet high, and was topped with an overhang. The edge of the overhang was wrapped in dull gray metal that glinted oddly in the orange sunlight. It looked very sharp.

The height of the wall seemed to imply that there was another story to the building, but there were no more windows above the set he had climbed through, nothing above them but blank concrete. It might simply be intended as an obstacle.

That wall was too high and bare for him to climb. He turned to look at the other sides. Before him was the edge of the roof; he crouched down and peered over.

The wall dropped sheer for a ridiculous distance, given that he was only one story up—at least thirty or forty feet, it looked like.

And about thirty feet away another wall rose, a wall that appeared to be hewn out of the mountainside itself, the space between the walls forming a sort of dry moat.

He worked his way around all three sides, and the moat went all the way around. Nowhere was it narrow enough to make an attempt to jump it reasonable; nowhere was it shallow enough to make a leap down into it reasonable; nowhere did it look possible to climb back out if he once did get in.

Frustrated, he climbed back down into the dormitory—and found four guards waiting for him.

They beat him soundly and removed his bedding, to prevent any attempts at making climbing gear from the fabric.

■

Major Johnston swore quietly under his breath, wishing he could think of some new obscenity. The old ones had all lost their flavor by this time.

"All of them," he said. "*All* of them."

"Yes, sir." The lieutenant stood beside the desk, trying to look suitably unhappy and hide the relief he felt that this wasn't his problem.

Johnston tapped his pen on the desktop and stared up at the lieutenant. He knew the man was glad to not have the responsibility on this one, and he didn't blame him. Johnston wished *he* didn't have the responsibility, either.

And to think he had *asked* for it, and had been pleased when the FBI decided to leave it all to the military.

"The cars are really theirs? The vehicle numbers match, not just the plates?"

"Yes, sir."

"And that damned phony spaceship hasn't moved? Nobody's been inside?"

"No, sir."

The major stopped tapping, and for a moment he sat silently. Then, abruptly, he hurled the pen across the room and roared, *"Where the hell did they go?"*

"I don't know, sir."

"You talked to the neighbors?"

"Someone did, sir, not me, personally."

"And searched the house?"

"Yes, sir."

"Legally?"

"Yes, sir; we got a warrant."

"Nobody saw anything?"

"No, sir."

"And there wasn't *anything* to say where they'd gone? Notes? Maybe something on a computer disk? *Anything?*"

"Nothing, sir. Some empty pizza boxes, a very hungry cat—nothing else out of the ordinary."

Johnston growled. "This is ridiculous. The spaceship appears out of nowhere, but does *that* disappear? No, it just *sits* there, and instead this . . . this marketing consultant bails the crew out of jail, and invites the Jewell woman and her lawyer over, and they all vanish. All the cars still there. Like the goddamn *Marie Celeste.* Lieutenant, does *any* of this make sense?"

"No, sir."

"Damn right it doesn't. Almost makes me believe in the fucking Bermuda Triangle and Charles Fort and all that crap." He slumped back in his chair.

For a moment he sat silently, and the lieutenant stood, equally silent, and waited.

"The cat," Johnston said at last. "What happened to the cat?"

The lieutenant cleared his throat. "Well, sir," he said, "I've got the cat at home. He's a cute little fellow."

Johnston chewed on his lip for a moment, then snarled, "Good. Keep it. And I want that place bugged. Both places. And watched. If anyone goes in or out of Jewell's house, or Brown's, I want to not just know it happened, I want to know who it was and every goddamn word they said. Bug that ship, too. Bug the lawyers' homes and offices. *Everything.*"

"Yes, sir." The lieutenant started to turn away, but the major's voice stopped him.

"Lieutenant. Do it legally. Get court orders."

"Yes, sir."

"Lieutenant."

"Yes, sir?"

"You think we'll ever find them?"

The lieutenant considered that carefully, then shrugged.

"No, sir," he said, "I don't think we will."

CHAPTER 24

By the end of the first month after the capture of *Emerald Princess*
Amy had given up any hope of rescue. She had also given up resisting Walter's advances. She still neglected the housework as
much as she dared, but when she received a direct order she
obeyed it without argument.

She had also made the rather startling discovery that Beth
was a slave, like herself, rather than Walter's wife. Walter had
never bothered trying to deal with free women; he had bought
Beth about twenty years ago, when they were both young, and had
kept her.

This revelation left Amy feeling betrayed—right from the first,
and at every point since, Beth had consistently sided with Walter
against her. It was bad enough that Beth had sided with a man
against one of her fellow women, that she had helped Walter to rape
and starve and torment Amy—but when she was herself a slave, and
at least theoretically in the same situation that Amy was?

When she learned the truth Amy refused to speak to Beth for
a day and a half.

She had just decided that this was a mistake, that she was
only making everybody's life more difficult and making Beth less
likely than ever to sympathize with her, when the whine of an
aircar made her look up from the sink.

Walter hadn't said anything about expecting company. He
and Beth were out in the fields somewhere.

Then another whine sounded, and another. Amy put the dish-
rag aside and reached for a towel to dry her hands.

Voices were calling back and forth out there; Amy tossed the towel on the counter and crossed to the window. She hesitated, then lifted the curtain and peered out.

There were a dozen men in purple uniforms out there, and three matching purple-and-gold aircars—or vehicles, anyway; they didn't look much like ordinary aircars. One of the vehicles had landed beside Walter's aircar, half on the gravel and half on the grass; the other two had set down on the corn, flattening it. The men had blasters drawn.

One of them saw her and pointed. She let the curtain drop, and her fingers trembled as she did. Her heart was racing, and her chest felt tight with excitement—was this *rescue*? Finally? Weren't those Imperial uniforms?

What should she do?

"All right, in there," an amplified voice called. "Come out with your hands up!"

That answered her question. For the last few weeks she had had lesson after lesson in not resisting—and Walter hadn't even had a blaster.

She opened the door and edged out, her hands raised, fingers spread, empty palms forward.

Half a dozen blasters were leveled at her by men crouching behind aircars—armored aircars, she realized. Each had a swivel-mounted weapon on top, something vaguely resembling a machine gun; all three of those were pointed at her, as well.

One of the men motioned for her to come forward; nervously, she did.

When she was well clear of the house, a man dashed forward, grabbed her by the arm, and pulled her away, across the little front lawn.

"Who else is in there?" another man—an officer, she supposed—barked at her.

"Nobody," she said. "They're out working the fields." She pointed with her thumb in the direction Walter and Beth had gone that morning.

The men exchanged glances.

"They must've seen us coming in, or heard us," someone remarked.

The officer nodded.

"Get her aboard," he said. "Jonas, Medfield, search the house."

After that, Amy didn't get to see much; she was dragged into the back of one of the vehicles and strapped onto a steel bench, sitting up with a purple-clad soldier on either side. A third man was perched in a raised seat nearby, his head and shoulders sticking up through an open hatch—manning the swivel gun, Amy realized. A fourth man sat up front, in the driver's seat.

A moment later the driver called, "Right," out a window and threw a lever into position; the car lifted off and began moving, but with the usual almost indetectible acceleration of antigravity vehicles, which made it impossible to judge speed or distance by feel.

From where she sat, Amy's only view of the outside was through a narrow strip of windshield that was visible between the two high-backed front seats; most of what she could make out through that was either sky or rapidly passing cornfield, and not enough of either one to mean anything to her.

She heard the whine of antigravity engines, the rush of wind, distant shouts, and once the electric hiss of a blaster, but she really had no idea what was going on outside the steel walls of the vehicle.

"What's happening?" she asked.

"You're a slave here, right?" the soldier on her right asked.

She nodded.

"Then we're rescuing you. The Empire's clearing out this whole planet, bringing it back under civilized control."

Amy felt a flood of relief; she had hoped, but hadn't dared believe, that that was what was happening. "Thank you," she said. She groped for more words, for some way of expressing what she felt, and could only repeat, "Thank you."

"Hey," the driver called back, "ask her who else is around here. Whose farm is it? Any other slaves?"

"A man named Walter," she said. "It's his farm. And a woman named Beth. She . . ." She hesitated.

Beth was a slave—but she hadn't acted the part, had she? She had sided with her master, every time. *Beth* wasn't beaten when she talked back. *Beth* wasn't raped almost every night. And she hadn't lifted a finger to stop it when *Amy* was.

Together, the two of them might have done something against Walter, but Beth had chosen to side with her master.

"She's his wife," Amy said.

■

Someone kicked Pel awake; startled, he raised his head.

Pain shot through his neck, which was stiff and bruised from his latest beating.

"It isn't really time, is it?" someone asked.

"Doesn't *feel* like it," someone else replied.

That was the truth; after three weeks, Pel was fairly well settled into the rhythms of his life in the mines, and it simply didn't feel like time to get up for breakfast.

Maybe it was just his bruises saying that, though. Reluctantly, he sat up.

"All right, boys," one of the overseers called, "line 'em up and march 'em out."

Grumbling, the slaves got themselves up, pulling their stiff, dry pants from the lines, and fishing malodorous boots from under cots.

One man refused to stir.

"Hey," an overseer said, prodding him, "rise and shine, boyo."

"The hell with breakfast," the slave said without moving. "I'll starve today, if it means I can have another ten minutes' sleep."

The overseer glanced at his boss, who was standing in the doorway. The head overseer shrugged.

"Listen, Sunshine," the guard said, "this isn't breakfast. Wouldn't be your shift for another two hours. This is special. Everybody out."

Pel blinked, and hesitated, with one leg in his pants and the other out.

Two hours early? No wonder everyone was sleepy.

What sort of special?

He pulled his pants on.

■

Raven's third owner had bought him as a personal plaything. He had no duties to carry out; he was simply to be there when Wilf was in the mood to inflict pain.

Wilf was astonished by just how stubborn his new acquisition was. Roland had told him the man was tough, but for someone not yet fully recovered from a serious whipping to take broken bones without even a whimper—that was impressive.

It drove him to greater efforts.

Raven had given up any idea of ingratiating himself with his owners; right now he was far more interested in surviving with his honor intact—honor that was far more important than his bones. To cry out in pain might not be unmanly, and the Goddess knew that any man would cry out if pressed hard enough, yet he was reluctant to give this filthy barbarian the satisfaction.

He knew that he could survive without breaking; it was just a matter of refusing to yield until eventually, his captors would give up.

Eventually, either they would give up, or he would die. He refused to admit any third possibility.

He was watching his new owner's face, studying the greedy look in his eyes, trying not to think about the pain, when the soldiers burst in.

■

For the long flight away from the farm the soldier on Amy's left traded places with the driver. The others stayed where they were. Walter and Beth, captured as they fled, were in one of the other vehicles, and Amy was relieved not to see them.

"Hi," the off-duty driver said, as he belted in.

"Hi," Amy replied.

"Listen, are you sure there were just three of you?" he asked. "And that the woman is this Walter Fletcher's wife?"

"Of course I'm sure," Amy said. "Why?"

"Oh, well . . . because she swears she's a slave, too."

"She's lying," Amy snapped.

The soldier nodded. "I figured she probably was—trying to get off, I suppose." He shook his head.

"I guess she tried to tell you *I* was . . . was that man's wife?"

"No," the soldier said, "she wasn't that stupid; nobody would buy that for a minute, not with that thing you're wearing, and that shiner, and all those bruises."

Amy felt an odd mixture of emotions in reaction to the man's words. He meant to be sympathetic, she was sure, but she was struck by anger, shame, embarrassment, and an uncomfortable sort of righteous self-pity, rather than taking any comfort from his words and presence.

After a moment of awkward silence, she asked, "Where are you taking us?"

The soldier glanced at her, then at the opposite bulkhead and the tangle of equipment that hung there. "Well," he said, "old Walter's going to a prison camp—and his wife along with him, I suppose. Keeping slaves is a felony. Beating them is assault—we'll want to have a doctor check you out, take some photos. You'll need to give a statement. We aren't going to bother with full-blown trials here—too many people for 'em. Besides, the whole planet's under martial law right now. We'll hold tribunals, a panel of judges'll check the evidence and figure out what to do with him." He shrugged. "He'll probably be in the camp for a good long time."

"Beth told me he killed a girl," Amy said. She wasn't sure why she was telling him this, but the words spilled out. "Her name was Sheila. They buried her out back, Beth said—I saw the grave."

The soldier frowned and stared at Amy for a moment. She returned his stare, unflinching.

She wasn't sure why she had told him, but she had, and it was true. If it meant Walter would be imprisoned longer, that was fine, it was what the son of a bitch deserved.

"That's murder," the soldier said at last. "If that's true, old Walter's going to hang. Or maybe they'll just shoot him, to save time. And his wife's an accomplice, I suppose, so she'll get the same."

"How'll they know?" Amy asked. "I mean, I don't think he and Beth are going to tell the judges about that."

"You'll put it in your statement. The grave will be there, if it's true."

It was not a question, saying she would put it in her statement. It was definitely not a question, and even after fighting

Walter, Amy knew she did not dare to refuse. She bit her lower lip.

Hang Walter? And Beth?

She hadn't meant that to happen, not really. She hated Walter, but . . .

Well, why the hell not, if they'd really killed Sheila? Why shouldn't the bastard hang?

But Beth hadn't killed anyone.

She would have to think very carefully about what she would put in her statement.

"What about me?" she asked.

"You," the soldier said, leaning back with his hands behind his head, "are on your way to what they call a repatriation center, where they'll sort you out and send you home—or if they can't do that, at least send you *somewhere*."

"Uh . . . where?"

He glanced at her. "You have any family? Anyone who'd be looking for you? Friends who might take you in?"

"Not in the Galactic Empire," Amy said bitterly.

"Well, where the heck are you *from*, then?" the soldier demanded. "You second generation or something?"

"I'm from a planet called Earth," Amy said. "In another universe." She shrugged. "Not that I expect anyone to believe that."

The soldier froze and stared at her. On her other side, the other soldier, who had been lounging and listening halfheartedly, sat up and stared as well.

"What did you say your name was?" the soldier on the right asked, fishing a clipboard out from under the bench.

"I didn't," Amy said. "It's Amethyst Beryl Jewell. Amy Jewell."

The man stared at the paper on the clipboard, then made a fizzing noise and said feelingly, "Son of a *bitch*. She's on here. Amy Jewell." He looked up at Amy. "Why didn't you tell us sooner?"

"I didn't know it mattered," she said timidly.

"Shit," he said. He looked down at the clipboard, then flipped a few pages. "Okay, if you're Amy Jewell," he said, "what was the last thing you ate before leaving Earth?"

Amy blinked.

Before leaving Earth?

Before her three weeks with Beth and Walter?

Before she was marched naked across a stage and auctioned off?

Before she was locked aboard a pirate spaceship for days on end?

Before those boring, pointless days wasted on *Emerald Princess*?

Before sitting out on that white sand desert for hours, freezing?

Before fleeing from black, monstrous creatures that had appeared practically from nowhere?

Before she had stepped through a concrete wall and found herself in a rather cold, damp corner of Fairyland?

Before taking five minutes to see another reality, five minutes that had turned into more than a month of hell?

How the hell was she supposed to remember that far back, remember that other life, when everything had been safe and sane and she had been free and in control of her own life? That was another universe entirely.

But of course, she *did* remember, which was, she supposed, the whole point.

"Pizza," she said.

"That's it," the soldier agreed. He flipped the pages back and tossed the clipboard aside, then leaned forward, between the two front seats. "Hey, Bill," he called to the driver, "we got a hot one here! Straight to the port!"

The new driver glanced back. "You serious?"

"Absolutely," the other replied.

"You got it," Bill said. He turned the wheel and began tapping at switches.

The others sat back and stared at Amy.

"You, my dear," the one on the left said, "are on your way to Base One."

■

They marched into the refectory in single file, but instead of taking seats they marched straight on, through the kitchen doors, through the courtyard, through the great black sliding door into a much larger yard, where a line of airbuses stood, surrounded by various smaller but equally wheelless vehicles, all of them at least partially purple, and crewed by men in purple uniforms. Blasters were much in evidence.

Another line of men was there, as well, coming along the central passageway from the mineshaft, through the other door of the refectory, the other door to the kitchen; at the door to the first courtyard the two lines merged into one.

They were being loaded onto the buses, Pel realized, all the slaves—the other line was the men of Red Shift.

One of them was Elmer Soorn, the crewman from *Ruthless*, Pel realized with a shock. He had never known that anyone else from the party captured on *Emerald Princess* was at this mine; the only part of Red Shift he ever saw was the gang that his own gang shared their shaft with.

And at the sight of the purple uniforms, Soorn began cheering.

The others stared at him at first, not comprehending; then someone else joined in, and a moment later all the slaves were whooping and shouting.

Dazed, battered, still sleepy, Pel was slow to understand, but at last it sank in.

Those were Imperial uniforms. Those were the soldiers of the Galactic Empire, and the Galactic Empire had outlawed slavery.

He didn't need to worry about escaping. He didn't need to be the hero. He could just be a minor character, somewhere in the background, while other people dealt with Shadow and Earth and the Empire.

They were rescued. The Galactic Empire had come for them at last.

Finally, they were rescued.

CHAPTER 25

They had offered him a set of fatigues, but Pel had kept his gray miner's pants. He had accepted a military-issue T-shirt, though—purple, of course, but comfortable and practical. Thus outfitted, he had settled in aboard one of the spaceships to wait while the other survivors from other universes were gathered.

Several ships were collecting freed slaves; two of them, however, were special. The passengers and crew from the *Emerald Princess* were being taken aboard one particular ship, where they would be treated, questioned, and taken home; the people from Earth, from Shadow's universe, or from ISS *Ruthless* were all sent to another.

It was a big ship, a military ship, and when the soldiers took him aboard they led him to a large room apparently intended for meetings or briefings of some sort. A long metal table stood at one end, with a row of chairs behind it, and a dozen uneven rows of folding chairs faced it from elsewhere.

Prossie Thorpe was there, behind the table, back in uniform, checking each person as he or she was brought aboard. She smiled at Pel.

Captain Cahn was there, also in uniform, but he was not behind the table. He was obviously not in command. Not only was he not in command of the rescue force, he did not seem to even be in command of himself. One side of his face was a huge purple bruise, the cheekbone obviously broken, lips swollen, drool seeping from the corner of his mouth; he sat motionless near the back, saying nothing, barely moving at all.

Arthur Smith and Bill Mervyn sat beside their captain, exchanging silent glances.

Stoddard stood against one wall, arms folded across his chest. He wore only a sort of fur loincloth and open black felt vest—Pel wondered how he had come by such a costume. It seemed to suit him. His sword and armor were gone, but even half naked he still looked dangerous enough; he had no bruises or welts, and his hair had been cut short, where the others, including Pel himself, had gotten rather shaggy. Pel wondered what could have happened to Stoddard while he was a slave to leave him thus. His expression gave no clue.

Elmer Soorn arrived just a few moments after Pel, back in uniform, and he seemed cheerful and healthy—but then, as Pel knew, life in the mines had not been all that harsh, really. Soorn greeted the others, grinning broadly, then got a look at Cahn.

The grin vanished.

"What the hell happened to the captain?" he asked.

Cahn closed his eyes.

Smith explained. "He tried to lead a revolt. Two days ago. Thorpe had told him help was coming, and he wanted to hurry things along a little. Didn't work. In the fighting someone threw him off a building."

Soorn dropped into a seat. "Shit," he said, "he couldn't have just laid low and waited?"

Smith shrugged; Cahn turned his head away.

Embarrassed, Soorn scanned the room. "Hey, Pel Brown," he called, "saw you at the mine—I'd hoped we'd be on the same bus, so we could talk."

Pel just shrugged.

"Looks like we'll get you home this time," Soorn said. "We must have half the Imperial Fleet here!"

"I hope so," Pel muttered.

"Don't everybody cheer at once, or I'll go deaf," Soorn said. "Hey, we've all just been rescued; why are you people so miserable?"

"Well," Mervyn said sourly, "we don't know how bad the captain's hurt, for starters. Pete Cartwright is dead. Jim Peabody is dead. Lieutenant Godwin is dead. Ben Lampert and Lieutenant Drummond are still missing. Nancy Brown's dead. Rachel Brown and Susan Nguyen are missing. That twit who called himself Squire Donald is dead—hanged, I heard. What's-her-name, Elani, is missing, and the lady gnome. Will that do?"

"You're sure Nancy's dead?" Pel asked.

Mervyn glanced at Prossie Thorpe, who nodded. "She's dead," Prossie said. "I'm sorry, Mr. Brown. They'll try to recover the body, so you can arrange a decent . . . burial, is it? Yes, you bury your dead." She winced at the pain her clumsy phrasing caused, and wished she could read the future, as well as minds—just a few seconds of precognition would let her avoid such awkward moments.

After a moment of uncomfortable silence, Soorn tried to change the subject. "What happened to *him*?" he said, pointing a thumb at Stoddard.

"I don't know," Prossie said. "I try not to snoop, you know. Sometimes I can't help it, but I do try."

" 'Twill bother me none that you read my thoughts," Stoddard said, startling everyone. He had looked so motionless that it was hard to remember he was alive and able to talk. "Doubtless you'd speak better than I on what befell."

Prossie smiled wryly. "I'd be none too sure of that," she said. She blinked, as if startled by her own words, then continued. "He was a wrestler," she said. "The woman who bought him challenged all comers to beat him, best two falls of three, in fair fight. She made that costume for him, called him the Space Barbarian, said he came from a lost colony somewhere. He was undefeated in twenty-three matches."

Stoddard nodded in acknowledgment.

Prossie started to say something else, then stopped, hesitated, and announced, "Latest reports are in. They've found Lieutenant Drummond and Susan Nguyen, both alive and well, but Alella is definitely dead—they've found her body, pickled in alcohol."

The men exchanged uneasy glances.

"What about the others?" Pel asked. "What about Rachel?"

Prossie shook her head. "Still no word on Rachel or Elani or Spaceman Lampert."

"What about the others?" Soorn asked. "That guy Raven, and the wizard, Valdakrul, or whatever it is. And the other Earth people?"

"Amy Jewell, Lord Raven, and the wizard Valadrakul are all alive and on their way here," Prossie said. "Miss Jewell will be coming aboard in just a few minutes—she may already be aboard, in fact. And Ted Deranian definitely is on board now, but he's in the ship's infirmary."

"They found Amy? Rachel isn't with her?" Pel demanded angrily.

"No," Prossie said, uncomfortably. "They were separated at the auction. I saw it happen, but there wasn't anything we could do."

"Damn it!" Pel growled. Then something else struck him. "You said Ted was in the infirmary," he said. "Why?"

Prossie sighed.

"Two reasons," she said. "First off, he got the crap beaten out of him several times when he just stopped what he was doing and refused to move, so they're setting broken bones, checking him over for internal damage, and so forth. Second, he did that because he's convinced himself that this entire universe isn't real, that he's still at home in bed, dreaming all this—either that, or that he's gone mad and is imagining it all. The alienists are trying to find some way to cure him of this delusion."

That led to another uncomfortable silence.

"What about the people from the *Princess*?" Mervyn asked at last.

"Well, they aren't really my department," Prossie said, "but last I heard there were three dead, a fourth probably dead, and eight still unaccounted for. But they aren't our problem anymore, the Empire's taking care of them."

"So," Soorn asked, "what happens when we're all present and accounted for here?"

"This group, you mean? We go to Base One," Prossie replied. "At full boost. About four days. In fact, we'll be leaving in a few hours even if the others aren't found. The Earth people, and Shadow people, are a top priority right now."

As she spoke, Amy Jewell stepped into the room. Pel looked up.

She looked older; her hair was partly grown out straight and a shade darker. One eye was spectacularly blackened. She wore a military-issue white blouse and purple slacks, but instead of the

shiny black boots that went with the uniform she had ragged bedroom slippers on her feet. She stood by the doorway, looking the
room over and listening.

She wasn't his problem, though. "What if they haven't found
Rachel?" Pel asked.

"Then we'll leave anyway," Prossie said. "And when someone
finds her they'll send her on another ship, as quickly as possible.
We don't have the time to wait around; the search might take
awhile. It's a big . . . well, no, it isn't really that big a planet, but
any planet is a big place."

"Who's going to take care of her?" Pel demanded. "Listen, if
she isn't found, I'm not going—she's my daughter. I need to stay
here until she's found."

Prossie shook her head. "I don't think they'll allow that," she
said. "You people are absolutely a top priority; they want you at
Base One as fast as possible."

Amy made an unpleasant noise, and all eyes turned toward
her.

"We're a top priority?" she asked, her voice a trifle unsteady.
"They want us there fast?"

Prossie nodded. "That's right."

Pel could see that Amy was angry—in fact, furious, and trying
hard to restrain herself, to calm herself down. He thought at first
it was because of Rachel, but then caught himself. Rachel wasn't
that important to Amy.

She wasn't that important to anyone, it seemed, anyone but
him.

"If we're so damned important," Amy said through her teeth,
"then why didn't they rescue us *sooner*? I've been through three
weeks of hell out there—I'd given up! I could have killed myself before these idiots bothered to come save us!" She lost control, and
began shouting wildly. "I could have *died* out there! I was beaten
and raped and abused, and they could have stopped it!"

"Miss Jewell," Prossie called, "please, Miss Jewell . . ."

Amy continued to shout.

The others looked helplessly at each other, impotent and embarrassed, while Prossie tried to make herself heard without
screaming.

All except Stoddard, who straightened up from where he had

leaned against the wall. Without a word, he crossed the room and put a hand on Amy's shoulder.

Startled, she broke off and looked up at him.

"Sit," he said, pointing to a chair. "Listen. An you be not satisfied, I'll side you, and we'll have what you will of them."

Slowly, Amy sat, watching Stoddard as if hypnotized.

When she was sitting, Stoddard turned to Prossie.

"And now, Mistress Thorpe," he said, "what is it you would say?"

Amy, too, turned to look at the telepath.

Prossie paused to catch her breath and clear her throat, then began, "Miss Jewell, I'm very sorry for whatever indignities you may have suffered. You aren't alone, you know; I was raped, too, and if you'll look around, I think you'll see bruises on several faces. And the preliminary report I got on your barrister seems to indicate she had it worse than any of us."

"Susan?" Amy asked.

Prossie nodded. "She's on her way. She's all right, more or less—just as you are. No permanent physical damage. Not everyone was as lucky—Mr. Brown's wife was killed, as were at least two of my crewmates, and some of the people from *Emerald Princess*. And there are some we still don't know about."

"So why didn't somebody *do* something . . ." Amy began. Stoddard silenced her with a hand on her shoulder.

"We did," Prossie said wearily. "I sent an alarm as soon as I knew *Emerald Princess* was under attack, and the Imperial High Command responded immediately—but space travel isn't instantaneous, and there were no warships nearby. So *Emerald Princess* was captured, and all of us were taken prisoner aboard the raider. I was able to disguise myself as a civilian passenger, and the pirates never found out I was a telepath; if they had, they'd have killed me instantly. Since they didn't, I was able to stay in communication with the High Command—but because telepathy is nondirectional, they couldn't use that to locate us. They knew where *Emerald Princess* was, but not the course the pirate ship took after capturing it."

Amy started to interrupt again, then glanced up at Stoddard and thought better of it.

"I tried to ask where we were going, but nobody bothered to tell me—I was locked in a room, just the way you were, with nobody who knew anything. I read a few minds, very carefully, trying to find out something useful, but I never managed it. So the pirates were able to reach their home base unmolested—and that made the job harder, because you can't defeat an entire planet with a single warship, no matter how much firepower it carries. You can't even free a bunch of slaves, not once they've been scattered all over two continents the way we were—you'll just wind up with a hostage situation, a standoff where you have to deal with criminals. In case you didn't notice, that isn't what happened; nobody sent just one ship. The Empire put together a task force—Task Force Umber, it's called, and you're currently aboard its flagship, ISS *Emperor Edward VII*. They put together a force that could do the job, could conquer the entire planet so fast that nobody would have time to fight back, to take hostages. They got eighty-two ships and eleven thousand troops organized and supplied in about two weeks, and then got them all here at top speed once my reports of the nighttime constellations had been analyzed and the planet located. It worked—you've seen that. It was a huge operation, but it worked, and it went as smooth as ice. They took the entire planet without losing a ship, without more than a dozen casualties, and you're complaining because they couldn't do the impossible any faster than they did."

"I didn't see any fighting," Amy muttered.

"You were way the hell out on the southern plains," Prossie reminded her. "Besides, they didn't put up much of a fight." She took a deep breath, and smiled crookedly. "I haven't done this much talking out loud since I was a girl," she said. "I think my voice is worn out!"

■

Raven had three broken fingers on his left hand. He walked stiffly, slightly bent, like an old man, and flinched when anyone came near his back. Ridges of fresh scar tissue broke the line of the borrowed shirt he wore.

Valadrakul's remaining braid had been cut off, but he was otherwise unharmed.

Susan Nguyen had burns on her back and arms, and scars on her back, but insisted she was fine. "I've had practice with this sort of thing," she said bitterly.

Elani was found, finally, hiding in a cave—she had been the only one to successfully escape from slavery, using tricks learned in years of avoiding Shadow's agents. She had, of course, avoided all contact with other people thereafter, so that she had been slow to learn of the planet's liberation by Imperial forces.

Ben Lampert seemed to have disappeared without a trace. The auction records listed him as sold for three hundred and ninety crowns, paid in cash, no name or address given—a dead end. No one who had been at the auction and was still alive was willing to admit knowing anything about him. Prossie could not locate him telepathically—but because he had no trace of psychic talent, no particularly distinctive thought patterns, that didn't mean much. She couldn't pick out one ordinary person on an entire planet without a little more to go on.

Several boxes of personal belongings were recovered from the auction house, to everyone's surprise—apparently the people in charge of sorting and pricing such things for resale had not been in any hurry. Susan's purse was found, apparently unopened, where she had hidden it—she would not tell the others where that had been—and it was returned to her intact shortly before *Emperor Edward VII* lifted off.

Prossie noticed Susan radiating a certain morbid pleasure upon the return of her purse, even while her face remained absolutely blank, and she couldn't resist snooping a little. She found that Susan was pleased because her gun was still there, untouched, apparently undiscovered.

Prossie also inadvertently shared Susan's wish that she'd had the gun with her on a few occasions during the past three weeks.

Emperor Edward VII launched on schedule, despite Pel Brown's protests. Rachel's probable location had been traced through the auction records and eyewitness reports, but she had not yet been found; Pel had to be sedated and confined to his assigned quarters to keep him from interfering with the flagship's departure.

Prossie tried to tell him that she would stay in touch with the search teams on the newly liberated Zeta Leo Three, and would let him know the minute Rachel was found, but that failed to comfort him.

And in fact, it was a lie.

Telepaths can lie quite effectively when they choose to. After all, they can tell when they're believed and when they aren't.

It was only partly a lie, though. She had every intention of telling him immediately when Rachel was found, on one condition—that she was found alive.

And Prossie didn't think she would be.

■

Nothing would interfere with an Imperial fleet at full strength, and nothing did. *Emperor Edward VII* reached Base One on schedule and without incident.

The body now called Base One had once been an asteroid of no special distinction. It was mostly nickel-iron, but so were a million other asteroids. The only things that marked out Base One were that it was about the right size, and it was about where the Empire wanted to put their military headquarters. By hollowing it out and using the material they thus removed to build on additional sections, the Empire had transformed it into a vast deep-space complex, the heart of the Imperial military and home to the High Command.

Pel never did see what it looked like from the outside during the approach; *Edward VII* didn't bother with unnecessary viewports. His primary impression of the inside was of endless corridors—not spotless, gleaming white corridors, as he had seen in any number of science-fiction movies, but steel corridors, painted in battleship gray or olive drab or maroon, most of them floored with worn linoleum tile in various colors—sometimes mismatched. He found black grit in the cracks between floor tiles, black streaks on the wall here and there where a cart had rubbed, and other signs of long and heavy use on every side.

He had to be dragged off the ship; he was demanding to be taken back to Zeta Leo Three to find his daughter. He was dragged off and given a small room, with a cot and a bureau and a chair, and he was locked in.

By the time he had been there a full day he had calmed down enough to be interviewed—they didn't call it interrogation, but that term would probably have been more accurate. He answered as honestly and completely as he could—and there was no reason not to, as a telepath always sat in on the sessions. It wasn't Prossie Thorpe; instead, it was a young man named Theobald Carver, who appeared, from comments various people made, to be Prossie's second cousin.

There were many sessions.

He was questioned about Zeta Leo Three, about Psi Cassiopeia Two, about Shadow's realm, about Earth, and he answered as well as he could.

Between interviews Pel was given a brief tour of parts of Base One, including an observation chamber where thick windows looked out onto the surface of the asteroid and gave a view of a gigantic complex of equipment—copper bus bars at least ten feet in diameter supported a ring of intricate crystal and metal gadgetry.

"That's the warp generator," his guide explained. "The gateway to your home universe."

Pel took more of an interest once he had heard that; he looked out at the huge tangle of machinery.

Soon, when they found Rachel and brought her safely back here, he would be going through that thing, back to the safety and sanity of his own world, his own home, his suburban quarter-acre twenty miles from Washington.

As soon as they found Rachel.

It was three days later when he was brought into the interview room again. This time, though, instead of his usual questioner in the standard purple uniform, he found himself facing an older officer in more ornate garb, with gold braid and a row of medals.

"Mr. Brown," the man said, folding his hands on the table in front of him, "this time, instead of asking you to tell us things, *we'll* be telling *you* what we've found out."

Pel took his usual seat and said nothing.

"You were captured by pirates and sold into slavery on Zeta Leo Three," the officer said. "While it's true that pirates and slavers are a recurring problem on the fringes of the Galactic Empire, they are a *minor* problem, and the odds of the particular ship that Captain Cahn had commandeered being attacked—well, let's just say that it was unlikely enough that we were very suspicious indeed."

Pel listened without much interest. The attack had happened, he didn't really care why.

"With that in mind, once we had taken control of Zeta Leo Three, we began a thorough investigation of pirate activities based there, and of the attack on *Emerald Princess* in particular. We took a dozen telepaths with us to aid in the investigation—an unheard-of measure. I don't suppose you realize just how extreme a measure that is, unfamiliar as you are with our society, but let me assure you, it's extreme. Never before have we allowed more than eight telepaths to gather in a single place, other than at military transfer points or this base." He raised a hand to make a gesture at the ceiling.

Pel sat, listening. He blinked occasionally.

"We found what we'd expected," the officer said. "Several people died inexplicably under interrogation, *not* from anything we did, but eventually we found what we were after. Agents of the extra-universal thing known as Shadow had secretly controlled the government of not just Zeta Leo Three, but an entire network of rebel worlds—the others are being reduced even as I tell you this. It was already expanding its sphere of influence from its own universe into ours, and it was this thing, this Shadow, that ordered the attack on *Emerald Princess*."

That was scarcely a surprise, really, Pel thought. They had guessed at it, without any evidence at all, aboard the pirate ship.

"That means that it was Shadow that was responsible for the death of your wife."

Pel blinked. He really hadn't thought of it that way, but it was true—Nancy hadn't just died. Someone had killed her. Some person had deliberately killed her.

He sat up a little straighter.

"And I'm afraid that I have some very bad news."

Pel knew, with a cold, crawling certainty, what was coming. His lips formed the word "No."

"I'm afraid we found your daughter, Rachel. And . . . well,

we'll be bringing the remains here to Base One, so you can make your goodbyes."

"No," Pel said, quietly.

"That's another death that this Shadow is responsible for, indirectly," the officer said. "More directly, of course, someone else was, and while I can understand it if you find this a disappointment, if you'd have preferred a more personal vengeance, I'm afraid that the procedures of military justice have already taken care of him. A man named Lemuel Burgess has been hanged for your daughter's murder. If you wish, transcripts of the tribunal and other evidence can be provided to satisfy you that we found the right man." He cleared his throat. "Your wife's killers were never specifically identified, but the entire crew of the ship *Reaper* has been apprehended and executed for piracy, slave trading, and other high crimes, so she, too, is avenged—in part."

Pel stared at him.

The Empire did things with despatch, certainly, if this man was telling the truth—and why would he lie?

They were all dead—Nancy and Rachel and the men who had killed them, all dead.

"Thank you," Pel whispered, unsure why he said it.

The officer hesitated. "There's a little more," he said.

Pel sat motionless, watching him.

"As I said," the man continued, "this Shadow is responsible for the deaths of your wife and daughter. And it's waging a sort of secret war against the Empire, as well. We can't just march in and bring Shadow, whatever it is, to trial; we can't hang it or shoot it, much as we'd like to. In plain truth, we don't know much about it. We do know, though, that it's evil, that it's criminal, that it's responsible for the deaths, not just of your family, but of hundreds of innocents." He paused dramatically.

Pel watched.

"We want it stopped," the officer continued. "It's a murderous, monstrous thing, intruding where it has no business, and we want it stopped as quickly as possible. What's more, we think that you can help us stop it. We want to send you into Shadow's world, as part of a team effort to track down and destroy it. This is the thing that gave the orders for your wife and daughter to die that we're asking you to fight; it's a chance for revenge. Will you take it?" He looked down at Pel, awaiting a reply.

Pel looked back. He stared up into the bright, brown eyes of this man from another universe, this officer in the military of a Galactic Empire, this figure from some pulp space opera, offering him a chance at lurid vengeance against the killer of his wife and child.

It was all like a scene from a novel or a movie, more than ever—he was James Bond being offered his assignment, Mr. Phelps listening to the tape, he was a man being offered a chance to be a hero. He was supposed to say yes, whereupon the officer would shake his hand, and the camera would cut away, and the next scene would be the determined little war party preparing for the assault upon the enemy's fortress.

It was all laid out in the books. This was where the hero differentiated himself from the lesser characters.

James Bond wouldn't hesitate in taking his assignment, no matter how risky. Horatio Hornblower would never turn down a command, no matter how outgunned he would be. Indiana Jones would go after the artifact, no matter how many booby traps there might be, no matter how many enemies might try to stop him. Any real hero would answer instantly.

But in the books the officer's breath didn't smell of the onions he'd eaten at lunch, and there wasn't an incipient pimple on the side of his neck; the table didn't have someone's initials scratched in it; the hero's stomach wasn't wrenched out of shape by the thought of his daughter's death, there weren't tears itching at the corners of his eyes, he didn't feel as if he was about to faint or vomit or, worst of all, burst out in hysterical laughter. In the books the world was all smooth and simple, not hard and solid and arbitrary; there were good guys and bad guys, right and wrong, and right always won out in the end.

Was the Galactic Empire right? Maybe it was better than the alternative, but it was no bastion of purity. Since leaving Earth he had not seen a single black person, or any Oriental except Susan Nguyen—where were they all? What had the Empire done with them? He had heard the Imperials openly voice hatred for "mutants," he had seen a society that to every appearance was racist and sexist and imperialist and saw nothing wrong with any of it. They had hanged every man aboard the pirate ship, had hanged or imprisoned most of the population of Zeta Leo Three—mercy was not one of the Empire's strong suits. Were these the good guys?

And in truth, all he knew about Shadow he had heard from its enemies. True, it had attacked him, but it might be acting in its own defense.

Was *he* one of the good guys, really?

The bad guys offered their people these choices, too—the agents Bond sent to gruesome deaths, the assassins assigned to kill the hero, they had these offers and they accepted them. Was the Empire in the right?

And if it was, so what?

This was no story. This was real life. There was no author making sure justice was done. Right hadn't won against Shadow before; why should it now? And how did he even know whether anything this man had said was true?

Rachel might still be alive; he had only the officer's word that she was not.

He didn't know what was true. He didn't know what was right.

The officer was still waiting for his answer.

This was his chance to be the hero, he knew that. All he had to do was say yes. Be brave and strong and true, and despite tragedy, the hero would win out, the evil would be destroyed, the survivors would live happily ever after.

All the stories said so.

Raven would say yes in an instant, he was certain. Raven had all the makings of a traditional hero. He believed in honor and courage and duty, in right and wrong, good and evil.

And look what it had gotten him; the doctors were still working on his back, and his traitor brother was still lord of Stormcrack Keep.

All Pel had to do was say yes.

James Bond would say yes; Indiana Jones, Horatio Hornblower, they'd say yes in an instant.

But Bond was a spy, Hornblower a sea captain, Jones an archaeologist—those were their *jobs*. Pel Brown was a marketing consultant; his job was telling small businesses why their ads didn't work.

All he had to do was say yes to be a hero, instead of just a marketing consultant.

All he had to do was say yes.

All he had to do was say yes.

. . .

"I don't know," Pel said.

ABOUT THE AUTHOR

LAWRENCE WATT-EVANS grew up in Massachusetts, fourth of six children whose parents were both inveterate readers, and both of whom read science fiction, among other things. He taught himself to read from comic books, and first attempted to write science fiction at the age of eight.

He was considerably older than that when he sold his first fantasy novel, *The Lure of the Basilisk*, to Del Rey Books, beginning his career as a full-time writer.

He is best known for the Ethshar fantasy series, consisting of *The Misenchanted Sword*, *With a Single Spell*, *The Unwilling Warlord*, *The Blood of a Dragon*, *Taking Flight*, and *The Spell of the Black Dagger*.

In addition to fantasy, he's written several science-fiction novels, of which his personal favorite is *Nightside City*, a twenty-fourth century detective story. He also writes horror. He has sold more than fifty short stories and novelettes, including "Why I Left Harry's All-Night Hamburgers," which won the Hugo Award for 1988.

He married in 1977, has two children, and lives in the Maryland suburbs of Washington, D.C.